A Nightingale
Christmas Wish

ı and brought up in south London, Donna Douglas
lives in York with her husband. They have a grown-
daughter.

Also available by Donna Douglas

The Nightingale Girls
The Nightingale Sisters
The Nightingale Nurses
Nightingales on Call

A Nightingale
Christmas Wish
Donna Douglas

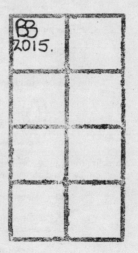

BB
2015.

arrow books

Published by Arrow Books 2014

2 4 6 8 10 9 7 5 3

First published in Great Britain in 2014 by
Arrow Books
Random House, 20 Vauxhall Bridge Road,
London SW1V 2SA

A Penguin Random House Company

Penguin
Random House
UK

www.randomhouse.co.uk

Addresses for companies within The Random House Group Limited
can be found at: www.randomhouse.co.uk/offices.htm

The Random House Group Limited Reg. No. 954009

A CIP catalogue record for this book
is available from the British Library

ISBN 978 0 09958 516 9

MIX
Paper from
responsible sources
FSC
www.fsc.org   FSC™ C018179

Penguin Random House is committed to a sustainable
future for our business, our readers and our planet.
This book is made from Forest Stewardship
Council ® certified paper.

Typeset in Palatino by Palimpsest Book Production Limited,
Falkirk, Stirlingshire

Printed and bound by
CPI Group (UK) Ltd, Croydon, CR0 4YY

Acknowledgements

It takes a great many people to make the Nightingale books happen, and I'd like to take the opportunity to thank them.

First of all, I'd like to thank my agent Caroline Sheldon for all her hard work and for putting up with my nonsense with great patience. The same goes for my wonderful editor Jenny Geras. Huge thanks also to the production team who work miracles with extremely short deadlines, especially the lovely Katherine Murphy.

There's no point writing a book if no one hears about it, which is why I'm so grateful to my enthusiastic and hard-working publicist Rachel Cain. And there is no point hearing about a book if no one can buy it either. So massive thanks to Andrew Sauerwine and his terrific sales team for working so incredibly hard to get my books on to the shelves. I'm so delighted to have you guys on my side!

Last, but not least, big thanks to my family and friends. Special thanks to my long-suffering husband Ken, who puts up with my long absences and short-temperedness with a ridiculous amount of patience; and to my daughter Harriet, who reads my work as I write it, and who manages to be both brutal and encouraging at the same time. I love you both and I couldn't do it without you.

To my sister Jane

Chapter One

On a freezing cold December morning in 1914, seventeen-year-old Frannie Wallace gathered with the rest of her Pennine village on a frosty railway station platform to see their loved ones off to war.

She barely recognised any of the men in their unfamiliar khaki uniforms, kitbags slung over their shoulders. Fathers, husbands and sons, all hugging their tearful wives and children, smiling as if it didn't matter.

'Come on now, love. Buck up, it won't be for long.'

'I'll be back home by Christmas, you'll see. Won't take us long to finish off that Hun!'

'Be sure to write to me when the baby arrives, won't you?'

In the middle of the platform stood Matthew, laughing and joking with his pals, their breath curling on the crisp winter air. They'd signed up together, all the boys. It was hard to believe that in a few days the lads Frannie had shared a classroom with would be in France, fighting for their country.

Especially Matthew. He looked so young and fresh-faced, his dark hair cut short over his ears, stamping his shiny new boots on the ground to keep out the cold. Tears stung Frannie's eyes but she blinked them away determinedly. She'd promised him she wouldn't cry.

Not that his mother and sisters kept their promise. Alice Sinclair was sobbing as she fussed over her son, straightening his collar and smoothing down his tunic.

Matthew brushed her aside impatiently. 'Get off, Ma. Do you want the other lads laughing at me?'

'Now, have you got everything?' Alice said, ignoring him. 'Did you remember that chocolate I gave you, and those extra socks?'

'Leave him be, Alice,' Matthew's father said, his voice hoarse with emotion. 'If the boy's old enough to fight a war then he's old enough to take care of himself!'

Of course that set his wife off crying again. Frannie couldn't imagine what Alice would do without her beloved only son. Even her three daughters knew he was the favourite, the one she truly doted on.

But then everyone doted on Matthew, including Frannie herself.

She looked around and suddenly noticed John. He stood apart from the others as usual, quiet and watchful. John had come from the local orphanage to work on the Sinclairs' farm when he was thirteen, and he and Matthew had become good friends. At eighteen years old John was already a tall, strapping man, making the others look even more like boys.

He had no one to see him off, no one fussing over him. But he stood proud, a look of defiant indifference on his square-jawed face.

Frannie went over to him. 'All ready, John?' She smiled at him.

He looked round at her, whipping the cap off his cropped dark head. 'Miss Wallace?'

'Frannie,' she reminded him. 'I'm only a school-master's daughter, you don't have to address me as if I'm a teacher!'

She regretted teasing him when she saw the blush creeping up from his collar. 'Sorry,' he mumbled.

Frannie felt so sorry for him, she handed him the bar

2

of Fry's Chocolate Cream she'd been keeping for Matthew. 'Here, have this.'

John looked at it, then back at her. 'Are you sure?' he asked. 'What about Matthew?'

'He already has more than enough.' Frannie glanced down the platform to where her sweetheart was still trying to squirm free from his mother's embrace. 'Look after him for me, won't you?' The words burst from her, though Frannie hadn't intended to say them.

'I'll make sure he doesn't get into any mischief, don't you worry.'

Frannie smiled ruefully. 'You'll have a job doing that! Matthew finds trouble wherever he goes.' A lump rose in her throat, choking her. Don't cry, she told herself. Please don't cry.

'I'll look after him, I promise,' John said quietly.

'And mind you look after yourself, too,' Frannie said, when she'd mastered her emotions enough to speak again.

John scuffed the frosty ground with the toe of his boot. 'Doesn't matter about me,' he mumbled.

'Yes, it does.' Frannie felt a sudden surge of pity for the orphanage boy who had no one to care about him. Impulsively she plunged her hand into her pocket and pulled out the only thing of value she had. 'Here,' she said, handing it to him.

He stared down at the rough grey stone in his palm. 'What is it?'

'A pebble I picked up from the top of Kinder Scout. I call it my lucky charm. Perhaps it will bring you luck, too?'

He didn't laugh. Matthew would have laughed, which was why Frannie had had second thoughts about giving it to him. She knew he would think her foolish, tell her he didn't need luck.

But John looked at her as if she'd just handed him one of the Crown Jewels. His eyes met hers, clear and green.

'Thank you,' he said, tucking it in the top pocket of his tunic. 'I'll treasure it always.'

The train let out a sudden hiss, belching a cloud of steam that shrouded them for a moment. The air was filled with the oily smell of burning coal as the guard blew his whistle.

'All aboard!'

Suddenly everyone was jostling towards the train. Frannie turned and ran back down the platform, just in time to see Matthew climbing aboard.

'Matthew?' she cried out, her voice lost in the hubbub. She pushed her way through to the front of the crowd, close to the platform's edge, lost in the billowing, acrid steam.

But then to her relief he appeared, hanging out of an open window. 'There you are!' He grinned down at her. 'I thought you'd forgotten about me.'

'How could I?' As she put up her hands to grasp his, the solitary diamond on her engagement ring caught the weak, wintry sunlight. It still gave her a surprise to see it there, less than a day after Matthew had slid it on to her finger.

To think yesterday she'd felt like the happiest, luckiest girl in the world. And now . . .

Panic seized her. 'I'm frightened, Matthew,' she whispered. 'I wish you didn't have to go.'

'I'll be home soon enough, you'll see.'

Frannie looked up into his smiling face. He was always so sure of himself. Not in an arrogant way, but his bright coppery-brown eyes gleamed with the confidence of someone who had never known a moment's self-doubt. It was one of the things she loved about him. She wished at that moment she had a shred of his self-assurance to bolster her.

'You will write to me every day, won't you?'

'Frannie! I'm going over there to fight, not to write love letters!' He laughed at her stricken expression. 'Don't look so worried, Fran. And for God's sake, smile. I don't want your long face to be the last thing I see here!'

'Sorry.' She tried to smile, but her lips were trembling.

'Oh, come here.' He leaned forward. Trapping her face between his hands, he kissed her long and hard. Frannie heard jeering and cheering around her and pulled away, embarrassed.

'Matthew!' She blushed to see all the faces around her, watching them.

'I'm allowed, aren't I? We're engaged.' Matthew lifted her hand and kissed the diamond on her ring. 'Wait for me,' he said. 'I promise I'll come home a hero and then we'll get married.'

'I don't want you to come home a hero. Just come home safe.'

His reply was lost in the shrill blast of the train whistle.

'All aboard!'

The guard was walking down the platform, waving his flag. Unseen hands dragged Frannie back from the platform's edge as the train started to inch away.

As it pulled out, the men all hung out of the windows, waving madly. Frannie caught a glimpse of John. He was sitting down, his face pressed to the glass. As the train rumbled past, he lifted his hand in the slightest of waves.

Frannie remembered Matthew's words and smiled until her cheeks ached and the train had disappeared out of sight.

She was glad she'd done as he asked. Especially when the telegram arrived.

Chapter Two

The young medical student made a perfect Assistant Matron.

It took all Frannie Wallace's self-control not to smile as he stood before her on the makeshift stage, grey dress skimming his hairy ankles, arms folded across his formidably padded bosom. Under the starched headdress, his frowning expression was exactly like Miss Hanley's.

'I'm sorry, Mr Evans, but it really won't do,' Frannie managed, when she could finally trust herself to speak.

Owen Evans looked put out. 'But, Sister, I've gone to so much trouble!'

'Then I'm afraid you've wasted your time. I can't allow you to appear in the Christmas show looking like that.'

There was a chorus of protest from the other young men gathered around him. Two of them were wearing the striped dresses of student nurses. Frannie shuddered to think how they'd acquired them.

At the other end of the vast dining room, the other would-be performers were preparing, clutching their sheet music, sliding up and down scales to warm up their voices, or huddled in groups waiting to take their turn on the crudely constructed dais where Frannie sat, directing the proceedings.

'This is supposed to be an entertainment for the patients and their families,' she reminded the students, raising her

6

voice above the din. 'I will not allow you to use it as an opportunity to lampoon members of staff. Poor Miss Hanley would be mortified.'

'Miss Hanley?' Mr Evans did his best to feign innocence. 'Oh, no, Sister, I don't know where you got that idea from. I wasn't making fun of anyone in particular, truly I wasn't. Really, I'm rather shocked that you should think that this – this gross parody remotely resembles our esteemed Assistant Matron—'

The other young men chortled. 'Come on, Sister, be a sport,' one of them piped up. 'It's only a bit of fun, after all.'

'Fun, is it?' Frannie shot him a chilly glance. 'I would like to see you having fun at one of the consultants' expense,' she said. 'Perhaps you could dress up as Mr Hobbs or Mr Cooper? Or what about Mr Latimer? I'm sure *he'd* see the funny side.' The young men shuffled their feet and stared at the floor like naughty schoolboys. 'I thought as much,' Frannie said. 'And yet you find it perfectly acceptable to poke fun at one of the senior nursing staff?'

There was an uncomfortable silence. Owen Evans whipped off his wig. He knew when he was beaten. 'I suppose you're right,' he sighed.

As they shuffled off the stage, one of the young students grumbled, 'You might let us have some fun, Sister. After all, we probably won't even be here next Christmas.'

'That's true,' another muttered. 'I expect we'll be in a trench somewhere, taking potshots at Germans.'

A chill brushed the back of Frannie's neck. 'Don't talk like that,' she said.

Owen Evans stopped and looked at her. 'Why not? We all know there's going to be a war.'

'Everyone except Mr Chamberlain!' his friend said.

'No one wants to go to war,' Frannie said quietly. 'Not after last time.'

7

'Yes, but we can't ignore what Hitler's doing in Europe,' Owen Evans insisted stubbornly. 'And it's not going to stop just because he's signed a piece of paper.'

'He needs to be taught a lesson,' another chimed in. 'You've got to stand up for what's right, haven't you? If we don't, it'll be us next.'

'Just let him try!' Another young man, a thickset chap with a pugnacious face, balled his hands into fists. 'Give me the chance to go over there. I'll show those Germans what for!'

'You don't know what you're talking about!' Tension made Frannie snap. 'You think it's all a big game, don't you? But war isn't like a football match. You don't shake hands and go home when you've had enough. Some of you won't come home at all—' She stopped talking, suddenly aware of the line of startled faces staring back at her from the makeshift stage. 'At any rate, things probably won't come to that,' she dismissed, shuffling the sheet music on the table in front of her. 'Now, about your act. If you want to take part in this Christmas show, you will have to come up with another sketch. That one simply won't do.'

'Yes, Sister.' This time they didn't argue. They hurried away, whispering among themselves.

'Well, I think you've given them something to think about.'

Frannie looked round to find Kathleen Fox standing behind her.

'Matron! I didn't hear you come in.' She started to her feet, but Kathleen waved her back into her seat.

'We're not on the ward now, Fran,' she said, smiling.

Kathleen Fox had been Matron of the Nightingale Hospital for more than four years now. But it was difficult for Frannie to look at her and not see the girl she'd shared a room with while training in Leeds. The girl she had been was still there in the warmth of Kathleen's grey eyes and the flash of auburn hair under her starched white headdress.

'You mustn't judge them too harshly, you know,' she said to her friend. 'You can't blame them for not under-standing what war is like. They're just boys, Fran. They can't take it in.'

'That's just it, isn't it? They're boys. Signing up for a lark. Just like—' Frannie stopped herself.

Just like Matthew. And look how that had ended.

'But we know what it's really like, don't we?' Kathleen continued, steadying her voice.

Like Frannie, Kathleen had worked as a voluntary nurse at a military hospital before they'd started their nurse's training. Frannie had volunteered as soon as she turned eighteen, so that she could feel closer to Matthew. But by the time she was posted to France, he was already missing, presumed dead.

'All this talk of war is bound to stir up bad memories,' Kathleen said to her kindly. 'It's everywhere you turn, isn't it?'

Frannie nodded. Owen Evans was right about that, at any rate. The streets were lined with sandbags, and trenches had already been dug in all the parks to shelter people caught in air raids. There was even talk of families being separated and children being sent away from the city.

It was hard to believe that only a few weeks ago the country had rejoiced when the Prime Minister returned from Munich clutching a piece of paper promising peace. That Sunday morning the bells had rung out in churches across the land, and everyone had breathed a sigh of relief that they might not be going to war after all.

But it had soon become clear that whatever Hitler had

promised, nothing was going to stand in the way of his ambitions. Gloom and resignation had settled over the country once more. Shortly afterwards, they had lined up to be issued with their gas masks by the council. Frannie's was still in its cardboard box in her room. She couldn't bring herself to touch it. Just seeing it on the shelf made her feel ill.

'I'm sure good sense will prevail eventually,' Kathleen said.

'I hope so. I only wish everyone would stop talking about it.'

They were both silent for a moment, lost in their thoughts. Then Kathleen smiled and said, 'Let's talk about something more pleasant, shall we? How are arrangements for the concert coming on?'

Frannie grimaced. 'Much the same as usual, I'm afraid.'

Every year the staff of the Nightingale Hospital put on a Christmas show for the patients and their families. And every year Frannie promised herself she wouldn't get involved with organising it. But as November rolled around and the festive season approached, she found herself confronted with all those hopeful faces and she couldn't say no.

Kathleen smiled at her. 'I'm sure you must secretly enjoy it?'

'Perhaps I do,' Frannie agreed ruefully. 'But not when I have to spend all my time sorting out their squabbles. Not to mention explaining to Sister Wren yet again why she can't do a duet with Mr Cooper.'

'Oh, dear.' Kathleen's grey eyes lit up with mischief. 'Perhaps Mr Cooper should just give in gracefully?'

Frannie leaned forward, lowering her voice. 'Between you and me, Mr Cooper has begged not to be put with her. He was very firm on that point.'

'Poor Sister Wren!'

'Poor Mr Cooper, you mean!' The ward sister's relentless infatuation with the obstetrics consultant had been going on for several years now, even though he was a married man and clearly not interested.

'Speak of the devil . . .'

Frannie followed Kathleen's gaze to the far end of the room. Miriam Trott, sister of Wren ward, was making her way towards them, sheet music tucked under her arm. 'Oh, lord. Don't leave me,' begged Frannie. 'Pretend we have some important ward business to discuss.'

'I can't, I'm afraid. I have a meeting with Mrs Tremayne in ten minutes.'

Frannie pulled a face, her own problems instantly forgotten. 'Oh, dear. What does she want?'

'Heaven knows. I'm just wondering what she can possibly have found to complain about now.'

'Perhaps she just wants a chat?'

Kathleen sent her an old-fashioned look. 'I don't think so. That woman is the bane of my life. And she's been even worse since she was made Chairwoman of the Board of Trustees.'

'You're more than a match for her.'

'I hope so. But I'm not really in the mood to do battle at the moment.'

There was something wistful about Kathleen's expression that made Frannie look twice at her friend. 'Are you all right, Kath? You look rather tired.'

'I'm quite all right, thank you.' Her smile was back in place. 'I just have better things to do than listen to Mrs Tremayne's complaints. And speaking of complaints . . .'

Suddenly Miriam Trott was standing beside them. 'Excuse me, Matron, but might I have a word with Miss Wallace?' she said, planting herself in front of Frannie and blocking her means of escape.

'Of course,' Kathleen said. 'I'll leave you to it.'

'No, really, Matron, there's no need—' Frannie sent her a silent, imploring look, which she blithely ignored.

'It's quite all right, Sister. I must prepare for my meeting.' And then she was gone. Frannie watched her making her way towards the dining-room doors, pausing here and there to exchange a few words with the nurses who had gathered to rehearse.

'Miss Wallace?' Sister Wren's voice insinuated its way into her thoughts. 'I wondered if I could talk to you about my music? I have a few ideas for duets. I thought perhaps Mr Cooper and I—'

'I want to talk to you about the Casualty department.'

Constance Tremayne was not a woman to beat about the bush. She sat on the other side of the desk from Kathleen, hands curled around her handbag. Everything about her was tightly drawn, from her ramrod-straight spine to the dark hair pulled into a severe bun at the nape of her long, thin neck. With her permanently pursed lips, she always put Kathleen in mind of a sucked lemon.

'What about it?' she asked. Behind her easy smile she was tensed, waiting for the blow to fall. In the four years she had been Matron of the Nightingale hospital, she had never known Mrs Tremayne come into her office without making a complaint of some kind.

'I understand Sister Percival is leaving?'

'That's right. She's moving down to Devon to nurse her sick mother.'

'So you'll be looking for a replacement. Do you have anyone in mind?'

Kathleen looked into Mrs Tremayne's inquisitive face and fought the urge to tell her to mind her own business. Be nice, Kath, she warned herself. She knew from experience

Constance Tremayne could be dangerous when crossed. 'I was planning to move one of the other staff nurses. Perhaps Staff Nurse Lund—'

'Is that wise?' Constance Tremayne asked. 'I mean, I'm sure Staff Nurse Lund is a perfectly adequate nurse, but wouldn't Casualty be better run by someone with Theatre experience? I was talking to Dr McKay the other day, and he told me they are dealing with more and more surgical emergencies these days. Road accidents and so forth. He would very much like to be able to deal with more such emergencies in Casualty, rather than waste valuable time sending them up to Theatre. But for that he would really need a qualified Theatre nurse . . .'

'I see.' Kathleen could already tell where this conversation was going, and why Mrs Tremayne had been so keen to see her. The Chairwoman of the Board of Trustees might think she was being clever, but she was as transparent as the cut-glass paperweight on Kathleen's desk.

'Of course, as Matron it's your decision,' Constance went on. But before Kathleen could draw breath, she added, 'Although it does occur to me that my daughter Helen might be a suitable candidate. After all, she has two years' experience in Theatre.'

There it was. Constance Tremayne had shown her hand, and now it was Kathleen's turn to respond.

'I agree, Helen is a very accomplished nurse,' she said. 'I've certainly heard good reports from Sister Theatre. But,' she added, as the self-satisfied smile widened on Mrs Tremayne's face, 'she is still very young. It's barely two years since she passed her State Final. She needs more experience as a staff nurse before she takes on the role of Sister.'

'I'm sure Helen would relish the challenge,' Mrs Tremayne put in swiftly.

I daresay Helen wouldn't have much choice in the matter, Kathleen thought. She wondered if Constance had troubled herself to ask her daughter's opinion. In Kathleen's experience, she seldom did.

She considered the suggestion. She had to admit, Constance Tremayne was right, they would benefit from having an experienced Theatre nurse in Casualty. Kathleen too had spoken to Dr McKay at length, and she knew he had high hopes of adding another operating theatre to the Casualty department.

But she worried for poor Helen. After only two years as a qualified nurse, she might be out of her depth.

As if she sensed Kathleen wavering, Mrs Tremayne pushed on. 'I must admit, I have a personal reason for suggesting it,' she said. 'As you know, the last two years haven't been easy for my daughter.'

'Indeed,' Kathleen agreed. Everyone knew Helen's tragic story. She had married her sweetheart in a rushed wedding at the hospital, only for him to die two weeks later. Poor Helen was so heartbroken that for a while it seemed she might not even get as far as taking her exams.

Now she appeared to be working well in Theatre, if the reports of her were anything to go by. Kathleen admired the young woman for her determination and courage.

'I think it would be good for her to take on a new challenge,' Mrs Tremayne said. 'She has shut herself away in Theatre for too long.'

Kathleen regarded the other woman across the desk. Perhaps there was a shred of humanity in her after all?

'I'll talk to her,' she promised. 'We'll see what she has to say on the matter.'

'I'm sure you'll find she's quite willing,' Mrs Tremayne dismissed this airily.

Kathleen sighed. Poor Helen. No doubt she would

succumb to her mother's implacable will, as they all did eventually.

After Mrs Tremayne had left, Kathleen watched her from the window of her office. She marched purposefully across the courtyard, rigidly upright, as if even the howling November wind couldn't bend her. The sky was a leaden yellowish-grey, heavy with the promise of snow. Kathleen shivered in spite of the warmth of the blazing fire in her office. She disliked this time of year: the deadening hand of winter settling on everything, the gusty wind that stripped the trees, leaving them bare and shivering. It felt too much like death for her liking.

Chapter Three

On a snowy Saturday morning in December, Helen Dawson laid flowers on her husband Charlie's grave. It would have been his twenty-fifth birthday.

'It was like this the day he was born.' His mother Nellie stood at the foot of the grave, her coat pulled tightly around her bulky figure. 'Snow piled up outside the door, it was. My old man had to dig a path down the alley for the midwife to get in.' She shivered. 'Charlie hated the cold, bless him. Never liked that his birthday was in the winter. "Why couldn't I have been born in the summer?" he used to say. "Winter's such a rotten time of year."'

She fell silent, her lips trembling. Helen pretended not to notice as she arranged carnations in an urn, a splash of scarlet against the white snow. She kept her eyes averted so she didn't have to look at Charlie's name, carved into the grey slab of a headstone. As long as she didn't allow herself to read the words, she could stay strong.

'It doesn't get any easier, does it?' Nellie seemed to read her thoughts. 'I know it's past two years, but I still miss him.'

'Me too,' Helen said quietly.

'Bless you, love, of course you do. It was cruel, him being taken so soon after you were married.'

'At least we *were* married.' Helen knew on her wedding day that they wouldn't have long together, but she was determined to take his name before he died. Sad as they were, those few days as man and wife had been the most special time she could remember.

16

She felt the hot tears brimming and dashed them away with her gloved hand. She wished she could be more like Nellie, letting her emotions spill out. But her own mother had taught her differently.

Nellie's hand settled on her sleeve, comforting her. 'Come on, love,' she said. 'I'll walk you to the hospital.'

They trudged back together through the streets of Bethnal Green. Thick white pelmets of snow clung to the roofs and window sills of the narrow terraces, but on the street it had turned to an ugly grey slush that seeped through their shoes. That didn't deter the children, who whooped with delight as they pulled their makeshift sledges up and down the middle of the street, laughing as they aimed gritty grey snowballs at each other. One whizzed past Helen's shoulder, narrowly missing her and Nellie.

'Sorry, missus!' A boy stuck his head around the corner and gave them a cheeky grin. 'That was meant for my mate!'

'Little perishers.' Nellie shook her head, smiling indulgently. 'My lot used to be just the same. As soon as it snowed they'd be out in it, getting up to all sorts.'

'William and I were too,' Helen recalled. 'He once decided to save himself the trouble of making a real snowman by covering me in snow instead. I had to stand still for so long, I couldn't feel my feet. I nearly had frostbite by the time Mother realised what he was doing.'

'That's big brothers for you,' Nellie chuckled. 'Charlie and his cousins were just the same with our Ivy.'

She fell silent again. Helen tucked her arm under Nellie's and they walked on, passing the end of Columbia Road Market. As it was a Saturday morning, the narrow street was already bustling with people. The stallholders, wrapped up in layers of coats, scarves, hats, mufflers and gloves, stamped their feet and blew on their hands to keep

17

out the cold as they plied their trade. A couple waved at Nellie as she and Helen passed by the end of the road. The Dawsons had been running a fruit and veg stall on the market for more than twenty-five years, and everyone knew them.

'Pity my poor Ivy on the stall this morning!' Nellie grinned. 'She won't be happy, getting up at the crack of dawn to set up in this weather.'

'Do you want to go down and say hello?' Helen asked.

'And listen to her complain? Not likely!' Nellie rolled her eyes. 'Ta very much, love, but I'd rather have a nice natter with you. You can tell me what's going on at that hospital of yours.'

'Well, it's funny you should ask . . .' As they walked, Helen told Nellie about starting her new job as acting Casualty Sister the following week.

'Sister, eh? Blimey, girl, you kept that quiet.' Nellie looked impressed. 'That's a step up for you, ain't it?'

'I suppose so.'

Nellie sent her a sideways look. 'You don't sound too sure about it, I must say.'

'I am,' Helen said. 'It's just – oh, I don't know.' She paused, searching for the right words to explain the worries that had kept her awake for the past week. 'I'm not sure if I'm up to the job. I've only been qualified as a nurse for two years. It's early to be promoted.'

'They must think a lot of you, then.'

Helen was silent. She suspected it had more to do with her mother's interference. Helen could almost see it in Matron's face when she'd told her about the job.

Nellie squeezed her hand. 'Come on, spit it out. You've got something on your mind, I can tell.'

Helen smiled ruefully. How strange that she could talk to Nellie more easily than she could to her own mother.

Constance Tremayne would only dismiss her fears and tell her she was being silly.

'I'm worried I don't have the first idea about running a ward, let alone a department as busy as Casualty,' she said. 'And the staff nurse under me is years senior to me. I don't know what she'll think of that.'

'Then you'll just have to show 'em what you're made of, won't you?' Nellie said. 'Besides, that Matron of yours wouldn't have given you the job if she didn't reckon you could manage it.'

'I suppose not,' Helen agreed reluctantly. 'But I didn't want to move from Theatre. I liked working there.'

Nellie shuddered. 'Rather you than me, love. I don't think I could watch people being cut about all day long!'

'You forget they're people,' Helen said. 'They're just cases to be treated.'

That was what she liked about it. In Theatre, the patients were brought in, put to sleep, treated and then taken away again. It wasn't like working on the ward. Helen never had to get to know them, or listen to their stories, or worry that they might not pull through. They were just names on a list, to be forgotten about as soon as the operation was over.

They skirted the tall, wrought-iron gates of Victoria Park. Beyond the gates it looked like a wintry wonderland, the dark, skeletal trees laced with snow.

'I suppose you'll be working over Christmas, if you're in charge?' Nellie said.

'I hadn't really thought about it,' Helen replied. 'I'll be in charge of the duty rosters. But it doesn't seem fair to give myself time off when the other nurses might have families they want to visit.'

'Don't you want to visit yours?'

Helen was silent for a moment. 'Well, my father will be busy in church most of the day, and I expect William will be on call at the hospital as usual, so there'll only be me and Mother . . .' She let her voice trail off.

'You could always spend Christmas with us?' Nellie suggested. 'We're only round the corner, and you know we'd love to have you. The kids are always asking when you're coming to visit.'

'That's very kind of you, but I wouldn't want to impose.'

'You wouldn't be imposing,' Nellie said. 'You're family, remember?' She put her hand over Helen's. 'Charlie would have wanted us to look after you.'

Helen smiled. She had been welcomed so easily into his rough and ready family, it made her feel ashamed to remember how badly her own mother had treated him. Constance Tremayne had never got over the fact that her daughter had married a costermonger's son.

'He wouldn't have wanted you to be a stranger,' Nellie said, then added, 'he wouldn't have wanted you to be unhappy either.'

There was something about the way she said it that made Helen turn to look at her.

'I am happy,' she said.

'Are you?'

'Of course. As happy as I can be,' she added in a low voice.

The truth was, she wasn't sure what happiness was any more. After two long years, the first sharp pain of Charlie's loss had subsided to a dull ache. She still yearned for him, but these days she could wake up in the morning and not dread the thought of dragging herself through her next waking hours. Only very occasionally did it catch her out. Like when she dreamed of him so vividly that she woke up believing he was still there with her. Then the fresh pain of loss would make her catch her breath.

But was the absence of pain the same as happiness? Helen wasn't sure. For the past two years it was as if the world had been shrouded in a fine grey mist. Through it, she could see the rest of the world, laughing and loving and going about its business, while she stood apart, detached from everything going on around her.

Nellie was silent for a moment. Then she said, 'Have you thought about courting again?'

Helen whipped round to look at her, shocked. 'What? No!'

'Why not? You can't be alone for ever, can you? How old are you? Twenty-four? You're still a young woman—'

'I don't want anyone else,' Helen cut her off firmly.

'You might say that now, but sooner or later someone's going to come along and catch your eye. And I know my Charlie wouldn't want you to spend the rest of your life alone. He'd want you to be happy.'

'I don't want anyone else,' Helen repeated, more firmly.

'Whatever you say, love. I just wanted you to know that if you did want to start courting again, it would be all right with me.'

Helen was silent, lost in her thoughts. Until Nellie mentioned it, it hadn't even occurred to her that she might fall in love again. Not just out of respect for Charlie, but because she genuinely couldn't imagine any other man stirring her heart the way he had.

The silence stretched between them, and Helen was relieved when they reached the hospital gates.

'Well, I'll be seeing you, love.' Nellie planted a warm kiss on her frozen cheek. 'Good luck with the new job tomorrow. And you won't forget what I said, will you? We'd love to see you at Christmas.'

'I'll try,' Helen said. Although deep down she knew she wouldn't. Even after two years, it hurt too much to go to Charlie's home, knowing he wouldn't be there.

Chapter Four

After a sleepless night, Helen was up, bathed and dressed well before the maid brought her tea in bed at half-past six on Monday morning.

'Oh! I beg your pardon, Sister, I didn't know you were up and about,' she said, as she placed the cup and saucer on the bedside table. 'Most of the sisters don't like to be woken before half-past, what with them not being on duty until eight.'

'I couldn't sleep,' Helen confessed. 'It's my first day today.'

'Ah.' The maid gave her a sympathetic smile. 'Will you be wanting your breakfast now? A nice poached egg, or a piece of toast, just to settle you?'

'Thank you, but I really couldn't eat a thing.' Helen put her hand over her stomach. It felt like a tight knot.

'Well, if you're sure, Sister? We don't want you going hungry, do we?'

After the maid had gone, Helen sat down at her dressing table to finish pinning up her hair. From the collar down, she was all bristling authority in her severe grey uniform. But from the neck up, all she could see was a pair of frightened brown eyes staring back at her from a pale, oval face. How on earth was she going to convince the other nurses in Casualty that she was a worthy sister, when she didn't quite believe it herself?

She had hardly slept all night. Not just from fear, but because the Sisters' quarters were so quiet compared to the nurses' home. Helen was used to voices and laughter in the passageways, but the ward sisters seemed to live in sombre silence.

After drinking her tea, pacing around her room, checking her dress several times and tying and retying the stiff bow of her headdress under her chin, it still wasn't seven o'clock. Helen decided to walk down to Casualty early, to look around and meet the nurses when they came on duty at seven. Surely setting foot inside her new department couldn't be as bad as sitting in her room with a churning stomach, worrying about it.

The Casualty department was open throughout the night for the ambulances to bring in emergencies. Light spilled from the high arched window above the double doors, piercing the wintry darkness as Helen made her way across the courtyard.

The main Casualty hall was a large, vaulted room as big as a tennis court, filled with rows of empty wooden benches. At the far end of the hall, a weary-looking night nurse had nodded off behind the booking-in desk, which sat on top of a raised dais.

She jolted awake when Helen walked in.

'Sister!' She stood up and glanced at the clock. 'I wasn't expecting you so early.'

'It's all right, I just wanted to have a look around and get my bearings.' Helen smiled at her. 'Busy night?' she asked.

'Very quiet, Sister.' The girl recovered herself. 'Dr McKay and Dr Adler came on duty ten minutes ago and sent Dr Ross home.'

'Where are they?'

The student pointed down the short stump of corridor beyond the booking-in desk. 'Consulting Room Three, Sister.'

'I suppose I'd better go and introduce myself.' Helen

turned back to the student. 'Thank you, Nurse. You may go off duty now.'

'Oh! Thank you, Sister.' The girl glanced at the clock again, her face lighting up. Helen remembered her own student days, and how grateful she'd always been to be sent off even five minutes early from night duty.

When the nurse had gone, Helen took off her cloak and hung it up in the nurses' cloakroom, then made her way to the consulting room. Her hand was raised to knock when she heard voices drifting from the other side of the door.

'All I'm saying is give her a chance, David,' she heard a man saying. 'We don't know what she's like yet, do we?'

'Oh, we all know exactly what she's going to be like. She's Mrs Tremayne's daughter, isn't she?' The other man's well-educated Scottish voice was full of disgust.

Helen froze, her hand still poised to knock.

'She might not be that bad. They think very highly of her in Theatre, so I understand,' the first voice said.

'It's a pity they didn't keep her, in that case.'

The man gave a rumbling laugh. 'David! I'm shocked at you. It's not like you to be so intolerant.'

'I have nothing against the girl, I promise you. But that's what she is – a girl. For heaven's sake, Jonathan, she's barely older than a student. We need someone with experience to run this department.'

Hot shame washed over Helen. She knew she should walk away, but her legs wouldn't move.

'You're only sulking because you weren't consulted.'

'Perhaps I am. But do you blame me? I take our work very seriously, and I resent having this – child foisted on us, just because she happens to be a Trustee's daughter who fancies a change of scene.'

Helen tiptoed away, hating herself for her own lack of courage. If she truly were her mother's daughter she would

24

have barged straight in and confronted them, instead of creeping off to hide in a corner.

She returned to the Casualty hall just as the other nurses were coming on duty. There were four of them, three students and a tall blonde in the royal-blue uniform of a staff nurse. They were all talking among themselves, but stopped dead when they saw Helen.

'Oh, hello. You must be our new Sister Cas?' The blonde nurse greeted her with a broad smile. She was a couple of years older than Helen, long-limbed and languid, with thickly lashed aquamarine eyes. 'I'm Staff Nurse Willard, and these are Perkins, Kowalski and French.' She nodded towards the three students who stood, still in their heavy cloaks, watching Helen warily.

'Would you like a cup of tea, Sister?' Nurse Willard offered. 'We usually put the kettle on as soon as we get in.'

'No, thank you.' Helen looked around her, completely wrong-footed. She had expected to walk into her department and immediately take charge, but instead she felt like a guest at a very jolly tea party. 'I would rather you showed me around, if you don't mind?'

'As you wish,' Nurse Willard said cheerfully, slipping her cloak off her shoulders. 'I'll give you a tour while Perkins puts the kettle on, how about that?'

Nurse Willard talked a great deal faster than she moved, Helen discovered.

'The Outpatients' clinics start at nine o'clock,' she said. 'On Mondays it's General Medical, Tuesdays is Orthopaedic, Wednesdays is General Surgical, Thursdays is Gynae and Fridays ENT. The consultants are all monsters, of course, apart from Mr Cooper, who looks like Tyrone Power. Mr Prentiss the ENT pundit is the worst. Do you know, he threw a basinful of water at poor little Nurse Kowalski last week, just for putting the wrong antiseptic in it? No wonder no one wants to assist in his clinic. Over there is the Plaster Room, and this is the Accident Treatment Room, where we deal with minor emergencies. The Cleansing Room is through that door there. Excuse me for asking, but you're Dr Tremayne's sister, aren't you?'

'That's right.' Helen opened the door to the operating theatre and looked inside. Just seeing the white-tiled walls of the theatre, with its glass-fronted cabinets full of gleaming instruments, made her feel at ease. This was what she was used to, everything shining, clean and orderly.

'I thought so. You look a lot like him. I went out with him once or twice, you know.'

'Really?' Helen inspected the instruments. Someone had done a good job of cleaning them, although they hadn't been put away quite as she would have liked.

'That was long before I met my Joe, of course. I mean, my fiancé,' Penny Willard said. 'He's a policeman,' she added importantly.

By the time they'd finished the tour of Casualty, Helen knew next to nothing about the running of the department, and everything she could possibly want to know about Penny's wedding plans, and her personal opinion of all the student nurses.

Penny spoke rapidly, her words tumbling out faster than Helen's brain could take them in. By the time they returned to the main Casualty hall, her head was reeling.

'You know, I was so pleased when we found out you were going to be taking over from Sister Percival,' Penny confided, settling herself comfortably behind the booking-in desk. 'She was all right in her way, I suppose, but it will be so much more fun to have someone my age running the place.'

'Fun?' Helen said.

'You know . . . someone I can chat to, have a laugh with. Ah, here's the tea.' She beamed as Perkins came in with a tray. 'I think you'll like it here, Sister. We're one big, happy family.'

Helen thought of the comments she'd overheard, and said nothing.

She knew she should set Penny Willard straight, make it clear right from the start that she was in charge and not there to have fun. But she was already so disheartened by what the doctor had said, she didn't want to make another enemy in the department.

Perhaps he was right, she thought miserably. Perhaps she was too young and inexperienced to take charge?

'Have you got a boyfriend?' Penny asked.

Helen stared at her, dumbstruck by the question. 'I'm a widow,' she said.

'Oh, gosh, yes, of course. I remember now. That was terribly sad.' Penny's lips pursed in the kind of sympathetic grimace Helen had grown to dread over the past two years.

Fortunately Penny changed the subject back to gossiping about the rest of the department. 'You won't have met the doctors yet, will you? There's Dr McKay – Scottish, terribly clever. And then there's Dr Adler. He's a great big bear, utterly adorable . . .'

'How very kind of you, Nurse Willard.'

Helen swung round. Two men stood behind them. One was a giant of a man, with a thick black beard and shaggy dark curls. The other was tall but of slighter build, with a sharp-featured face and keen brown eyes.

'You'll notice, Dr McKay, that Nurse Willard referred to me as utterly adorable, but the best she could come up for you was "clever"?' the big man went on, his black eyes twinkling. 'What does that say about you, do you think?'

'I think it probably says more about you than it does about me,' Dr McKay replied dryly. Hearing that well-spoken Scottish voice again filled Helen with fresh mortification.

She was even more mortified that she'd been caught drinking tea and gossiping with the other nurses. Another black mark against her, she thought.

But Nurse Willard seemed oblivious to any undercurrents. 'Oh, you!' She batted Dr Adler playfully on the arm. 'Have you met our new Sister Cas? Sister, these are the two I was telling you about, Dr Adler and Dr McKay.'

'How do you do, Sister?' Dr McKay's professional smile and firm handshake gave away none of his true feelings.

'I suppose Nurse Willard has been telling you all our secrets?' Dr Adler grinned. 'How will we ever gain your respect, I wonder?'

'I think it's *your* respect I have to gain,' Helen said, shooting a sideways look at Dr McKay.

If he noticed her barb he didn't react. 'Should we get these doors open, so we can start seeing some patients?' he said. 'That is what we're here for, after all.'

Chapter Five

No sooner had he said it than the telephone rang, shattering the silence. Nurse Willard pounced on it.

'That's the emergency telephone,' Dr Adler explained to Helen in a low voice. 'It rings when there's an ambulance on its way.'

Helen listened carefully, trying to piece together what Willard was saying.

'Right, yes. A car and a motorcycle, you say? Three casualties, I see. And how bad is the head injury?' She scribbled notes on the pad in front of her.

'What do we have?' Dr McKay asked, when she'd put the receiver down.

'Traffic accident. A car went into a motorcycle on Mile End Road. The motorcyclist got away with cuts and bruises and possible concussion, but the car driver is unconscious with possible spinal injury, and the passenger has a deep cut to his thigh and an injury to his wrist.'

All eyes turned to Dr McKay. 'We'll send the spinal injury straight to Theatre,' he said. 'Dr Adler, you can look after the motorcyclist, and I'll take care of the leg.'

'Right you are,' Dr Adler said. 'Sister, perhaps you could assist me?'

'No, she'll be assisting me,' Dr McKay interrupted him.

Helen caught his sharp brown-eyed stare and realised this was a test for her. The first of many, she was sure.

'As you wish, sir.' She turned to the student nurses, who were waiting keenly for their instructions. 'Perkins, telephone Theatre and let them know there is a head and possible spinal injury on the way down. Organise a dresser to be sent up here, too. French, get some blood ordered – Type O, since we don't know what group our patient might be.'

'Forget the blood,' Dr McKay snapped. 'We won't need it.'

'But with a deep cut . . .'

'The ambulance men didn't say he was bleeding to death, did they?'

'No, but—'

'Then we won't be needing the blood.'

He strutted off before she could reply. A shocked, embarrassed silence followed. Even Dr Adler looked a little shaken as he hurried off to his consulting room to prepare for his patient.

Helen pulled herself together quickly and turned to the students. 'I will be acting as scrub nurse for Dr McKay,' she told them briskly. 'Kowalski, I want you to help me. And French, please order that blood,' she added as an afterthought.

'But Dr McKay said—'

'Please,' Helen interrupted her. 'To be on the safe side,' she added.

'Yes, Sister.'

She had just finished scrubbing up when the patient arrived. Helen could hear his screams of agony from the other end of the passage.

She shouldered open the door to the operating theatre as the ambulance men were bringing him in.

'Got a right one here!' the driver said, rolling his eyes at Helen. 'Been cursing like a good 'un all the way from the Mile End Road, he has. Honest to God, you'd think he was dying!'

Helen looked down at the patient. He was young, in his early twenties. His face was the pale, translucent colour of candle wax, slick with sweat.

'My leg!' he screamed. 'Jesus, my leg!'

'Oi, stop the language! There are young ladies present.' The driver shot Helen an apologetic look. 'Sorry, Sister.'

'It's quite all right.' Helen fixed her attention on the young man. 'Get him on to the table, as quickly as you can, please.'

He screamed as Helen carefully removed the makeshift splint. His dressing was soaked in blood, and as she peeled it off she caught a sickening glimpse of raw, glistening muscle.

'Making a hell of a fuss, isn't he?' The ambulance man grinned at her.

'So would you, if you'd gashed your leg open like that.' Helen peered into the wound. It was deep, and there seemed to be fragments of broken glass embedded inside, but she had seen worse. The ambulance man was right, he did seem to be in a great deal more pain than he should have been. Unless there was something else going on, something she couldn't see . . .

She was aware of the man watching her, and smiled down at him reassuringly. 'Don't worry, I'll give you something for the pain and then we'll get you cleaned up.'

She gave him an injection of morphia and was carefully swabbing his wound when Dr McKay swept through the doors, his gloved hands raised.

His eyes looked so forbidding above his surgical mask, Helen's nerve started to fail her. She was probably mistaken anyway. But if she wasn't . . . She took a deep breath. 'Doctor, I think this patient might have a femoral fracture,' she said.

Dr McKay's brows puckered in a frown. 'The ambulance men didn't mention it,' he said shortly.

'The ambulance men don't have access to X-rays,' Helen replied.

'Neither do you, Sister.'

'No, but I know when a patient is in more pain than he should be.'

She knew arguing with a doctor was the worst crime she could commit. Even as a sister, her job was to carry out his instructions to the best of her ability and not to question his judgement in any way. But she knew from her experience in Theatre that doctors and surgeons were only human. They could make mistakes, just like everybody else. Helen had seen patients die on the operating table because a consultant had missed something, and no one had had the courage to question them.

They faced each other across the table and for a moment Helen thought he was going to ignore her and carry on stitching up the patient. But to her relief he looked down at the young man and said, 'Right, let's see what you've been doing to yourself, shall we?'

The patient groaned, already groggy from the shot Helen had given him.

She waited tensely while Dr McKay took up his forceps and gently probed the open wound. She didn't want to humiliate herself by being wrong, but she didn't want to be right, either, for the poor young man's sake.

When Dr McKay looked up it was at Kowalski, who hovered by the door. 'Nurse, please telephone Theatre and let them know there is a fractured femur coming down. And alert the X-ray department, too.' He glanced at Helen. 'It seems you were right, Sister,' he murmured.

Helen said nothing. The silence became uncomfortable

as they waited for the porters to come and collect the patient.

Five minutes later, they were shifting the young man on to the trolley. 'Be careful,' Dr McKay warned. 'There's still some broken glass in the wound, which needs to come out. If a piece shifts it could sever the femoral . . .'

No sooner had the words left his mouth than a fountain of blood spurted violently from the wound. Helen grabbed a towel and started to mop at it, but the blood soaked straight through, flowing over her hands in a warm, sticky crimson tide.

Dr McKay reached for a tourniquet as Helen dropped the towel and moved to place her hands around the rim of the man's pelvis, her thumbs pressing down on the artery, feeling the hard bone underneath. She threw her weight against it, her feet slipping on the slick of blood under her shoes.

She'd lost the feeling in both her thumbs by the time Dr McKay got the tourniquet strapped into place and stemmed the tide of blood. Then he moved quickly to ligate the wound, tying off the two ends of the artery and bringing them together.

'How is he doing, Sister?' he asked, not looking up.

'His breathing is very shallow.' Helen felt for his pulse, leaving sticky red fingerprints on his skin. His heartbeat skittered underneath her fingertips. 'And his pulse is irregular.'

'We'll need some blood. Telephone down to—'

'I've already got it.' Helen nodded to Kowalski, who hurried off to prepare it.

'How . . . ?' She saw Dr McKay's expression change behind his surgical mask. She could see he didn't know whether to be angry that she'd defied his orders, or grateful that she had anticipated his needs. In the end, neither won.

'I'll give him a shot of Vasopressin, while his blood pressure is still up to it. Then we'll pack the wound and get him down to Theatre. They can sort him out from there,' he said shortly.

While Dr McKay administered the drug and packed the wound with Vaseline-soaked gauze, Helen set to work in the adjoining room, filling hot-water bottles and preparing blankets to keep the patient warm and prevent him from going into shock.

Fifteen minutes later, the young man was on his way down to Theatre, and Helen and Dr McKay were alone in the Cleansing Room.

She cast a quick sideways look at him as he scrubbed his fingers in the sink. His surgical gown was smeared with blood, but Helen knew that was nothing to how she looked herself. Her own white gown was soaked through.

He didn't say a word to her, or even acknowledge her presence. But he didn't have to. Helen knew she'd proved her worth in that operating room.

Whatever happened, she would make Dr McKay eat his words.

Chapter Six

The new patient arrived on Blake ward in the middle of the morning. By midday he was awake and letting everyone else know it.

Frannie could hear his voice ringing the full length of the Male Orthopaedic ward as she did her rounds after lunch.

'You don't understand, I need to know!' the young man roared from behind the screens around his bed. 'Why won't someone tell me what's happened to him?'

'Someone's in a good mood,' Mr Anderson, an arthritic patient, remarked with a grin.

'Indeed.' Frannie picked up his chart from the end of the bed. 'Now, Mr Anderson, Nurse tells me you weren't satisfied with your meal?'

'Oh, it was right enough. There just wasn't a lot of it.'

'That's because you need to lose weight.'

'But I'm starving!'

Frannie looked at the man, his bulk almost filling the narrow hospital bed. Starving wasn't a word she would ever use to describe Freddie Anderson. 'It's for your own good, Mr Anderson. You're putting too much strain on those joints, and it isn't helping your arthritis.'

'I know that, Sister. But have a heart. A fellow like me can't live on that rabbit food you dish out. A nice steak and kidney pud, that's what I fancy.' He smacked his lips.

'I'm sure you do, Mr Anderson, but I'm afraid I can't allow it. Doctor's orders.'

'Couldn't I at least have a biscuit or something? Just to see me through till teatime?'

Frannie looked at his round, appealing face, then at the patient in the bed next to him. 'Why don't you just ask Mr Maudsley to give you his, as usual?' she said.

'Me, Sister? I don't do anything of the kind!' Eric Maudsley tried and failed to look innocent, but all he managed was a sheepish grin at his neighbour. He was as thin as Mr Anderson was fat, and Frannie knew the two men were firm friends.

'I reckon we've been rumbled, Eric,' Mr Anderson sighed.

'True,' his friend agreed. 'Sister's got eyes and ears everywhere.'

'Indeed, I have,' Frannie said. 'Really, Mr Anderson, we haven't put you on this diet to punish you. If you could just—'

'But I need to know!' The young man's voice bellowed again, drowning Frannie out. 'Where's Richard? What have they done with him?'

'I know what I'd like to do to that noisy beggar!' Mr Anderson muttered.

'Quite. Now, as I was saying—'

'Is he dead? Is that why no one will tell me anything?'

'Listen to him going on!' Mr Maudsley tutted. 'Strewth, I hope he ain't going to keep that racket up!'

'Oh, he won't. Believe me.' Frannie replaced the chart and smiled sweetly at the two men. 'Excuse me for a moment, would you?'

As she walked away, she heard Mr Anderson chuckling, 'That's done it, Eric. He's got her on the warpath now.'

'That's right, Sister. You give him what for!' Mr Maudsley called after her.

Effie O'Hara, the student nurse, whipped round as

Frannie swished aside the screen. 'I-I'm sorry, Sister,' she stammered, her blue eyes wide with panic. 'I've been trying to calm him down, but—'

'It's quite all right, Nurse, I know you were doing your best.' Frannie turned a severe expression on the young man in the bed. He was in a sorry state, his leg raised in a Hodgen splint, a complex metal contraption of wires and pulleys. His right hand and arm were also in a plaster cast, and his face was splotched with bruises. But there was a truculent expression in his green eyes as he looked at her.

'Who are you?' he demanded. 'Are you in charge here?'

Frannie had already studied his notes when he was first brought up to the ward. Adam Campbell, twenty-one years old from Pimlico. Fractured forearm and femur and a severed femoral artery. He seemed very angry for someone who had narrowly escaped death.

'Indeed I am, Mr Campbell,' she replied. 'Now, what seems to be the matter?'

'I want to know what's happened to Richard.'

'Richard?'

'Richard Webster. My friend. He was driving the car when it—' He swallowed. 'Is he all right? I keep asking, but no one will tell me anything.'

'That's because we don't know anything. And shouting at poor Nurse O'Hara is not going to change that.'

'But . . .'

'But,' she held up her hand as he started to argue, 'if you do as you're told and try to stay calm, I will find out what's happened to your friend.'

He eyed her warily. 'And you'll let me know?'

'Of course. But you have to stop shouting and disturbing the other patients. Do we have an agreement?'

'I suppose so,' he said grumpily.

'Good.' Frannie nodded to Effie O'Hara, who followed her through the curtains. 'Now, Nurse,' Frannie said. 'Do you think you can cope with this patient, or would you like me to find another nurse to take over?'

Effie O'Hara squared her shoulders. She was a tall, slender girl with typical Irish colouring – milky-white skin, startling blue eyes and an abundance of wavy dark hair escaping from her cap.

'I can manage, Sister,' she said.

'Keep him as quiet as you can. You have nursed a post-operative patient before?'

Yes, Sister.'

Frannie glanced towards the screens. 'Try to find out if he has any friends or family, too. Surely someone must be looking for him.'

Adam Campbell drifted off to sleep shortly after Sister Blake left. Effie sat at his bedside, watching him anxiously, trying to work out whether he'd lost colour or whether his breathing was too shallow. She didn't want to admit it to Sister, but she dreaded looking after post-operative patients on her own. She was always convinced they would die and it would somehow be her fault.

Mr Campbell seemed much nicer when he wasn't awake and being a nuisance, she thought. Not bad-looking either, in a way. He was well built, his dark hair unfashionably long with just a hint of a curl at the ends. She could imagine his pale skin freckling in the sun.

She watched the rise and fall of his chest under his hospital gown. Was it her imagination or was it rising and falling a little less than it had before? Panic assailed her. Come to think of it, was it rising and falling at all?

She had laid her head against his chest and was trying

to gauge his breathing when he suddenly opened his eyes and stared at her.

'What are you doing?' he asked. He spoke in a well-educated drawl, like a medical student.

'Making sure you're still breathing.' Effie straightened up, shamefaced at being caught out.

'Have you been sitting here all this time, watching me sleep?'

'It's my job to keep an eye on you.'

'It's very disturbing.'

'I have to do it until we know you've recovered properly from the operation.' Effie reached for his pulse. 'How are you feeling?' she asked. 'Any nausea or pain?'

'No.'

'Do you want me to fetch a bottle for you?'

'A bottle?' He looked mystified for a moment, then suddenly it dawned on him what she was talking about, and his expression turned to outrage. 'Certainly not!'

'You'll have to use one sooner or later.'

'Not in front of you, I won't.'

'Oh, I've seen it all before,' she said airily. 'Besides, I'll need to take a sample.' She finished taking his pulse and noted down the figure on the chart. She could feel him watching her.

'Do you know if Sister's found out anything about Richard?' he asked.

Effie shook her head. 'But I'm sure she'll tell you as soon as she knows anything.' She looked down at him. 'Is there anyone we can contact, to let them know what's happened? Any family?'

His face turned to stone. 'I don't have any family.'

'A friend, then?'

He thought for a moment. 'You could contact Adeline,' he said.

'Who is she?'

'My girlfriend. She'll want to know where I am.'

'Where will we find her?'

He gave her an address in Bloomsbury, and Effie wrote it down carefully.

'You will let her know, won't you?' Adam said.

'Of course.'

Sister Blake was sitting at the table in the middle of the ward when Effie gave her the slip of paper with the address written on it.

'Adeline Moreau? What a pretty name,' she commented. 'Thank you, O'Hara, I'll inform the Almoner's office. I daresay it will make the patient feel a lot better to see a familiar face.'

'Yes, Sister.'

Sister Blake looked up at her. She was by far the prettiest of the sisters, small, dark and lively-looking. She was one of the nicest, too. In the month Effie had been working on the Male Orthopaedic ward, she had never known Sister raise her voice to anyone. All the patients adored her because she was always willing to have a laugh and a joke with them.

'You've done very well, O'Hara,' she said. 'I don't think Mr Campbell is going to be the easiest patient to deal with, do you?'

'No, Sister.' Effie glowed with quiet pride. Wouldn't her elder sisters be surprised to hear her being praised for once? she thought.

Sister Blake went back to her paperwork, but Effie hovered at her shoulder. She wondered if she should ruin it all by asking her next question.

Finally, Sister Blake looked up. 'Was there something else, O'Hara?'

'Please, Sister, I wondered if you'd had any news about

Mr Campbell's friend – Mr Webster? Only he seemed very anxious to know . . .'

'Ah, yes. I'm glad you reminded me.' Sister Blake looked troubled. 'I'm afraid it isn't very good news, Nurse. Unfortunately, Mr Webster sustained a serious head injury during the crash. The doctors have had to operate to relieve some of the pressure inside his skull, but he's still unconscious. And there is some doubt as to whether he has severed his spinal cord, too.'

'Will he live, Sister?'

'I don't know, Nurse,' Sister Blake admitted heavily. 'The doctors have done all they can. He's recovering on Holmes ward.'

'I see. Thank you, Sister.' Effie paused, taking it in. 'Poor Mr Campbell.'

Sister Blake looked up at her with a quizzical smile. 'Don't you mean poor Mr Webster?' she asked.

Effie blushed. 'Yes, of course, Sister. I just meant – Mr Campbell seemed so worried.'

'It does you credit to be so concerned about him,' Sister Blake said. Then she added, 'But don't get too concerned about him, will you?'

'No, Sister.'

On her way back down the ward, Effie was waylaid by her elder sister Bridget, a senior staff nurse on Blake.

'What did Sister want with you?' she demanded. Unlike smiling Sister Blake, Bridget never missed the excuse to bully her. 'I hope you're not in trouble again?'

'If you must know, Sister was telling me what a good job I did with the new patient in bed one,' Effie preened.

'Hmm. I noticed you were with him a long time.' Bridget's eyes narrowed. 'I hope you weren't flirting with him?'

Effie's mouth fell open. She might have known it would

kill her sister to spare her a kind word or a bit of praise. 'Honest to God, Bridget, what makes you say that?'

'I've seen you with the patients, especially the young and good-looking ones. You're often over-familiar with them. And you must call me Staff while we're on the ward,' Bridget reminded her haughtily.

'I can't help it if I'm naturally friendly – *Staff*.' Effie emphasised the word. 'Besides, I'd have to be as desperate as you to flirt with someone unconscious!'

Bridget sent her a narrow look. They looked alike, with their dark colouring, blue eyes and willowy height, but there the similarity ended. Bridget had turned into a bitter old spinster before she was thirty, and Effie had no intention of ending up like her.

'I've a good mind to send you to Matron for your cheek,' her sister snapped. 'Now go and make yourself useful. It's almost time for the tea round.'

As Effie's luck would have it, her middle sister Katie was in the kitchen. After passing her State Finals, she had chosen to join Male Orthopaedic as a junior staff nurse. Effie couldn't imagine why she would willingly choose to work alongside their bossy elder sister.

As they prepared the tea trolley, Effie complained to Katie about what Bridget had said.

'She's just jealous because the patients like me more than they like her,' she fumed as she set out the teacups on the saucers.

'You weren't flirting, then?' Katie asked. She was as dark-haired as her sisters, but smaller and plumper.

'Not you, too!'

Katie shrugged. 'Bridget's right, you are over-familiar with the patients. You're here to look after them, not to find a boyfriend,' she said primly.

Effie stared at her. Katie used to be man mad, but since

she'd got engaged to her boyfriend Tom she'd turned as priggish as Bridget.

'If I wanted to find a boyfriend, I certainly wouldn't be looking at Adam Campbell, believe me!' said Effie with feeling.

'All the same, you should watch it.' As usual, Katie had to have the last word.

Effie ignored her and shoved the trolley through the kitchen doors. She loved the patients on Blake ward, and Sister Blake was an angel. But thanks to Katie and Bridget, she couldn't wait for her three-month stint there to end.

Chapter Seven

Friday morning was the Ear, Nose and Throat Outpatients' clinic, run by Mr Prentiss.

Patrick Prentiss was a brilliant surgeon, but he had a reputation at the Nightingale Hospital for being difficult. Helen had prided herself on being able to handle his explosive rages during her time in Theatre, which was why she'd volunteered to assist him instead of subjecting the poor students to his temper.

But after two hours of overgrown adenoids, infected sinuses, deflected nasal septums, polyps and mastoids, she was beginning to wonder why she'd agreed so readily. She'd forgotten what a hard taskmaster he could be.

She prepared the instruments and filled bowls with water, administered anaesthetic and grimly held on to patients' heads while Mr Prentiss set to work, syringing ears, piercing sinuses with terrifying pointed instruments, and banging away at infected mastoids with a hammer and chisel. Then, when the operation was over, she would usher the patient away, tidy up and remove the instruments for cleaning, then replace them with fresh ones from the steriliser.

And all the time, Mr Prentiss was barking orders at her. 'Adjust the light, Sister, I can't see a thing.' 'Where is the Siegel's speculum?' 'For God's sake, dry that ear. How am I supposed to examine it?'

Thankfully, by one o'clock it was all over. The last infected sinus had been drained and sent home, and Helen could relax.

She was putting the last of the instruments into the steriliser when French, one of the students, stuck her head around the door.

'Please, Sister, come quickly!' she panted. 'A patient's just dropped dead in the waiting room!'

In the main Casualty hall, all hell had broken loose. Helen arrived just in time to see the porters carrying away a stretcher draped in a blanket, while all around people were crying and shaking their heads and talking loudly among themselves. Penny Willard was handing out cups of tea to everyone.

'If you could just calm down, please . . .' she called out, her voice lost in the commotion.

Another student, Perkins, sat white-faced in the corner, her arms wrapped around herself.

Before Helen could reach her, Dr McKay bore down on her out of nowhere, looking like an avenging angel in his flapping white coat.

'Where the hell have you been?' he demanded.

'In the Outpatients' clinic. What happened?' Helen looked around.

'I'll tell you what happened. A man has just collapsed with a cardiac failure, right in front of the other patients. And you weren't here to deal with it!'

Helen looked at Perkins. Her face was blotchy with tears. 'I-I'm sorry, Sister, I didn't know what to do,' she stammered. 'He said he felt sick, so I went off to fetch a dish. But then he suddenly turned a funny grey colour and started sweating, and the next thing I knew he was on the floor – I didn't know whether to stay with him or to fetch the doctor.' She wiped the tears from her face with a shaking hand.

'Why didn't you get Nurse Willard to help?' Helen asked.

'Please, Sister, she was on her break. There was no one here but me.' Perkins started to cry again, great heaving sobs that shook her body.

Helen hurried over and sat down beside her, putting her arm around the girl's shaking shoulders. 'Don't cry, Perkins, it's all right. You have no reason to blame yourself,' she soothed her.

'Quite right. She isn't to blame – you are!' Dr Mckay snapped. 'The poor girl should never have been left in charge of the Casualty department on her own.' His brown eyes blazed. 'That man might have been saved if you'd been here to act. But instead you're off in Outpatients, merrily cleaning instruments while chaos descends!'

Dr Adler stepped in. 'Now I'm sure there's no call for that. Sister Dawson is doing her best—'

'Then her best obviously isn't good enough, is it?' Dr McKay turned on her accusingly. 'You're supposed to be the sister. You're supposed to be in charge.'

Helen stared at him, forcing herself to stay calm in the face of his blistering anger. 'I *am* in charge.'

'Are you? You could have fooled me. Perhaps if you started acting like a real sister instead of a glorified probationer, we wouldn't have situations like this.'

With one final, quick scowl at Helen, he was gone. She heard the door to his consulting room slam, sending a shudder through her.

She looked around. Penny Willard, the students and a line of patients were all staring back at her. Seeing their shocked expressions was almost too much for Helen. She could almost feel herself shrinking before their eyes, becoming diminished and insignificant. A creature to be pitied, not respected.

She roused herself, squaring her shoulders and drawing herself to her full height. She would not, could not, allow herself to be treated in such a way, not in front of her nurses. If she lost their respect, she would lose everything.

She turned to little Nurse Perkins. 'Perkins, you may take five minutes off to gather yourself. Nurse Willard, will you take over, please?'

Helen didn't wait for a reply before she marched off to Dr McKay's consulting room.

She was so fired up with anger she walked straight in without knocking. Dr McKay looked up at her in surprise.

'What the—'

But before he could begin his sentence, Helen got in first. 'How dare you speak to me like that in front of my nurses?' she snapped. 'I realise you were upset over the death of a patient, but you were rude and disrespectful, and I won't stand for it. Would you ever have spoken to Sister Percival like that? I doubt it.' She saw his eyes narrow, but she was too angry to care. 'I know you don't like or approve of me, Doctor, but nevertheless I have been given a job to do, and I intend to do it to the best of my abilities,' she continued. 'I would appreciate it if you could refrain from trying to humiliate me in front of my nurses, and treat me with the respect and courtesy I deserve!'

Without waiting for a reply, she left the room. Her legs were shaking so much she could hardly walk.

Rather than go back and face the other nurses, Helen sought refuge in the Plaster Room to give herself time to calm down. As her anger abated, she began to realise what a foolish thing she'd done. Had she really just given a senior doctor a dressing down? Even if Dr McKay had deserved it, it was a shocking thing to do. It would probably also spell the end of her short career as a ward sister. Once he told Matron what she'd said, that would be it for her.

47

Not that she really cared. She couldn't go on working for Dr McKay the way things were. He had been spoiling for a fight for the past week, ever since she'd arrived.

Perhaps this was what he'd wanted all along, she thought. Perhaps he'd been deliberately goading her, trying to make her lose her temper so he could have her removed? If so, she'd played right into his hands.

She jumped guiltily when the door opened and Dr Adler stuck his head round. 'Is this a bad time?' he asked.

'No, not at all.' Helen hurriedly turned away, smoothing down her apron. 'I'm sorry, Doctor, did you need me?'

Dr Adler smiled. 'I came to see if you were all right.'

His kind face almost undid her composure completely. 'I'm quite all right, Doctor. Thank you,' she said.

'I also came to apologise for Dr McKay. He shouldn't have spoken to you like that.'

'I'm afraid I was rather rude to him in return,' Helen said.

'So I understand.' Dr Adler looked more amused than angry.

Helen bit her lip. 'Is he going to tell Matron?'

'Not if I can help it.' Dr Adler grinned at her. 'Don't look so worried, Sister. Dr McKay isn't one to bear a grudge, I assure you.'

All the same, Helen knew she hadn't made things better between them.

'He had every right to be angry,' she said. 'A man died because of my negligence.'

'If it's any consolation, he would have died anyway,' Dr Adler said. 'We've seen that patient in here before. He's had myocarditis since he contracted diphtheria as a child. His heart was barely functioning. Truly, it was only a matter of time.'

'That's not what Dr McKay thinks.'

Dr Adler let out a sigh. 'I don't know what's troubling Dr McKay. He doesn't usually take things so personally. And he isn't usually so difficult, either.'

'I know what's wrong with him. He doesn't like me.'

'I'm sure that's not true—' Dr Adler started to say, but Helen cut him off.

'Dr Adler, I heard the two of you talking on the morning I first arrived,' she said. 'Dr McKay made it quite clear he feels I'm too young and inexperienced, and can't cope with the job.'

The worst of it was, she proved him right every day. He made her so nervous, she had started making silly mistakes. Things she'd done a hundred times, things she had never got wrong even as a student, were suddenly impossible for her. She handed him the wrong forceps, or set out the wrong instruments for a procedure, or she gave an injection clumsily and caused the patient to yelp in pain.

And all the time she could feel David McKay watching her, judging her. She didn't have to look at him, she could just imagine him silently shaking his head in reproof.

'I'm sorry you had to hear that,' Dr Adler said solemnly. 'And you know I don't agree, don't you? I think you're a first-rate nurse.'

'Thank you.' Helen finished washing her hands and reached for the towel. In the week she'd been in Casualty, she'd come to realise what a kind, generous, open-hearted man Jonathan Adler was. He'd gone out of his way to welcome her and to make up for his colleague's mean-spiritedness. She felt she could confide in him. 'Do you want to know the real reason I was helping at Mr Prentiss's Outpatients' clinic?' she said.

'Nurse Willard said it was because all the students were terrified of him?'

'That wasn't the only reason. I also wanted to escape from Dr McKay and his constant criticism.'

'Is he really that bad?' Dr Adler frowned.

'I would rather assist Mr Prentiss with a hundred tonsil ops than clean a scraped knee for Dr McKay,' Helen replied.

Dr Adler was silent for a moment, taking it in. 'But he's usually so kind.'

'I know.' That was what made it even more difficult. She'd seen Dr McKay show great tenderness to his patients. He comforted distressed parents, made fractious children laugh, and even slipped a shilling to a homeless tramp who'd wandered in out of the cold. He was also kind and patient with the student nurses, forgiving them their endless mistakes.

But not with her. Helen couldn't remember a time when he'd even looked at her with any real warmth.

'It's only been a week,' Dr Adler said. 'Perhaps he just needs more time to get to know you?'

'I don't think so.' Helen shook her head. 'I think it might be easier for everyone if I left. Then at least you could find someone more experienced for the post.'

'No!' Dr Adler's broad, bearded face was full of dismay. 'Don't even think about leaving, Sister, please. You're a wonderful nurse, and you've done such a good job here already. We'd be lost without you.'

Helen smiled wryly. 'Thank you, but I don't think Dr McKay sees it that way.'

And after the way she'd just spoken to him, she was sure it would be all-out war between them.

Chapter Eight

As usual, Effie was given the job of changing Adam Campbell's dressing. She caught the other nurses' sympathetic looks as she made her way up the ward with the trolley, but no one offered to help her. In the fortnight he'd been there, Adam had managed to upset everyone on Blake ward except her. And that wasn't for the want of trying on his part.

'Oh, it's you,' he greeted her sullenly.

'Good morning, Mr Campbell,' Effie replied through gritted teeth, determined to maintain her sunny disposition come what may.

'I don't know what's good about it.' He eyed her gloomily. 'I suppose you've come to poke and prod me again?'

'I've come to change your dressing.' She checked the traction on his splint, as Sister had shown her.

'Why does it always have to be you?' he demanded. 'You're so clumsy.'

'I'm afraid you're stuck with me because no one else will do it.' She inspected his leg closely. 'No sign of splint sores, which is a good thing.'

He shifted himself upright, a look of genuine interest on his face. 'Really? Why not?'

'I suppose it's because the splint isn't rubbing against your skin—'

'No, I mean why won't any of the nurses come near me?'

Effie paused. 'They find you – difficult,' she said.

'Don't you find me difficult?'

'Oh, I find you impossible. But I'm only the junior, so I get stuck with all the jobs no one else wants. Still, it could be worse.' She shrugged. 'I could be scrubbing the toilets, I suppose.' She smiled brightly. 'Right, let's have that leg.'

He lay there in martyred silence as she removed his old dressing, checked and cleaned his wound, then applied a new one. It wasn't until she'd almost finished that he suddenly blurted out, 'Has there been any word from Adeline yet?'

Effie's heart sank. Every day he asked the same question, and every day she dreaded it. 'Not yet, Mr Campbell,' she said briskly. 'But I'm sure she'll be in touch soon.'

'But it's been two weeks.' His eyes narrowed suspiciously. 'Are you sure they've written to her?'

'Sister gave her address to the Almoner's office.'

'But did she give them the right address? I wouldn't put it past you to get it wrong.'

Effie gritted her teeth. 'I'm sure she'll be in touch,' she repeated doggedly.

Adam thought about it for a moment. 'I should write to her myself,' he said. 'Where can I get some writing paper?'

She considered it for a moment as she finished dressing his wound and collected up the used dressings. 'I suppose you'd have to ask someone nicely to bring some in for you,' she said.

He turned to her. 'Will you—'

Effie held up her hand. 'Only if you ask nicely,' she reminded him.

He sighed. 'Please, Nurse O'Hara, please, please, will you be so kind as to get hold of some writing paper for me? If you don't mind. Please?' he said with exaggerated humility.

Effie smiled. 'Well, since you put it like that . . .' she said, pushing back the screens. But Adam wasn't listening to her. He was staring beyond her shoulder. Effie turned to see a man standing at the foot of his bed. He was in his forties, tall, dark and distinguished-looking in an army officer's uniform.

'Can I help . . .' she started to say, but Adam interrupted.

'What are you doing here?' he demanded.

'I came as soon as I heard.'

'I didn't send for you.'

'Nevertheless, I'm here.' The man's face, shadowed by his peaked cap, gave nothing away. 'How are you, Adam?' he said stiffly.

Adam looked sullen. 'Why should you care?'

Effie looked around the ward for one of her sisters to help her, but for once neither Bridget nor Katie nor any of the other staff nurses were lurking around. And it was Sister Blake's afternoon off.

'Could someone please tell me what's going on?' she asked.

'Allow me to introduce Major Campbell, of the Lancashire Fusiliers,' Adam said, a mocking edge to his voice.

Effie saw the man wince. 'I'm also his father,' he said.

'Support the Peace Society! No war at any cost!'

It was a Saturday afternoon three weeks before Christmas, and Oxford Street was packed with Christmas shoppers. Lights blazed in every window, illuminating the freezing twilight. The inviting aroma of roasting chestnuts hung in the air. On the corner, a group of carol singers joined in with a rousing 'O Come All Ye Faithful'.

Wet slush seeped through Frannie's shoes as she stood shivering on the street corner, pressing pamphlets into the hands of passers-by.

'Support the Peace Society. Tell the government we don't want war!' she cried.

'Never mind the government, it's that Hitler you want to tell!'

Frannie turned round. Two young soldiers in uniform were looking down at her.

'What's this, then?' One of them took the pamphlet and flicked through it. 'You one of them Communists, missus?'

'No, I'm not,' Frannie said, facing him. 'I'm just someone who believes that war is wrong.'

'So you reckon we should just roll over and let Hitler do what he likes, is that it?' the other soldier sneered, an insolent expression on his face.

'I'm saying we shouldn't get dragged into someone else's fight like we did last time.'

The soldier's chin lifted. 'My old man fought for his country in the last war and he was proud to do it,' he said.

Frannie turned on him. He looked so young, twenty years old if that. He reminded her of Matthew and his friends, little boys in men's uniforms. Perhaps one day his sweetheart would see him off on a train, never to return.

'But he wasn't fighting for his country, was he? He was fighting for a few hundred yards of mud that meant nothing to anyone,' she said. 'Do you know how many British boys lost their lives on the Western and Eastern fronts? Thousands of young lives wasted, and for what? So some general could stick a pin in a map of a place no one's heard of.'

The soldiers looked at each other, and Frannie could sense their uncertainty.

'The Germans are our enemies,' one of them insisted. 'They were our enemies then and they're our enemies now.'

'Why?'

The young man's face puckered in confusion. 'Eh?'

'Why are they your enemies? How many Germans do you know? I bet you could walk past dozens on this very street and not even know them. They're not monsters, they're just ordinary people like you and me, going about their business and looking forward to Christmas.'

'Tell that to the poor Jews who've had their shops smashed up!' one of the young men said. 'Tell that to the poor sods who've been turned out of their houses and put into camps. And you reckon we should turn a blind eye to that?'

'Of course not,' Frannie said. 'But I don't want to see young men like you and your friend dying either. Do you want to die?' she challenged them. 'Do you want your mothers to get a telegram, telling them you've been lost?'

'I've heard enough!' the soldier stopped her. 'This is what I think of your stupid ideas!' He ripped her pamphlet up and scattered the pieces into the air. Frannie watched them fluttering down like confetti, soaking into the slushy ground.

'Good riddance to bad rubbish!' The soldier laughed, and he and his mate sauntered off.

Frannie bent down to pick up the pieces, and her friend Ruth joined her.

'Take no notice of them' she said, helping to pick up the scattered fragments. 'They're just ignorant.'

'No, they've got a point,' Frannie said. 'That's the problem. It's hard to argue against standing up to someone who's walking all over everyone else. But the thought of going to war again . . .' She shuddered. 'I just

55

feel so sorry for them. I don't want to see them go off and get killed.'

They stood up, pulling their coats tighter around them.

'Shall we call it a day?' Ruth said.

Frannie nodded. 'I've got to get back on duty at five,' she said. 'And I don't know about you, but I'm frozen to the marrow!'

She was still cold to her bones when she went back on the ward later. Thanks heavens the maid had a nice crackling fire going, she thought as she warmed her icy fingers in front of the flames.

'Sister?' Bridget O'Hara approached her. 'I thought you should know, Mr Campbell's father is here.'

Frannie frowned. 'His father? I didn't think he had any family?'

'Apparently he has. His father has been ringing round the hospitals for days, wondering where he is.'

'Well, I never. Where is he now?'

'He's waiting in your office. I thought you might want to see him?'

'I do. Thank you, Staff.'

Still shivering, Frannie made her way down the short corridor to her office. As she reached the door, she could see a man's blurred outline through the frosted glass.

'Mr Campbell?' She said, opening the door. 'Sorry to keep you. I'm—'

The man turned round in his seat and she stopped talking, the greeting dying on her lips, as she found herself staring into a face she hadn't thought she would ever see again.

Chapter Nine

He rose to his feet, and Frannie gasped, as if she were seeing a ghost. He stood there, tall and broad-shouldered, in his army uniform, just as he had when she'd last seen him on that railway station platform.

'John?'

There were threads of grey in his close-cropped dark hair and fine lines fanning from the corners of his green eyes, but she would have known Matthew's best friend anywhere.

'Miss Wallace?' He frowned, uncertain. 'Is it you?'

'Yes, it's me.' She gave an embarrassed smile, her hand going up to touch her hair, hidden under her linen bonnet. 'Although it's a wonder you still recognise me, after all these years.'

'I'd know you anywhere.'

Her legs felt weak with shock and Frannie crossed the room quickly to sit behind her desk before they gave way. She motioned for John to sit down opposite her.

'I can't believe it,' she marvelled. 'Seeing you, after all these years . . . I thought you were dead,' she said frankly. 'When you didn't come back to the village after the war, we all assumed—'

'That I hadn't made it?' John said grimly. 'I'll admit, there were a few close calls. But then after the war I decided to re-enlist. The army was my family by then.'

Frannie regarded him across the desk and felt very sad for the orphanage boy with no home to go to and no family to wonder what had become of him. She suddenly wished she'd looked for him, or at least mourned him. But she'd been too consumed with grieving for Matthew to give his friend a second thought.

She felt herself drifting back to those days, and quickly dragged her thoughts back to the present. 'You've seen your son?'

'Oh, yes, I've seen him.' John's tone was chilly.

'I have to say, Mr Campbell led us to believe that he had no family.'

John's mouth twisted. 'That sounds like Adam. We're not close,' he explained. 'Having a father who's an officer in the British Army is rather an embarrassment when you're a dedicated pacifist, I think.'

That was a hint of mockery in his tone that made Frannie think of the soldiers she'd encountered on Oxford Street.

'How is he?' asked John. 'I understand there was an accident of some kind?'

'Hasn't he told you?'

He gave a small smile. 'As I said, we're not close. He has never been inclined to confide in me about anything.' He leaned forward. 'Perhaps you could tell me what happened?'

His face paled as Frannie explained about the accident, and the extent of Adam's injuries. They might not have been close, but there was no doubting John's concern for his son.

'And he will recover, you say? There won't be any permanent damage?'

Frannie nodded. 'As long as he's patient, does as he's told and allows us to look after him, he should be back on his feet soon enough.'

'Patience has never been my son's strong point. Neither has being told what to do.'

'We're beginning to realise that,' Frannie admitted ruefully.

John was silent for a moment, and she could see the emotion building behind his calm face. 'But what on earth was Adam doing, racing cars around the streets in the early hours of the morning?' he said at last.

'You'd have to ask him that.'

'Much good that would do me, I daresay.' A muscle twitched in John's jaw. 'I'm just relieved I've found him at last. I've been ringing around the hospitals for days. I was beginning to fear the worst.'

'As I said, he should make a full recovery.' Frannie paused, then said, 'Will your wife be coming to see him?'

'My wife is dead.'

'Oh. I'm sorry, I didn't realise.'

She tried to read John's face, but his expression gave nothing away. She couldn't stop staring at him as he got to his feet and put his cap back on. He looked every inch the officer, tall and strapping with his gleaming leather boots and belt. Even with her dislike of anything military, Frannie couldn't help being impressed.

She also couldn't stop thinking about the boy she'd grown up with, the strong, silent young man in his rough work clothes, pushing the plough through the fields behind the heavy horses. Seeing him here made her think about Matthew again. She could picture the two of them laughing together, and it gave her a sharp pain that she hadn't felt for many years.

'I must be getting back,' he said, interrupting her thoughts. 'Thank you for sparing the time to speak to me.'

'It's no trouble.' Frannie followed him to her office door. 'Are you based in London?'

'For the time being. I'm staying at my club in Piccadilly while Adam is in hospital. I thought it might be best.'

'I'm sure he'll appreciate that,' Frannie said.

John gave her a sad smile. 'Then you don't know my son,' he said.

As he went to leave, she said, 'It was good to see you again, John.'

'And you, Miss Wallace.'

'Frannie,' she said. 'Please call me Frannie.'

'Why didn't you tell us you had a father?' Effie asked that night as she handed Adam Campbell his cup of bedtime cocoa.

'I don't want anything to do with him.'

'Why not? He seems like a nice man.'

'That's all you know, isn't it?'

Effie picked up the magazines Major Campbell had brought with him, and tidied them away in Adam's locker. 'Did you have a falling out?' she asked.

'How can you fall out with someone you barely know?' His expression was bitter. 'The only time he ever speaks to me is to remind me what a disappointment I am to him.'

'He certainly seemed as if he cared.'

'As I said, you know nothing about it.'

'You never know, perhaps this will bring you together?' Effie suggested brightly.

'It's too late for that. I told you, I want nothing to do with him.' Adam glared into his cocoa. 'This tastes odd. Are you sure you're not trying to poison me?'

'Don't put ideas in my head,' she murmured under her breath.

His brows lifted. 'That's not a very caring thing to say. You're not a very good nurse, are you?'

'You're not a very good patient.'

'I suppose you'd rather I flirted with you, like the others?

Don't deny it, I've seen you,' he accused. 'You're always laughing and joking with the patients.'

Effie sighed. He sounded just like her sisters! 'I'm being friendly. Time goes quicker when you're having a laugh. You should try it sometime.'

'What have I got to laugh about?'

'You're alive, for one thing. You could have died in that crash.'

She knew she'd gone too far when she saw his face darken. 'It might have been better if I had,' he muttered.

Effie stared at him, shocked. 'That's a horrible thing to say! And it's ungrateful, too, to wish yourself dead when your friend is lying unconscious . . .' She saw his stricken expression and stopped abruptly. As usual, she'd let her mouth run away with her and gone too far. 'I'm sorry, I shouldn't have said that,' she murmured.

'No, you're right,' Adam said heavily. He looked up at her. 'I keep asking Sister how he's getting on, but she always says there's no more news. He's not going to get better, is he?'

Effie thought about Richard Webster, lying in a coma on Male Surgical. She didn't know a great deal about brain injuries, but she couldn't imagine him making a full recovery after so long.

'I don't know,' she admitted. 'Truly, I don't.'

'It should have been me,' Adam said. 'Richard is a good man, a kind man. He's never hurt a soul in his life. I should be the one who's dying, not him.'

'You mustn't talk like that.'

'Why not? He doesn't deserve to die!'

'Neither do you.'

'How do you know?' Adam's eyes turned to green ice. 'You don't know anything about me, or my life. You don't know what I've done.'

61

Effie felt a blush rising in her cheeks. 'I was just trying to make you feel better, that's all.'

'Well, don't,' he said sourly. 'Save your Florence Nightingale act for someone who appreciates it!'

Her friend and fellow student Jess Jago was already in their attic room when Effie returned to the students' home that evening. Jess lay on her narrow bed, still in her uniform, arms outstretched.

'I can't move,' she complained. 'Sister's had me running around all day, changing dressings and sorting out drips and drains and taking samples and testing urines, and I haven't had time to think.'

'Poor you,' Effie sympathised. 'You should be on Blake, it's much more fun.'

She went to the chest of drawers and started rummaging around inside. Jess lifted her head to look at her.

'What are you looking for?'

'I had some writing paper in here.'

'Writing paper?' Jess propped herself up on her elbows, weariness forgotten. 'Who are you writing to?'

'It's for a patient, if you must know.'

Jess's dark brows shot up. 'You're writing letters to a patient? Won't Sister Blake mind? Sister Holmes doesn't even approve of us looking at our patients, in case they become infatuated with us.'

Effie grinned. 'Some chance, in this horrible old uniform! No, it's for Mr Campbell. The young man who was in the car crash?'

'Don't tell me you've got a soft spot for him?'

'No! Actually, he's the most horrible man I've ever met. But I feel sorry for him. He seems sort of – lost.'

'You *do* have a soft spot for him!'

'No, I don't,' Effie denied heatedly. 'I'm just being a good nurse, that's all.'

'A good nurse doesn't get personally involved with her patients, Nurse O'Hara,' Jess mimicked Sister Holmes's strict tones. 'But it's hard not to sometimes, isn't it? Some of them are so sad.'

'I know.' Effie found the writing paper at last and put it beside her bed so she wouldn't forget it. Then she set about patiently folding up all her belongings and putting them back in the drawer. The Home Sister would create merry hell if she found a pair of stockings out of place.

'Like your friend Mr Campbell's mate,' Jess went on. 'He's a very sad case. Tragic, in fact.'

Effie turned round. 'You mean Mr Webster?'

'That's him.' Jess shook her head. 'Did you know he was engaged? Due to be married in the spring, apparently.'

'Poor man.' No wonder Adam Campbell felt so wretched about him.

'Not much chance of that now, of course,' Jess went on. 'You never know.'

Jess sent her a pitying look. 'Sister Holmes doesn't think he'll make it to Christmas. Not that anyone's told his fiancée that,' she went on. 'Poor girl comes in every day, just to sit by his bed and hold his hand. So sad.' She sighed. 'Still, that's love for you, I suppose.'

'I suppose,' Effie agreed. Not that she'd ever experienced such devotion herself. In spite of her best efforts, none of her boyfriends had ever shown more than a passing interest in her.

That was why she felt such sympathy for Adam Campbell. His girlfriend was treating him with similar indifference, and Effie knew he was breaking his heart over it.

Not that Jess seemed to understand, when Effie

explained it to her. 'I hope you're not getting too involved,' she warned.

'Of course not. I don't know why you'd think that.'

'Because I know you.' Jess smiled. 'You're far too soft-hearted for your own good.'

Effie frowned, irritated. 'You sound just like my sisters!' Why did everyone always think the worst of her?

When she returned to the ward the following morning, she went straight to Adam's bed. Typically, he looked put out to see her.

'You again,' he groaned.

She smiled. 'Did you miss me?'

'Not really. You nurses are all the same to me.'

'You're a cheery soul, aren't you?' She reached into the bib of her apron. 'I've a good mind not to give you this present.'

He looked sideways at her. 'A present?'

She handed him the packet of writing paper. 'I've brought this for you. So you can write to Adeline.'

'You brought it for me?' He stared at it, then at her. For a moment she thought he looked almost touched.

Then he lifted the notepaper to his face. 'Why does it smell of cheap scent?' he complained.

Effie sighed. And to think everyone imagined she would want to get involved with someone like him!

Chapter Ten

'I need your help,' William said.

Helen paused halfway through pulling the red rubber mackintosh sheet off the bed. She and her brother had just finished the Gynae Outpatients' clinic. William, a junior registrar, had taken the clinic, as the consultant Mr Cooper was away in France with his wife.

'How much do you want?' she sighed.

William looked offended. 'I don't need your money, thank you very much.'

'There's a first time for everything, I suppose.'

'Do you mind? I'm not a penniless medical student any more.'

'You could have fooled me. You certainly dress as if you are.' Helen looked pointedly at his scuffed shoes. 'So what do you want?'

William paused. 'The thing is, I'm in rather a sticky situation. It's not what you think,' he insisted, as she rolled her eyes. 'It isn't woman trouble this time. Well, not entirely. Anyway, the long and the short of it is, I need someone to do a duet with me in the Christmas show.'

'I thought your latest girlfriend was singing with you?'

'Ah, well, you see, that's the trouble. She is no more, I'm afraid.'

'Not another one?' After his long love affair with an orthopaedic doctor had ended a year earlier, William had returned to his old womanising ways. Much to Helen's dismay and to the delight of the other nurses.

She regarded him across the consulting room. Tall and lanky, with a permanently dishevelled air and cowlick of dark hair that never seemed to lie flat, she couldn't see what it was about him that other women found so irresistible. To her, he would always be an annoying big brother.

'I know, I know,' he sighed. 'But it wasn't my fault this time. She was the one who ended it, not me.' He paused. 'Admittedly, it was after she caught me kissing that delightful nurse on Male Medical, but all the same . . .' He put on his appealing look, the melting dark eyes that she supposed worked a treat on other women. 'Will you help me out, Helen? You don't have to do much, just join in with the chorus and look pretty. You can do that, can't you?'

'The last thing I'd want to do is stand on a stage with you.' Helen went back to stripping off the bed. 'Why don't you ask that delightful nurse on Male Medical?'

'Delightful she may be, but her voice is as flat as a pancake.' William grimaced. 'Honestly, Hels, she'd make a cat sound like Dame Nellie Melba. You, on the other hand, have the voice of an angel.'

'Oh, no.' Helen shook her head. 'You can't get round me as easily as you can your empty-headed nurses, William Tremayne.'

'Want to bet?' He grinned. 'Please, Helen. Just this once? I'm begging you. I've tried everyone else.'

'So I'm your last resort? Thank you very much.'

'Actually, Sister Wren is my last resort. She's been hinting.'

Helen smiled. 'That would serve you right. Come to think of it, Sister Wren is probably the one woman who hasn't succumbed to your charms.'

'Only because her heart belongs to Mr Cooper.' William wrung his hands in supplication. 'Please, Helen, even you wouldn't be that heartless.'

'We'll see.'

'Thank you.'

'No promises,' she said, but she could already feel herself weakening.

'Of course not,' William agreed, solemn-faced.

As Helen finished cleaning up, she said, 'So is your girlfriend very angry with you?'

'Utterly furious. It makes life rather difficult, actually, since now none of the staff on Wren is talking to me.'

'Serves you right. I can't feel sorry for you, William, because you bring these things on yourself. When are you going to learn that romance between doctors and nurses is a recipe for disaster?'

'So there's no chance for you and Dr McKay, then?' he teased.

Helen shot him a warning look. 'Don't even mention that man's name to me.'

'You two still not getting on?'

'Hardly.' Helen sighed. In fact, things were even more frosty since their confrontation. He had stopped trying to humiliate her in front of the nurses, but now he barely spoke to her at all. It made the atmosphere inside the Casualty department almost as icy as the weather outside. 'I've tried everything, William. I've done everything I possibly can, but no matter how hard I try, nothing I do is right.'

William frowned. 'That doesn't sound like the David McKay I know. I've always found him to be a thoroughly decent chap. Do you want me to have a word with him?'

'No, thanks. I've got to fight my own battles.'

On Thursday afternoon, just over a week before Christmas Eve, Richard Webster surprised everyone by waking up.

Jess told Effie about it when she came off duty that night.

'Everyone was amazed,' she said. 'They'd all given up on him after he'd been unconscious for so long. You should have seen Sister Holmes's face, anyone would have thought she'd witnessed a Christmas miracle. She practically ran to fetch the doctor, which of course is unheard of.'

'How is he now?' Effie asked.

'Well, there's still some spinal damage and they don't know if he's going to make a full recovery, but at least it's looking brighter than it was yesterday. I thought you'd want to know, so you can pass on the good news to your friend?'

'Adam Campbell isn't my friend,' Effie said emphatically. If anything, he treated her worse than any of the other nurses. But unlike the others, Effie felt sorry for him. She wasn't sure why, but she sensed that somehow under that gruff, surly exterior he was very sad.

He seemed to go out of his way to push away anyone close to him. Like the way he treated his father, for instance. When poor Mr Campbell had turned up on the previous visiting day to see his son, Adam had barely looked at him, let alone spoken. Effie wondered if he'd been as offhand with his girlfriend. Perhaps that was why the mysterious Adeline hadn't come to see him?

As they got ready to go on duty the following morning, Effie asked Jess if she could go with her to Holmes to see Richard Webster for herself.

'Certainly not!' Jess replied, shocked. 'Sister Holmes would have a fit. She'd never allow a student to wander in and out of her ward.'

'She doesn't come on duty until eight, I'll be long gone by then,' Effie said. 'I have to be on duty myself by seven, so I'll just pop in for a minute. Please? I want to make sure before I give Mr Campbell the news. I don't want to raise his hopes.'

'I don't suppose I can stop you, can I?' Jess said grudgingly. 'But only a quick look, mind. And if the Night Sister catches you, I'll deny I even know you.'

'Fair enough.' Effie grinned.

The surgical ward was in chaos, with extra beds lined up down the centre of it. The weary-looking night staff buzzed back and forth, serving breakfasts.

'We had an appendix and two perfs in yesterday,' Jess said. 'Sister isn't best pleased. We're supposed to be getting patients home before Christmas, but as fast as we send them away, we keep getting more in.'

'Which one is Mr Webster?' Effie asked, gazing around.

'They put him in a side room. Number three. Don't be long, will you?' Jess hissed. 'If Staff sees you, pretend you're one of the night students.'

The door to Room Three stood open. Richard Webster lay still in the bed, staring ahead of him. A tired-looking young woman in a red velvet coat sat at his bedside, holding his hand.

Effie had only intended to take a quick peek. But as she started to tiptoe away, the young woman looked up and spotted her.

'Nurse?' she called out. 'Did you want to check on Richard?'

Effie put on her most professional smile and walked into the room. 'I just wanted to make sure he was awake,' she said truthfully. She picked up his chart and pretended to read it, her eyes skimming over the figures.

'Yes, he is. Isn't it wonderful?' The young woman smiled, eyes shining. She was very pretty, with the kind of sleek bobbed blonde hair that Effie had always dreamed of having. 'The doctor says it's nothing short of a miracle. But I always knew he'd wake up. I prayed for him every day, you see. I never gave up hoping.'

'It's wonderful news, to be sure.' Effie glanced at the diamond sparkling on the woman's left hand. 'I hear you're engaged?'

'Yes, we're going to get married in the spring. I was beginning to think it might not happen, but now . . .'

Effie smiled back, but deep down she knew it would still be a miracle if Richard Webster were well enough to make his vows.

But the young woman was so radiant with happiness, Effie didn't want to bring her down to earth. Besides, a Christmas miracle had already brought him out of his deep sleep; why shouldn't there be another one?

Effie returned to Blake ward in high spirits. As on Holmes ward, the night staff were clearing away the breakfast dishes while the day nurses prepared to take over.

Her sister Bridget descended on Effie the moment she came through the double doors. 'What's the matter with you?' she demanded. 'Why have you got that silly grin on your face?' Her eyes narrowed. 'What have you been up to?'

'Nothing!' Effie said. 'I'm just in a good mood, that's all. You should try it sometime,' she added in an undertone.

'Less of your cheek,' Bridget snapped. 'Let's see if you're still in a good mood when you've finished testing all those urines in the sluice. Go on, get to it. I want them all done and the charts filled in before Sister arrives.'

The sluice room was freezing as usual. The high mesh-covered windows were no match for the icy December wind, which blew straight through.

Tilly Turnbull, another first-year student, turned to greet her as Effie came in. Her nose was blue with cold.

'This is ridiculous,' she complained. 'One day they're going to forget about us in here, and we'll end up frozen

70

stiff.' She shoved the rack of test tubes towards Effie. 'Here, you do albumen and I'll do sugars.'

As Effie plodded through her tests, laboriously adding nitric acid to each test tube, Turnbull managed to race through hers by testing a few drops from each sample all together. Most of the students did this if they didn't think they would be found out. It made it much quicker and easier than testing each sample on its own, especially if they all turned out to be negative.

But not today. 'Oh, look, we've got at least one positive,' Turnbull said, pointing to the brick-red test tube. 'Let's try to guess who it is, shall we? I reckon Mr Anderson.'

Effie shook her head. 'Mr Pilcher, definitely.'

'How much do you want to bet?'

'Sixpence.'

'You're on!' Tilly Turnbull giggled. 'Listen to us! Did you ever imagine you'd be freezing to death in a sluice, taking bets on people's urine samples?'

As it turned out, Effie won the bet. So she was in an even more high-spirited mood when she was finally able to see Adam Campbell later that morning.

He was half propped up, his fractured leg still suspended in mid-air, reading a newspaper.

'You don't want to be reading that,' Effie said. 'I never bother with newspapers, they're always too full of bad news.'

He sent her a withering look. 'That'll be why you're so well informed.'

'As a matter of fact, I've got some news for you that you won't find in your newspaper.'

'Oh, yes? Don't tell me, the man in bed five has had a bowel movement. That's the kind of thing you nurses talk about, isn't it? When you're not discussing your love lives, that is.'

Effie thought about keeping her news to herself to punish him for his meanness. But she was so excited she couldn't wait to tell him.

'Your friend Mr Webster has woken up,' she said.

Adam looked at her sharply. 'He's awake? Really?'

She nodded, hardly able to hide her glee. 'He regained consciousness yesterday. It's still early days, but that's good news, isn't it?'

'Oh, thank God. You don't know what a relief that is.'

For a moment they stared at each other. Then Effie collected herself. 'Anyway, I'd better get on,' she said, straightening his bedclothes for something to do. 'Heaven forbid anyone should think I'm standing here discussing my love life.'

Adam looked sheepish. 'Sorry,' he mumbled.

As she walked away, he called after her, 'Thank you, Nurse. For letting me know about Richard.'

'That's all right. I'll tell you if I hear any more.'

Effie walked away, smiling to herself. Getting a thank you from Adam Campbell was even better than winning sixpence from Tilly Turnbull.

Chapter Eleven

Snow had fallen heavily overnight, burying the hospital courtyard and the yard outside the Casualty department under deep drifts of crisp whiteness, marred only by lines of black footprints where the nurses had trudged through it that morning.

'It looks smashing, doesn't it? Like a winter wonderland,' Penny said as they stood at the doors, gazing out.

Helen frowned. 'I'm more worried about how ambulances will get through.'

Penny laughed at her. 'Trust you to think of that!'

'It's my job.' Helen turned to the students. 'Kowalski, telephone the Porters' Lodge and ask them to come down and clear the snow away from outside our doors, would you?'

'Yes, Sister.' Kowalski scuttled off, but returned a moment later. 'Please, Sister, Mr Hopkins says to tell you all his men are already out clearing the main driveway. He can't spare anyone else.'

Helen frowned. 'What are we supposed to do if an ambulance arrives? We can't very well ask them to haul stretchers up from the main gates, can we?'

'She'll have us clearing it ourselves in a minute!' one of the students, French, whispered to Perkins.

Helen smiled. 'That sounds like an excellent suggestion, French,' she said. 'Get your cloaks on, Nurses. Then you three can go down to the Porters' Lodge and beg some shovels. Mr Hopkins might not be able to spare us any men, but I'm sure he can manage something for us to dig with!'

Ten minutes later the five of them were ankle-deep in snow, clearing a broad path from the courtyard up to the doors. The metallic scrape of their shovels across the cobbles and the chatter of the nurses sounded oddly loud in the snow-muffled silence. The students, at first not very keen to venture out, were soon enjoying themselves immensely, laughing and egging each other on, their cheeks bright and glowing. But Penny Willard moved even more slowly than usual. She scarcely seemed able to lift her spade.

'Put your back into it, Nurse Willard!' Helen called out to her across the yard.

'I'm doing my best, Sister.' Helen noticed Penny's strained smile and trudged over to her.

'Are you all right, Nurse?'

Penny nodded. 'Just a bit stiff, that's all. I – slipped in the bath last night and hurt my ribs.'

'Oh, I'm sorry to hear that.' Helen stuck her shovel into a drift of snow. 'Let me see. Where does it hurt—' She went to examine her, but Penny stepped away.

'It's nothing,' she said.

'But if you're still in pain this morning you might have cracked a rib. It'll need strapping.'

'Really, I'm fine.' Penny's smile was suddenly over-bright. 'No need to make a fuss.'

Helen frowned. There was something Willard wasn't telling her, she was sure of it. But before she could ask any more, she was distracted by a soft thump behind her.

She swung round. Three very guilty faces stared back at her.

'I hope you aren't throwing snowballs?' she warned. 'You're supposed to be clearing this lot, not messing about.'

74

They exchanged even more guilty looks. Then French spoke up. 'Please, Sister, we weren't throwing them at each other,' she explained. 'Perkins bet me I couldn't hit that tree over there.' She pointed to a plane tree in the distance. Its dark, skeletal branches were weighed down by snow.

'And did you?'

'No, Sister. It's too far away.'

Helen narrowed her eyes on the tree. Then, still keeping it in her sights, she bent down and scooped up a handful of snow. She formed it into a ball between her gloved hands, took aim and then bowled the ball overarm. They all watched as it soared high through the air, before coming down in a graceful arc right on its target.

The students clapped their hands in an admiring smatter of applause. 'Well played, Sister!' Perkins cried.

'I used to bowl for my brother when we played cricket,' Helen said modestly, patting the snow off her gloves.

'Are you sure it wasn't just a lucky throw?' Penny asked, leaning on her shovel.

'Certainly not! I'll prove it to you.' Helen picked up another handful. 'It's all in the arm movement, you see. You have to make sure you give it just the right amount of spin . . .' She skimmed the snowball through the air – just as the figures of Drs Adler and McKay came round the corner.

Her aim couldn't have been better if she'd tried. Helen knew exactly what was going to happen, seconds before the snowball arced downwards and hit Dr McKay square in the face with a soft *thwump*.

The students couldn't contain themselves. They doubled up, clutching each other for support, their hands pressed over their mouths to stop themselves from laughing out loud. Penny Willard had turned away, unable to watch. Helen felt the sudden, terrible urge to run away.

Why did it have to be him? If it had been anyone else . . .

Dr Adler gave a shout of laughter. 'Good shot, Sister,' he cried.

Helen rushed forward, flapping at Dr McKay with her hands, trying to brush off the snow. 'Doctor, I'm terribly sorry. I didn't mean—'

'Just leave it,' he said, shrugging her off.

'It was an accident, truly. If you come inside, I'll fetch a towel.'

'I said, leave it!' His brown eyes blazed with anger. 'I think you've done enough damage don't you?' he snapped.

Jonathan Adler was still laughing about it when David McKay went round for dinner that night.

'You should have seen the look on your face! It was priceless,' he chuckled.

David stared at his plate, his pride still prickling. 'I really don't think it was funny,' he said.

'You weren't standing where I was!'

'Stop teasing our guest, Jonathan,' Esther Adler protested mildly, but David could see she was trying not to laugh herself.

'Someone could have been hurt,' he insisted.

'Nonsense, it was only a snowball,' Jonathan dismissed. 'Although you're lucky she didn't throw anything worse. I might have been tempted to aim a rock at you, the way you've been treating her!'

'Really?' Esther turned to him. 'Don't you like this girl, David?'

'It's not a question of liking or disliking her,' he said. 'I've just expressed my concerns about her suitability as a sister, that's all. And surely today should have proved I was right,' he added.

76

'Nonsense, she's a first-rate nurse. And you know it,' Jonathan said, pointing his fork accusingly at his guest across the dinner table.

'I'll admit she hasn't been quite the unmitigated disaster I expected,' David conceded. 'But she's still young and irresponsible, as she proved today. She sets a bad example to the younger nurses.'

'Bad example, my eye. The nurses love her.'

'No wonder, if she lets them cavort about in the snow. This chicken is wonderful, by the way, Esther,' added David, changing the subject determinedly.

'Would you like some more?'

'Yes, please.' He held up his plate for her to serve him. 'I think you must be the best cook in East London,' he told her.

Esther's face coloured. 'Oh, it's nothing grand,' she murmured.

'Nothing grand? Eating here is like dining at the Dorchester compared to what our housekeeper serves up at the doctors' house.'

'You should get married, then you'd be able to eat like this every day,' Jonathan said.

'Oh, yes?' Esther's eyebrows shot up in mock reproof. 'And is that the only reason you married me?'

'You know it isn't, my love.'

David saw the look that passed between them, and marvelled all over again at his friend's new-found domestic bliss. He and Jonathan Adler had been close friends for years. As well as working together in the Casualty department, they had also lived in adjoining rooms in the doctors' house. But two years ago, at the ripe old age of thirty-six, Jonathan had married Esther, a Jewish woman who ran a local garment factory with her elderly father. They now lived in a tall Edwardian house overlooking Victoria Park.

'All the same, I do recommend married life,' Jonathan said. 'You really should try it, you know.'

'I'll bear that in mind,' David said, helping himself to the roast potatoes Esther offered.

'I'm sure Esther could introduce you to a suitable woman, if you're interested? You have a lot of friends who would love to meet an eligible doctor, don't you, my dear?'

'Stop it, Jonathan. David didn't come here to be teased,' she said with a glance at him.

'Of course he did, he loves it. Besides, it makes a nice change from the lonely bachelors' home!'

'It was good enough for you once,' David reminded him.

'So it was. Until I found out what I was missing.' Jonathan reached for his wife's hand and kissed it.

'Not everyone is as fortunate as you,' David muttered.

'That's because you're not looking hard enough. As I said, I'm sure Esther would be able to introduce you—'

'Leave him alone, Jonathan,' she warned again. 'I'm sure he doesn't need your help to find a wife.'

'Thank you, Esther.' David shot her a grateful look.

'Besides,' she went on, 'when the right woman comes along, he'll be the one doing the chasing. And he won't need any assistance from us,' she added firmly.

'Well said.' David nodded. 'Now, can we change the subject, please?'

'If we must,' Jonathan agreed. 'As I was saying, about Sister Dawson . . .'

'Not again! I'd rather go back to discussing my love life, if that's the only other topic on offer.'

'I just don't know what you've got against the girl, that's all,' Jonathan persisted. 'Sister Dawson is the most conscientious nurse I've ever met.'

David stifled a sigh of irritation. 'She makes endless mistakes.'

'Only because you make her nervous.'

David put down his knife and fork with a clatter. 'I make her nervous?'

'Surely you must have noticed? The poor girl is a nervous wreck around you.'

'I hardly think that's true.'

'She told me so herself.'

David stared at him, shocked into silence for a moment. 'I had no idea . . .' he murmured.

'No, because you're too busy barking at her to notice.'

David glanced at Esther. Her kind, plain face was appalled.

'David would never do such a thing,' she defended him. 'He's far too nice.'

'You haven't seen him,' Jonathan said. 'For some reason, poor Helen Dawson has got right under his skin.'

David stared down at his plate, troubled. He knew he'd been hard on Sister Dawson, but didn't realise he'd made her so unhappy. It was a revelation to him.

'Well, if she takes offence that easily, it just proves my point that she's too young and inexperienced for the job,' he defended. But even he had to admit his protests sounded very feeble. And he could see in his friends' reproachful faces that they thought the same.

He thought about it all the way home. Jonathan was right, Helen Dawson had got under his skin, and he didn't know why. At first, he'd had genuine concerns about her suitability for the post. And he thought he'd been proved right by her endless mistakes. But the revelation that he made her nervous had come as a complete surprise to him. Up until that moment he hadn't realised how much his behaviour had affected her.

He should have known after that day when she'd confronted him in his consulting room. He could still remember her standing before him, quivering with rage and wounded pride. At the time, he'd felt completely justified in the way he'd treated her. But now he wasn't so sure why he'd reacted so badly. It was almost as if he'd been looking for an excuse to let fly at her.

He was shocked by his own callousness, and even more so because he had been completely unaware of it. He prided himself on rarely losing his temper and being able to get on with everyone.

Everyone, it seemed, except Helen Dawson.

Chapter Twelve

The arrival of the Christmas tree was always a big occasion on the ward.

The porters brought it in just before visiting time was due to start on Sunday afternoon, and Frannie and her nurses set about decorating it, to a chorus of cat calls and general amusement from the patients.

'Need a hand, Sister?' joked one of the patients as he lay strung up in traction from head to foot like a broken puppet. 'Just say the word and I'll hop up that ladder and help you.'

'That's very kind of you, Mr Wilson,' Frannie answered with a smile, 'but I think we can manage.'

'Ooh, Nurse, I can see your stocking tops from here!' another voice shouted from the other side of the ward.

Frannie shook her head in mock disapproval. 'Really, Mr Pilcher, you should be ashamed of yourself,' she scolded. 'I've a good mind to tell your wife when she comes in.'

'Sorry, Nurse,' he mumbled, turning bright red. Frannie wasn't surprised he looked so nervous. She'd met Mrs Pilcher and she wasn't a woman to be trifled with.

She was still perched on a ladder trying to fix a glass bauble to one of the upper branches when the visitors started to arrive. Wives, sweethearts and mothers poured in, eagerly clutching their visitors' tickets, laden down with gifts for their loved ones. They gave Frannie a wave as they passed.

'You want to be careful on that ladder, Sister,' one of the women called out. 'That's how my old man ended up in here!'

'Oh, I won't fall. It's quite safe, I assure you—'

No sooner had she said it than the ladder started to wobble. Frannie put out a hand to steady herself, and the bauble fell from her fingers.

A hand shot out and caught it inches before it hit the ground. Frannie found herself looking straight into John Campbell's green eyes. Halfway up the ladder, she was on a level with his face.

'Here you are,' he said, handing it back to her.

'Thank you.'

He wasn't wearing his uniform today. But he looked just as distinguished in his trench coat and trilby hat, a brown paper package tucked under one arm.

Frannie watched him as he made his way down the ward towards his son's bed at the far end. Below her, she was aware of the other nurses' hushed whispers.

'Gosh, he's handsome, isn't he? You can see where his son gets his looks from.'

'Pity he hasn't inherited his father's manners!'

'I think I prefer him in his uniform, though.'

I don't, Frannie thought.

She watched from the ladder as John reached Adam's bedside. She saw him lean forward as if to embrace his son, then he seemed to change his mind. He placed his package down carefully on the locker and sat on the chair farthest from the bed.

Speak to him, Frannie silently begged Adam. But the young man turned his face away to stare into space. John sat for a few minutes, addressing the back of his son's head. Then, defeated, he picked up his hat, slung his trench coat over his arm, and left.

'Gosh, that visit didn't last long, did it?' One of the nurses below her voiced Frannie's thoughts. 'They can't have much to say to each other, can they?'

Frannie looked back to where Adam lay, staring at the ceiling. She suspected the opposite was true. They had a great deal to tell each other, they just didn't know how to say it.

They finished decorating the tree, and all stood back to admire their handiwork.

'Now we just have to put the star on the top.' Frannie turned to the nurses. 'Who would like to do the honours?'

'You do it, Sister,' Bridget O'Hara said.

But as Frannie started up the ladder, a voice blurted out, 'Wait! You have to make a wish first.'

Frannie looked over her shoulder. Effie O'Hara was blushing bright red while her sisters standing to either side of her stared her down furiously.

'We always do it at home,' she defended herself in a small voice. 'You all make a wish on the Christmas tree star, and see whose wish comes true.'

'Good idea.' Frannie smiled. 'Right, Nurses, let's all make a wish, shall we?'

'I wish my sister would learn to shut up!' Bridget O'Hara muttered. But the other nurses all closed their eyes and wished. Katie O'Hara in particular had her eyes screwed tightly shut, and Frannie smiled, knowing the young staff nurse would be wishing her fiancé Tom would name the date.

Frannie paused and closed her eyes, too. She wished as she always did that Herr Hitler would come to his senses and leave everyone in peace, and take away all thoughts of war.

When visiting time was over and all the patients had been settled, Frannie went off duty. It was starting to snow again, the drifting flakes illuminated in the pale light from the ward windows.

She was supposed to be helping the sisters' choir rehearse their songs for the Christmas show, but as she crossed the courtyard Frannie noticed John Campbell sitting on a bench under the plane trees. He looked alone and forlorn, elbows resting on his knees, head cradled in his hands.

Frannie hesitated for a moment, then went over to him. 'John?'

He looked up, distracted at first. Then he stood up. 'Frannie.'

'Have you been sitting here all this time? You must be frozen.'

He looked down at his hands. Even in the fading light, Frannie could see his fingers were tinged blue with cold.

'I hadn't really noticed,' he said.

He looked so lost, Frannie's heart went out to him. 'Would you like a cup of tea?' she offered. 'Come back up to the ward and I'll get the maid to make us one.'

Hope flared in his eyes. 'Are you sure? I don't want to take up your time, I'm sure you must have things to do.'

Frannie smiled. 'Nothing I can't cancel.' The choir could practise without her for once, she decided. She was in no mood to listen to their bickering anyway.

'In that case – thank you. That would be very welcome.'

Bridget O'Hara seemed most put out to see Frannie back on the ward so soon after she was supposed to have left. The junior nurses were also clearly fascinated to see her with the father of one of the patients. But Frannie ignored their curious looks as she directed John to her sitting room at the far end. All the sisters had private quarters attached to their wards, where they occasionally took refuge. Frannie hardly used hers, preferring to spend her time with her nurses and patients. But she was grateful that the ward maid always insisted on making up the fire just in case. The small room was wonderfully warm and cosy as she and John sat down in armchairs to either side of the fireplace.

She watched him as he leaned forward, warming his hands in front of the flames. The flickering golden light softened his chiselled profile.

She started the conversation. 'It didn't seem to go very well with Adam earlier?'

He smiled thinly. 'You noticed?'

'You didn't stay very long.'

'I'd already outstayed my welcome, believe me.'

The maid brought their tea, and set the tray down on the low table between them.

'Why is he so hostile towards you?' Frannie asked, when they were alone again.

'I told you, I offend his beliefs.'

'It must be more than that,' she said. 'The way he reacted to you earlier – it's more than just a dislike of your uniform.'

John was silent for a moment, weighing his words. 'You're right,' he agreed heavily. 'I haven't always been the best father in the world.'

Frannie drew his cup towards her and picked up the teapot. 'In what way?'

'It's a long story.'

'Then start at the beginning.' She poured tea into the cups. It was a deep, coppery brew, just as she liked it.

He hesitated again. 'His mother and I didn't have a very happy marriage,' he said. 'To be honest, we probably shouldn't have married at all. But Eileen got pregnant, and—' He paused. 'She didn't want to get married, either. She wanted to have the baby quietly and give it

85

up. But I couldn't stand the thought of my child growing up unwanted in an orphanage, like I did.'

Seeing his desolation, it was all Frannie could do not to reach out to him. She passed him his cup, saying nothing.

'And so we were married, and it all went wrong from the start.' John spooned sugar into his tea. 'I can't blame Eileen. She didn't ask for a soldier for a husband, but that was what she ended up with. And it made her very unhappy.'

'What happened?'

'She left me for someone else.' He stirred his tea slowly, the spoon clattering around in the cup. 'She took Adam with her, and I didn't see him for years. Eileen didn't think it was a good idea,' he said. 'She reckoned he had a new father, and she wanted nothing to do with me.'

'And you accepted that?'

'I was stationed in India at the time, so there wasn't a great deal I could do about it,' he said. 'Besides, I agreed with her. I thought Adam would be better off without me.'

'But you were his father!'

'I know,' he sighed. 'Looking back on it, I can't imagine what possessed me to give him up. But as long as he was loved, that was all I really cared about.'

'And then what happened?'

'Eileen died, and Adam's so-called loving new step-father couldn't wait to get rid of him.' John frowned. 'The first I found out about it was when my commanding officer sent for me and informed me I had to collect my son.' He shook his head. 'Suddenly I had a very angry, grief-stricken twelve-year-old boy to look after. We were father and son, but we were strangers to each other.'

'What did you do?'

'Well, I couldn't look after him myself. Looking back on it, I know I should have resigned my commission then

86

and taken a desk job somewhere so I could be with him. But I didn't. The army was the only life I'd known, and I didn't know what else I'd do. So I sent Adam to boarding school.'

'Oh.'

He watched her closely. 'You don't approve?'

'Well, I can see why he would grow up resenting your uniform, can't you?'

'Yes, I know,' John agreed heavily. 'I can see it myself now. But at the time I wasn't thinking clearly. I did my best.' His green eyes met hers, pleading for understanding. 'Or what I thought was best at the time,' he amended. 'But now I can see I made one big mistake after another, and I've been doing so ever since.' He put down his cup. 'At any rate, now I've lost my son. Adam's made it very clear he doesn't want to know me.'

'You can't give up hope,' Frannie urged.

'But you've seen how he is with me. He doesn't want anything to do with me.'

'On the contrary, I think he needs you more than he's willing to let on.'

John's brows drew together. 'Do you think so?'

'I know he does. You have to keep trying. Be patient.'

John let out a deep sigh. 'I don't have much choice, do I? I'm not going to abandon my son. Even if he does despise me.'

'I'm sure that's not true.'

His mouth curved. 'Then you don't know Adam. Over the years he's gone out of his way to embrace everything I detest.'

'You detest pacifism?' Frannie said.

'No one who has been through a war can detest peace,' John said. 'But I've been trained to do my duty. And I'm afraid Adam finds that idea rather laughable. He'd rather be with his high-minded friends, discussing poetry and politics.'

'There's nothing wrong with poetry and politics,' Frannie said.

'I suppose not. But I'm just a simple soldier.' He considered her across the table. 'You were always the clever one, as I recall. I thought you might become a teacher like your father?'

'I thought about it,' she said. 'But after I'd served as a VAD in France, I thought I might as well continue training as a nurse.'

He blinked. 'You were with the Voluntary Aid Detachment?'

She nodded. 'I signed up when I was eighteen. I went out to be closer to Matthew. But by the time I was posted out to France, he was already missing.'

John was silent for a long time. Frannie felt his mood shift and realised that even after all these years, Matthew's death still affected him as much as it did her.

'I'm sorry,' she said quietly. 'I suppose you must find it difficult to talk about what happened?'

'Yes,' he murmured. 'Yes, I do.'

He didn't meet her eye when he said it. There were so many questions in Frannie's mind, things she longed to know, but she didn't dare ask them.

'And yet you joined up again,' she said.

'I told you, the army was the only place I'd ever felt I belonged,' he said.

'But I thought you liked working on the farm?'

'Oh, I did. Don't get me wrong, I'm grateful to Matthew's family for taking me in, and they treated me very well. But I was never going to be more than a farm worker to them. In the army, I learned that if I worked hard I could earn respect. I managed to work my way up through the ranks and when the war ended, I had the chance of a commission. Suddenly people were looking up to me as an officer, not down on me as a workhouse boy.'

'I hope you don't feel I ever looked down on you?'

His eyes met hers. 'No,' he said in a low voice. 'You were one of the few people who treated me as if I belonged. I was always grateful to you for that.'

They finished their tea shortly afterwards, and John stood up to leave.

'Thank you,' he said. 'It's good to be able to talk to someone about Adam.'

'You can come and speak to me any time,' Frannie assured him. 'My door is always open.'

'Thank you. You're very kind.'

She watched him striding down the passageway, his military bearing evident even in civilian clothes. Seeing his tall, straight stance, his head held high, no one could possibly guess he carried the weight of the world on his shoulders.

Frannie sighed. She'd wished on the Christmas tree star that the world would see sense and stop all the talk of war. Now she longed for another wish so she could bring John Campbell and his son together.

Chapter Thirteen

Dora Doyle – or Riley, as she was now – was a no-nonsense East End girl. She had been one of Helen's best friends while they were training, but she'd left nursing when she married a hospital porter. Now she and Nick lived on the ground floor of a neat little terraced house off Old Ford Road.

It was a modest place, just two rooms and a kitchen, but Dora had turned it into a warm and welcoming home. Helen always enjoyed visiting, and sharing in her friend's new life and happiness.

'I wasn't sure you'd come, in this filthy weather.' Dora helped her visitor off with her coat in the narrow hallway. It was strange to see Dora out of her nurse's uniform and wrapped in a flowery pinny. But her freckled face and mop of untidy red curls were just the same. 'Come through to the kitchen. You'll have to excuse the mess, I'm making the Christmas pudding with Danny. We've left it a bit late this year.'

'It all smells delicious,' Helen said, as she followed her friend down the passageway into the brightly lit warmth of the kitchen. It was filled with a warm, aromatic fug of baking fruit and spices.

'That'll be the batch of mince pies I've got in the oven,' Dora said.

A young man stood at the scrubbed kitchen table, stirring pudding mixture in a big earthenware bowl. When he saw Helen he dropped the wooden spoon and darted into the scullery.

'Don't be shy, Danny, it's only Helen. You know her, don't you?' Dora said gently. 'Come on, mate, come in and say hello. She ain't going to bite you.'

Helen watched Dora coax her brother-in-law back into the kitchen. He edged towards the kitchen table, still not looking at Helen.

'That's it,' Dora said. 'You finish off that mixture while I put the kettle on.' She ruffled the young man's hair affectionately and picked up the kettle. 'Cuppa?' she said.

'Yes, please.' Helen watched Danny from the other end of the kitchen table as he moved slowly to pick up his wooden spoon again, his wary gaze still turned away from her. She'd been shocked when she first met him and found out he was Nick Riley's brother. His pale hair, translucent skin and slack, vacant expression were nothing like Nick's dark good looks. He was in his early twenties but he had the mind of a child – the result of an accident, Dora had told her.

'Come on, then. I'm dying to hear all your news,' Dora said as she bustled around making tea. 'What's been happening at the Nightingale?'

'I'm surprised Nick doesn't tell you.'

Dora laughed. 'My husband ain't exactly the chatty type, in case you hadn't noticed! Besides, he says the last thing he wants to talk about when he gets home is work. But I like to hear what's been going on.'

'Do you miss it?' Helen asked.

Dora paused for a moment. 'Sometimes,' she admitted. 'I mean, I'm happy with what I've got,' she added hastily. 'I wouldn't swap my life for all the tea in China. But, yes, I miss being on the wards, and having a laugh with the other nurses. We had some good times, didn't we?'

'Yes,' Helen agreed. 'We did.'

Sometimes she longed for the old days when they'd

shared the draughty attic room at the student nurses' home, giggling and grumbling and crying together. It had all seemed so simple then, when all they had to worry about were their exams, or whether the Home Sister would catch them climbing through a window after lights out.

'There you are.' Dora put a cup down in front of her.

'Aren't you having one?'

Dora shook her head. 'I don't really fancy it. Besides, I've got to get this pudding on.' She moved around the table to inspect the mixture Danny had been stirring. 'How are you getting on, Dan? That's lovely. I reckon it could do with some more fruit though, don't you? Fetch us some from the cupboard, there's a good boy.' She looked up at Helen. 'Come on, then. Let's hear all your news. How are you getting on in Casualty?'

Helen sighed. 'Not too well, I'm afraid.'

It was a relief to unburden herself to someone. She told Dora all about her problems with Dr McKay. Dora listened sympathetically as she worked, her arms going back and forth, adding the fruit Danny had brought from the larder, and stirring the mixture. From time to time she stopped to blow one of her red curls off her face.

'Oh, my gawd!' She shrieked with laughter when Helen told her about the snowball incident. 'I wish I'd been there. Fancy you smacking someone in the face with a snowball, Helen Dawson! And a doctor, no less.'

'Don't,' Helen groaned, covering her face with her hands. 'I want to die every time I think about it.'

'Did he say anything about it afterwards?'

She shook her head. 'It's been stony silence ever since.'

At least he'd stopped seeking her out to criticise her. Now he just seemed to avoid her.

'Well, that's peculiar,' Dora said. 'It ain't like Dr McKay

not to have a sense of humour. He was a real sweetheart when I worked with him. Couldn't do enough for people.'

'I know, that's what everyone tells me,' Helen sighed. 'I'm beginning to think I'm the only one in the world he doesn't like. Anyway, I'm not going to let him spoil my afternoon,' she said determinedly, picking up her teacup.

'Good for you.'

She watched Dora go to the oven, take out a tray of hot mince pies and dump them unceremoniously on the draining board.

'Aren't you going to take them out of the tin?' Helen asked.

'In a minute. To be honest, the smell's making me feel a bit queasy.'

Dora went back to the big pudding bowl. 'Right, now we've all got to take turns to stir this and make a wish,' she said. 'Come on, Helen, you can go first.'

Helen did as she was told, closing her eyes as she scraped the spoon around the bowl. Danny took his turn and then Dora. Helen watched her friend as she stirred the pudding round and around, her eyes tightly shut.

'I bet I know what you've wished for.' Helen smiled.

A frown crossed Dora's freckled face. 'What do you mean?'

'Come on, Dora! I've never known you say no to a cup of tea before, and as for the smell of your delicious baking making you feel sick . . .' She looked down at her friend's waistline. 'And covering yourself up in that pinny doesn't fool me, either.'

Dora grinned, her hand moving down to smooth the folds over her stomach. 'I might have known I wouldn't be able to pull the wool over a nurse's eyes!'

'So I'm right, then? You're pregnant?'

Dora nodded, her eyes sparkling. 'I'm due in June. We

didn't want to tell anyone until we were sure.' She smiled sheepishly. 'You're right, that's what I was wishing for. That my baby will be born healthy.'

'You don't need to wish for that. You'll be fine,' Helen reassured her.

'I will if my husband has anything to do with it. He's treating me like I'm made of glass. Won't let me do anything.'

'Quite right, too. You deserve to be thoroughly spoiled.' Helen smiled at her. 'For heaven's sake, Dora, why did you let me go on rambling about my problems when you had such big news?'

'I wasn't sure if I should tell you.' Dora sent her a cautious look from underneath her lashes.

'Why not?'

'I dunno . . . it didn't seem right somehow.' She went back to stirring the pudding. 'I was worried you might be upset.'

'But why on earth should I be—' Helen stared at her, and the truth slowly dawned. 'You mean because of Charlie and me?'

Dora nodded not looking up. 'I just feel a bit guilty that I'm so happy,' she mumbled.

'Well, don't be,' Helen said firmly. 'What kind of friend would I be if I resented you for something like that? Anyway, you deserve to be happy, Dora Riley. And I'm really happy for you. But I'm warning you now, I'm going to spoil this baby!'

'You're not the only one,' Dora said. 'I reckon his dad's going to be worse!'

Just at that moment, the back door banged open and Nick came in, stamping the snow off his boots.

'All right, my darling? Give us a cuddle to warm me up, it's perishing out there . . .' He stopped talking when he saw Helen. 'Oh, sorry. I didn't know we had company.'

'It's all right, I was just leaving.'

'You don't have to go on my account,' Nick said. He shrugged off his overcoat and it struck Helen how handsome he was – tall, lean and muscular, with a shock of dark curls and inky blue eyes.

'Stay and have some more tea,' Dora offered. 'Someone's got to eat those mince pies,' she added. 'I ain't going to touch them myself.'

'No, honestly, I'd best go.'

'At least let Nick walk you back to the hospital. I don't like the thought of you walking on your own in the dark.'

Helen shot a quick look at him. 'Really, I'll be quite all right. I've brought my bicycle with me.'

'That thing!' Dora rolled her eyes. 'You'd never get me on one of those.'

'They're very handy, once you get used to them.'

'I'll take your word for it.' As she saw her friend to the door, Dora lowered her voice and said, 'Don't go chucking snowballs at anyone else, will you?'

'Definitely not,' Helen promised. 'And you take care of yourself, won't you?'

Dora glanced over her shoulder at Nick. 'Not much chance of me doing anything else, with His Lordship watching over me.'

The cold wind slapped Helen in the face as she stepped outside. Even with her coat pulled around her, the sleet stung her cheeks. As she mounted her bicycle, she looked back through the window into the brightly lit kitchen. Nick and Dora were standing close together, his hands closed protectively around her waist. He leaned forward to whisper something to her, nuzzling her ear as he did. Dora laughed and squirmed away. Then her arms went up, winding around his neck, and they kissed.

Helen felt a pang of dreadful loneliness, watching them.

She desperately wanted someone to look at her the way Nick looked at Dora, the way Charlie used to look at her.

She cycled home carefully through the darkened streets. Lights spilled out from the houses. As she passed, Helen caught tantalising glimpses of Christmas trees, and front parlours festooned in decorations, and happy families.

Would it always be this way for her? she wondered. Would she always feel like an outsider, looking in on other people's happiness but never being able to share it?

She thought about her own Christmas wish as she'd stirred the pudding. She'd wished that she wouldn't be lonely any more. But as she headed back to the hospital and her solitary room, it felt as if her wish would never come true.

Chapter Fourteen

'I need your help.'

Frannie paused at the end of Adam Campbell's bed. He was propped up on the pillows, a truculent look on his face.

'Certainly, Mr Campbell, if I can,' she replied pleasantly. 'What is it you want?'

'I need to write a letter and I can't do it myself.' He held up his bandaged wrist.

Frannie smiled to herself. She'd watched him struggling for days, trying to write with his left hand. She'd wondered how long it would take him to admit he needed help.

'Very well,' she said. 'I'll make a deal with you.'

His brows drew together. He looked so like his father when he frowned, she thought. 'What sort of deal?'

'I'll allow one of the nurses to write your letter for you, if you promise to speak to your father the next time he comes to visit.'

Adam looked outraged. 'No!'

'I'm not asking for a miracle, Mr Campbell. Just talk to him for ten minutes, that's all.'

'I won't do it.' He shook his head. 'I'm not trying to be rude, Sister, but if you knew anything about me and my father you wouldn't even ask.'

'Why? Because he abandoned you as a child?'

Adam stared at her. 'How did you – I suppose he's been crying on your shoulder?' he said bitterly.

'Your father is the last person to cry on anyone's

shoulder, as you well know,' Frannie said. 'But he feels very sorry for what happened to you. And I know he'd like the chance to make it up to you.'

'Well, he's too late.' Adam's mouth was a tight line of resentment. 'He should have thought of that when he packed me off to boarding school.'

'He didn't know what else to do,' Frannie said. 'It was a difficult situation for both of you . . .'

'But I was a child!' Adam shot back. 'He should have tried to take care of me, but he abandoned me just like everyone else did. He put the army before his own son, and I'll never forgive him for that.'

'If it's any consolation, I don't think he'll ever forgive himself,' Frannie said quietly.

Adam was silent for a moment. She wasn't sure if her words had had any effect on him.

'He knows he made mistakes, but all he's asking for is a chance to put things right,' she urged. 'Just spare him ten minutes, that's all.'

'No.'

Frannie sighed. 'Then I'm afraid I can't spare anyone to write your letter for you.'

As she turned to go, Adam said sulkily, 'All right. I'll talk to him, if I must. But you needn't think we'll end up the best of friends.'

'I'm not asking for that,' Frannie assured him.

'Well?' Effie prompted.

'I'm thinking!' Adam shot her a stony look. 'I've got to think what to write, haven't I?'

'You've had weeks to think about it,' she pointed out. He ignored her.

He cleared his throat. 'Right, here goes. "*Chère* Adeline . . ."'

'I'm sorry?'

'It's French.'

'Oh.' Effie hesitated, not wanting to show her ignorance. Then she said, 'How do you spell that?'

'C-h-e-r-e. Honestly, don't you know how to speak French?'

'There isn't much call for it where I come from,' Effie snapped back, a blush rising in her cheeks.

Adam looked disappointed. 'I was going to write the whole thing in French, but I don't suppose I can now.'

'Would you like me to see if one of the other nurses can help?'

'No. No, it's all right.' He lay back against the pillows, a frown creasing his handsome features. Effie waited, her pen poised. Cramp started to creep into her fingers as they both sat in silence, and she had just put down her pen to stretch them when he suddenly said, 'I know. Write this down. "Take, oh take, those lips away, that so sweetly were forsworn . . ."'

Effie stopped. 'I beg your pardon?'

'It's a poem,' Adam said, a touch of irritation in his voice. 'By John Fletcher. I don't suppose you've heard of him, either?'

'I didn't really pay much attention to poetry at school,' Effie confessed.

'You don't know what you're missing.' Adam sent her a pitying look. 'Anyway, you don't need to understand this to write it down, do you?'

'I suppose not,' Effie agreed. 'So what comes next after "forsworn"?'

'"And those eyes, like break of day, that do mislead the morn. But my kisses bring again—"'

'Hang on, I can't keep up with you.'

'Can't you write any faster?'

99

'I can, if you don't mind a lot of spidery scrawl.'

Adam sighed. 'Very well, then. "But my kisses bring again, seals of love, though sealed in vain . . ."'

He went on quoting, and Effie struggled to keep up with him. She didn't understand most of the flowery language about hills of snow and hearts in icy chains, but it all sounded terribly romantic. It almost made her wish she'd paid more attention during those dry old poetry lessons.

It also made her wish she had a man who cared enough to send her poems about their heart being bound in icy chains by their love for her.

Finally, he finished dictating his letter, and Effie signed it for him. 'Shall I add a few kisses?' she suggested.

Adam sent her a withering look. 'Certainly not,' he said.

'Why not? I think it's nice.'

'Yes, well, that says a lot about you, doesn't it? Just put it in the envelope and seal it up. You will make sure it's posted?' he said.

'I'll put a stamp on it and post it myself,' Effie promised.

'Thank you.' As she walked away, he called out, 'And don't even think about drawing hearts on the envelope.'

'Spoilsport!' Effie looked back at him over her shoulder. He was half smiling.

The following Sunday afternoon, Frannie was at the final rehearsal for the Christmas show. She sat at her table in front of the makeshift stage, and wondered how many more times she could listen to the sisters' choir warbling their way through 'Blow, Blow, Thou Winter Wind'. She was beginning to hear it in her sleep now, complete with Sister Wren's excruciating flat soprano.

And as if that wasn't enough to give her a headache,

Mr Hopkins the Head Porter was making a terrible fuss about the lighting for the stage.

'I don't think it's safe, Sister, I really don't,' he said. He stood over Frannie, a dapper little Welshman, his bushy grey moustache bristling with indignation. 'I mean, what if someone trips over it? They could have the whole lot down. And then you only have to have it catch the curtain and . . .' He broke off, miming a complete catastrophe. 'A deathtrap,' he concluded finally.

'So you've said, Mr Hopkins. Several times.'

'Yes, but I don't think you realise the seriousness of the situation, Sister. And there's talk of the medical students lighting matches on stage, too. I'm sure I don't need to tell you what I think of that?'

'I'm sure you don't, Mr Hopkins.'

But he did anyway. Frannie propped her elbows on the table and buried her head in her hands and prayed for someone, anyone, to rescue her.

And then someone did.

'Sister?'

She looked up sharply. There, towering behind Mr Hopkins, was John Campbell.

'I hope I'm not disturbing you?' he said.

'No! No, not at all.' Frannie turned to the Head Porter. 'Would you excuse us for a moment, please, Mr Hopkins?'

As he strode off to bully the porters who were rigging up the curtains, Frannie smiled with relief at John. 'That was a very timely interruption,' she said. 'You saved me from another lecture from our Head Porter on why the whole production is going to go up in flames.'

'And is it?' John said.

'At the moment, I don't think I really care.'

He smiled. 'Oh, dear, is it that bad?'

'Not exactly,' she said ruefully. 'I think I've just been

101

through it all too many times. I stopped laughing at the medical students' comedy sketch about a week ago.' She looked up at him. 'Anyway, I'm sure you didn't come here to listen to me going on. What can I do for you?'

'I wanted to thank you.'

'Whatever for?'

'Persuading Adam to talk to me. We actually exchanged a few words this afternoon.'

'Really?'

John nodded. 'It might not have seemed like much to anyone else, but it's the closest we've come to a conversation in years.'

'I'm glad,' she said. 'Although I can't imagine why you're thanking me.'

'My son has barely spoken to me in five years, and suddenly he's making small talk. You must have had something to do with it.'

'Or perhaps he's finally come to his senses?'

'Perhaps,' John said. 'Either that or someone blackmailed him with the promise of a letter?'

Frannie looked up at him sharply. 'He told you that?'

'He was most put out about it. But I'm very grateful.'

'You're welcome.'

Their eyes met and held for a moment. He didn't seem to want to leave, and Frannie realised she was in no hurry for him to go either.

'So this is your Christmas Show?' he asked, looking at the stage. 'I didn't realise it was such a big production.'

'It isn't, really. Everyone puts a little act together to entertain the staff, patients and their families on Christmas Day. It's all rather amateur, but people seem to enjoy it.' A thought suddenly struck her. 'You should come and see it,' she said, 'if you're not doing anything else, that is?'

He smiled. It was a genuine smile this time, warming

his green eyes. 'I'd love to,' he said. 'To be honest, I wasn't looking forward to the prospect of spending Christmas Day alone at my club. It would be nice to have something to look forward to.'

'Then we'd love to see you,' Frannie said. She looked into his face and realised that she meant it, too.

Chapter Fifteen

They were coming to the end of the Christmas Eve shift when the news came in.

It had been a busy day. Saturdays always brought their fair share of accidents and brawls, but it was much worse on Christmas Eve. Helen felt as if she'd spent the whole day patching up black eyes and broken ribs, tending to cuts and bruises, cleaning up vomit and even breaking up a fight between two drunks in the Casualty hall.

As nine o'clock approached, she was dead on her feet. She could see her own exhaustion reflected in the grey faces of the student nurses as they trudged around, cleaning and tidying and readying the department for the arrival of the night staff.

Dr McKay seemed just as worn out. Dr Adler had taken the day off, so his colleague had been coping alone with the steady stream of casualties.

Dr Ross the night relief doctor turned up while Helen was giving report to the student nurses on night duty. He was still in evening dress and in a bad mood.

'I had to leave an excellent party,' he grumbled, pulling off his bow tie. 'I hope tonight is worth it.'

'I'll be sure to pray for a catastrophe for you,' Dr McKay said drily. Helen smiled before she remembered herself and pressed her lips together. It wouldn't do to show any emotion in front of Dr McKay.

No sooner had he said the words than the telephone rang.

Dr Ross burst out laughing. 'How bizarre! Looks as if your prayers have been answered.'

'You answer it,' Penny Willard told the night student. 'I'm not getting involved, I've got a date. It's probably just another silly, drunken fight anyway.'

The student answered the telephone. As Helen fiddled with the fastening on her cloak, she saw the girl's expression change, her face draining of colour. Helen glanced at Dr McKay. He was watching the student keenly too.

Moving as one, they both crossed to the desk just as the student put down the receiver.

'Well?' Helen said.

'There's a fire at the Mission Hall on Hetton Road.' The girl spoke quietly and calmly, but shock was written all over her face. 'They were having a party for the local children.'

'Dear God,' Dr Ross muttered under his breath.

'Casualties?' Dr McKay asked.

The student nodded her head. 'They don't know how many. They're still trying to bring the fire under control. But the ambulances are bringing in the ones who've managed to get out, and then they'll start looking for the others . . .' Her voice trailed off.

Without thinking, Helen started to unfasten her cloak, then realised Dr McKay was taking off his coat too.

'What are you doing?' Dr Ross looked from one to the other of them.

'What does it look like?' Dr McKay said. 'I'm not going to abandon you with all this happening.'

'I'm sure I can manage.' Dr Ross said defensively. 'I don't need—'

'Don't be a fool, man!' Dr McKay snapped, shrugging on his white coat. 'Any minute now, dozens of wounded and dying could be coming through those doors, and you're going to need all the help you can get. So swallow that pride of yours and let's get on with it, shall we?'

Helen turned to her nurses. They were already taking off their cloaks, looks of grim resignation on their ashen faces. Only Penny Willard stood defiant, her navy cloak still wrapped around her shoulders.

'I can't stay,' she insisted. 'I'm supposed to be meeting Joe.'

'You heard what Dr McKay said. We could have dozens of casualties coming in.'

'But this is important!'

'More important than saving lives?'

Penny's voice was choked. 'You don't understand. Joe will be so upset. I can't disappoint him—'

But Helen wasn't listening. She had already picked up the telephone to ring Theatre for extra help.

'When the casualties come in, they'll need to be processed and assessed as soon as possible,' she told the students. 'There's a risk of shock, so they must be kept warm. Kowalski and French, go and round up as many blankets as you can from the wards, and start to prepare hot-water bottles.'

'What about me? What do you want me to do?' Helen turned to see Penny Willard had taken off her cloak and was now standing with the other nurses.

Helen acknowledged her with a grateful nod. 'Thank you, Nurse Willard,' she said. 'You can start to prepare the tannic-acid compresses, and make sure we have enough saline drips set up.' Helen looked around. 'The consulting rooms might not be enough to cope with all the injuries, so we'll need to set up extra beds in here,' she said. 'Perkins, you can make a start on that.'

'Yes, Sister.'

'Good Lord, you make it sound like the field hospital

at Scutari!' Dr Ross laughed nervously. 'Honestly, Sister, there's no need to frighten the poor girls. How many casualties do you think there'll be?'

As if in answer to his question, the stillness of the night was suddenly shattered by the harsh clamour of alarm bells, as three ambulances screeched to a halt outside the double doors.

Helen looked at Dr Ross. 'I think we're about to find out.'

The next hour was a blur. Flanked by a string of porters with stretchers and trolleys, Helen waited, shivering with cold and apprehension, as the ambulance men flung open the doors.

At first the injuries were minor. Smelling of smoke, their eyes terrified white orbs in blackened faces, they coughed and choked and clutched burned hands and wrists.

But then the more serious casualties started to arrive, screaming in agony, reeking of burned flesh. Men, women, children, clothes stuck to them like blackened skin, hair, lips and eyelids missing, seared, blistering skin stretched over bone. Beside her, Penny retched and swayed on her feet and Helen put out a hand to steady her.

There were over fifty casualties that night. Helen hurried to and fro, assessing them as they came off the ambulance, sending them for treatment by nurses or doctors depending on the extent of their injuries. Others, who had already died in the ambulance, were sent to the mortuary. At some point the Night Sister Miss Tanner appeared and Helen left her in charge of the ambulances while she went to help the nurses in the Casualty hall.

As she'd predicted, there were not enough consulting rooms to cope with the demand, so she and the nurses moved between makeshift beds, keeping patients warm with blankets and hot-water bottles, setting up drips, giving morphia injections, cutting and soaking off clothing where they could, splinting limbs and applying tannic-acid compresses to raw, blistered flesh.

Matron arrived and Helen was so preoccupied she didn't even notice her at first, almost pushing past her in her rush to get to the next stretcher.

'I came to see if I could help, but you seem to be coping, Sister,' she said.

Helen wanted to laugh. She might seem as if she was coping, but inside she was teetering on the verge of hysterical terror. Couldn't Matron see the chaos that surrounded her, stretchers and trolleys flying here and there, nurses hurrying past, patients' screams filling the air?

'Is there anything I can do?' Matron asked.

'You could make tea for the families?' Helen said without thinking. 'We've left them out in the courtyard because there's no room for them in here, and I'm worried they'll freeze.'

For a brief moment Matron stared at her, and Helen realised what she'd done. Then Miss Fox nodded and said, 'I'll have them moved to the dining room straight away.'

'Thank you, Matron.'

'Not at all, Sister Dawson. Keep up the good work.'

And then she was gone. Helen paused for a moment, wondering if she had really just ordered Matron to put the kettle on. But before she could think about it, one of the students called out,

'Sister! Sister, come quickly, I don't know what to do!'

Helen rushed over to where French, one of the students, was kneeling beside a little girl.

'I thought she was doing all right, but her breathing is erratic,' she said.

'Let me see.' The child, a tiny thing of about six, didn't seem badly injured, just a slight burn across her hands.

But Helen could hear the fearful croaking whoop as she fought for breath, her little ribcage rising and falling under her scorched pink party dress. Beneath the black smoke smuts, her translucent skin had taken on a bluish tinge.

Helen looked up just as Dr Ross swept past, on his way back to the consulting rooms. 'Doctor?' she called after him. 'Doctor, this child needs to be seen.'

Dr Ross retraced his steps and stood over them. 'She seems all right to me. No obvious sign of injury.'

'She's having trouble breathing. I think the smoke has got into her lungs.'

'I'll see her in a moment,' he said. 'When I've dealt with my other patients.'

'Doctor, please, she's suffocating!' Helen called out, but Dr Ross was already walking away.

'Not now, Sister,' he threw over his shoulder.

Helen looked at Nurse French. Then she gathered the child up and carried her across the Casualty hall to Dr Ross's consulting room. The child lay in her arms, as light and limp as a rag doll.

She pushed open the door to the consulting room. Dr Ross looked up with a frown as he stood poised to give an injection to a man with a burn the length of his arm.

'Doctor, you've got to see to this child,' demanded Helen.

'I told you, I will when I've finished with this patient.'

'Now, Doctor!'

Dr Ross pulled himself up to his full height and looked as if he was about to let fly, but the patient sitting in front of him broke in quickly.

'It's all right, Doctor,' he said. 'You see to the kiddie, I can wait.'

'Very well. Put her on the bed.' Dr Ross didn't hide his annoyance as he gestured to Helen. But she didn't care.

She didn't care if she spent the whole of Christmas Day explaining herself to Matron, so long as he saved the little girl.

But as soon as she laid the child down on the bed she realised it was too late. The little chest was still, and her breath no longer rattled in her throat.

Dr Ross gave her a cursory glance. 'She's dead,' he said flatly.

'No!' Helen heard the patient he was treating cry out. But she couldn't react. All she could do was stare at Dr Ross.

'Well, don't just stand there, Sister. Take her away.'

Helen didn't move. She stood, rooted to the spot, unable to do anything but stare at him.

Something in her eyes must have unnerved Dr Ross, because when he spoke again his tone was gentler.

'I'll fetch a porter,' he said, moving towards the door. 'I suggest you go outside and get some air, Sister. You look quite pale.'

But Helen didn't take his advice. She straightened her cap and smoothed down her apron and went back to work, calming and soothing and applying compresses and hot-water bottles and blankets, moving like an automaton until the porters took the last of the patients up to the ward.

Only then did she go outside and sit on the bench in the middle of the courtyard. It was a beautiful, sharp winter's night and the bare black branches of the plane trees sparkled with frost. She'd left her cloak behind but hardly noticed the cold as she sat there, trying to make sense of the terrible events she had witnessed.

The courtyard was silent, but Helen could still hear the screams of the afflicted echoing around her head, and the painful rasping of the poor little girl's chest as she'd desperately sucked air into her smoke-clogged lungs.

On the other side of the courtyard, through the lighted windows of the dining room, she could see families huddled around tables, anxiously waiting for news. Somewhere among them was the child's family. Someone would have to tell them, to break the news that their little girl had died on Christmas Eve.

A tremor of emotion went through her, and she shuddered violently. A second later she felt the warm weight of a jacket being placed gently around her shoulders.

Helen looked up and found herself staring into Dr McKay's surprisingly kind brown eyes.

'I thought you might be cold,' he said.

'Thank you.' She started to her feet, steeling herself for the inevitable criticism. 'I must get back, everyone will be wondering where I am.'

'I'm sure they can spare you for a few minutes.'

'But I need to make sure everything is all right—'

'For God's sake, Sister Dawson, sit down before you fall down. You haven't stopped for hours.'

Helen hesitated, then sank back down on the bench.

Dr McKay pointed to the seat next to her. 'May I?'

'Of course.'

He sat down heavily beside her and stared up at the sky. 'It's been a hellish evening,' he commented.

'Yes, it has.'

They sat in silence for a moment. 'Ross told me what happened,' Dr McKay said. 'He couldn't have saved her, you know.'

'But she wasn't even hurt. Hardly a burn on her.'

'That's the awful thing about fire. It can kill in ways we can't see. The smoke would have badly damaged her lungs.' He paused. 'I know young Ross has his faults, and he can be arrogant, but he feels wretched about this.'

'I know he's not to blame really,' Helen said. 'But I just

wanted it to be someone's fault. Otherwise it seems so cruel and unfair . . .'

'Life is cruel and unfair sometimes.'

Helen turned her gaze back to the dining room. Light streamed from the windows, and she could see the outline of people sitting, standing and pacing, waiting anxiously for news of their loved ones.

Dr McKay was right, life could be cruel. She knew what it was like to lose someone she loved. And tonight someone else would know it too. This would be a Christmas they would never forget, and for all the wrong reasons.

'Those poor people,' she said.

'I know,' Dr McKay agreed heavily. 'But don't forget, we saved some lives tonight, too.'

'I suppose so. But I can't really think about them at the moment. It all just seems so horrible and sad . . .'

She broke off, turning her face towards a curious sound. The sound of singing. At that moment the doors to the ward block swung open and a group of nurses came out, their dark cloaks turned inside out to reveal the scarlet lining. They held jam-jar lanterns, and the dim light bathed their faces as they sang in the frosty moonlight.

'Silent night, Holy Night . . . All is calm, all is bright . . .'

It was all too much for Helen. The sweet poignancy of their song, their clear, beautiful voices, was too much of a contrast with the awful sights she'd witnessed that night. The smell of smoke, the charred skin, the screams of agony. A little girl in a scorched pink party dress, struggling to breathe . . .

Helen started to cry, and suddenly she couldn't stop. Juddering sobs shook her whole body and she doubled over, roaring with pain.

'Sister Dawson . . . Helen . . .' She felt Dr McKay's arms around her, pulling her close to him. She allowed herself to rest her head on his shoulder, feeling the smooth warmth of his cotton shirt against her cheek. He smelled faintly of smoke and cologne.

'There . . . it's all right . . .' he whispered, stroking her back. She felt the tension melt from her body as she was drawn against him, reassured and protected. Their faces were only inches apart. If she turned towards him just a fraction, their lips would almost touch.

And suddenly she badly wanted to kiss him.

But as she shifted towards him he stiffened and pulled away, and the spell was broken.

Dr McKay shot to his feet as if he needed to put as much distance between them as possible. 'I'd better go back inside,' he said.

Helen could feel him watching her in the darkness. 'Are you sure you're all right?'

'Quite all right, thank you.' She couldn't look at him.

'Good . . . good. Then I'll be off.'

He was already on his way, walking briskly back across the yard towards the Casualty hall.

Chapter Sixteen

Effie always looked forward to Christmas on the ward. Lots of the nurses moaned about being away from their families on Christmas Day, but much as she missed her mother and father back in Ireland, Effie loved the festive atmosphere at the hospital.

And it was especially festive in Male Orthopaedics. The high-ceilinged ward was festooned with decorations, swags of paper chains hanging down from the light fittings. The towering Christmas tree stood beside Sister's desk, weighed down with so much tinsel and so many baubles it was difficult to see the green branches beneath.

The patients on Blake weren't as poorly as those in Medical and Surgical, so they were able to join in with the fun. There was much laughter as Sister Blake handed out small gifts to each of them.

'A handkerchief?' Mr Carson, an amputee, mocked as he unwrapped his package. 'You might have got me a bottle of brandy, Sister.'

'Could have been worse, mate. She could have got you socks!' the man in the next bed shot back, and they both roared with laughter.

After the beds and backs had been done and the patients were all washed and comfortable, the nurses crowded into Sister's tiny office for coffee. She presented them each with a gift. Effie got a small bottle of scent, Californian Poppy, which she dabbed on to her wrists when no one was looking.

They also presented Sister Blake with the gift they'd clubbed together to buy. Effie steeled herself as she watched her unfasten the wrapping paper, knowing her sister Bridget had chosen it for her.

Sure enough, it was a suitably improving book.

'*Reflections on the New Testament*. Oh, how thoughtful.' Effie could see Sister Blake putting on her best smile as she read the cover. She knew how the poor woman felt. She'd worn the very same expression herself many times when she received her sister's gifts.

'Told you she'd prefer a cigarette case,' Katie muttered out of the corner of her mouth.

Later, Christmas dinner was served. The turkey was brought to the ward amid much ceremony by Mr Hopkins, then Mr Hobbs the Orthopaedic Consultant came up to do the honours and carve the bird, much to the amusement of the patients.

'Blimey, I know how that poor bird feels,' Mr Maudsley groaned as he watched Mr Hobbs struggling inexpertly with a wing. 'He did the same thing to my hip!'

After dinner, the nurses hurried to clear everything away and get the ward straight again before visiting time.

It meant a great deal to the families to be able to spend at least part of Christmas Day with their loved ones. Effie could see the children's faces shining with excitement as they crowded outside with their mothers and grandparents, waiting for the doors to open.

As usual, she found herself watching Adam Campbell. He was propped up, his eyes fixed avidly on the doors. Effie knew who he was waiting for. She wondered if the mysterious Adeline would finally answer his plea and come today. Surely she couldn't abandon him on Christmas Day?

But it seemed she could. As the doors opened and the

visitors streamed in, Effie watched Adam's hopeful expression slowly fade. Her own hopes began to fade with them.

'She's not coming,' she said to Katie.

'Hmm? Who are you talking about?'

'Adeline. Mr Campbell's mystery girlfriend.'

'Oh, her.' Katie shrugged. 'I expect she's ditched him and found someone else by now.'

'No!'

'It happens all the time,' her sister said airily. 'Out of sight, out of mind, I suppose. Go and put the kettle on, will you? Sister wants us to serve tea to the visitors.'

Sister Blake also produced a tin of shortbread biscuits her mother had sent her, much to Bridget's dismay.

'Biscuits, Sister?' Effie's sister frowned, as if she had never heard the word. 'We don't usually offer the visitors biscuits.'

'Yes, well, it's Christmas, isn't it? Don't look so worried, O'Hara,' Sister Blake grinned. 'One tin of biscuits isn't going to turn the ward into Sodom and Gomorrah!'

Effie was glad of the excuse to go over to Adam Campbell. She parked her trolley at the end of his bed. 'Would you like some tea?' she asked.

She half expected him to snap her head off as usual, but all she got was a listless, 'No, thank you, Nurse.'

'Are you sure? I can make coffee for you, if you prefer? And there are biscuits, look.' She proffered the tin.

'I'm fine, thank you.'

Effie looked at her watch. 'You never know, she might still come.'

'She won't.'

'How do you know? It's only a quarter-past two.'

'She won't come,' Adam repeated, more firmly this time.

Effie stared helplessly at him. She wished she had the

power to make him feel better, but all the splints and poultices in the world couldn't mend a broken heart.

'You did post the letter, didn't you?' he asked.

'I put it in the postbox myself,' Effie said. He'd asked her that question so many times, she was tired of hearing it.

'I'm sorry.' Adam gave her a sad little smile.

Just then the doors opened and they both looked up sharply. But it was only Adam's father. He came down the ward, smiling hopefully, a brightly wrapped parcel tucked under one arm.

'At least you have a visitor,' Effie said brightly.

It was a relief to be able to leave Adam with his father. But his depression seemed to hang over her as she pushed her tea trolley around the rest of the ward.

'Why are you so long-faced?' Katie accused when she found Effie washing up in the kitchen later.

'I feel sorry for Mr Campbell, that's all.'

'Well, don't,' Katie said. 'It's none of your business. And you'd better not even think about making it your business, Euphemia.' She pointed a warning finger at her sister. 'Do you hear me? Don't get involved.'

'I won't,' Effie muttered, plunging her hands into the hot soapy water so Katie wouldn't see her crossed fingers.

'You do understand, don't you?' William said.

He was giving Helen his big puppy-dog eyes look again, but even he knew that didn't make up for the fact that he'd left her in the lurch.

'Understand? Oh, I understand, all right,' she snapped. 'I understand I gave up Christmas at home so I could be here to help you, and now you're telling me you don't need me after all.'

'I know, Hels.' William tried his best to look wretched.

'And I'm truly sorry. But I couldn't say no, could I? The situation is far too – delicate.'

The 'situation' was that William and his erstwhile girlfriend had kissed and made up the night before, and now she was insisting on taking back her part in their Christmas show duet. Mainly, Helen suspected, to prove a point to her love rival in Male Medical.

'I don't want to let Sue down,' he said piously.

'But you don't mind letting me down, is that it?'

William looked thoughtful. 'I'll have a word with Sister Blake for you, if you like?' he offered. 'I'm sure she could find another part for you somewhere in the show . . .'

'I don't want a part in the show! I didn't want to be in it in the first place, if you recall. That's the point, William. I could have been at home in Richmond, and instead I'm stuck here at a loose end for the rest of Christmas Day. What am I supposed to do now?'

'You could always come and watch the show?' he suggested.

Helen glared at him. 'That's the last thing I want to do at the moment, thank you very much.'

She rubbed her eyes, which were still stinging from lack of sleep. William regarded her sympathetically.

'Are you all right, Hels? I heard you had a bad time on Casualty last night?'

'It wasn't the best Christmas Eve I've ever spent.' Her whole body felt as if it was stuffed with cotton wool.

'Poor Helen. I'm so sorry.' William put his arm around her shoulders. 'Why don't you go to bed?'

'I tried that. I couldn't sleep.' Every time she closed her eyes, her head filled with horrible visions of charred flesh and blackened, blistering skin. She constantly jerked awake, with screams of agony echoing inside her head.

'You should take something to help you. I could prescribe you something, if you like?'

'No, thank you. I'll manage.' Helen managed to smile at him. Her brother had a good heart. He just lost it too easily.

'I'm sorry, Hels,' he said again. 'I will make it up to you, I promise.'

'Just don't ask me to do you any more favours,' she growled at him. 'Because next time I'm definitely saying no!'

Helen watched her brother sauntering off across the courtyard, hands in his pockets, not a care in the world. It wasn't his fault, she thought. He didn't realise how difficult Christmas was for her, without Charlie.

The past two Christmases she'd managed to keep herself busy. The first year she'd been on duty, the second she'd spent with her family. Christmas with Constance Tremayne wasn't the most festive experience in the world, but at least it helped distract Helen, and stopped her thoughts from straying.

But now she was all on her own, and she wasn't sure how she would cope if the loneliness crept up on her.

She thought about going into Casualty and making herself useful. She was sure one of the nurses would be grateful to be relieved of their duty for a few hours. But that would mean facing Dr McKay, and Helen was worried she might have made rather a fool of herself with him the previous night.

It wasn't all her fault, she thought. It had been a long, hard night, she was worn out and distraught. And when Dr McKay had comforted her, she'd let her guard down and allowed her emotions to get the better of her. She was still too mortified by her behaviour to want to face him for a while.

And then, suddenly it occurred to her where she should be. Somewhere she knew she would be welcome.

Her nerve started to fail her as she stood on Nellie Dawson's doorstep, her hand poised on the doorknocker.

Nellie had told her to come round any time, but now she was here Helen wasn't sure it was such a good idea. She could hear laughter, piano music and the sounds of a lively party going on inside. What if she wasn't welcome after all?

She had turned to go when the door suddenly opened and Nellie stood there. 'Helen, love! I just looked out of the window and saw you. Why didn't you knock?'

'I – I wasn't sure if I should,' she murmured, embarrassed. 'You're entertaining, and I didn't want to be in the way . . .'

'It's only family, love. Besides, you're family too.' Nellie took charge, ushering her in. 'Come inside and have a drink.'

She pulled Helen into the narrow hallway and shut the door. The passageway was filled with welcoming warmth. 'You poor little mite, you're frozen to death.' Her mother-in-law rubbed Helen's icy fingers between her big hands. 'Go through and get warm by the fire. Everyone's in there.'

Terror seized her. 'I'm not staying . . .' Helen started to say. But Nellie was already herding her into the front parlour.

As soon as she stepped inside Helen was immediately engulfed in a fug of heat, noise and people. A thick pall of cigarette smoke hung in the air, mingling with the smell of beer and cheap scent. Over in the corner, a man was pounding out a tune on the piano. And everywhere she looked, there were faces. Men and women of all shapes and sizes, elderly folk and children: squeezed into armchairs and sofas, standing in corners, crouched on the floor. Helen could never have imagined such a small room could hold so many people. And they all seemed to be talking at once.

But the chatter stopped when she walked in, and all eyes turned to look at her.

Helen felt her mother-in-law's arm slide around her shoulders protectively. 'You all remember Helen, don't you? Our Charlie's wife.'

There was a general murmur of greeting. Helen caught a couple of people giving each other sideways looks. Charlie's father, a big man with red-gold hair like his son's, stepped forward.

'Helen love, it's a treat to see you. Sit yourself down, girl. What will you have to drink?' he offered.

Helen was about to protest that she couldn't stay, but Nellie had already shooed two children off the moquette settee to make space for her. 'Just a lemonade, please,' she said.

'You'll have something stronger than that, surely? It is Christmas, after all. How about a nice drop of sherry?'

'Really, lemonade is fine.'

'Suit yourself. You make yourself comfy there. A rose between two thorns!' He grinned at the two large ladies sitting like bookends either end of the settee.

'Cheeky!' One of them, a tinsel-bright redhead with crimson lipstick, handed him her empty glass. 'Just for that, you can fetch me a top up.'

'I bet you don't want a lemonade?'

She cackled. 'A milk stout, if you wouldn't mind.'

Charlie's father took her glass and shuffled off. Helen smiled nervously at the women she was sitting between. The one to her left was an equally bright redhead, except she was wearing cerise lipstick. The women fixed her with interested stares.

'We met you at our Charlie's funeral, although I daresay you won't remember,' one of them said.

'She's Auntie Mabel. And I'm Auntie Midge,' the other woman said.

'Pleased to meet you,' Helen replied. Both women sighed with pleasure.

'Aw, listen to her. Ain't she got a lovely speaking voice?' Auntie Midge said.

'Lovely manners, too,' Auntie Mabel agreed.

'You're a nurse, ain't you?'

Helen nodded. 'That's right. At the Florence Nightingale hospital.'

'Lovely,' Auntie Mabel said.

'We know it well,' Auntie Midge chimed in. 'My husband had his appendix out there.'

They fell silent after that but Helen could feel their eyes on her, watching her with that look she'd come to know so well over the past two years, a look that hovered between affection and pity.

Charlie's father returned with the drinks. As he handed her the lemonade, Helen began to wish she'd chosen something stronger after all.

Then the pianist struck up another rousing tune, and soon everyone was singing again. Helen tried to join in, swaying in time to the music with Midge and Mabel, but her heart wasn't in it.

This was a mistake, she realised, staring into the depths of her glass. She'd thought being with others might be the answer to her low spirits, but if anything she felt even more lonely in a crowded room full of people enjoying themselves.

What's wrong with me? she wondered. Charlie had

been dead for two years now. Everyone kept telling her to move on, and she desperately wanted to. And yet . . .

She put down her glass and struggled to her feet, disentangling herself from Auntie Midge and Auntie Mabel.

'You ain't going, are you?' Mabel looked up at her, her crimson lipstick smudged at the corners.

'I – I just need some fresh air,' Helen said.

'You hear that, Midge?' she heard Mabel say as she pushed her way towards the door. 'She said she wanted some fresh air. I expect she wants to use the lav.'

'Lovely manners,' Midge said approvingly.

Nellie was at the front door, gossiping with a neighbour who'd dropped round. Helen turned and headed down the narrow passageway towards the kitchen, planning to slip out of the back door and through the gate. Everyone else at the party was so tipsy, she was sure no one would miss her.

Still craning her neck to make sure Nellie wasn't watching, she reached out to open the back door. But suddenly it swung open from the outside, nearly knocking her off her feet.

'Sorry, love, I didn't see you there,' said a cheery, deep voice.

'That's all right, I was just—' Helen looked up, and the words died in her throat.

There, standing on the back step, was Charlie.

Chapter Seventeen

'Hello there,' he said. 'Going somewhere?'

As soon as he stepped into the light from the kitchen, she realised it wasn't her husband. The man framed in the back doorway, a duffel bag slung over one shoulder, had the same reddish-gold hair and blue eyes as Charlie, but everything else about him was different. He was taller, broader in the chest and shoulders, and there was a lazy insolence in his smile that her Charlie had never had.

Before Helen could speak to him, Nellie appeared in the kitchen doorway.

'Helen love, where are you—' Then she saw the stranger and a broad smile lit up her face. 'Well, I never! When did you get home? We weren't expecting you for another week at least.'

'I left my ship in Liverpool last night and got a lift on a wagon as far as Essex,' the man said. 'I couldn't miss spending Christmas with my favourite auntie, could I?' He held his arms out to her. 'You got a kiss for me, then?'

He grabbed her and planted a noisy kiss on the top of her head. A girlish blush rose in Nellie's plump cheeks.

'Oh, you!' She fought him off playfully. 'I ain't got time for your nonsense.'

'I bet you say that to all the boys.'

'Cheeky little sod! You never change, do you?'

'Not if I can help it.' He glanced at Helen. 'Who's this, then, Auntie Nell?'

'Oh, I forgot, you two ain't met, have you? Helen, this is my nephew Christopher. Chris, this is Helen.'

His expression changed. 'Charlie's Helen?'

'That's right,' Nellie said. 'She's come to spend Christmas with us.' She sighed with satisfaction. 'Now all my family's together. Ain't that nice?'

'Very nice,' Charlie said, still looking at Helen. The intensity of his stare made her feel awkward, but she couldn't tear her gaze away from those blue eyes.

Nellie didn't seem to notice as she bustled around. 'Come in, son, let's see about getting you something to eat. I expect you're hungry?'

'Famished.' Christopher stepped into the kitchen. Helen moved back to let him pass, but his body still brushed against hers. He smelled of stale sweat mingled with the salty tang of the sea.

'You always are, as I recall!' His aunt smiled fondly at him. 'You've missed Christmas dinner, but I can fetch you some cold meat and pickles, if you like?'

'Smashing.'

'Go through to the parlour and I'll bring it in to you. They'll all be pleased to see you, especially the kids.'

'To be honest, Auntie Nell, I could do with a good wash first,' Christopher said, unhooking his duffel bag from his shoulder. 'I've been curled up on the back of a coal wagon all day, so I ain't really fit for company.'

'Of course, I should have thought of that. You can have a scrub down in the scullery.'

'I'll heat the water up,' Helen offered quickly.

She darted into the scullery, filled the heavy iron kettle and put it on the hob. She picked up the matches and tried to light the gas, but for some reason her hands were suddenly shaking so much she couldn't hold a match steady enough to strike it.

'Here, let me.' She jumped as Christopher came up behind her and took the box out of her hands.

'Thank you.' As he bent over the hob, Helen let her gaze travel up the breadth of his shoulders. His fair hair was neatly trimmed, revealing sunburned skin on the back of his neck.

'You looked like you'd seen a ghost when I walked in.' He turned and caught her looking at him.

'I thought you were Charlie,' she admitted.

He frowned. 'I'm nothing like him!'

'I can see that now.' She blushed to think she could have been so stupid. Imagine her thinking her dead husband had returned to her. But Christmas wishes did sometimes come true, and she'd wished often enough that she didn't have to be lonely any more.

But it wasn't just the shock that had disturbed her. Her reaction to Christopher had been too intense for her own liking. It was as if seeing him had ignited something deep within her.

He paused, his eyes fixed on the dancing blue flames of the gas ring. 'I'm sorry I couldn't get back for the funeral, but I was stuck on a cargo ship in the middle of the Atlantic. I would've liked to pay my respects to Charlie. He was a good mate. One of the best.'

'He was,' Helen agreed.

The silence stretched between them. Helen was aware of him standing close to her, their bodies almost touching in the narrow confines of the scullery. She was also suddenly aware that she hadn't breathed in a long time.

'I'll go and help with your supper,' she said.

Nellie prattled on as she made sandwiches, sawing great doorsteps of bread from the loaf she'd retrieved from the larder.

'Chris is my sister-in-law Ada's boy,' she explained. 'She

passed away when he was just a nipper and he's never got on with his dad, so we took him in. Charlie must have mentioned him to you, I'm sure?'

'I don't think so. I can't remember.'

'They were close as two boys could be until Chris went off and joined the Merchant Navy when he was fifteen,' Nellie went on. 'We don't see as much of him as we'd like these days because he's away at sea so often. He keeps in touch, though. Sends me postcards from wherever he goes. I keep them all, too, in a tin under the bed. I've got postcards from all over the world.'

'Nellie?' She looked up at the sound of her husband calling her name from up the passageway. 'Nellie, you're wanted!'

'I'm busy,' she called back, and went on sawing away at the loaf.

'I can do that, if you like?' Helen said.

'Oh, no, love. You're a visitor.'

'You're always telling me I'm family, remember?' Helen reminded her. 'And I'd like to make myself useful,' she added.

'Go on, then.' Nellie straightened up, pushing a stray curl off her face with the back of her hand. 'Just finish buttering this bread, I'll be back in a minute.'

Helen buttered the bread, conscious all the time of the sound of splashing water coming from the other side of the thin scullery curtain. She went to the larder to fetch the pickles, but as she turned back, the curtain suddenly swished aside and Chris stood there, naked to the waist, water gleaming off the smooth, sleek muscles of his chest. His hair was wet and dripping and he was wiping it out of his eyes with one hand as he groped about blindly with the other.

'Pass us a towel, will you, Auntie?'

Helen grabbed the towel off the fireguard and thrust it at him. Try as she might, she couldn't tear her eyes away from his leanly muscled torso, the broad chest tapering into the narrow waistband of his blue serge trousers.

He wiped his face, then looked up and saw her. 'Oh!' He covered his chest with the flimsy towel. 'I thought you were Auntie Nellie.'

'She's not here,' Helen whispered, suddenly dry-mouthed.

'So I see.' He grinned at her. 'I beg your pardon, I didn't mean to shock you.'

'You didn't.' Helen found her voice. 'I'm a nurse. I see people undressed every day.'

'And do you stare at them, too?'

His words broke the spell. Helen flicked her gaze away quickly and hurried to the table to finish making the sandwiches. But she was aware of Christopher behind her, crossing the room, delving into his duffel bag and pulling out a clean shirt.

'Is that for me?' he asked, nodded towards the food.

Helen pushed the plate towards him. 'Would you like a cup of tea to go with it?' she asked.

'I'd rather have a beer, if you don't mind?'

He sat down at the table. Helen went to the larder, found the jug of beer and filled him a glass. She was aware she was blushing. If she wasn't careful she would lose her composure completely.

She put the glass down and was about to move away when he said, 'Ain't you going to keep me company?'

'I thought you'd want to join the others in the parlour?'

He grinned. 'What, and listen to my aunties squawking and Uncle Harry murdering tunes on that old piano? I'm in no hurry, believe me!'

Helen smiled reluctantly. 'They're not that bad.'

'Then why were you running away?'

His eyes met hers across the table, direct and challenging.

'I wasn't,' Helen said. 'I just needed some fresh air, that's all.'

'A likely story! Come on, you can tell me. I won't tell a soul.'

She smiled furtively. 'I am finding it quite – difficult,' she admitted.

'I daresay you are. Brings back a few memories, I suppose?'

Helen nodded. She traced a pattern on the scrubbed wood of the kitchen table with her thumbnail. 'I know I'm being silly, but—'

'Not silly at all. But I'm glad you didn't run away before I met you,' he said.

Nellie came back into the kitchen. 'Sorry about that,' she said, looking from one to the other of them. 'Oh, I see Helen's been looking after you, has she? That's good.'

'She's been looking after me very well.'

Helen was aware of him watching her across the table but she kept her eyes lowered.

She got to her feet. 'I'm going back to join the party.'

In the parlour, all the talk was of Christopher's unexpected arrival.

'I wonder what's brought him back now?' Auntie Mabel said.

'I expect he's in trouble again.' Uncle Harry shook his head. 'He only ever comes home when he's worn out his welcome everywhere else.'

'Now, Harry, you know Nellie won't hear a word said against him,' Charlie's father warned. 'You and I might have our own opinion of him, but we'd best keep it to ourselves.'

'Besides, all that's in the past now,' Auntie Midge joined in. 'Chris is a changed man since he joined the Merchant Navy.'

'A leopard can't change its spots, Midge, as you well know.'

Helen looked from one to the other. She desperately wanted to find out more, but good manners prevented her from asking.

The party went on, with more music and singing and laughter. Helen fixed a smile on her face and joined in, but all the while she kept looking up at the door, waiting for Christopher to come in.

And then, finally, he did. Helen was at the piano at the time, turning the pages of sheet music for Uncle Harry. She didn't need to look round to know that Christopher had walked in. It was as if an electric current had run through her body, lighting up her nerve endings.

The family greeted him like a prodigal son. Helen watched as he worked his way around the room, charming the aunties until they blushed and flapped at him with their hands and told him not to be so saucy. He joked with the uncles, telling them outrageous stories that made them roar with laughter. He played with the boys, swinging them up on his broad shoulders, and danced with the little girls.

The only one he didn't speak to was Helen. But she was aware of him all the time, could feel his every move like a brush across her skin. She was grateful he didn't speak to her. She felt sure that if he did, she would blush and stutter like a tongue-tied schoolgirl.

Shortly afterwards, Helen went home. She wanted to slip away quietly, but Nellie found her putting on her coat in the hall.

'You can't go out on your own,' she said. 'Wait a minute, and I'll get Chris to walk you back to the hospital . . .'

'No!' Helen said, so sharply that Nellie blinked at her. 'It's all right, honestly. It's not late.'

'But I'm sure he won't mind . . .'

'No, really. I don't want to spoil the party.'

Helen hurried away, out into the frosty darkness, before Nellie could press her further. The last thing she wanted was to be alone in the dark with someone like Christopher. She had a feeling that might be very dangerous indeed.

Chapter Eighteen

After supper on Christmas Day, the staff gathered in the dining room for the long-awaited Christmas Show.

Those taking part concealed themselves in the kitchens beyond the makeshift stage to prepare, while everyone else filed in to take their seats among the rows of chairs set out for the audience. Porters brought in patients in wheelchairs and positioned them along the walls.

Frannie sat at her piano at the front of the stage, running her hands lightly over the keys in an improvised overture. All the time her eyes scanned the room, waiting for John to arrive.

'Looking for someone?' Kathleen Fox asked. She sat beside her friend, sorting the sheet music into order for her.

'Just someone I invited to come this evening.' She glanced at the clock on the wall. Five minutes to curtain up.

'Oh, yes? Anyone I know?'

Frannie shook her head. 'He's an old friend of Matthew's. From when we were growing up.'

'I see.' Kathleen paused, then said, 'Is that a new dress you're wearing, Fran?'

'Yes, as a matter of fact. Why?'

'And your hair's looking rather nice this evening. You've done it differently, haven't you? Those waves suit you.'

Frannie came to the end of her improvised piece. 'It's not what you're thinking,' she whispered, over the final flourish.

'I'm not thinking anything, I assure you.'

'Yes, you are. I can see that gleam in your eye. Anyway, even if I did make an effort it looks as if it was wasted,' she said.

But then, just as the lights dimmed, John strode in looking every inch the officer in his smart uniform. He caught Frannie's eye and waved as he took his seat at the back of the room.

Kathleen grinned. 'I can see why you wore the new dress,' she said.

'Stop it.' Frannie shook her head and propped the piece of introductory music on her stand. But she could feel herself blushing like a schoolgirl as the first act began.

The show was the usual mixture of comedy, chaos and choral singing. Unfortunately, too many of the laughs were unintentional, such as when a slightly tipsy Dr Bertram forgot the punchline of his comedy monologue, or when Owen Evans tripped over his skirt on his way off the stage and sprawled headlong at Frannie's feet. But somehow they muddled through, and the audience seemed to enjoy every minute.

Afterwards, John approached Frannie as she was tidying away her music.

'Thank you,' he said. 'That was a most enjoyable show.'

She grimaced. 'It's all right, you don't have to be kind!'

'No, I mean it. It was most – entertaining.'

'We do our best.' Frannie started to collect up her music, conscious that John was still behind her, waiting.

Finally, he said, 'I don't suppose you'd consider joining me for supper at my club? As a way of saying thank you for this evening, I mean. Although I expect you're busy,' he went on, his words coming out in a rush. 'You probably already have plans . . .'

She looked at him, and suddenly it was as if the years

had rolled back and she saw again the diffident orphanage boy gazing warily back at her.

'Thank you,' she said. 'I would like that very much.'

John's club was in an elegant Georgian building off Piccadilly. As befitted an officers' club, it was full of men in uniform. In spite of her feelings towards the military, Frannie couldn't help but be impressed by the number of men who saluted John as they passed. It gave her a quiet lift of pride to be by his side.

'I really don't feel as if I belong here,' she whispered, as they headed down the long wood-panelled passage to the lounge.

'I'll let you into a secret – neither do I,' John whispered back. 'I keep thinking at any moment someone is going to realise I'm that boy from the workhouse and throw me out on my ear.'

'But you're an officer!'

'I don't feel like one. I never have. Even when I got my commission after the war, I never felt as if I quite belonged.'

They sipped their cocktails in the hushed atmosphere of the lounge, watched over by suits of armour and paintings of imperious-looking men in Napoleonic uniform.

'I really don't know what my friends in the Peace Society would make of this,' Frannie laughed as she sipped her cocktail.

'Just because we wear uniforms, it doesn't make us the enemy,' John pointed out quietly. 'I bet if you asked any of the men here, they would sooner choose peace over going to war any day. And talking of going to war, I have something for you.' He reached into the top pocket of his tunic. 'This is yours, I believe?'

Frannie gazed down at the smooth grey stone he'd placed in her palm. She recognised it straight away. 'My lucky charm! You mean to tell me you've kept it all these years?' she said.

He nodded. 'It's seen me through a great many sticky situations, I can tell you. I always hoped to be able to return it to you one day.'

She laughed. 'It's just a pebble.'

'It was a great deal more to me than just that.' He looked down at it, then lifted his gaze to meet hers. 'I still remember the moment you gave it to me, as clearly as if it were yesterday,' he said. 'I was standing by myself on that railway platform, watching everyone say goodbye to their loved ones and wishing I had someone to tell me how much they'd miss me. And then suddenly there you were.' His voice was gruff with emotion. 'You were the only one who noticed me that day. I was more grateful than you could ever imagine.'

Frannie looked away, embarrassed by his intensity. Her fingers closed around the pebble. 'I remember that day, too,' she said. 'It was the last time I ever saw Matthew.'

'Of course. I'm sorry, I didn't think . . .'

'It's all right. It's been more than twenty years, I'm hardly a tearful girl any more.' Frannie leaned back in the leather-covered wing chair and stared into the crackling flames of the fire. She knew she shouldn't ask, but she couldn't stop herself. 'How did he get on out there?'

He frowned. 'Didn't Matthew tell you in his letters?'

'At first he did. When he arrived in France his letters were typically Matthew, full of fun and stories about the things you all got up to. But then gradually they became – well, less like him, I suppose.' She thought about those letters, and how she came to dread reading them. Gloom and despair dripped from every page. There was sickness, disease and death all around him, and Matthew had told her he didn't know how much more he could take.

Frannie had done her best to cheer him up, sending him little gifts of socks and chocolate and his favourite tobacco, when she could. She tried to reassure him it wouldn't be for ever, the war would end soon. She gave him news of home to try and make him feel less far away.

But then, suddenly, the letters had ceased.

'I don't know why he stopped writing,' she said. 'Poor Matthew, I think he just found it so difficult to cope with it all . . .'

'We all found it difficult to cope, not just him!' John's voice was harsh. 'It wasn't easy for any of us, watching our mates being picked off one by one, wondering if the next day it would be our turn.'

'Yes, but he was right to be afraid, wasn't he?' Frannie snapped back. 'Matthew was one of the ones who didn't come home.'

John didn't reply. He gulped down his drink and gazed moodily into the fire. Frannie followed his gaze towards the dancing flames.

'I waited for him, you know,' she said. 'Even after that telegram arrived, I refused to believe it. I thought there must be some mistake, that he'd been forgotten about, perhaps he'd lost his memory. It had happened before, you see. We'd get men dragged in to the field hospital off the battlefield, so shocked and injured they had no idea who they were or where they'd come from. It was so easy, wasn't it, to lose track of someone in all that chaos . . .' She felt the old familiar emotion rising in her chest and paused for a moment to gain control of herself. 'I was sure he would be found injured in a hospital behind the lines,' she said, more calmly. 'That's why I waited for him. I never gave up hope that one day I'd be working in the hospital, and I'd look up and there he'd be, standing in the doorway. I thought he'd find his way back to me one day.'

'Oh, Frannie, I'm so sorry.' John looked at her, his eyes dark pools of sorrow.

She turned to him. She had been putting off asking the question since the first moment she'd seen him, but she knew she couldn't put it off any longer.

'Do you know what happened to Matthew?' she asked.

John shook his head. 'I only know what it said in the telegram.'

'Missing, presumed dead.' Frannie recited the words dully. 'But that could mean anything, couldn't it? Was it a mortar shell? Did he get hit by a sniper?'

'I don't know.'

'But you were in the same section, surely you must have seen something.'

'I told you, I don't know anything about it!'

His voice was harsh, shocking her into silence. For a moment neither of them spoke.

'I'm sorry,' John said heavily. 'I didn't mean to lose my temper. It's just I find it very hard to think about.'

'I understand.' Frannie nodded. 'I shouldn't have brought it up – I'm sorry.'

He drained the last of his drink and put down his glass. 'It's late,' he said. 'I'll take you back to the hospital.'

'I can make my own way back.'

'I want to take you.'

They made the taxi journey back to Bethnal Green in awkward silence. Frannie stared unseeingly out of the window as they left the bright lights of the West End behind, passing through the City of London and out the other side, into the darkened streets of the East End, with its narrow terraces, cobbled back alleys and slightly menacing air. The stark outlines of the towering dock cranes stood out against the moonlit sky, and the air was filled with the salty, tarry tang of the factories that lined the river.

Frannie dearly wished she hadn't said anything. It was as if a yawning gulf had opened up between them.

The taxi drew up at the hospital gates and John asked it to wait while he got out with her.

'Thank you for a lovely evening,' he said.

Frannie looked rueful. 'I'm sorry it ended so badly.'

He frowned. 'Has it ended badly?'

'You don't have to be polite, John. It's my fault. If I hadn't brought up the past . . .'

He put his finger to her lips. 'Don't,' he said. 'I don't mind talking about the past, Frannie, truly I don't. But in my experience it rarely does any good to keep looking back. We need to look forward if we're going to live our lives to the full.'

'You're right,' she sighed.

He looked down at her and for a mad moment she was sure he was going to kiss her. But then he took a step back and started towards his waiting taxi.

As she watched him get back into his cab, Frannie put her hand up to her mouth. She could still feel the gentle touch of his finger against her lips.

Chapter Nineteen

The following day was Effie's afternoon off, and she caught the bus up to the West End. In the two years she had been in London, she had only ever ventured past St Paul's with one of her sisters or some of the other girls from her set. Now she wished she'd brought someone with her as she traipsed the wintry streets of Bloomsbury alone, the cold wind flaying her cheeks. She would have felt better if she'd had her sister Katie or her friend Jess with her. But she knew they wouldn't approve of this mission. They would tell her she was getting too involved, as usual.

After losing her way several times and trudging down many wrong streets, Effie finally found Adeline's address. It was on a street of tall, grey-brick houses in Bloomsbury. Effie's heart was in her mouth as she climbed the short flight of stone steps and rang the front doorbell. Now she was here, it occurred to her that she hadn't the first idea what she was going to say.

She was still wondering when a man answered the door. He was in his twenties, reed-slim, with slicked-back hair and a thin moustache. Even though it was past two in the afternoon, he was wearing dishevelled evening dress. The sound of laughter and jazz music drifted from inside the house.

He looked her up and down. 'Yes?'

Effie's courage nearly deserted her. 'I've come to see Adeline,' she said.

He frowned. 'She isn't here.'

'Who is it, Charles?' A woman's voice drifted from inside the house.

'Some girl wants to see Adeline,' he called back over his shoulder.

'Tell her to go away.'

'I'm trying,' the man laughed. He turned back to Effie. 'You'll have to come back another time.'

He started to close the door, but she stood her ground. 'When is she expected back?'

'I haven't the faintest idea. She's hardly ever here at the moment. She spends all her time at the hospital.'

'Hospital? Which hospital?'

'How should I know?' The young man sighed impatiently. 'Hold on a moment,' he said, and disappeared.

Effie peered into the shadowy hallway. Every inch of the walls was covered with paintings. But these weren't the sort of pretty landscapes her mother liked. These were strange, disturbing, filled with splashes of colour that didn't resemble anything at all as far as she could see.

Effie was still staring, trying to fathom them out, when her eye snagged on something else. A red velvet coat, hanging on the coatstand at the far end of the hall.

An uneasy feeling started to grow inside her. She had seen that coat before.

The man returned and handed Effie a piece of paper. 'Here you are. This is the address. You're bound to find her there. She's visiting her fiancé.'

'Thank you.' Effie stuck the piece of paper in her pocket. She didn't need to look at the address. She already knew where she'd find Adeline.

Two days after Boxing Day, Father Christmas came to Casualty, escorted by a policeman.

'Bit late for Christmas, aren't you?' Dr McKay commented.

'He was caught breaking in through a warehouse window,' Helen told him. 'He thinks he may have broken his ankle.'

'A window, eh?' Dr McKay said. 'You should've come down the chimney as usual, then you wouldn't be in this mess.'

'Don't you start!' Father Christmas mumbled irritably, pulling off his beard to reveal a dark, stubbly chin. 'I've had that all the way here from the copper. Right comic cuts, he is!'

'Well, if you will dress up as Father Christmas to go robbing, what do you expect?'

'I thought no one would think anything of it if they saw me,' he mumbled.

Helen did her best not to smile, but when she caught the doctor's twinkling eye it was difficult to keep a straight face. 'Let's have a look at that ankle, shall we?' he said.

As it turned out, the 'broken' ankle was nothing more than a severe sprain. Dr McKay applied a firm bandage, then sent the patient up to the ward.

'You've done a nasty job on it,' Dr McKay said. 'I'd like to have the consultant look at it. He might decide you need a splint.'

'Suits me, Doctor.' The man grinned. 'I ain't in any hurry to go to the cop shop. Besides, that rozzer's got a nasty look in his eye, if you know what I mean. Got a bit rough with me on the way here, he did. I don't fancy my chances against him.'

'Nonsense, I'm sure he was only doing his job,' Dr McKay dismissed. 'Sister, will you go and break the news to him?'

The policeman was leaning against the booking-in desk, talking to Penny Willard. From the look on her face, they seemed to be arguing.

They stopped speaking abruptly as Helen approached.

'Is everything all right?' she asked, looking from one to the other. Penny stared down at the ledger in front of her and said nothing, but the policeman turned to Helen with a smile. He was tall, fair-haired and handsome, but there was something cold about his arrogant grin.

'Couldn't be better, Sister. How's the patient?'

'Severely sprained ankle,' she said. 'Dr McKay wants the consultant to look at him, so he's sending him up to the ward.'

The policeman's smile disappeared abruptly, like a light going off. 'But he's under arrest!'

'Nevertheless, Dr McKay has decided—'

'I don't care what Dr McKay has decided! That little toerag needs to come to the station with me. He's probably putting it on anyway. I've seen it happen before. They make out they're at death's door, then the minute the nurse's back is turned they have it away on their toes out of the door.'

'I don't think this patient will be having it away anywhere with his ankle in that state.'

They turned around. Dr McKay stood there, notes tucked under his arm.

The policeman gave a derisive snort. 'I wouldn't be surprised if he was pulling the wool over your eyes.'

'Are you suggesting I don't know a sprained ankle when I see one, Constable?' Dr McKay replied. He was smiling, but there was a steely look in his brown eyes.

A muscle twitched in the policeman's tense jaw. 'No,' he snapped.

'I'm glad to hear it. Because I also found some bruising

to his arms and neck that can't be explained by falling heavily through a window. I'm sure you wouldn't like me to ask too many questions about that, either?'

The silence stretched to breaking point. 'I'm going up to that ward with him,' the policeman muttered. 'He ain't getting away from me that easily.'

He gave Penny a brief nod, then he was gone. Helen watched him disappear through the doors, letting them crash shut behind him.

'What a charming man,' Dr McKay remarked.

Penny looked uncomfortable. 'That's Joe,' she mumbled.

'Your fiancé?' Helen caught Dr McKay's eye. He looked as dismayed as she felt.

'He's not always like that,' Penny defended him stoutly. 'He just gets angry when he's not allowed to do his job properly.'

'I'm sure he's very – conscientious.' Dr McKay put the notes down on the desk. 'See these are sent up to the ward, will you? And send the next patient through.'

As he disappeared back to his consulting room, Helen heard a sniff, and turned to look at Penny Willard. Her fair head was bent so Helen couldn't see her face. 'Nurse Willard? Are you crying?'

'I'm fine, really.' Penny wiped her fingers across her cheek, still not looking up from the ledger. 'I just don't want anyone thinking badly of Joe. He's a good man, really. It's my fault he's in a bad mood.'

'Your fault?'

She nodded. 'We had a bit of an argument. He's still upset with me for standing him up on Christmas Eve.'

Helen shuddered at the memory of that awful night. 'But that was an emergency,' she said. 'Surely he wouldn't blame you for that?'

'No, he was just – disappointed, that's all.'

Helen stared at the top of Penny's head, her fair hair tucked under her cap. Her hands were locked together on the desk in front of her. Looking at them, Helen caught a glimpse of yellowing bruises under her starched cuffs.

'What have you done to your arm?' she asked.

'Nothing.' Penny slipped her hand under the desk, out of sight.

Cogs began to turn and whirr inside Helen's head, slowly clicking into place. 'Nurse Willard—' she started to say, but Penny cut her off.

'I'd best get the next patient sent in,' she said, picking up the list. 'Who's that?'

'I think that would be me.'

Helen turned around. Standing in the busy Casualty hall, addressing them both, was Christopher.

There it was again, the same powerful jolt Helen had felt when she first saw him. It took all her self-control not to run into his arms.

'What are you doing here?' she greeted him, as coolly as she could manage.

'I've done my shoulder in.' He nursed his left arm across his broad chest, his jacket slung loosely around his shoulders.

'Oh, dear, how did you manage that?'

'Would you believe, I fell off a roof?' He looked rueful. 'I was trying to fetch a ball out of the gutter for the kids and I slipped.'

'I'm not surprised, in this icy weather.' Helen shook her head. 'You'd better come with me.'

In the consulting room, Dr McKay was similarly unimpressed. 'You're lucky it's only your shoulder. You could have broken your neck.'

'Not me, doc.' Christopher grinned confidently. 'I'm

like a cat. I've got nine lives.' He turned to Helen. 'Anyone would think I'd done it deliberately, to see you again,' he said in a low voice.

Helen blushed. Dr McKay looked from one to the other. 'Do you two know each other?'

'We met on Christmas Day, didn't we?' She could feel Christopher's warm gaze on her but she couldn't meet his eye. 'Except she disappeared like Cinderella before I had a chance to talk to her properly.'

'Mr Dawson is – was – my husband's cousin,' Helen explained quietly.

'I see.' She could feel Dr McKay's disapproval as he turned back to Christopher's shoulder. And just when things were starting to improve between them! Ever since Christmas Eve she'd sensed him thawing towards her. Now he was bound to have something to say about Christopher flirting with her in front of him. 'Well, it's definitely dislocated. I'm going to have to reset it.'

'You go ahead, doc,' Christopher said, still grinning at Helen.

'It might hurt . . .'

'I'm a big lad, I'm sure I can take it.' Christopher shook his head. 'I've put it out a couple of times and it's gone back right as rain – ow!' He flinched as Dr McKay started to rotate his upper arm.

'I told you it would hurt.'

'It's never hurt that much before.' Christopher stared at him balefully.

'I'm sure you can take it.' Dr McKay parroted his words back at him. 'Now, put your elbow across your chest for me. This will probably hurt a bit more . . .'

Christopher caught his lower lip between his teeth to stop himself roaring in pain, but Helen could see the sweat standing out on his brow as Dr McKay rotated his arm again. She had never known a patient complain so much. Perhaps Christopher wasn't as tough as he looked, she thought.

Finally, Dr McKay finished and stood back. 'Right, Sister, you can strap him up now,' he said.

Helen felt very self-conscious as she applied the heavy adhesive strapping. Once again, she could feel Christopher watching her, even though she kept her eyes fixed on her task. She could sense his lazy amusement, as if he knew exactly the effect he was having on her. She couldn't finish the job quickly enough.

'You'll have to make an appointment for Outpatients in a week's time to have it taken off,' Dr McKay said, scribbling his signature on the notes.

'A week?' Christopher laughed. 'That's a bit much, ain't it? Last time I did it I was hauling crates on deck the next day.'

'That's probably why it keeps dislocating.' Dr McKay handed Helen the notes. 'A week, and then you'll need massage to get the joint moving again.'

'He's a miserable old stick, ain't he?' Christopher said, as Helen followed him back into the Casualty hall.

'Sometimes,' she agreed.

'Anyway, he's not going to stop my fun. I was thinking of going up to Trafalgar Square on Saturday night, to see in the New Year. D'you fancy coming with me?'

Helen stared at him. 'Are you sure that's a good idea?' she managed finally. 'You really ought to avoid crowds, with that shoulder . . .'

'There's a lot of things I ought not to do, but I still do 'em!' Christopher grinned at her, and Helen found herself smiling back.

'I've never been to Trafalgar Square on New Year's Eve before,' she said.

'Me neither,' he admitted cheerfully. 'It'll be an adventure for both of us, won't it?' He looked at her. 'So what do you reckon, Helen? Do you fancy being reckless with me?'

Their eyes met, and she saw the direct challenge in his gaze. Her first instinct was to refuse, to back away, to stay safe. But as she was beginning to realise, safe was also very lonely.

She smiled up at him. 'Why not?' she said.

Chapter Twenty

'Something wrong with your tea, love?'

Effie looked up at the café proprietor standing over her, wiping his hands on his greasy apron, then back down at the cup of tea cooling in front of her.

'No, thank you,' she replied.

'Only you ain't touched it for half an hour. I just wondered if you wanted a fresh pot?'

'I'm waiting for someone.'

The proprietor looked down at her. He was a big man, an Italian cockney with strands of greasy black hair smeared over his shining bald patch. 'Been stood up, have you?' He grinned.

'No!' Effie stared back at him, affronted.

The man shrugged his shoulders. 'You wouldn't be the first.' He nodded towards her teacup. 'Sure I can't get you a crumpet to go with that? Or a teacake? Or a plate of assorted fancies?'

'No, thank you.'

The man went off, grumbling about how he was never going to afford to retire if all his customers were like her. Effie didn't blame him for being cross. She had been sitting there for nearly an hour, eking out one cup of tea while she waited for Adeline Moreau.

She cleared a spot in the steamy window with her sleeve and looked out into the grey, slush-covered street. According to Jess, Adeline left her fiance's bedside at one o'clock every afternoon to have lunch here. Effie had had to wait three days before Sister Blake moved her off-duty time from morning to afternoon and she could come here.

But now she wondered if she'd got it wrong. What if Adeline visited some other café? This was the closest one to the hospital, but it was nearly half-past one and she should have been here by now, if she was coming.

Typical, Effie thought, toying with her teaspoon. This would be the one day Adeline decided to break her routine and stay at her fiancé's bedside.

And what was she going to say if the girl did come? Effie had mentally rehearsed a million ways to say what she had to say, but nothing sounded quite right.

She wondered what her sisters would think about it. Katie would probably pretend to disapprove, but then she'd want to hear all about it. And Bridget would have a fit and march Effie straight to Matron herself.

But she wasn't doing anything wrong. It wasn't as if she'd fallen in love with a patient. Exactly the opposite – she was trying to reunite him with someone else.

It was a noble thing she was doing, Effie decided. She was being a good nurse, trying to heal Adam Campbell's broken heart for him. Florence Nightingale herself would probably approve.

Except she'd completely wasted her time.

But then, as she was fumbling in her purse to pay, she glanced up and caught a flash of red crossing the street towards the café. A moment later the door opened and Adeline walked in, swathed in her crimson coat, a feathered hat on her sleek blonde head.

'I've changed my mind,' Effie said to the proprietor, as she sat back in her seat. 'I will stay, after all.'

She watched as Adeline sat down at her table and waved at the proprietor.

'Usual, love?' he called across to her.

'Yes, please, Lou.' Adeline smiled back at him. She was very beautiful, Effie thought, with dark, almond-shaped eyes, flawless porcelain skin, and what Effie's mother would call 'good bones'. No wonder everyone seemed to be in love with her. Even the grumpy café proprietor seemed charmed as he placed a pot of coffee in front of her.

Effie breathed in the rich aroma. Coffee seemed terribly sophisticated, just like the stylish clothes Adeline wore. She dressed to be noticed, in colourful floaty layers, her blonde hair caught up in a silk scarf.

Effie picked up her own cup and clumsily slopped cold tea into the saucer. The thought of confronting Adeline made her feel ill. But the thought of not confronting her, of going back to the ward and seeing Adam Campbell's sad, wistful face, worried her even more.

All her carefully rehearsed lines deserted Effie as she put down her cup, rose to her feet and made her way across the café.

Adeline was reading a book. She looked up with a smile as Effie approached.

'Can I help you?' she said. Then, as Effie struggled to speak, she added, 'We've met, haven't we?'

'I'm a nurse at the Nightingale,' she said.

A small frown gathered between Adeline's perfectly shaped brows. Then she nodded. 'Of course, I remember now. You came to see Richard.' She put down her book. 'Won't you sit down?' she offered.

Effie stared at the empty chair, momentarily non-plussed. In all her imaginary conversations, she hadn't expected Adeline to be quite so charming.

In the end, she pulled out the chair and plonked herself down in it. 'How is Mr Webster?' she asked.

'He's improving every day, thank you.' Adeline smiled,

showing perfect white teeth. 'He's sitting up and talking, which the consultant thinks is nothing short of a miracle, considering . . .' Her voice trailed off and she looked troubled.

'Does he remember anything about the accident?'

Adeline shook her head. 'Nothing at all. He has no memory of anything up to the moment he woke up. We're having to piece everything together very slowly for him. Although he remembers me, thank God!' She smiled.

'What about Adam? Does he remember him?'

The smile faded from Adeline's face. 'How do you know Adam?'

'He's a patient on my ward.'

Adeline didn't react, but Effie noticed her hands shaking slightly as she topped up her coffee cup.

'The Almoner's office wrote to you. And so did he,' Effie said.

'I know.'

'Why didn't you reply?'

'It's complicated.'

'Because you're engaged to someone else?'

'Something like that.' Adeline sipped her coffee, her gaze fixed on a distant point beyond Effie's shoulder.

'Does he know you're engaged to Richard?' Effie asked.

'Of course he knows!' Adeline snapped, turning her dark gaze to meet Effie's. 'Richard and Adam are – were – best friends.'

'Until you came along?' Effie guessed.

Adeline's mouth tightened. 'I told you, it's complicated,' she said. 'You wouldn't understand.'

'I'd like to try.'

She put down her cup. 'I suppose Adam sent you? Did he ask you to plead his case for him?'

'Actually, he doesn't know I'm here.'

'So why did you decide to come?'

'Because I feel sorry for him.'

'Do you?' Adeline's brows lifted. 'Is that the only reason, I wonder?'

Effie felt herself blushing. 'I don't know what you mean.'

'I wouldn't be surprised if you'd fallen for him. I suppose it was bound to happen. He's an attractive man, after all. It's very easy to fall for someone like Adam Campbell. I should know,' she murmured.

'What happened between you?' Effie asked.

'That's none of your business.'

'It is my business,' Effie insisted. 'I'm worried about him. He's upset and pining for you, and that's not helping him to get better.'

Adeline shot her a quick glance, and Effie caught the flash of something like smugness in her expression before her eyes hardened again. 'Well, I'm sorry, but I can't help,' she said shortly. 'Adam has caused far too much trouble already, and the last thing I want to do is encourage him any more.'

'But—'

'Look, I understand you're trying to help, but you really don't know anything about it,' Adeline interrupted her. 'I made a terrible mistake with Adam. It was supposed to be a harmless flirtation, nothing more. But he took it all too seriously.'

'You had an affair behind your fiance's back, and Adam fell in love with you,' Effie guessed.

Adeline gave a slight shrug. 'I suppose so,' she said. 'But it wasn't supposed to be that way,' she insisted. 'I thought he understood . . . but then he suddenly announced that he wanted to tell Richard about us. He wanted to do the right thing, he said. Reckoned he felt wretched lying to his best friend.' Her mouth twisted. 'He acted as if ours was some great, doomed love affair.'

Effie stared at Adeline's beautiful, petulant face and fought the urge to slap it. Then a thought occurred to her.

'Do you suppose that's what caused the accident?' she asked.

'I'm afraid it must have been.' Adeline picked at her thumbnail. 'Richard was an excellent driver, he would never have lost control like that, unless – I'm afraid he might have tried to kill them both because he thought he'd lost me,' she sighed.

Effie gazed at her. In a strange kind of way, Adeline seemed to be enjoying the drama surrounding her.

'Anyway,' she went on, 'nearly losing him brought me to my senses,' she said. 'It made me realise how much I truly love him.'

'And what about Adam?' Effie said.

'What about him?' Adeline eyed her coldly. 'As far as I'm concerned, he's the reason Richard nearly died. He tried to take away everything I care about. I want nothing more to do with him.'

'Don't you think you should tell him that?'

'I didn't reply to his letter. Surely that should tell him everything he needs to know?'

'He deserves better than that. You should write back to him, tell him where he stands. He's breaking his heart, wondering what he's done to upset you.'

'You tell him, then, since you're so concerned about him.' Adeline's dark eyes flashed.

Effie stared at her. Adeline was the cause of all this, not Adam. She'd played with two men's hearts, set them against each other, and when it all went wrong she'd tried to step away from it on those dainty, expensively shod little feet of hers.

'I'm not doing your dirty work for you,' said Effie. 'The least you can do is tell him face-to-face.'

'I'm tired of listening to you.' Adeline pulled a ten-shilling note out of her purse and put it on the table. 'I have to go back to the hospital. Richard will be wondering where I am.'

'So is Adam,' Effie said pointedly.

As Adeline went to leave, Effie blurted out, 'I could tell him, you know.'

Adeline froze. 'What?'

'I could tell Richard about the accident – the real reason he crashed.'

The colour drained from Adeline's face. 'You wouldn't!'

'You never know, do you?' Effie shrugged. 'Promise me you'll go and see Adam? Please?' she begged.

Adeline shot her a sulky look. 'I'll think about it,' she said.

Chapter Twenty-One

Snow fell heavily on New Year's Eve, burying the streets of the East End under another deep white blanket. But in spite of the freezing winds and leaden skies, the Casualty hall was still crowded with people who had trudged through the winter night. They huddled around the crackling fire, warming swollen, chilblain-covered hands, men and women and children, all muffled in layers of scarves, coats and woollen hats.

Helen stood at the booking-in desk and listened to the chorus of deep, chesty coughing that rattled around the high-ceilinged hall. Bronchitis and chest infections were always rife in the East End, with its damp houses and air thick with factory smoke. But when the cold weather set in it was even worse. She'd lost count of the number of patients they'd sent up to the medical wards. Sister Everett had already telephoned down to tell them she'd had to put in extra beds. Any more and they'd be sleeping in the passageways.

'We should just send them away.' Penny Willard seemed to read her thoughts. 'Tell them to go home and sit by their own fires.'

'Some of them don't have fires to go home to,' Helen reminded her.

Penny shrugged. 'It's not our problem if they can't look after themselves, is it?'

But it wasn't just the patients who couldn't look after themselves. In the middle of the afternoon, Helen was summoned to Matron's office.

'I'm afraid we have had several nurses admitted to the Sick Bay with chest infections, including the student assigned to night duty in Casualty,' she said. 'Miss Tanner and I are doing our best to find other nurses to cover for them, but I've also had to assign extra help to the medical wards, as we've had so many new admissions recently.' She looked up at Helen, her grey eyes serious. 'It may be that we'll have to close Casualty tonight, if we can't find cover.'

'But what about emergencies, Matron?' Helen asked.

Miss Fox shook her head. 'They'll have to go elsewhere. Miss Tanner has offered to fill in, but given the situation I daresay she will already be very busy with other wards.' She paused. 'Of course it would be better if we could stay open for ambulances, especially as New Year's Eve tends to be rather busy. But if we don't have the staff to cope . . .'

'I'll do it,' Helen said.

Matron frowned. 'You, Sister?'

'If I go off duty now, I can have a few hours' rest and be ready for night duty at nine o'clock. If that will help?'

Matron frowned. 'I can't deny it would, but surely you already have plans for this evening?'

'I can cancel them,' Helen said promptly.

Miss Fox sat back in her chair and considered her. 'Are you sure, Sister? When I summoned you, I wasn't expecting you to give up your free time. I merely wanted to apprise you of the situation.'

'I appreciate that, Matron. But I would rather keep Casualty open, if you don't mind?' Helen replied. 'As you've said yourself, New Year's Eve is a very busy time. I wouldn't like to think of someone being denied treatment or having to find their way to a hospital further afield, when they could be seen here.'

'Very well.' Matron smiled. 'In that case, I will inform

Miss Tanner, I'm sure she will be very relieved. Between ourselves, the poor woman is tearing her hair out!' she confided.

'Thank you, Matron,' Helen said.

'No, Sister Dawson. Thank *you*,' Miss Fox said warmly. 'You've done the hospital a great favour.'

Helen felt a pang of guilt as she hurried back to Casualty. Matron had acted as if Helen had made a supreme sacrifice, but the fact was she had been looking for an excuse not to go out with Christopher. The thought of spending time with him unnerved her. He attracted her like the flames of a blazing fire on a freezing cold night. But like a fire, he had the power to burn. It was far safer to keep her distance than to get hurt.

She went back to the Casualty hall and left instructions for Penny Willard and the students in her absence, then returned to the sisters' home. On the way, she left a quick note at the Porters' Lodge to explain to Christopher why she couldn't meet him.

You're a coward, Helen Dawson. The thought ran through her mind as she sealed up the envelope. There was nothing to stop her going to see Christopher and telling him face-to-face. Nothing except her own fear that if she saw him again she might realise she was making another terrible mistake.

On the evening of New Year's Eve, David McKay went to visit his sister Clare and her family in Middlesex. Much as he loved his elder sister and her children, it wasn't a visit he generally looked forward to.

They made a strained group as they sat around the dinner table. His niece and nephew sat at the far end, heads down, eating in silence.

'You two are very quiet.' David smiled at them.

'We don't encourage talking at the table,' their father Graham said sternly.

David ignored him. 'How are you getting on at school?' he asked his nephew. 'Still mad on sport, are you? I remember you were keen to get into the cricket team?'

Philip, eight years old and the younger of the two, turned large, fearful eyes to his sister. She shook her head at him.

'How about you, Beth?' David turned to her. 'How are your studies going? Do you still want to be a doctor when you grow up?'

'You may leave the table, if you've finished,' their father cut across him brusquely. 'Go and get ready for bed, then you can come back down and say goodnight. Quietly, please,' he added.

They slipped off their chairs and hurried out, eager to escape. David listened to their footsteps scuttling up the stairs and their voices, whispering to each other.

He turned to his brother-in-law, seated like a king at the head of the table, stern-faced. 'I haven't had a chance to talk to them properly.'

'I told you, I don't allow talking at the table.' Graham gave him a small, tight smile. 'Really, David, I don't appreciate your encouraging my children to break the rules.'

'They're hardly running amok,' he pointed out.

'Nevertheless, they are my rules,' Graham stated firmly.

David glared at him in dislike. There had never been any love lost between the two men. Graham was a schoolmaster, fifty years old and once handsome but now running to seed. His body was soft and paunchy, face falling into jowls either side of his mean little mouth.

David glanced at Clare, picking at her food. He scarcely recognised his beautiful, vivacious sister any more. Twenty years of marriage to a miserable older man had turned her into a nervous wreck.

Graham dabbed his lips with his napkin and leaned back in his seat. 'Anyway, I expect you will have a chance to run riot with them while I'm out,' he said.

Clare glanced up at him. 'You're going out?'

'Didn't I tell you? My friend Roger telephoned me this morning. You remember Roger, don't you? We were at college together. He's in town for the evening, and wants us to meet for a drink.'

David looked at Clare. Her gaze still fixed on her plate, she said timidly, 'But I'd hoped we might all spend the evening together, as it's New Year's Eve?'

'Yes, but I've made other plans.' There was a hard edge to Graham's voice that David didn't like. 'Besides, you've got your brother to keep you company, haven't you?'

David caught sight of his sister's disappointed expression. 'I have an idea,' he said. 'Why don't you two go and meet your friend together? I could look after the children.'

'I'm sure Clare doesn't want to spend the evening listening to my friend and me reminiscing about the old days!' Graham gave a forced laugh, but his eyes glittered with anger.

'Nonsense, a night out would do her the world of good.' David turned to his sister. 'What do you think, Clare?'

'Well, Clare?' Graham's voice had a hard edge to it. 'Answer your brother.'

Clare hesitated a fraction too long for David's liking. 'Graham's right,' she murmured finally.

'You see?' he said. 'Really, David, as if we would be so ill-mannered as to invite you for dinner and leave you to mind the children while we go out!'

David started to reply, but saw his sister's warning look and said nothing.

Half an hour later Graham had left. As soon as he'd gone out, it was as if a heavy cloud had lifted. Beth and Philip came back downstairs, freshly scrubbed, in their nightclothes and slippers. David noticed the way they looked around anxiously before they came in, as if to satisfy themselves that their father was really gone, before they allowed themselves to relax.

Clare seemed more at ease, too. 'Have you washed properly?' she asked the children, putting her arms around them.

'Yes, Mother.'

David turned to Beth and said, 'Are you sure you've washed behind your ears?'

A solemn twelve-year-old with dark hair fastened in tight plaits, she frowned at him. 'Yes, Uncle.'

'I don't think you have. Look.' He reached up towards her ear and produced a farthing between his fingers. 'You see?' he said, handing it to her.

Beth and Philip both stared at the coin, then at each other.

'Your turn, Philip.' David reached forward, fingers brushing the little boy's silky dark hair. 'Well, I never,' he declared, as he produced a penny. 'Look at that.'

Philip grinned sheepishly and scratched his ear. 'Do it again!' he said.

'Well, I'm not sure . . .' David grinned. 'Oh, all right, then. If you insist.'

By the time he'd emptied his pockets of all his change, both children were giggling. Then he played horses with them, going around the floor on all fours while they took turns to jump all over him, until their mother declared, 'That's enough! You've worn your poor uncle out!'

'I don't mind,' David said, collapsing under the weight as both children hurled themselves on top of him.

'All the same, it's time for bed.'

The children protested. 'Oh, Mummy, can't we stay up until midnight, just this once?'

David looked appealingly at her. 'Go on, Clare. It is New Year's Eve, after all.'

She shook her head. 'Can you imagine if your father were to come home and find you still up?'

The children sobered immediately, shocked to their senses. They jumped off David's back and stood to attention, as if Clare had somehow summoned the spectre of their father into the room.

'Get up to bed,' she said, more gently. 'I'll come and tuck you in.'

'Can Uncle David do it?' Philip pleaded.

He gave an exaggerated sigh. 'If you insist.'

'I'm sorry,' Clare said, as they listened to the children hurrying back up the stairs, chattering loudly this time.

'I don't mind at all. You know I love spending time with them.'

'You're very good with them. That's the first time I've heard them laugh in a long time.'

'I'm not surprised. They're like different children when their father isn't here.'

'I know,' Clare said quietly. She went over to the drinks cabinet and poured them both a brandy. 'Graham can't help it, you know,' she said. 'It's just his way, that's all. He was nearly forty when Beth was born, he's bound to be set in his ways . . .'

'Stop making excuses for him,' David cut her off. 'He's a monster. He treats you and the children appallingly.'

Clare was shocked. 'Don't say that,' she begged. 'Graham is a good man.'

'Is that why he's gone off to spend the evening with his mistress?'

He saw his sister wince, and immediately regretted speaking so bluntly. 'I'm sorry,' he said. 'I didn't mean to upset you. But you know as well as I do that's where he is.'

He had been shocked and outraged when Clare first confided in him that her husband had another woman. David had immediately wanted to confront Graham, but his sister had begged him not to say anything. It was becoming more and more difficult for him to stay silent, let alone be civil.

'I know,' she said quietly. 'But I don't want to talk about it.'

'Why not? I can't understand how you can ignore it, go on pretending it's not happening.'

'Because it's easier that way.' Clare looked at him, defeat in her eyes. 'If I say something, it would only start another fight. It might even push him further away from me. And then what would I do?'

'You could always leave him?'

'And where would I go? A woman on her own with two children. How would I support them?'

'I'd look after you, you know that.'

She shook her head. 'I couldn't ask you to do that.'

'You're not asking me. I'm offering.' He leaned forward. 'I want to help you, Clare. I could set you up with a place to live. I could look after you.'

'What about the children? They need their father.'

'They don't need a father who makes their lives a misery, and you don't need a husband who treats you badly either. Please, Clare? I can't bear to see you in this state.'

She stared into the flickering flames in the fireplace. 'You don't understand. I know my marriage isn't perfect. But I made my vows, and I need to abide by them.'

David stared at her in frustration. They'd had the same conversation many times, and it always ended the same way.

Clare would never leave Graham, no matter how badly he treated her. She still clung to the idea that marriage was for life. She refused to admit that she'd made a mistake in marrying him.

And he understood why, too.

'If we'd inherited Father's house in his will you would be free,' he said. 'You would have enough money to be independent.'

'Yes, well, that didn't happen, did it?'

'No, it didn't,' he said bitterly. 'Instead you're married to a monster, and our wicked stepmother living in our house. She's got exactly what she wanted, hasn't she?'

Clare sighed. 'There's no point in getting upset about it, David.'

'I can't help it. She made all our lives a misery. If it hadn't been for her, you would never have run off and married Graham.'

'That's not true. I didn't have to marry him.' Clare refilled her brother's glass. 'I know you don't care for him, and I realise he can be difficult. But he's good to us in his own way. And if I hadn't married him, I would never have had the children. So I have to be thankful for that, don't I?'

David gazed into his sister's face. 'I wish I had your optimistic nature.'

'Uncle David!' The children's voices drifted down from upstairs before he could say any more.

He left just after midnight. He hugged his sister fiercely and wished her a happy New Year. He also pressed a £10 note into her hand.

'I can't take this!' She tried to give it back, but David insisted.

'Treat yourself to something nice,' he urged. 'I just wish I could do more.'

'I know – and thank you.' She gave him a brave smile.

'I mean, it, Clare. Any time you decide you want to leave, just let me know.'

He couldn't stop thinking about her all the way home in the taxi. Whatever she said, he knew the real reason she had married Graham was to escape from their unhappy home, and their stepmother. She had made everyone's lives such a misery that Clare had run off and married the first man who'd showed her any kind of affection. She had sought solace in marriage and creating a family of her own . . . much good it had done her. David had sought his own comfort by avoiding making any kind of commitment altogether.

He returned to the doctors' house. The home for lonely bachelors, as Jonathan mockingly called it these days. As if he hadn't been grateful enough for it for so many years!

But it did feel like a different place to David since his old friend had left. One by one, David had seen his fellow doctors get married and move out, to be replaced by other eager young housemen. Even though he was only thirty-five, David had begun to feel out of place surrounded by so many young men.

Even so, it didn't bother him. He would rather grow into a crusty old bachelor like Mr Hobbs than settle for the compromise his sister's marriage had been.

A sudden image of Helen Dawson came unbidden to his mind, sitting on a bench in the snow, crying over a dead child. He'd understood her pain, so of course he'd had to comfort her. He ruthlessly pushed from his mind the thought that there might be anything more to it than that.

Chapter Twenty-Two

It was just as well they'd decided to keep the Casualty department open, Helen reflected as she closed the doors on the last patient just after eleven o'clock. Even though she and Dr Ross had mainly been dressing wounds and consoling tearful drunks, they had also dealt with an elderly man with a cardiac arrest and a young mother who'd gone into premature labour during a family party. In both cases, being admitted to hospital quickly had saved them.

But now the night and the year were almost over, and for the next eight or nine hours the department was only open to admissions by ambulance.

'And hopefully we won't have too many of those this evening,' Dr Ross had said as he dragged himself off to sleep in the consulting room. 'Good night, Sister.'

'Good night, Doctor. And Happy New Year to you.'

'What? Oh, yes, of course,' he yawned, shrugging off his white coat. 'See you in nineteen thirty-nine.'

And so Helen was seeing in the New Year alone. As she pulled the bolt across the double doors, she thought wistfully of the merry evening she could have been spending in Trafalgar Square with Christopher, if only she hadn't been so cautious. Though she knew it wouldn't have been a good idea, she still couldn't help wondering what it would have been like to kick up her heels and have fun, just for one reckless night.

She was turning down the lamps in the Casualty hall when she heard a sharp rap on the doors.

'We're closed,' she called out. 'Emergencies only.'

'This is an emergency,' a muffled voice called out from the other side.

'Oh, for heaven's sake.' Helen sighed as she crossed the hall to unbolt the doors. If this was another drunk looking for a bed for the night, she would not be amused. She had only just finished scrubbing the floor with Lysol after the last one.

'I told you, it's emergencies only . . .' Her voice trailed off as she saw Christopher standing there, a bottle of brandy in his hand. Flakes of snow sparkled in his hair. 'What are you doing here?'

'I came to see you.' He sauntered past her and looked around. 'On your own, are you?'

'Dr Ross is resting. We've had a busy night.' Helen closed the door behind him, shutting out a rush of cold air. 'I thought you'd be up West by now, seeing the New Year in?'

'I was. But then I realised I'd rather spend it with you.'

Helen opened her mouth, then closed it again. She caught sight of her reflection in the lamplit window. She looked a terrible mess, her apron stained and the laces of her bonnet hanging loose. Her face was drawn, dark shadows like bruises under her eyes. Why Christopher didn't run away screaming at the sight of her, she had no idea.

'I was surprised when I got your note,' he said. 'I've never had a girl stand me up before. Proper wounded my pride, it did.'

'I'm sorry.'

'I forgive you.' He grinned at her.

Helen looked up into his laughing eyes. She could believe girls didn't say no to him very often.

She dragged her gaze away. 'Would you like a cup of tea?' she offered.

'I'd rather have a drop of this.' He held up the bottle. 'Get a couple of glasses and we'll have a drink together.'

'This is a Casualty department, not a cocktail party!' Helen replied, shocked. 'Dr Ross would report me in a moment if he caught me drinking on duty.'

'But it's New Year's Eve!'

'It's still against the rules. He'd report me if he knew you were here, too.'

'Then I'll have to be quiet, won't I? And if he comes in, I'll lie down and pretend to be dying.'

Helen smiled in spite of herself. 'Let's sit down by the door,' she said. 'Then you can get out quickly if Dr Ross wakes up.'

They sat on the bench closest to it. Christopher was relaxed but Helen perched on the edge of her seat, her gaze fixed on the passageway leading to the consulting rooms.

'Am I making you nervous?' Christopher joked.

'I told you, I don't want Dr Ross to catch us.'

'Do you always follow the rules?'

'Of course.'

'Why?'

'Because . . .' She stared at him. The question had never occurred to her before. She had been following rules all her life; first her mother's, then the hospital's. 'Because it's all I've ever done,' she said.

'That doesn't sound like much fun.'

'No, but it's a lot less trouble.'

'I don't mind a bit of trouble now and then,' Christopher said.

Helen smiled sideways at him 'I can imagine.'

He was silent for a moment. 'Is that why you didn't come out with me tonight?' he asked. 'Because you thought I'd be trouble?'

Guilty heat rose in her face. 'I told you, I had to work.'

'And is that the only reason?' Helen didn't reply. 'Only I wondered if it was because you felt bad about Charlie.'

Helen glanced up at him. But before she could reply, he went on, 'Because I feel bad, too.'

His comment took her by surprise. She stared at him in the darkness. 'You?'

He nodded. 'Charlie and I were so close, I looked up to him. That's why when I met you . . .' He shrugged expressively. 'I knew straight away I liked you. But you being Charlie's wife – well, it doesn't make it easy, does it?'

'No,' Helen said. 'It doesn't.'

He looked so honest, so vulnerable, she wanted to be honest too.

'I suppose I was nervous about seeing you,' she confessed. 'I've never – spent time with any man since Charlie. I wasn't sure if it would be right. Especially . . .'

'Especially with me being Charlie's cousin?' he finished for her. Helen nodded. 'You can't live your life in the shadows,' he said softly. 'I know Charlie would never have wanted that for you. I mean, would you have wanted him to be alone for the rest of his life if you'd died?'

'Of course not,' she said. 'But it's just so difficult . . .'

'Then I'll help you,' said Christopher.

Helen looked down at her hands. Five years of nursing had left her long, slender fingers raw and callused.

'Why me?' She asked the question that had been niggling at her from the moment he'd asked her out. You could have your pick of girls, I'm sure. Why choose someone as complicated as me?'

'I don't know,' he admitted. 'All I know is there's something about you. I could see it from the minute I set eyes on you.' He sent her a sideways smile. 'This is going to sound daft, but I sometimes wonder if Charlie didn't send you to me. Because he knew I'd look after you.'

Helen smiled at him. For some reason, that didn't sound daft at all. In fact, it sounded like just the sort of thing her loving husband would have done. Perhaps her Christmas wish was going to come true, after all.

'I think I will have some of that brandy,' she said.

With a grin Christopher handed her the bottle. 'Go on, live dangerously.'

Helen took a gulp, wincing as the fiery liquid burned its way down her throat. 'I'm not sure I know how,' she admitted.

Christopher's eyes met hers, alight with intent. 'Then I'll have to show you, won't I?' he said.

Chapter Twenty-Three

It was New Year's Day, and after the excitement of celebrating with her friends up West, Effie O'Hara was back to earth with a bump, enduring Mass with her sister Bridget.

It was too cruel to make her get up so early, she decided. It had been past two o'clock in the morning when she and the others had finally tumbled through the skylight window into their room. And after far too many glasses of champagne, she had nearly broken her neck shinning up the icy drainpipe. Now her head was pounding and the smell of the incense was making her feel decidedly sick.

Not that Bridget was sympathetic. She sat beside Effie, ramrod-straight as usual, hands folded in her lap, listening primly to the priest droning on in Latin as if she understood every word. Each time Effie allowed her eyelids to droop over her prayer book, Bridget dug her sharply in the ribs, making her wake up with a yelp. No need to wonder where she'd spent New Year's Eve, Effie thought. Bridget's idea of reckless abandon was a cup of cocoa and an improving book.

After what seemed like hours, the service was finally over and Effie was able to escape into the cold, bright sunshine. The sun had broken through the leaden clouds and glittered off the thick blanket of snow, transforming the mean, ugly little streets of the East End into a place of magical beauty. Children ran to and fro, pulling makeshift sledges made of old tin trays. Others tossed snowballs at each other, laughing and shrieking as they ducked into doorways.

On the pavement the snow had been churned up to muddy slush. Effie's shoes slipped and slithered as she picked her way along. Bridget, of course, had no such difficulty. She seemed as sure-footed as ever as she strode ahead of her sister, lecturing her over her shoulder as she went.

'Fancy falling asleep in the middle of Mass!' she snapped. 'I'm ashamed of you, Euphemia O'Hara, I really am.'

'I didn't fall asleep,' Effie mumbled.

'You were snoring during the Our Father! Everyone was looking at us, I didn't know where to put myself.' Bridget shot her a look of disdain. 'When are you back on duty?'

'Not until five.'

'Good. That should give you time to smarten yourself up.'

Effie looked down at herself. 'What's wrong with me?'

'What's right with you?' Bridget stopped and turned on her heel to face her sister. 'You're a disgrace. Your hair looks like it hasn't seen a brush in weeks, you're pasty-faced and your eyes are bloodshot.' Effie backed away as Bridget leaned in towards her. 'And you smell like a brewery,' she declared.

'If you must know, I don't feel well,' Effie defended herself. 'I think I might be coming down with something.'

'The only thing you're coming down with is a hangover. I suppose you were out until all hours last night?'

'No,' Effie lied.

'Show me your hands.'

'No, you can't – let me go!' Effie yelped as Bridget seized

her fingers in a tight pinching grasp and pulled off her glove.

'Just as I thought,' she said, releasing her. 'They're covered in scratches. You've been climbing up drainpipes.'

'I bet you did the same when you were a student,' Effie said, pulling her glove back on.

'I most certainly did not!' Bridget turned on her heel and stalked off again. 'We're not all like you,' she threw over her shoulder. 'Some of us respect the rules. Some of us would prefer to stay out of trouble. Some of us – ow!'

Effie squawked with laughter as a snowball came out of nowhere and hit her sister squarely in the back of the head, sending her hat spinning sideways into the snow.

A moment later a grinning little face appeared around the corner.

'Sorry, missus!' a cheeky voice called out.

'Why, I—' Bridget spluttered, shaking snow off her hat. She looked so outraged, Effie could hardly breathe for laughing.

But then a snowball hit her in the face, stinging her cheeks. As she wiped the grimy slush from her eyes, she saw Bridget standing a few yards away, dusting snow off her hands. A rare smile lit up her face.

'That should wake you up a bit,' she said.

Effie felt a little better when she returned to the ward at five o'clock, thanks to several cups of tea, a brisk wash in cold water and a bar of chocolate that her room-mate Devora Kowalski had carelessly left in her bedside drawer.

Sister Blake met her at the door and told her to prepare a warm salt bath for the arthritis patient, Mr Anderson. Her sister Katie found her in the bathroom as she was filling the tub.

'You missed all the excitement at visiting time,' she said, closing the door behind her.

'What excitement?'

'Mr Campbell's girlfriend came to see him.'

Effie straightened up. 'Adeline was here?'

'She arrived just as visiting time was over,' Katie nodded. 'At least I'm assuming it was her. Very fancy-looking piece in a feathered hat. She strutted up the length of the ward with her nose in the air, didn't even look at us. I don't know what he sees in her,' she sniffed.

'What happened then?'

'I don't know, do I? She didn't stay long, I know that much. Barely five minutes.'

'What did she say?'

'I told you, I don't know.' Katie sighed with exaggerated patience. 'Unlike you I don't make a point of eavesdropping on patients' conversations.'

Effie knew that wasn't true, but she let it pass. 'How is he now?' she asked.

Katie shrugged. 'A bit quiet, I suppose,' she says. 'It's hard to say, since he never talks to anyone but you.'

'Doesn't he?'

Effie preened herself on hearing this, but then Katie ruined it by saying, 'By the way, that bath is overflowing. You really ought to watch what you're doing.'

Effie longed to talk to Adam and find out what had happened, but Sister Blake kept her busy with lots of other jobs so she didn't have the chance.

It wasn't until she was helping with the bedtime cocoa round that she finally managed to spend a moment alone with him.

He was very quiet, staring vacantly into space as Effie pushed the trolley to the end of his bed. 'Can I get you a cup of tea?' she asked.

'No, thank you.'

'Cocoa? Horlicks?' He shook his head. 'You might feel better if you have something,' Effie suggested.

He sent her a withering look. 'Do you really think a cup of cocoa is going to make all my problems go away?'

'It can't make you feel any worse.'

He stared at her for a moment, then turned his head to one side. Effie waited patiently for him to speak. Silence stretched between them.

Then, when she was about to give up and push her trolley to the next bed, he suddenly said, 'I suppose you've heard Adeline came to see me?'

Adam turned his head to look at her, just as she was trying to compose her features into a suitably surprised look.

'Don't pretend you hadn't heard,' he said. 'I know you nurses love to gossip.'

'I did hear something about it,' Effie replied, unable to lie. 'How was she?' she asked cautiously.

'It's over between us.'

Even though she'd been expecting this, it still felt like a punch in the stomach. 'Oh, I'm so sorry.'

'Why? It's not your fault.' Adam's voice sounded quiet, almost resigned. 'If anyone is to blame, it's me. If I hadn't been so stupid and pig-headed, if I hadn't tried to force the situation . . .'

'You weren't stupid,' Effie said. 'It wasn't your fault she led you to believe there was more to it than—' She stopped abruptly, realising what she'd said. It was too much to hope Adam hadn't noticed.

His eyes narrowed. 'How did you know that?' he asked.

Effie stared back at him, panic-stricken. Then, thank goodness, she heard her sister Bridget calling her. She had never been so pleased to hear that eldritch shriek in her life.

'I'd better go,' she said, taking hold of the handle of the trolley.

'You talked to her, didn't you?'

Effie felt a blush rising in her face. 'I had to,' she admitted quietly. 'I was worried about you. I could see what it was doing to you, waiting every day to hear from her.' She darted a quick look at him. 'But I shouldn't have interfered,' she said. 'You have every right to be furious . . .'

'I'm not furious,' he said. 'I'm grateful to you.'

She eyed him warily. 'Grateful?'

'You're right, I needed to know for sure, one way or the other. And it was kind of you to take the trouble to find her. Even if it wasn't quite what I wanted to hear,' he added, his mouth twisting.

'Nurse O'Hara!' Bridget's voice rose from the other side of the ward. 'When you've quite finished, there are other patients waiting!'

'Coming,' Effie said. She gave Adam a quick smile. 'I'll see you later,' she said.

As she left, he called after her, 'Nurse O'Hara?'

She turned back. 'Yes?'

'Perhaps you're right,' he said. 'Perhaps I should have put some hearts and kisses on that letter after all.'

Chapter Twenty-Four

It was late on a chilly Thursday afternoon in February, and Victoria Park was almost deserted. A damp grey mist hung low over the grass, the avenue of bare skeletal black trees rising out of the gloom.

'At least we've got the place to ourselves!' Christopher joked.

'That's true,' Helen replied, pulling her coat tighter.

Christopher looked sideways at her. 'We could go somewhere else, if you like? Catch a bus up West, have tea in Lyons?'

She shook her head. 'I have to be back on duty at five, remember?'

'Another time, then.'

'Another time.' Helen smiled with relief. Every time she saw Christopher, she felt a little flutter of panic that today might be the last time they met. Sooner or later, she thought, he would go back to sea, or meet someone else, or just grow bored with her.

But it hadn't happened so far. In fact, after nearly six weeks he still made sure he saw her every day, even if it was only for a snatched half-hour at the hospital gates after Helen came off duty. If she had the evening off, they would go to the pictures or dancing. Or sometimes they would just walk down to the docks and Christopher would point out to her the various ships and where they'd come from. He'd been all over the world, seen places Helen could only imagine.

She couldn't remember the last time she'd been so happy, and it frightened her. She couldn't trust it. She knew too well how quickly happiness could be snatched away. She was so wary she hardly dared allow herself to enjoy the moments she had, just in case she lost them.

Christopher had laughed when she told him how she felt.

'Nothing lasts for ever,' he'd said. 'You just have to make the most of the good times while you can.'

But that was easy for him to say. He approached every day with the same breezy confidence that something good, or funny, or exciting would happen. Unlike Helen, he never planned, never worried or looked round corners, expecting something dreadful to be lurking there. He never stared up at the sky, searching for rain. It made him laugh that she took an umbrella with her everywhere, even on the brightest of days.

But gradually, under the warmth of his sunny personality, Helen felt the chill around her heart thawing. Sometimes she caught herself smiling for no reason.

They skirted the lake, and Christopher reached for her hand.

'I'd forgotten how much I love this place,' he said. 'Charlie and I used to hang around here all the time, when we were kids.'

Helen waited for the pain that usually lanced her whenever Charlie's name was mentioned, but for once it didn't come. Christopher often talked about his cousin, dropping his name into the conversation as easily as if Charlie were still alive. And after a while Helen had got so used to it, it stopped hurting so much.

She smiled at Chris. 'I bet you were always getting into trouble, weren't you?'

'I was a right little tearaway!' He grinned. 'No one really

taught me right from wrong when I was growing up, what with my mum being ill for so long and my dad not being bothered. I thought I could just go on doing as I pleased when I moved in with Charlie's mum and dad, but Aunt Nellie soon taught me different!' He grimaced at the memory. 'Even then, I was always getting into scrapes, and Charlie would have to wade in and help me. The times he saved me from a hiding!'

'That sounds like Charlie.' Helen smiled.

'But he didn't mind teaching me a lesson himself, if he thought I needed it,' Christopher went on. 'One time, when I was a nipper, I nicked a couple of apples from that stall over there.' He nodded towards the small wooden hut on the far side of the lake, closed up for winter. 'Charlie caught me eating one and gave me such a clout! He can't have been much more than twelve himself, but it didn't half hurt. Then he got me by the collar and marched me back round to the stall and made me give the other apple back. And the woman behind the counter gave me a clout too! I hated Charlie for that, but I learned my lesson, I can tell you.'

'You never stole anything again?'

'I made sure I never got caught!'

For some reason Helen remembered a comment she'd overheard at that Christmas party, the night she'd first met Christopher.

A leopard can't change its spots.

They stood at the edge of the boating lake, a flat expanse of pewter-coloured water with the mist hanging low over it. A few miserable-looking ducks paddled around the shallows, searching for scraps in the soggy earth.

'This was where Charlie and I had our first date,' Helen recalled. 'The park was closing but he persuaded the park-keeper to let us take a boat out. It was lovely, having the lake to ourselves.'

'We could have it to ourselves now, if we took one out?' Christopher suggested.

Helen frowned up at him. 'Surely it's closed down for the winter? The boats are all locked up.'

'Yes, but I know where they keep them.' Christopher grinned mischievously. 'Come with me.'

Helen followed him around the edge of the lake to the boathouse. 'Chris, you can't steal one!' she protested.

'I ain't stealing it. I'm just borrowing it for a little while.'

'But what if someone sees us?'

He gave her a teasing smile. 'Trust me, Helen!'

They picked their way across the soft mud to the boathouse doors. Christopher tested the padlock.

'I reckon I could get into this,' he said. 'Got a hairpin I can borrow?'

'But . . .' Helen started to argue, then gave up. She took off her hat, pulled a pin from her hair and handed it to him. 'Just be careful,' she warned.

'You keep watch for me,' Christopher said, huddling over the lock. Helen thrust her gloved hands into her pockets, shivering with cold and fear as she looked this way and that.

'This is silly,' she declared. 'I don't know why you're insisting on—' She broke off as Christopher emerged from the shed, dragging a rowing boat across the damp shingle behind him. He looked so pleased with himself, Helen couldn't help smiling.

He hauled the boat into the shallows, then turned to her. 'Your carriage awaits, madam,' he said, with a sweeping gesture of his hand.

'No, thank you,' she said. 'I'm not getting in that thing.'

His face fell. 'You mean I've gone to all this trouble for nothing?'

'I didn't ask you to break in and steal a boat.'

'No, but I've done it now. So we might as well enjoy it, don't you think?' he coaxed. 'Go on – just for a few minutes? We can stick close to the shore, I promise.'

Finally, he managed to persuade her into the rickety little craft. She yelped as it swayed and rocked beneath her feet, nearly knocking her off balance.

'Shhh!' Christopher hissed. 'We don't want the whole world to hear us, do we?'

He hopped in and sat down on the seat opposite, then rolled up his shirtsleeves and picked up the oars. Helen was very aware of him as they glided out on to the still, misty water. They were so close, their knees were brushing. She found herself watching his strong, sinewy forearms as he pulled on the oars.

And then, suddenly, she thought of Charlie, and how she'd watched him in the same way when he rowed them across the lake on that fine evening in early summer. She remembered how she'd teased him about his rowing, so he'd handed over the oars and made her try instead. They'd laughed, and the sun had shone down on them and the birds had sung and she'd thought her happiness would last for ever.

'Helen?' She looked up. Christopher was watching her closely. 'Are you all right? You were miles away.'

She forced a smile. 'I'm fine.'

He gave a wry smile. 'I can see you're not,' he said. 'We'll turn back, shall we?'

No sooner had he turned the boat round than they heard a shout from the shore. Looking over Christopher's shoulder, Helen saw the distant figure of the park-keeper waving from the open doorway of the boathouse.

'Blimey, now we're for it!' Christopher laughed.

'It's not funny!' Helen said. 'What if he catches us?'

'We'll have to make sure he doesn't, won't we?'

Christopher swung the boat around again and headed away from the boathouse, skirting the shore as closely as he dared. But the park-keeper was keeping pace with them on the opposite bank, waving his fist and threatening to call the police.

'It's no good,' Christopher admitted. 'We'll have to row back and face the music.'

'We can't!' A horrible vision came into Helen's mind of being frogmarched in handcuffs back to the hospital. She would be sacked for sure, and sent home in disgrace to face her mother's wrath.

She looked desperately about her at the grey, weed-choked water. 'We'll have to jump,' she said.

'Abandon ship, you mean?' Christopher stared at her. 'But we can't do that. The water will be freezing. It'll kill us.'

'My life won't be worth living anyway, if my mother finds out what I've done.' Helen was already on her feet.

'Helen, don't . . .' But she didn't wait to hear the rest as she pitched herself headlong into the lake.

It wasn't deep, but the icy water made her gasp, robbing her of breath. The weeds caught at her, entangling her legs as her heavy coat dragged her down. The water closed over her head, cold and murky, filling her nose and mouth and ears in a roaring rush.

And then suddenly she was aware of strong arms grasping her around the waist, pulling her gasping to the surface. She opened her eyes and saw Christopher, his hair slicked off his face.

He swam backwards, threshing strongly through the water with one arm while dragging her with the other. As they reached the shore, Helen felt the rough shingle scraping against her legs and scrambled to her feet.

'Come on,' he said, grabbing her arm.

They ran as fast as they could, weighed down by their soaking-wet clothes, pushing their way through the dripping branches of the weeping willows that edged the lake, then out into open land.

'This way.' He half dragged her through some bushes. The spiky branches snagged and tore at her stockings, but Helen barely noticed in her desperate hurry to escape the park-keeper. On the other side of the bushes was the bandstand, and beyond that a small wooden hut where the deckchairs were kept. Helen struggled to keep up as Christopher sprinted towards it.

They reached the far side of the hut and collapsed on the damp, mossy ground. They lay wedged into the narrow space between the peeling painted walls and a rhododendron bush, and listened as the park-keeper came pounding towards them, still shouting and threatening. Helen was shivering so violently from cold and wet and fear she was sure he would hear her teeth chattering, but she couldn't stop herself.

She looked at Christopher. He pressed his finger over her lips to quieten her. They waited. The park-keeper was getting closer, closer . . .

And then, by some miracle, his footsteps started to recede towards the bandstand. They both froze, waiting and listening, as his shouts grew more distant.

'Looks like we got away with it.' Christopher grinned.

The pent-up tension flowed out of her and Helen collapsed back on the ground. As she lifted her hands to push her soaking-wet hair off her face, she saw that they were shaking and blue-tinged with cold.

'I thought he was going to get us,' she whispered.

'So did I.' Christopher propped himself up on one elbow and looked down at her. Admiration shone in his eyes. 'Well, you're full of surprises, ain't you? Fancy jumping in the water like that! And I thought I was the one who liked living dangerously.'

'I couldn't think what else to do.' She struggled to sit up. 'Oh, God, I thought he was going to get us. I was just wondering how to explain it to my mother.'

Christopher laughed. 'It was fun though, wasn't it?'

'No, it wasn't. And I've lost my hat.'

'You look better without it.' He put up his hand to smooth a tendril of wet hair off her face. His thumb brushed her lips and Helen caught her breath. She was suddenly aware of how close he was.

His eyes met hers. The pupils had expanded, turning his blue eyes almost black. 'You're a bad girl, Helen,' he said softly.

And then he kissed her, and it wasn't a chaste peck like the kind they exchanged at the hospital gates. It was deep, and urgent, and like nothing she'd ever experienced before. Christopher expertly parted her lips, his tongue invading her mouth, shockingly intimate and terrifying. And yet Helen wanted more. Almost of its own accord, her body arched towards his as his arms went round her.

He pulled away from her, his face inches from hers. 'Let's go inside the hut,' he said hoarsely.

Helen looked up at him, and suddenly realised what he meant. It was as if she'd hit that icy water again, all her drowsy senses shocked into alert.

'No.' She started pulling away from him, disentangling herself from his embrace.

He looked bewildered. 'Don't worry, the park-keeper ain't going to find us. We'll be safe in there.'

Helen risked a glance at him, his shirt clinging damply to the muscular contours of his chest. Safe wasn't a word she would ever use to describe Chris.

'I can't,' she murmured, looking away. 'It wouldn't be right.'

'Why not?' He frowned at her, then something in her expression must have given her away because suddenly his face cleared and he said, 'You mean to tell me you've never . . .'

'No!' She inched away from him, pulling her coat around herself, wishing she had more layers to swathe herself in because she didn't like the way his gaze seemed to sear through her clothing.

'But surely you and Charlie must have . . .'

She felt the heat rising in her face. 'We wanted to wait.'

He watched her, his expression full of wonder, as if he were seeing her for the first time. 'I'm sorry, I just assumed—' His voice broke off then continued, 'It didn't even occur to me you were a virgin.'

Helen looked away. 'I suppose you must think me very naïve?' she mumbled.

'Not at all.' He smiled at her. 'I'm glad. It just makes me love you more.'

Her startled eyes met his. 'Don't say that.'

'What? I'm not allowed to tell you I love you?' He grinned. 'I do love you, Helen. I'd shout it from the roof-tops if it weren't for that damn park-keeper.'

'You mustn't,' she said. 'It feels like bad luck.'

'What's bad luck about being in love? It's the best feeling in the world.'

She sent him a shy, sideways look. 'I wish I could believe that,' she said.

He winked at her. 'Then I'm going to have to prove it to you, ain't I?'

Chapter Twenty-Five

It was Effie's final day on Male Orthopaedics, and she wasn't looking forward to her move. During her stint on Blake she'd grown fond of all the patients on the ward. They were a cheery lot, always laughing and joking among themselves, and she knew she'd miss them. Wherever she was sent next was bound to be dreary by comparison.

And there was one patient she would particularly miss, even though she didn't want to admit it.

But at least she got the chance to see Adam Campbell back on his feet before she left. His fractured femur was knitting together so well he was allowed to get out of bed, albeit with his leg heavily splinted. After so long without walking he wobbled unsteadily on his crutches.

'You look like a newborn foal!' Effie said.

'Don't laugh at me.' He tried to scowl at her, but was so pleased with himself he couldn't help smiling as he tentatively tried out a few steps, Effie hovering at his side, ready to catch him. Even leaning on crutches he was taller than her, she was pleased to see. At five foot ten in her stout black shoes, it was rare to find a man who didn't look ridiculous next to her.

'You're doing very well,' she encouraged him.

'About time, too,' he grunted. 'I only wish this wretched hand would hurry up and improve.' He flexed his fingers, wincing at the pain.

'Sister says a broken arm can be tricky,' Effie said. 'You need to be patient.'

'Don't you think I've been patient enough, stuck in bed for nearly three months?'

'If you will go around breaking your bones, you've got to give them time to mend,' Effie replied primly. 'I think that's enough exercise for one day. Come and sit down.' She took his arm to guide him back to the bed, but he shook her off.

'Just a few more steps – please?' he begged. 'You don't know what it's like to be able to stand on my own two feet after all this time.'

Effie sighed. 'Just a few more,' she said. 'But try not to put too much weight on that leg. You don't want to undo all your good work, do you?'

'I suppose not.' He allowed her to help him back on to the bed. As she pulled the covers up around him, he suddenly said, 'Will you write another letter for me?'

'Of course,' Effie said, smoothing down the top sheet. 'I'm sure Sister will let me have the time. Who are you writing to?'

'Adeline.' There was a touch of defiance in his voice. 'And before you start, I don't want to hear it,' he added, holding up his hand. 'I've been thinking about this, and I've decided it's the right thing to do.'

'Is it?' Effie sighed. Adam had been very quiet about his erstwhile girlfriend since her visit nearly two months earlier, but it was too much to hope that he'd forgotten about her.

'I know it's not my place to say anything, but are you sure that's a good idea? I mean, she's already told you where she stands.'

'Yes, but that's the point,' Adam said eagerly. 'That's what I've been thinking about. I've been wondering what made her say what she did, and I've realised it must be guilt.'

'Guilt?'

He nodded. 'That's why she's staying with Richard, because she feels bad about what happened to him. She knows he's never going to be the man he was, and she feels responsible. She's sacrificing her own happiness for his sake.' He leaned forward, his green eyes full of fervour. 'That's why I need to write to her. I need to let her know I understand, but that she doesn't have to waste her life tied to a man she doesn't love. It won't help Richard for Adeline to punish herself.'

Effie looked back at him without speaking. She thought about the tearful girl at her fiancé's bedside, clutching his hand as if her own life depended on it. Adeline Moreau might not be Effie's cup of tea, but she loved Richard. It was written all over her face.

Effie picked up Adam's crutches and tucked them into the corner behind his locker. 'I'm sorry, but I can't write your letter,' she said shortly.

'Can't?'

'Won't,' she corrected herself.

Their eyes met. An angry muscle flickered in Adam's jaw. 'Why not?'

'Because . . . because I think you'd be wasting your time,' she said. 'Adeline isn't interested in you. I'm sorry if that sounds cruel, but that's the way it is.'

'You're wrong,' Adam snapped. 'She loves me.'

His stubbornness wore away at her patience until it snapped. 'Then why isn't it your bedside she's sitting at?' she said. 'Why isn't it your hand she's holding? Why isn't she crying for you the way she is for her fiancé?'

'I told you, she feels guilty—'

'No, she doesn't! I've seen her . . . seen the way she looks at him. She's doing it out of love.'

Adam flinched. 'No! She loves me. She loves me,' he repeated with quiet insistence.

But Effie saw the desolation on his face and knew he didn't believe what he was saying.

'I'm sorry, Mr Campbell, I really am,' she said. 'I wish there was something I could do to help.'

'I've asked for your help and you turned me down.'

'Only because I don't want to see you getting hurt any more.'

He turned on her angrily. 'What do you know about it anyway? You have no idea how I feel.'

'You're not the only one who's ever been in love, you know.'

He looked up at her with eyes like flint. 'You can't possibly know how I feel, or how Adeline feels. She's a sensitive, passionate woman, and you're just a silly girl.'

Effie held on to her temper. 'She's not sensitive, she's just selfish and vain. When it all became too difficult for her, she tried to stuff you back in the toy box as if your feelings didn't count. That doesn't sound very sensitive to me.'

A dull flush spread up his throat to his face. 'Go to hell.'

'I beg your pardon?'

'I said, go to hell. I should never have asked you to get involved. You're an idiot. You have no comprehension of how intelligent people think or feel.'

Effie stared at him, waiting for him to apologise. But he kept his face averted from hers, his mouth in a stubborn line.

'And you're a sulky, spoiled child,' she hissed. He didn't react but she knew he was listening. 'You wonder why Adeline wants nothing to do with you? Look in the mirror.' She straightened up, smoothing down her apron. 'I daresay I'm not as well read as you and your friends. I don't go to political meetings, or quote poetry. But I do know how horrible it is to love someone when they don't love you back.'

She turned and walked away with as much dignity as she could muster, her chin held high in the air. It was only when she was in the safety of the sluice, with the door closed firmly behind her, that she allowed herself to cry.

Effie leaned against the big stone sink, hugging herself against the freezing February wind whistling through the grating above her head, and wept. She was still weeping when Katie stormed in five minutes later.

'What did he say to you?' she demanded.

'Nothing,' Effie sniffed, dabbing her eyes on her apron.

'Yes, he did. It's written all over your face. He's upset you again, hasn't he? I swear, if that man says another wrong word, I'll – I'll put cascara in his cocoa!'

'You'll do no such thing, Nurse O'Hara.'

Effie looked up sharply. Sister Blake stood in the doorway, arms folded over the bib of her immaculate apron, watching them both. 'What's all this? A mothers' meeting?' she asked. 'You're supposed to be helping with the dressings.'

'Sorry, Sister.' Effie went to leave, but Sister Blake stopped her. 'Not you,' she said. She turned to Katie. 'You go. I want a word with your sister in my office.'

'Yes, Sister.' Effie caught Katie's despairing look at her as she slipped past out of the door. Being summoned to Sister's office was usually for more than just a telling off. And Effie deserved it, too, sobbing in the sluice like an eejit probationer.

But to her amazement Sister Blake had the ward maid bring them a pot of tea. She poured Effie a cup and then handed it to her, together with a clean, lavender-scented handkerchief.

'Now, what's all this about?' she asked kindly.

Clutching her cup in one hand and the handkerchief in the other, Effie told her about Adam Campbell, Adeline and the letter he'd asked her to write. Sister Blake listened carefully, her bright dark eyes fixed on Effie.

'Well,' she said, when the girl had finishing telling her tale, 'it was very wrong for Mr Campbell to speak to you the way he did, and I will have a word with him about it. But,' she went on, before Effie could reply, 'I must also say it isn't your place to decide who he should or shouldn't be corresponding with.' She eyed Effie severely. 'How many times have you been told not to get too close to the patients, Nurse O'Hara?'

Effie hung her head. 'I know, Sister.'

'But I think it's probably already too late to warn you about that in this case, isn't it?' Sister Blake guessed shrewdly. Effie heard her sigh. 'It's all very well to care for the patients, but you have to stop yourself getting involved in their personal lives. It really isn't your business, and it can only ever lead to trouble.'

'Yes, Sister.'

Effie risked a glance at Sister Blake's face. Her bright brown eyes had a knowing look.

'I think it's just as well it's your last day on Blake ward today,' she said. 'Now go and wash your face and smarten yourself up and get on with looking after the other patients. And make sure you stay away from Mr Campbell,' she added. 'I will get one of the other nurses to write his letter for him.'

'Yes, Sister. Thank you, Sister.'

Effie threw herself into her work for the rest of the day. She changed beds, washed faces and bodies, combed hair, scrubbed false teeth, rubbed surgical spirit into backs and liniment into legs.

'You're a right little whirling dervish today, ain't you?'

Mr Anderson commented, as she skimmed around the ward with the tea trolley.

'Got to keep up, Mr Anderson. Too much to do and too little time.' Effie smiled brightly at him. 'Now, would you like some tea, coffee or Bovril?'

'I'll have some tea, please, love. And mind you don't get it wrong like you did last time. I didn't think much to the Bovril with milk and sugar in it!'

All the patients made her laugh, teasing her about how much they would miss her.

'You and those sisters of yours are a hoot, the way you argue among yourselves,' Mr Maudsley said. 'You're like Elsie and Doris Waters!'

'More like the Crazy Gang!' his neighbour put in. They both roared with laughter and Effie smiled along with them, even though she didn't have the faintest idea what they were talking about.

And all the time she was aware of Adam watching her from the far end of the ward. She was sorely tempted to pass by the end of his bed, just to see what he'd say to her. But she was even more aware of Sister Blake watching her keenly, and even Effie wasn't silly enough to risk being summoned to her office again. She didn't think she would be offered tea and sympathy a second time.

At nine o'clock the night staff came on duty and Effie and the other nurses hurried around finishing off their chores before the end of their shift.

Afterwards, Effie went around saying goodbye to all the patients. Mr Maudsley gave her a humbug as a parting gift.

'Thank you, but you know we're not allowed to eat on duty,' Effie said.

'Stick it in your pocket for later. No one will know. Besides, Sister's too busy having a chinwag with the night nurse to notice,' he said.

Effie glanced over cautiously to where Sister Blake was giving her report to the two second years. Miss Tanner the Night Sister was also with them. Mr Maudsley was right, no one was paying any attention to Effie.

She popped the humbug in her mouth. 'Don't tell anyone, will you?'

'My lips are sealed, love.' Mr Maudsley leaned forward, lowering his voice. 'By the way, I think your young man wants to speak to you. He's been trying to catch your eye this past half an hour.'

Effie glanced over her shoulder. As soon as she did, Adam lifted his hand and waved at her, beckoning her over.

'He's certainly not my young man,' she said.

'If you say so, love. But he seems very keen to have a word with you.' Mr Maudsley gave her a twinkling smile. 'Go on, what harm will it do? Like I said, Sister ain't even watching. Put the poor devil out of his misery. He's going to miss you, you know.'

'I doubt it,' Effie muttered through a mouth full of humbug.

'Don't you believe it, ducks,' Mr Maudsley said. 'I was young myself once. I know what young love is like.'

Effie was determined to be cool and aloof as she sauntered over.

'Did you want something, Mr Campbell?' she asked icily. 'Only the night nurse is coming on duty, if you'll wait a minute.'

'I don't want the night nurse. I want you.'

'Oh? Why's that?'

He blushed. 'I wanted to apologise,' he muttered. 'For earlier. About the letter.'

Effie pressed her lips together and forced herself to say nothing. Cool and aloof, she kept telling herself. She tried to imagine what her sister Bridget would do.

'You were right,' he said eventually. 'I'd be wasting my time. If Adeline really cared about me, she'd be here now.'

Effie looked at his downcast face and forgot all about being cool or aloof. 'I'm sorry,' she said.

He shrugged his uninjured shoulder. 'It doesn't matter,' he said. 'Anyway, that's all I wanted to say. Sorry – and thank you.'

'What for?'

'For putting up with me.' His mouth twisted wryly. 'I know I haven't been an easy patient.'

'That's true!' Effie laughed. 'You won't be able to get away with that kind of behaviour with my sisters!'

'I know,' he said. 'It won't be the same without you.'

'You mean you'll get your bed made properly, and no one will spill your tea in the saucer,' Effie said.

'I mean I'll miss you,' he said.

Their eyes met. Cool and aloof, Effie muttered to herself, even though perspiration was beginning to prickle at the back of her neck.

Then, just as she thought he was going to make some heartfelt declaration, he added, 'I must say, I am looking forward to a properly made bed, though.'

Effie grinned, relieved they were back on safe ground, teasing each other again. 'And I'm looking forward to going somewhere my efforts are better appreciated,' she said.

'Do you know where you're going yet?'

She shook her head. 'They put the notice up on the dining-room wall. I'll find out when I go to supper.'

'I hope wherever it is they like their coffee like soup and their eggs boiled like tennis balls!' he joked.

'Whether they like it or not, I expect that's what they'll get!' Effie glanced down the ward. Sister Blake had finished giving her report to the night nurses. Any moment now she would turn around and see them. 'I'd better go,' said Effie.

As she walked away, Adam called after her, 'Don't forget me, will you?'

She looked over her shoulder at him. 'How could I?' she replied.

Chapter Twenty-Six

'Parry, one receiving dish – enamel. Blake, two pillowcases. Everett, three test tubes and one bucket with lid . . .'

Kathleen Fox stared out of the window while Miss Hanley's droning voice washed over her, reciting the weekly inventory.

Every week, all the ward sisters had to complete a full inventory of their store cupboards and report back to the Assistant Matron. Miss Hanley would then report the missing items to Kathleen. Every week she would have to sit at her desk, listening patiently to the tedious list of what was missing from where, and why.

As she allowed her attention to wander over the courtyard and the haphazard arrangement of ward blocks, clinics and outbuildings that surrounded it, she wondered how many precious hours of her life she had already wasted listening to the Assistant Matron's endless lists.

'Can't they just order another one?' she interrupted, when Miss Hanley reported that a catheter tube had disappeared from Hyde ward.

Miss Hanley stared at her, her broad, mannish features blank with incomprehension. 'I beg your pardon, Matron?'

'It's only a catheter tube. Can't Sister Hyde get another one from the stores?'

'Well, yes, she could. But that's not the point.'

'Then what is the point?' Kathleen kept her voice level, but inside she wanted to scream.

'Matron?'

'Why do we carry out these checks every week, Miss Hanley? Can't we trust these women to organise the running of their own wards without looking over their shoulders, constantly checking if they have enough pillowcases?'

Miss Hanley's face reddened. 'The point is they shouldn't have gone missing in the first place,' she said. 'These things have to be accounted for. Surely you as Matron should be concerned . . .'

I have bigger things to worry about than a missing bucket! Kathleen wanted to blurt out, but she held her tongue. The last thing she wanted to do was burden anyone else with her problems.

'You're right,' she sighed. 'Please go on.'

At last it was over. As Kathleen stood up, pain lanced through her, making her catch her breath. She clenched her teeth to stop herself from crying out.

It was too much to hope that Miss Hanley wouldn't notice. 'Matron? Whatever is the matter?' she asked, springing to her feet.

'It's nothing. Just a little pain, that's all.'

'Can I get you something? A glass of water?'

'Honestly, I'm fine.' She straightened up gingerly. 'There, you see. It's gone now.'

'You're still very pale. Perhaps you should see Dr McKay?'

Wouldn't you love that? Kathleen thought. Miss Hanley would be behind her desk in a moment, making lists and driving all the ward sisters mad.

'Oh, no, I wouldn't want to bother him. It's just a bit of abdominal cramp, that's all. Women's troubles, as the patients on Wren would say!' She forced a wry smile.

'If you say so, Matron.'

Kathleen closed the door, and finally allowed herself to

succumb to the wave of pain that washed over her. It was worse today. And the bleeding was getting worse, too.

Automatically, Kathleen's hand strayed down to her abdomen. She hated herself for doing it, but she couldn't stop herself feeling for the swollen curve through the thickness of her uniform. Was it her imagination, or had it grown bigger in the past couple of days?

'It's nothing,' she told herself aloud. Just the fears and fancies of a silly woman, that's all.

But those fears and fancies had been giving her sleepless nights since before Christmas. For months before that, she'd ignored the twinges and odd spells of bleeding. It was the change of life, she told herself, only to be expected in a woman her age. But as the weeks went by, the twinges had turned into a constant pain that gnawed away at her as she tried to go about her duties. It was getting harder and harder to push it from her mind.

It was time she talked to someone about it, she decided. She was supposed to be going to a concert with her friend Frannie that night. Surely she could talk to her? They'd shared their secrets and troubles since they were trainees together in Leeds. There was nothing Kathleen couldn't tell her.

But as soon as she met her friend outside the hospital gates and saw the broad smile on her face, Kathleen knew she couldn't dampen her spirits. Frannie was in such a good mood, Kathleen didn't want to worry her. And besides, desperate as she was, she didn't want to put her thoughts into words, because then her nameless fear would become real and she would have to face it.

So instead she pinned a smile to her face and listened to the concert and tried her best to ignore the nagging pain deep inside her belly and the troubled thoughts that crowded into her mind.

Afterwards, as they walked back through the darkened streets to the hospital, she asked Frannie about her admirer, John Campbell.

'Don't call him that!' Even in the darkness she could see the blush rising in her friend's face. 'He's just a friend, that's all.'

Kathleen thought about the tall, good-looking soldier. The way he'd stared at Frannie that night at the Christmas Show was far more than just friendly. 'But you've been seeing a lot of each other?'

'We've been to a few concerts and exhibitions together. I like his company,' she admitted shyly.

'Have you talked about Matthew much?'

Frannie shook her head. 'I've tried asking about him, but John always changes the subject. I think the memory of his death still hurts him.'

'And does it still hurt you?'

Frannie was silent for a moment. 'I'll always miss Matthew,' she said finally. 'He was my first love, and it was tragic that he was killed so young, before he'd even had a chance to live. I suppose I'll always think about what our lives might have been like if he'd come home . . .' She smiled bracingly. 'But you can't live in the past, can you? As John says, you have to keep looking to the future.'

The future. It wasn't something Kathleen liked to dwell on too much these days.

'And do you think you have a future with John?' she asked teasingly.

'I don't know,' Frannie replied quietly. 'But I'd like to think so.'

Kathleen grinned at her friend. 'Imagine you, of all people, with a soldier!'

She'd meant it as a joke, but Frannie's face clouded over. 'Don't,' she said shortly. 'I don't want to think about it.'

Kathleen was instantly sympathetic. Whatever Frannie said, her fiancé's death had left scars on her heart. They'd all lost loved ones in the last war, but it had left Frannie with a deep fear of conflict.

But sooner or later she would have to confront the fact that the man she was falling in love with was a soldier.

'Anyway, it doesn't matter,' she went on. 'He's never going to be called to fight again, is he?'

Kathleen knew better than to argue. If her friend had decided to close her mind to awful possibilities, who was Kathleen of all people to judge her for it?

Chapter Twenty-Seven

The atmosphere on Holmes, the Male Surgical ward, was very different from that on Male Orthopaedics. There was no laughter, no fun, no teasing the nurses or calling out to each other between the beds. It was unnervingly quiet, the only sound the slow, steady ticking of the clock on the wall and the muffled squeak of the nurses' shoes on the highly polished floor. There were screens pulled around several of the beds, and even the patients Effie could see lay still and silent under their covers. One or two brave souls at the far end of the ward were propped up on their pillows, reading or doing the crossword with studied concentration. But she noticed how their eyes darted around the ward, as if they were expecting a reprimand at any moment.

Sister Holmes was very different from Sister Blake, too. They were roughly the same age, both in their early forties, but while Sister Blake was small, slim-boned and dark, Sister Holmes was rounded, bosomy and blonde. Her face was as round and pretty as a doll's, with prominent blue eyes, pink cheeks and pert rosebud lips that looked as if they'd been painted on. Wisps of honey-coloured hair escaped from under the edges of her goffered bonnet.

But looks could be cruelly deceiving. For all her rounded curves, there were no soft edges to Sister Holmes. As Effie and Devora Kowalski skidded around the corner just on seven o'clock, Sister Holmes was standing in the doorway with her watch in her hand.

'A minute late,' she tutted. 'Not a good start, is it?' She

looked them both up and down. 'And that hem is more than eight inches from the ground, O'Hara. Report to Matron at nine o'clock.'

'I can't help it if I've got long legs, can I?' Effie grumbled as they unfastened their cloaks. 'I've already sent it to the sewing room twice to have the hem taken down. There's nothing left to stitch!'

'I don't know what she's doing here so early anyway,' Devora joined in. 'Sisters aren't supposed to come on duty until eight.'

'I don't suppose she ever goes off duty,' Effie said. 'She probably sleeps standing up in the broom cupboard, waiting to catch out unsuspecting students.'

Devora snorted with laughter. 'Shhh! She'll hear you.'

'What are you two doing?' Anna Padgett, another student from their year, loomed out in front of them. She was the self-appointed leader of Effie's set, and always top of the class.

'I might have known you'd be here early,' Effie said. 'You could have waited for us.'

'And make myself late? No, thank you. Anyway, you'd best hurry up. Sister wants us to hear the night report.'

After the night nurse had stammered her way through her report – timed, of course, by Sister Holmes – the ward sister went through their instructions for the day.

'We have several patients due down to Theatre,' she announced. 'Two hernias, a haemorrhoid and a partial gastrectomy. Wilson, you'll be accompanying the patients down to Theatre and bringing them up again. I assume you have all dealt with a post-operative patient before?'

'I have, Sister.' Anna Padgett's hand shot up first as usal. Effie and Devora rolled their eyes at each other.

'Good,' Sister Holmes said. 'You and Foley can sit with them until they regain consciousness, check their temperature, pulse and respiration, and make sure they're comfortable and that there are no complications. As for the rest of you . . .' She looked around and her china-doll gaze fell on Effie. 'O'Hara and Kowalski, I want you both to assist Staff Nurse Lund in specialling Mr Webster, our head injury in Room One. Kowalski, you can help this morning, and O'Hara can take the afternoon shift. Nurse Lund will tell you what you have to do.'

Effie glanced at Anna Padgett, who looked furious. She always thought she should get the most interesting cases because she was the cleverest. Now, thanks to her hasty actions, she was going to spend the day sitting with a haemorrhoid op. Served her right for always having to be first, she thought.

But Effie wasn't sure how she was going to enjoy specialling Mr Webster. Sooner or later she knew it would bring her into contact with Adeline Moreau. How would she be able to smile and act normally around her, knowing what a scheming, calculating heartbreaker she was?

Sister Holmes went through the other post-operative patients, and the care they needed, and once again Effie was struck by how astonishing ward sisters' memories were. They knew, without consulting their notes, every patient's name, their condition and everything about them, right down to their last bowel movement. Effie doubted if she would ever be able to achieve such a feat. Her mammy always said she was far too much of a scatterbrain.

When she'd finished giving out the work lists, Sister Holmes dismissed them all with a sharp, 'Well, don't just stand there. Hurry up!'

It was a phrase Effie heard a great deal during that morning. Sister Holmes did everything at double speed, and always with her watch in her hand. She operated like a machine, and nothing was allowed to get in the way of the smooth running of her ward.

'She's really not that bad once you get used to her little ways,' Daphne Anderson, the junior staff nurse, said breathlessly as they whizzed around making the beds. Sister Holmes had already warned them she expected each bed stripped and made in under two minutes.

'I might not live that long,' Effie sighed. At the rate they were going, her heart would give out long before her off-duty time came.

And if her heart didn't give out, her feet definitely would.

Effie was making her last bed when Adeline Moreau came strutting down the ward in her red coat. She was smiling at everyone, nodding to the nurses as if she were visiting royalty. But when she saw Effie her smile froze into a grimace of dismay.

'Mr Webster's fiancée,' Daphne Anderson whispered. 'So elegant, don't you think? That coat didn't come from Columbia Road market, I'm sure.' She sighed. 'And she's so devoted, poor thing. Comes in every day just to sit beside his bed.'

'I'm sure that must drive Sister mad,' Effie said, but Daphne shook her head.

'Oh, no, she's been a great help to us. Having her there watching over Mr Webster means we don't have to sit with him all day every day. Although Nurse Lund makes sure there's always at least one of us in sight of him,' she added.

'Nurses! Stop whispering at once!' Sister Holmes hissed furiously. 'Weren't you taught in training that it's very rude to talk over a patient? And you've taken two minutes and twenty-five seconds to finish that bed,' she added.

'Anyone would think we were in the Olympics!' Effie muttered at her retreating back, then jumped as Sister

Holmes shot back, 'If you were then you would hardly qualify for a medal, O'Hara!'

At twelve Nurse Lund summoned Effie to take Mr Webster his lunch, which had been sent up from the kitchen.

'You'll need to feed him, of course,' she said as she led the way down the short passageway of private rooms set aside for patients who were particularly poorly or who had paid for private care. 'He's still very weak and can't do much for himself at the moment, but his improvement is remarkable when you think he was barely conscious a few weeks ago. He's a very determined young man, as you'll find,' she said.

'Can he do anything for himself, Staff?' Effie asked.

'Not very much at the moment. He's having to relearn everything from scratch, so it's bound to take time. His speech is coming on very well, but you'll need to be very patient with him.' She nodded towards the tray Effie was carrying. 'You've fed a patient before, I take it?' Effie nodded. 'That's good. Remember, always treat him with dignity and respect. He may be helpless but he isn't a child.' She smiled. 'Although I daresay he'll remind you of that soon enough, if you go too far.'

'His mind is quite sharp, then?'

Mary Lund smiled. 'Sharper than yours, I daresay. Although he gets confused sometimes and his memory is still very patchy. The consultant has also directed that he needs to be stimulated if he's to recover fully, so keep talking to him and asking him questions, but don't over-tax him.'

Effie's mind was racing with all these instructions as they entered Mr Webster's room. Adeline was at his bedside. Effie deliberately didn't look at her, focusing her attention on the young man in the bed.

Richard Webster looked a great deal better than he had the last time she'd seen him. The bandages that had swathed his skull were gone, and his shaved head was covered with a soft down of light brown hair. He was pale and delicate, his skin translucent, his wasted limbs as slender as a dancer's. But his hazel eyes shone with warmth and intelligence as they regarded Effie.

'And who's this?' His voice sounded thick and slurred, as if his tongue were too large for his mouth and he couldn't quite master it.

'This is Nurse O'Hara, Mr Webster. She'll be helping me look after you this afternoon.'

Effie sneaked a sideways look at Adeline. Her smile was fixed on her face, but her eyes were dark and cold.

'O'Hara . . . you're Irish?'

'That's right,' Effie nodded.

'I like the Irish nurses. They're the pretty ones. And I reckon you're the best-looking so far.'

'Now, Mr Webster, what have I told you about flirting with the nurses?' Mary Lund chided him. 'And in front of your fiancée, too.' She turned to Effie. 'Nurse O'Hara, this is Miss Moreau.'

'Call me Adeline.' She was a brilliant actress, Effie had to give her credit for that. She rose from her seat and held out her hand in greeting, wearing the brightest, warmest smile Effie had ever seen. She gave away no hint that they were anything but cordial strangers.

But then she was probably used to covering up, Effie thought. After all, she'd had an affair with her fiance's best friend behind his back.

'Pay no attention to Richard,' Adeline went on, shaking her head at the young man in the bed. 'He's quite incorrigible, aren't you, darling?'

Richard's slack mouth curved in a sheepish grin.

'Miss Moreau has been a tremendous help to us in looking after Mr Webster,' Staff Nurse Lund went on. 'We really don't know where we'd be without her.'

'Neither do I,' Richard mumbled.

Effie watched Adeline turn towards him and reach for his hand. She might be a brilliant actress, but the affection for him in her face was quite genuine. Effie was touched, until she remembered the heartless way Adeline had treated Adam.

'Now, Mr Webster, Nurse O'Hara will be giving you your lunch,' Mary Lund said.

'I can do it,' Adeline put in quickly. 'I don't want to put you to any trouble, and I'm sure Nurse O'Hara is very busy.' Her panicked eyes fixed on Effie.

'That's very kind of you, Miss Moreau, but it's no trouble,' Mary Lund said.

'But I'd like to—'

'We'll do it, Miss Moreau,' Mary Lund said firmly, putting an end to her protests. 'Nurse O'Hara will look after him, don't you worry.'

'Why don't you take a break?' Effie suggested.

'Good idea,' Richard agreed. 'You've been sitting here for hours, you need some fresh air.'

'I'd like to stay,' Adeline said tightly.

Richard gave Effie a lopsided grin. 'She's worried about what I'll get up to while her back is turned,' he confided.

Effie looked at Adeline's tense, white face. She's more worried about what I'll get up to, she thought. 'I'm sure we can be trusted together,' she said.

Finally, Adeline gave in. 'I'll be very quick,' she said. 'Just a five-minute walk and then I'll be back.'

With a quick, warning glance at Effie, she was gone.

'She worries about me,' Richard said, when they were

alone and Effie was feeding him his lunch. 'I know I've put her through hell recently.'

'She seems very – devoted,' Effie said carefully.

'She is.' He sighed. 'Poor Adeline, it can't be much fun for her, being stuck with an invalid.'

'You won't always be an invalid.'

'Won't I?' He looked up at her, his eyes full of despair. 'I don't know how I'll end up. Even the doctors can't tell me. They just keep saying, wait and see.' He attempted a twisted smile. 'I daresay this isn't what Adeline had in mind when we got engaged.'

Effie put another spoonful of food carefully between his slack lips. 'Do you remember getting engaged?'

'Sometimes I think I do. And other times . . . I don't know if I'm just remembering what Adeline's told me. It all gets confused, you see.'

'But you remember Adeline?'

'Oh, yes. That's the odd thing. I knew her instantly. The moment I woke up and saw her sitting there, I knew who she was. But everything else . . .' He shook his head. 'That's love for you, I suppose.'

'So you don't remember anything else?' Effie asked.

'Not really. Nothing at first. But recently . . . It's as if I'm staring into a thick fog and every so often something will emerge from the mist – a picture of someone's face, a name. But then they'll slip away, back into the fog, before I can grasp them.'

'I'm sure it will come back to you.'

'I wish I had your confidence, Nurse.'

Effie thought for a moment as she dabbed his chin with the linen napkin.

'What about the accident?' she ventured. 'Do you remember that?'

His head wobbled on his shoulders. 'I didn't even know

there was an accident until the doctor told me. I've tried asking Adeline about it, but she won't discuss it. She says it's too upsetting.' He turned to her. 'Do you know anything about it?'

Effie paused, wondering how much she should tell him. 'I know you were in your car, on the Mile End Road.'

'Was I?' He looked blank. 'I don't know why. I'm not sure I'd ever ventured into the East End before. Was I with anyone?'

'Well—'

Before Effie could say any more, a sharp voice behind her said, 'That's enough.'

She swung around in her seat. Adeline stood in the doorway, her pretty face taut. 'Really, Richard, how many times have I told you, you're not to tax yourself and get upset? And you should know better, Nurse.' She turned to Effie. Her smile was bright and brittle, but Effie glimpsed the angry warning in her eyes.

'It's not her fault,' Richard said. 'She was just trying to help me remember.'

'And you will remember, all in good time,' Adeline said. 'But you're not to try to force it.' She looked at Effie. 'Have you finished giving him his lunch, Nurse?'

Effie looked at the empty plate. 'Yes, but—'

'Then we won't keep you. I daresay you have a great deal else to do.'

As Effie left, Adeline followed her into the passageway.

'What do you think you're playing at?' she hissed, closing the door behind her.

'I was just trying to jog his memory. Staff Nurse Lund said—'

'Never mind what she said! I *know* what you were trying to do. You want to ruin things for me, don't you?'

'I don't know what you mean,' Effie said.

'Don't play the innocent with me. You don't approve of me, of what I did. You want to punish me.'

'It's none of my business.'

'You're right. It isn't. So I'll thank you to stay out of it.' Then, just as Effie was reeling from this assault, Adeline switched on an appealing smile. 'You know, there's no reason why we should be at odds,' she said. 'I'm sure things would be a lot easier for both of us if we could be friends, don't you think?'

Effie looked at her. She could see from the calculating look in Adeline's eyes that she wasn't remotely interested in Effie's friendship. All she really wanted was to avoid trouble for herself.

'Just as you like.' Effie shrugged.

As she took Richard Webster's tray back to the kitchen, she met Staff Nurse Anderson.

'What do you think of Adeline Moreau?' she asked. 'Isn't she beautiful? And so devoted, too.'

'I suppose so.' Effie gritted her teeth. If she had to listen to one more person telling her what an angel Adeline was, she might not be responsible for her actions.

'Mind you,' Daphne went on, 'I'd probably be devoted to someone who had that much money.'

Effie looked over her shoulder at Daphne Anderson as she stood at the sink. 'What do you mean? What money?'

'Don't you know? Richard Webster's family are rolling in it. Apparently he pretends to be some kind of impoverished writer, but he's the heir to an absolute fortune, so I've heard. That could explain a lot about Miss Moreau, don't you think?' said Daphne with a sly smile.

Effie was thoughtful as she turned back to the sink. 'I should say it does,' she murmured.

Chapter Twenty-Eight

War was coming. On 15 March Hitler's tanks rolled into Prague, and now even the government who had insisted there would be no war had to admit that Chamberlain's scrap of paper meant nothing. Factories began producing guns, bombs, battleships and aircraft, and people began to volunteer as air-raid wardens, ambulance drivers and auxiliary firemen – 'just in case'.

On the Saturday morning when the *Picture Post* called for women to volunteer, Helen was at Dora's house, helping her to knit a matinee jacket for the baby.

'I'm going to sign up as a volunteer nurse,' Dora announced as they sat side by side on the sofa, their needles clicking. Helen's clicked a lot faster than Dora's. As she'd already told Helen, she was a lost cause when it came to knitting. She had to stop every couple of minutes to sort out a dropped stitch or a tangled piece of wool. 'They're bound to have me, don't you think, with my training?'

Helen laughed, eyeing her distended belly. 'In your condition? You'd never get a uniform to fit!'

'I won't be pregnant for ever. At least, I hope not.' Dora grimaced, stroking her bump. 'I can hardly walk, I'm so big. And the kicking! Drives me mad all night, it does. Nick reckons this little one's going to play for West Ham!'

Helen caught the light in Dora's eyes. For all she pretended to complain, she was the happiest and most content Helen had ever known her. 'It's not due for another couple of months yet, is it?'

'Early June, so the doctor reckons. You never know, I might have finished this ruddy jacket by then!' She pulled a comical, cross-eyed face at her knitting.

'Here, let me sort it out for you.' Helen put down her own needles and took Dora's from her.

'Anyway, what do you reckon? About me signing up as a volunteer nurse?'

'I think it's a very good idea. I daresay we'll have need of extra help, once the bombs start coming down. Especially if there are gas attacks. Dr McKay reckons there could be hundreds of casualties every night.'

'Don't!' Dora shuddered, her face milky pale under its scattering of freckles. 'I don't want to think about it.'

'I don't either, but Dr McKay says we have to. He plans to ask the Board of Trustees to extend the Casualty department and carry out emergency training.'

She handed Dora back her knitting. Dora stared down at it glumly. 'It's a horrible thought, isn't it? Let's hope we won't need it.'

'Let's hope not,' Helen agreed.

They went on knitting, but the thought had taken hold of Helen and wouldn't let go. She kept thinking of the Casualty hall, extended to the size of a football pitch, with bodies stretched out as far as the eye could see. She imagined herself rushing here and there, not knowing who to help first, deafened by the screams of agony.

The thought must have taken hold of Dora, too, because she suddenly said, 'I can't imagine what it would be like, can you?'

'No,' Helen said, but the truth was she could, only too well. She was haunted by that fire on Christmas Eve, all those people crying out, the stench of burned flesh. She never, ever wanted to hold another dying child in her arms.

'It's Nick I'm worried about,' Dora went on. 'He's bound to be called up sooner or later. I don't want him going off to fight . . .' Her voice trailed off, thick with emotion. Helen looked away and pretended not to notice. Dora wasn't one to show her feelings very often.

'I know what you mean,' she said. 'I'm frightened for Chris, too. Even if he stays on the merchant ships he'll be risking his life out there at sea.'

Dora didn't reply. She'd gone very quiet, her curly red head bent over her knitting. Helen guessed she was still thinking about Nick being called up and sent off to fight.

She tried to change the subject. 'Did I tell you, Chris has found another ship? He sets sail for Russia next week. He'll probably be gone for a couple of months this time.' She sighed. 'It'll be strange without him again. I don't think we've gone a day without seeing each other in weeks.'

She'd expected some sympathy from Dora, so was taken aback when she said quietly, 'Perhaps that's for the best.'

Helen looked up at her. 'What do you mean?'

'You said yourself, you've been spending a lot of time together.'

'What's wrong with that? It's what courting couples do, isn't it?'

'Yes, but you don't want to get too reliant on him, do you?'

Helen frowned. There was a look in Dora's eyes, as if she knew something Helen didn't.

'What are you saying?' she asked.

'It's none of my business,' Dora said quickly, going back to her knitting.

'No, go on. I want to hear what you've got to say.'

Dora let her knitting rest in her lap. 'I just worry that you're getting too serious about him,' she said. 'You said yourself, he's going to be away for weeks. I'm afraid he might not come back and then you'll be hurt.'

'Of course he'll come back,' Helen said.

'Are you sure? You know what they say about sailors having a girl in every port.'

Helen stared at her. 'Is that all you think I am to him? Just one of his girls?'

'I don't know,' Dora said. 'I'm just warning you not to get too involved, that's all. I don't want you to get hurt again,' she insisted.

'Chris won't hurt me. He loves me,' Helen declared. 'And I love him,' she added.

Their eyes met for a moment, then Dora went back to her knitting. 'Like I said, it's none of my business,' she mumbled.

They were silent for a long time. Helen's needles clicked furiously, in time with the turmoil inside her head. She was so angry, she could hardly focus on the line of stitches.

How dare Dora be so high-handed! She was implying that Chris was taking Helen for a fool, and that she was pathetic enough to believe he was truly in love with her. Anger burned inside her until she burst out, 'I don't know why you can't just be happy for me!'

'I am happy for you,' Dora said gently. 'I told you, I'm just worried for you, that's all.'

'Well, don't be,' Helen said. 'Charlie loves me, I know he does. And I don't really care what anyone else thinks anyway, because for the first time in ages I'm not sad or lonely any more.' She stopped talking abruptly, seeing Dora's expression. 'What is it?' she demanded.

'You called him Charlie,' her friend said quietly.

'No, I didn't.'

'You did.' Dora paused. 'Are you sure that's not why you've fallen for him . . . because he's Charlie's cousin?'

'Don't be ridiculous,' Helen said, shifting in her seat. 'He's nothing like Charlie.'

'No,' said Dora, 'you're right. He's nothing like Charlie.'

Helen's eyes narrowed. 'You don't like him, do you?' The couple of times they'd met, Christopher had gone out of his way to be friendly, but Dora had been decidedly cool in return.

'It's not that. I hardly know him. And neither do you,' she said. 'I'm just worried you've fallen for him for the wrong reason. Because you're lonely, and he reminds you of Charlie . . .'

Helen's hackles rose. 'Do you think I'm some kind of simpleton, falling for a man because he reminds me of my dead husband?'

Dora blushed. 'I didn't mean—'

'But that's what you just said. You think I'm so desperate and gullible I'd let myself get taken in by the first man who pays me any attention.' Helen felt her anger rising. 'Why can't you be happy that for the first time in years I have someone who cares for me? Or is that something that only happens to the likes of you? Everyone else has someone who loves them, is it so strange I should have someone too?'

'Of course not. Helen, I didn't mean . . .'

'I know what you meant.' Helen slammed down her knitting and got to her feet.

'Where are you going? Please don't leave.'

'I've got to. I won't stay here and listen to you telling me I don't know my own mind.'

'Helen, please. I'm sorry. It's none of my business, I shouldn't have said anything.'

'You're right, you shouldn't. And in future, I'll thank you to keep your nose out of my business!'

Helen was still simmering when she met Christopher that night.

They walked down to the docks. It seemed eerie there in the darkness, with the skeletons of the towering cranes silhouetted against the night sky, the dark, hulking shapes of the huge vessels on the inky water.

It was a cold, starry night and Chris put his arm around her, pulling her close. But for once the solid warmth of his body pressing against hers failed to re-assure Helen.

He turned to her, his handsome profile outlined by the moonlight. 'What's wrong? You've been in a funny mood all night?'

'Nothing.' But she couldn't force Dora's warnings from her mind. Was she being foolish? Helen wondered. She had fallen headlong for Christopher, without any thought of where it might lead. Now, as they stood together in the darkness, it began to occur to her that he had another life, one she could never share.

'Good, because it's our last night together and I don't want anything to spoil it.'

Our last night. It seemed so final when he said that.

'You're right,' Helen said determinedly. If this was to be their last night together, then she wanted to remember and enjoy every minute of it.

'You see that one?' Christopher pointed out a particular ship in the distance. 'That's the one I'm sailing on. The *Troubadour*, she's called. In a few days I'll be in Norway, and then off around to Russia.' He hugged her closer, so she could feel the steady beat of his heart against hers. 'It'll be a lot colder there than it is here, I can tell you.'

He shivered. 'I won't know what to do without you to warm me up.'

Perhaps you'll have someone else in your arms by then. The wretched thought scratched at Helen's mind.

'Will you come back?' she asked.

"Course I will.' He smiled down at her. 'Why do you look so worried? You don't think I'm just going to disappear, do you?'

'I wasn't sure,' she admitted, staring down at the cobbled street. 'I suppose you must have a girl in every port?' she echoed Dora's words.

'True. But none of them as special as you.' He laughed, seeing her dismay. 'I'm having you on, Helen!'

She tried to smile, but her face felt stiff and cold.

He put his finger under her chin, turning her face so that she looked up into his eyes. 'I wasn't joking about you being special, though. You are, Helen. You ain't like any other girl I've ever met.'

She felt herself blushing. 'I'm not special,' she mumbled.

'That's where you're wrong. I'm lucky to have you.' His face grew serious. 'You might be wondering if I'm going to come home, but I'm wondering if you're going to be snapped up by one of those clever doctors while I'm gone.'

'Don't be silly! Of course I won't be.'

'Are you sure? I'd hate to come back and find out you'd got someone else.'

She gazed up at him. For once, he seemed deadly serious, his eyes full of intent.

'I won't,' she promised.

'All the same, I'd like to be certain.' A strange feeling came over Helen as he released her and took a step back. She already knew what he was going to do before he sank down on one knee on the wet cobbles. 'Helen, will you marry me?'

She stared at him, shocked laughter bubbling up inside her. 'I – I don't know what to say,' she stammered.

'You could say yes? And quick as you like, before this wet ground gives me rheumatism!'

Well, Dora, what do you think of that? Helen thought. She could just imagine her friend's face when she heard. And she'd thought Chris wasn't serious!

But then she heard Dora's voice again, loud and clear. *He's nothing like Charlie.*

No, he was nothing like Charlie. But Helen loved him, and more than anything she wanted to be like Dora, full of contentment, knitting little jackets for her baby and waiting for her husband to come home.

'Helen?' Christopher prompted. He was looking up at her, his eyes full of hope.

'Yes.' She smiled at him. 'Yes, Chris, I will marry you.'

Chapter Twenty-Nine

David McKay stood at the head of the table and surveyed the Board of Trustees gathered before him. They were a mixed bunch, to say the least. Reginald Collins, a timid little accountant, scribbled figures on the blotter in front of him, while local MP Gerald Munroe examined his fingernails and the aged Lady Fenella Brake snoozed quietly. On the opposite side of the table sat Malcolm Eaton, the newest member of the Board, a fresh-faced young lawyer. Next to him was Matron, a distant expression on her face.

But it was to the lady at the far end of the table that David addressed his remarks. Whatever anyone else said, everyone knew it was Mrs Constance Tremayne who really made all the decisions for the Nightingale Hospital Board of Trustees.

He cleared his throat and met her steely gaze. 'Last Christmas Eve we experienced an emergency in the Casualty department,' he said. 'A local church hall caught fire, and we had to deal with the victims. More than fifty people were brought in that night, some slightly injured, others fatally.' He looked around the table. Everyone but Matron stared back at him, politely blank-faced. Lady Fenella snored quietly.

'The incident proved to me that we are woefully unprepared to cope effectively with such an emergency,' he said. 'Treating fifty people stretched the Casualty staff to its limits. Imagine how much worse it would be if it were a bomb dropping, or a gas attack.'

He saw the uncomfortable looks exchanged around the table. No one wanted to imagine such a thing.

Only Constance Tremayne didn't flinch. 'What point are you making, Dr McKay?' she asked pleasantly.

David cleared his throat. He had no idea why such a slightly built, middle-aged lady should make him so nervous, but she did.

'We need to make provision for war,' he said. 'An extension to the current Casualty department if possible, with more staff and more emergency operating theatres.' He saw the expressions of dismay around the table, but carried on without drawing breath, 'We will also probably need to set up some kind of cleansing station, in the event of gas attacks.'

'Extensions? More staff and operating theatres? And where is the money coming for all this?' Reginald Collins asked.

'Desperate times call for desperate measures. At the very least, we need to carry out an emergency drill,' went on Dr McKay, his confidence dwindling. He could feel perspiration trickling down inside the collar of his shirt, in spite of the coldness of the room.

'Emergency drill?' Constance Tremayne said. 'Please explain.'

'We would replicate a large-scale emergency – for instance, a gas attack – so we could practise our response,' David explained. 'Several London boroughs have held such drills, I believe.'

'I read about one in the papers,' Gerald Munroe chimed in. 'Chelsea, I think it was. Bodies strewn about all over Sloane Square, apparently. Sounded quite a lark!' he guffawed.

'I'm not sure if it would be a lark,' David said quietly. 'But it certainly would be very useful practice.'

'Where would you find the bodies?' Reginald looked worried.

Gerald laughed again. 'My dear man, if you can't find bodies in a hospital, where can you find them?'

'We would use real people, not cadavers,' David put in quickly, seeing Reginald go pale.

'And would we have to pay them?' He scribbled a few more figures on his blotter. 'Because this could prove very expensive . . .'

'Perhaps he'd rather we did use cadavers!' David heard Malcolm Eaton mutter to Matron. She didn't reply.

David's exasperation mounted. If they were quibbling over paying people to take part in an emergency drill, it was unlikely he was going to get his extension to the building.

'I'm sure we can find some local people willing to volunteer,' he said. 'If not, we could use medical students, or some of the junior nurses. Or perhaps you yourselves would like to offer—' He saw the frozen look on Constance Tremayne's face and stopped talking.

'Well, I'm sure this all sounds very jolly,' she said through a tight smile. 'And I've no doubt our young nurses would love to spend a few hours larking about with the medical students, pretending to be unconscious. But I wonder who would look after the patients while your – drill – was going on?' Her lip curled over the word.

David turned to Kathleen Fox, hoping she might speak up for him. But she stared back at him blankly. 'Nevertheless, I believe it's very important we are as prepared as we can possibly be in the event of war,' he ploughed on.

'That's all we seem to hear about these days,' Gerald Munroe grumbled. 'Anyone would think we were already at war, the way people go on.'

They all turned to look at him.

'Dr McKay is right,' Malcolm said. 'We should be prepared.'

'We're as prepared as we need to be,' Gerald said, leaning back in his chair with a complacent look on his face.

Something about his self-satisfied expression made David's patience snap. He leaned forward, gaze sweeping round the whole table. Even Lady Fenella woke up. 'Let me be clear on this,' he said. 'When those bombs start dropping, London is going to be the worst-hit place in England, and the East End is likely to bear the brunt. Think of it. Such a dense population, and so close to the docks – we're an obvious target. We could see hundreds – no, thousands – of casualties. We need to be able to deal with them.'

'Why?'

David looked up sharply. Constance Tremayne had spoken quietly, but her voice still carried all the way around the table.

'I beg your pardon?' he asked.

'If things are going to be as terrible as you say, then perhaps we shouldn't be asking ourselves how we can prepare for such an emergency. Perhaps instead we should be asking whether we should even try?'

There was a stunned silence. David wondered briefly if she'd gone mad.

'But we're a hospital,' he said.

'I'm aware of that, Dr McKay.' Mrs Tremayne's voice held an underlying note of steel. 'I'm also aware that should war break out, it's highly likely that the Nightingale will close down.'

'Wait a minute . . . did you say we're going to shut down?' Gerald Munroe said.

'I think we should certainly consider the possibility.'

221

'But – that's absurd!' David didn't realise he'd spoken out loud until he saw all eyes turn towards him. 'We can't close the hospital. It's unthinkable!'

There was a general murmur of agreement around the table. Only Mrs Tremayne remained icily silent.

'As you said yourself, Doctor, this area is likely to be the worst affected,' she said eventually. 'It's highly unlikely that we would be able to function normally as a hospital if the dreadful events you describe come to pass. It would be highly dangerous for the staff and the patients.'

'And what about dealing with casualties? Who is going to look after them?'

'I daresay they will be transported to another hospital, out of harm's way. It makes no sense for them to be treated in a place where they're likely to be in danger, does it?'

'But time is of the essence when treating emergencies. Transporting them miles by ambulance could mean the difference between life and death.'

'So could staying in a hospital with bombs dropping through the roof,' Mrs Tremayne pointed out mildly.

Frustrated, David directed his gaze to Miss Fox. Surely she couldn't sit and listen to this? She must be as outraged as he was. But she scarcely seemed to be paying attention, her pen moving restlessly over her blotter, sketching abstract shapes on the thick white paper.

Malcolm Eaton broke the tense silence. 'I'm sure we don't need to come to any drastic decisions just yet,' he said, looking around the table. 'Besides, we don't even know if there's going to be a war.'

'Quite right,' Gerald Munroe agreed. 'Could all just be a lot of fuss over nothing.'

'Why don't we just wait and see what happens, and then think about it?'

'I agree,' Constance Tremayne said. But David could

see from her expression that whatever discussions might follow, her mind was already made up.

The meeting drew to a close shortly afterwards. He was still feeling shaken as he gathered up his notes.

'Is it always that bad?' he asked Kathleen Fox.

'Hmm?' She looked up at him, smiling vaguely.

'The Trustees' meeting. Is it always such an ordeal?'

'That depends if Mrs Tremayne has a particular bee in her bonnet about something.'

'She certainly had one today.' David paused, considering. He was still reeling from the shock of what he'd heard. 'You don't think she really means it, do you? About closing down the hospital?'

'Who can say?'

David frowned. Miss Fox's expression was so bland, they might have been discussing the new linen order, not the future of the hospital.

He peered at her. She was usually a handsome woman, but today she looked rather pale and drawn. 'Miss Fox, are you quite well?' he asked.

She looked at him sharply. 'Why do you ask?'

'You just seem rather distracted, that's all.'

'I'm fine, thank you.'

David had reached the door when Miss Fox suddenly said, 'Actually, Dr McKay—'

He turned to face her. 'Yes?'

Their eyes met for a second. Then she shook her head. 'No, it's nothing,' she said, forcing a smile.

He returned to the Casualty department and went straight to see Jonathan Adler in his consulting room.

'Well, that was a complete waste of time,' David said, slamming his papers down on the desk.

'Oh, dear. We're not getting our extra resources, then?'

'Hardly. In fact . . .' He stopped talking abruptly. This

223

was no time to start spreading doom and gloom about the hospital's future. Rumour spread around the Nightingale faster than the influenza virus.

'I daresay you did your best, old man,' Jonathan said mildly.

'Yes, but I'm still no match for Mrs Tremayne. I don't know what it is about that woman, but she really infuriates me.'

'Like mother, like daughter, eh?'

David frowned at him. 'I beg your pardon?'

'Sister Dawson is Constance Tremayne's daughter, remember?'

'Helen Dawson is nothing like her mother,' David said firmly.

'Yes, but she still gets under your skin, doesn't she?'

David thought about Helen Dawson, and what a great asset she'd been to the Casualty department. He'd been wrong about her, he didn't mind admitting it. She knew her job, and she ran the department better than it had been run in years.

'I've got used to her,' he admitted grudgingly. 'And she's good at her job, I must say.'

Jonathan grinned. 'High praise indeed, coming from you! The poor girl couldn't do a thing right a few months ago.'

'As I said, I've got used to her.' More than that, in fact. Helen Dawson might be young, but she wasn't the silly, empty-headed girl he'd feared she would be. She was calm, patient and unfailingly good-humoured, whether she was soothing an angry drunk, consoling a frightened child or dealing with a stomach-churning injury. David liked having her at his side when he treated patients. Her serenity seemed to wash over everything around her.

'I don't know how we're going to manage without her.'

David looked up at Jonathan, not sure he'd heard

correctly. 'What do you mean? Why should we have to manage without her?'

'When she gets married, of course.' Jonathan looked at him. 'Oh, you won't have heard the news, will you? Our Sister Dawson is engaged.'

David froze. It was as if all the air had suddenly been sucked from his body, making it too painful for him to breathe.

'Since when?' he said.

'Well, she only told us an hour ago, but it all happened a couple of days ago, apparently. Quite a whirlwind romance, so Nurse Willard reckons. Some young merchant seaman she met at Christmas. You know what they say, I suppose. All the nice girls love a sailor!' he laughed.

David had a sudden image of a handsome, fair-haired young man swaggering into his consulting room, so full of himself. Just the kind to bowl a naïve girl right off her feet . . .

'She can't,' he said.

Jonathan's brows rose. 'I'm sorry, old boy?'

'I mean, she can't do this to the department,' David amended, seeing his friend's look of surprise. 'Does she know what she's doing? Does she even care that she's leaving the rest of us in the lurch?'

'I didn't think you cared much for her? You've always said we needed someone older, more experienced—'

'Yes, well, I was wrong, wasn't I?' David snapped. 'She's been a real asset to this department, and now we're losing her without a by your leave. How are we supposed to cope without her? This place will descend into chaos!'

'I hardly think it will be that bad.'

'And fancy getting engaged to someone she's only known five minutes,' David went on, not listening. 'It's the height of lunacy, in my opinion.'

'Surely that's her business?'

'It's our business too, if it means we lose a damn good nurse! Honestly, I don't know why this hospital goes to so much trouble and expense to train these girls for three years, when all they do is run off and marry the first man they meet. It's a complete waste of everyone's time.'

'You didn't say that when Nurse Willard got engaged. I seem to remember you bought her a bunch of flowers,' Jonathan pointed out mildly.

'That's different!' David said. 'I wasn't surprised by her getting married. It was pretty obvious she was only ever biding her time here. And besides, Nurse Willard isn't half the nurse Helen Dawson is. I'm very disappointed in her, I really am.' He stopped, aware that his friend was studying him with interest. 'What?'

'Well, I never,' Jonathan said wonderingly. 'So that's the reason she got under your skin so much. You've fallen for her!'

'Don't be absurd,' David dismissed this, turning away. 'I'm just put out, that's all. And so should you be,' he said.

'Oh, I am. You're right, Sister Dawson is an excellent nurse, and I'll certainly miss her. But not as much as you, by the way you're acting.' Jonathan regarded him consideringly. 'But this has got nothing to do with her abilities as a nurse, has it? You're jealous.'

'And you're mad,' David declared, snatching up his notes.

'I don't know why I didn't see it sooner,' Jonathan went on, ignoring him. How did Shakespeare put it? "My only love sprung from my only hate?"'

'Sister Dawson and I are hardly star-crossed lovers,' David snapped. Embarrassment prickled like spreading heat up the back of his neck. If this was his friend's idea of a joke, he didn't find it very funny.

Once again, Jonathan ignored him. 'But what are you going to do about it? Are you going to tell her how you feel?' he asked.

David stared at him, appalled. 'What?'

'You can't just keep quiet about it, surely? Good heavens, David, this is the first woman you've ever lost your head over. You can't possibly let her walk out of your life!'

'Jonathan, if anyone has lost their head, it's you,' David said flatly. 'I think you've been spending far too long gossiping with Nurse Willard. You're as foolish and romantic as each other. You'll probably be braiding each other's hair soon.'

'You can deny it all you like, but I can see I've hit a nerve.' Jonathan's voice followed David as he left the consulting room, closing the door behind him. 'Just wait until Esther hears about this. She won't be able to believe it either.'

Chapter Thirty

'Do we have to do this now?' Helen pleaded. 'Why can't we wait until later, when things are more settled?'

'Everything *is* settled,' Christopher said firmly. 'Unless you're having second thoughts?' he asked with a smile.

'Of course not,' Helen replied, although she'd thought of little else over the restless weekend since his proposal.

'Good.' He lifted her hand to look at the ring he'd given her. The diamonds and sapphires sparkled in the spring sunshine. 'Don't look so worried, love. She'll be delighted, I promise.'

'Will she?'

"Course she will. Anyway, we've got to tell her sooner or later. And I'd rather do it before I go away. It's been hard enough keeping it to myself all weekend. I reckon I'll burst if I have to wait any longer!'

He looked so excited, just like a child, Helen couldn't help smiling.

But her heart was still sinking to her shoes as Christopher pushed open the front door.

'Anyone home?' he called out. 'Auntie Nellie?'

'I'm out the back, love.'

Helen followed Christopher down the narrow passageway, through to the kitchen. The scullery door was open, and Nellie was in the yard, bent over the galvanised tin tub, scrubbing her husband's shirt with a slab of green soap.

She looked up. 'All right, Chris? You were out and about early. You usually like a nice lie-in.'

'I'd promised to meet someone.'

He pushed Helen forward as she cowered in the shadows behind him. Nellie straightened up, smile fading to a bewildered frown.

'Helen? What are you doing here, love?'

She would have fled then if she could, but Christopher held on to her hand so firmly she could feel her brand-new engagement ring cutting into her finger.

She opened her mouth to speak, but he jumped in first. 'The thing is, Auntie Nell, we've got some news. We're engaged.'

Beyond them, in the street, a pot mender went by on his bicycle, his tools clanking as he pedalled. Further down, someone whistled tunelessly. All around them life went on, while in the tiny square of sunlit backyard, time seemed to have stopped completely.

'Oh!' Nellie wiped her soapy hands on her apron. Helen couldn't meet her eye but she could feel the older woman's gaze on her. She was afraid to look at her, worried she would see her own shame reflected in her mother-in-law's face.

Why had she done this? Why had she let Christopher persuade her this was a good idea? She wanted to blurt out that it had all been a terrible mistake, that she had got carried away by her own happiness, that she'd never meant to betray Charlie.

Because that was what she'd done – betrayed him. And she'd betrayed his family, too. The very people who had taken her in and treated her as one of their own.

She was so consumed with her own guilt and misery, she hardly knew what was happening when Nellie rushed to her, gathering her in her arms.

'Oh, my love, that's smashing news. I'm so pleased for you.'

Helen stayed rigid, crushed against Nellie's pillowy bosom. She smelled of Sunlight soap.

Christopher nudged her. 'I told you she'd be pleased, didn't I?' he grinned.

'Of course I'm pleased. Come into the kitchen, I'll put the kettle on.'

'Celebrate with a cup of tea? You must be joking!' Christopher looked scornful. 'I reckon Helen could do with a nip of brandy,' he said, grinning. 'She was nearly fainting dead away with nerves about telling you.'

'Was she?' Helen cringed under Nellie's curious gaze.

'She reckoned you wouldn't approve of us getting wed.'

Helen caught Nellie's eye, feeling helpless. It was as if she were sitting on a galloping horse, trying to slow it down but not knowing how. All she could do was cling on and hope for the best.

'Tell you what, Chris, why don't you go down to the pub and fetch a jug of beer?' said Nellie, her eyes still fixed on Helen. 'I'll finish this washing and get it hung up for when you come back. You could give me a hand if you like, Helen?'

Christopher let himself out through the back gate. Helen listened to him sauntering down the street, whistling.

'He's happy, ain't he?' Nellie said. 'Like the cat that got the cream.' She smiled. 'Come on, you rinse this lot through for me, then we'll put them through the mangle.'

Helen rolled up her sleeves and got stuck in, rinsing the soapy clothes in a big galvanised tub of cold water. Perspiration cooled the back of her neck as she laboured in the spring sunshine, but she was glad of something to do. If she had to have a heart-to-heart with her mother-in-law, it was far better if they were both occupied.

It wasn't long before Nellie spoke up. 'When did all

this come about, then? I didn't even know you two were courting?'

'Christopher came to the hospital with a dislocated shoulder just after Christmas,' Helen said, not looking up from her work. 'He asked me to go out with him on New Year's Eve, and it all started from there.'

'Well, I never. I knew he was going out with someone, but I had no idea it was you. I thought it must be a local girl.'

Helen flicked a quick, anxious glance at her. 'You don't mind, do you?'

'Mind? Bless you, love, why should I mind? You're both over twenty-one, you can do as you please.'

'I know, but I was just worried . . . I didn't want you to think I was betraying Charlie's memory, or anything like that?'

Nellie sighed. 'Our Charlie is past caring, God rest his soul,' she said. 'And as for me, I'm just happy you're happy. Didn't I say you should find someone else? You can't mourn Charlie for ever.'

'I know,' Helen said. 'I suppose I just feel guilty for being so happy.'

'If anyone deserves a bit of happiness it's you, my love.' But then a troubled expression crossed Nellie's face and she said, 'You are happy, ain't you?'

'Of course,' Helen said. 'Why shouldn't I be?'

'I'm just worried it's all happening a bit quick, that's all. You ain't known each other long, have you?'

'Chris wanted us to get engaged before he went back to sea.'

'That sounds like our Chris! When he sets his sights on something, he generally can't wait until he gets it. Act first, think later—' Nellie stopped abruptly. 'Not that I'm saying this is too quick or anything . . .'

'No, you're right. It is very sudden. But it's what I want,' Helen said firmly. If she stopped to think about it, she might allow the doubts to creep in and ruin everything. Christopher told her she thought too much, and he was quite right.

Besides, the sooner she married him, the quicker she could start her happy new life.

Nellie straightened up, massaging the small of her back. 'As long as you're sure, that's all that matters. Now let's get all this through the mangle, shall we?'

Helen fed the clothes through the giant rollers while Nellie turned the handle, squeezing out the water, which dripped into a tin tub at their feet. Helen felt more relaxed now she knew Nellie wasn't angry with her.

As they worked, they chatted about the wedding. Nellie asked her all kinds of questions about her dress, and her bridesmaids, and where they would get married, and Helen laughingly confessed she hadn't had time to think about it at all.

'And what does your mother think of all this?'

Helen blushed. 'I haven't told her yet.'

Nellie sent her a shrewd look. 'Don't you think you should? She's bound to have something to say about it.'

That's what I'm afraid of, Helen thought. She didn't want her mother bursting her bubble of happiness before she'd had time to enjoy it.

'Well, I'm glad for you anyway,' Nellie said. 'Chris is a nice lad, and he'll look after you. And it's about time he settled down,' she went on. 'Marriage could be the making of him.'

Helen watched her as she picked up the basket of damp washing and hauled it over the washing line. Nellie's comment troubled her, although she didn't know why.

Helen took her engagement ring out of her pocket and slipped it back on her finger, admiring it as it sparkled in the sunshine.

'It's a beauty,' Nellie commented from the other side of the yard. 'Bit different to that old scrap of silver paper my Charlie gave you, ain't it?'

When they'd got engaged, Charlie was already in hospital fighting for his life. He'd given Helen a makeshift ring fashioned out of a twist of paper from a cigarette packet. He made up for it later, with a beautiful emerald that had once belonged to his grandmother. But Helen still treasured that silver-paper ring.

A thought struck her. 'I'm sorry, I didn't think . . . do you want Charlie's ring back? I know it belonged to your mother, and I'm not sure if it's right for me to keep it now?'

'Of course I want you to keep it, love.' Nellie smiled at her. 'Charlie gave it to you, and I know he'd want you to have it.' She picked up Helen's hand and gazed down at the diamonds and sapphires. 'I must say, it seems peculiar, though, seeing you wearing another man's ring.'

'I know,' Helen said. 'It almost feels as if it shouldn't be there.'

'You'll get used to it, I'm sure.'

'I hope so.'

They were in the kitchen making tea when Christopher returned, a jug of beer in his hand, smiling broadly.

'Sorry I took so long,' he said. 'I had to keep stopping to tell the neighbours our good news.' He put his arm around Helen. 'I suppose you two have been talking about weddings, haven't you?'

Helen shot a quick glance at Nellie

'Never you mind what we've been talking about, young man,' the older woman said briskly. 'Fetch yourself a glass and get that beer poured before it goes flat.'

Helen and Nellie sipped tea while Christopher drank his beer. 'Do you know when you'll be getting wed?' Nellie asked, then paled and added, 'Don't tell me you're going to do it before you go back to sea tomorrow? I don't think my poor old heart can take another shock!'

Christopher laughed. 'Much as I'd like to, we wouldn't be able to get a licence.' He reached for Helen's hand. 'But I'd like to get married as soon as I can after I get back in the summer, I reckon.'

Helen stared at him. This was news to her. 'Does it have to be so quick? I thought we might wait . . .'

'You'll get used to our Chris,' Nellie chuckled. 'Impulsive, that's what he is.'

'I ain't impulsive, I just know what I want. Besides, I want to marry Helen before she gets the chance to change her mind!'

'Don't be silly,' she murmured, blushing.

Christopher leaned back in his chair. 'I'm happy to leave all the arrangements to you, love,' he said. 'It's your special day, and I want you to have it just as you like. No expense spared!'

'I'd rather just have a quiet wedding,' she said.

'You're joking, ain't you? I want this to be a day everyone remembers for years to come. The day Chris Dawson got wed to the best-looking girl in Bethnal Green!'

'Yes, well, I'm sure you can sort out the arrangements later, when you're back from sea,' Nellie said quickly. She passed Helen a plate of biscuits. 'I suppose you're going to have to get used to him being away for weeks at a time,' she said. 'He's never in the same place for long.'

Helen opened her mouth to reply, but Chris interrupted.

'I've been thinking about that,' he said. 'The Merchant Navy's no life for a married man. I don't want to be stuck on a ship for weeks and months when I've got a wife and a family waiting for me at home.'

Helen put her cup down. 'You're giving up your job?'

'Don't look so surprised. You didn't think I was going to abandon you once we're married, did you?' His thumb circled the gems on her finger. 'I want to spend every minute I can with you,' he said softly.

'What are you going to do for a job, then?' Nellie asked.

'I reckon I might get myself a job at the docks. Or perhaps Uncle Harry might have something for me at his furniture factory?'

'Where our Charlie worked, you mean?' Nellie said slowly.

'That's right.' Christopher swigged his beer. 'I know Harry's never had much time for me in the past but I reckon he'll want to take me on once I'm a respectable family man, don't you?'

'I suppose so, love.' Helen glanced at Nellie. She couldn't tell what she was thinking, but her mother-in-law looked suddenly troubled.

Chapter Thirty-One

Adam Campbell was going home. The evening before, the Lady Almoner had been to visit him and Frannie had filled out his discharge slip, which had been signed by Mr Hobbs the consultant. That morning one of the nurses had cleaned out Adam's locker and packed up his personal belongings, and Frannie had taken his watch and wallet from the safe for him.

'Now, you understand what you've been told about coming back to Outpatients to get that bandage changed, don't you?' she said.

'Yes, Sister,' Adam replied solemnly.

'And you've checked you have all your belongings? We wouldn't want you to leave anything behind.'

'I have everything.' He held up the brown paper package Frannie had made up for him. 'I suppose you'll be glad not to see me again,' he said in a quiet voice.

'Heavens, why on earth should you think that?'

He looked at her ruefully. 'I haven't been the easiest patient, have I?'

'It's been – interesting,' Frannie conceded. 'But we'll miss you.' She smiled kindly at him.

'Will you?' His face brightened for a moment, and Frannie once again caught a glimpse of the lost, lonely little boy beneath his surly exterior.

'Of course. Although I daresay I'll see you at a Peace Society meeting sometime,' she said.

'I daresay you'll see my father before you see me!'

he grinned. Then, with a glance at Frannie's expression, he added, 'Don't worry, Sister, I won't tell anyone! And I'm pleased for you both, honestly. If I'm going to have a stepmother I would rather it was you than anyone else!'

'Mr Campbell!' Frannie glanced around her in dismay to make sure none of her nurses was listening. But inside she couldn't stop the bubble of happiness rising inside her.

She didn't want to allow herself to think that far ahead, but the truth was she had been thinking more and more of what it would be like to spend the rest of her life with John Campbell. And she could tell he was thinking the same.

It was so strange that they should end up together, she reflected. If anyone had told her when she was a girl that she would fall for John Campbell, she would never have believed them. She liked him, but she hardly noticed him.

But then, it was hard to notice anyone else when Matthew was there. His bright dazzling presence cast everyone else into shadow.

Years on, however, Frannie could appreciate John Campbell for the good man that he was. Strangely, she felt as if they were better suited than she and Matthew had ever been. She and John spent their free time at galleries and museums or attending concerts. Matthew had never had any patience for what he scathingly called her 'boring' love of culture. Matthew always had to be the centre of everyone's attention. John was still as quiet as he had always been, but Frannie realised now that he was more thoughtful and considered than shy.

Frannie knew she had fallen in love with him, but it was a deeper, more satisfying feeling than the heady, girlish infatuation she had felt for Matthew. She sometimes wondered what Matthew would have made of them, and whether he would have approved.

'Speak of the devil,' Adam said, nodding towards the doorway. Frannie turned, her heart lifting at the sight of John walking down the ward towards them with a suitcase in his hand.

'Good morning, Major Campbell.' Frannie sought his gaze, smiling.

'Sister.' He shot her a quick glance, then turned to his son. 'Ready to go?' he said gruffly.

'I'll leave you to get changed.' Frannie nodded to a nurse to bring the screens from the other end of the ward, then returned to her desk.

She was called away to help adjust a patient's splint. By the time she returned, Adam was emerging from behind the curtains, leaning heavily on his sticks, his father at his side.

She approached them, smiling. 'All ready? I'll walk you down to the doors. Got to see you safely off the premises,' she said to Adam. 'Hospital rules.'

He looked uncomfortable. 'I was wondering, Sister – would it be possible to call in at Male Surgical on the way? There's someone I want to say goodbye to,' he said shyly.

She gave him a stern look. 'I take it you mean Nurse O'Hara? You know nurses aren't supposed to talk to men, don't you? If Sister Holmes caught her . . .' She saw his disappointed expression and smiled. 'I'm just teasing you. I happen to know Sister Holmes is off duty this morning, so the coast will be clear. I'm sure we can make a quick trip there on the way. As long as you keep an eye out for Staff Nurse Lund,' she warned.

'Thank you, Sister. You're a sport!'

They reached Holmes ward, and Adam limped off to find O'Hara.

'Young love, eh?' Frannie grinned at John. 'I know it's against the rules and I'm meant to discourage it, but I can't help feeling it's rather sweet. I'm just a born romantic, I suppose.' She caught sight of his troubled expression and said, 'You're very quiet today, John. Is everything all right?'

'I have to go away,' he blurted out.

'Where?'

'Wiltshire. I've been ordered down there to help with this compulsory military training they're bringing in.'

Frannie suppressed a shudder. The news that all twenty- and twenty-one-year-old men were to be given six months' compulsory training in weapons and combat had sickened her. But all the young men on the ward seemed very taken with the idea, and couldn't wait to get their hands on a rifle. Everywhere Frannie went, she was driven mad listening to them boasting about how they were going to take on Hitler single-handed.

'How long will you be gone?' she asked.

'I don't know.' John's face was a blank mask. Unease curled in the pit of Frannie's stomach. There was something he wasn't telling her, she was certain of it.

'I suppose you could always come back and visit?' she suggested. 'Or I could come and see you, if I have a free weekend?'

'Perhaps,' he said. 'But I don't know how much free time I'll have. I'll write to you.'

She looked up into his chilly green eyes and understood what he was trying to say to her. But she couldn't quite believe it.

'John?' she could feel her smile wobbling uncertainly. 'Is everything all right?'

'Of course.' He directed the remark over the top of her head, his gaze still fixed in the direction his son had gone.

239

'Are you sure? You seem very – distant.'

'I have a lot on my mind, that's all.'

Frannie looked up at him. His face was closed, his green eyes blank. 'Is there something you're not telling me?' she asked.

He didn't reply at first. Frannie felt her bewilderment turning to anger. 'John, if your feelings for me have changed, then at least have the goodness to tell me to my face,' she said. 'I deserve that at least, don't you think? Coming up with some feeble excuse and then telling me you'll write to me is cowardly, and you and I both know you're hardly a coward.'

He hesitated. 'You're right,' he agreed heavily. 'You do deserve better than that, I'm sorry.' His eyes met hers at last. 'The truth is, this is very difficult for me, because I do have feelings for you. But I don't think we should see each other any more.'

Frannie felt the lump rising in her throat and swallowed it down determinedly.

'And may I ask why?'

John shook his head regretfully. 'I'm a soldier, Frannie. The army is my life and always will be. I don't have room for anyone or anything else.'

Frannie looked into his rigid face. 'I thought you'd learned your lesson after you almost lost Adam?'

'Perhaps it's too late for me to change.'

'Or perhaps you don't want to?'

He flashed a look at her, and Frannie glimpsed something in his unguarded gaze. He wasn't telling her the truth, she was sure of it.

But the next second the shutters were back in place. 'Perhaps you're right,' he conceded.

'Then you're going to be very lonely.'

'It's what I'm used to.' He sent her a wary look. 'I'm

so sorry, Frannie. I should never have let it get this far. But I couldn't help myself. I very much enjoyed your company, perhaps more than I should . . .'

Then don't go, she urged him silently. But she had more pride than to beg.

'It's all right, John, you don't have to look so worried,' she scorned. 'I'm not some lovesick girl, I'm hardly going to scream and rage and dissolve in tears at your feet!'

His mouth twisted in a heartbreaking smile. 'Your anger is no less than I deserve.'

'Well, I shan't give you the satisfaction,' Frannie replied with mock haughtiness.

They looked at each other, and once again Frannie saw the flash of pain in his green eyes. This was hurting him more than he wanted to admit. There was still something he wasn't telling her, but she knew this time she wouldn't be able to get the truth out of him. It was buried too deep.

'Thank you,' he said.

'What for?'

'For giving me the happiest few months I've ever known.'

His voice was thick with emotion, and Frannie felt the sting of tears in her eyes. It doesn't have to end, she wanted to cry out. But deep down she knew it did. She might never understand John's reasons, but she had to trust them.

The man opened his eyes and stared around him. 'Where am I?' he murmured groggily, his voice gruff from the anaesthetic.

Effie leaned towards him. 'You're back on the ward, Mr Bennett. You've had an operation.'

'Operation?' He frowned.

'For your hernia.' She reached for his wrist to check his pulse. Post-operative patients made her nervous. She was always worried they might not wake up, and it would somehow be her fault. But Mr Bennett's colour was good, and he was breathing normally. 'How are you feeling?'

'I – I—' He turned his head towards her. 'I don't feel too clever, Nurse.'

Effie saw the colour drain from his face. 'Oh, wait!' she cried, making a grab for the enamel bowl. But she was too late. Mr Bennett promptly vomited all over her.

'Sorry, Nurse,' he croaked.

'Not to worry, Mr Bennett. I should have been quicker with the bowl.' At least Sister wasn't there to tell her off about it. Sister Holmes liked to make an example of students, and Effie was relieved she and her vomit-stained apron wouldn't be paraded in shame before the other nurses.

She cleaned him up, adjusted the blankets and hot-water bottles around him and made him comfortable, then when he had drifted off back to sleep, she went to find Staff Nurse Lund, to ask if she could go and change her apron.

Mary Lund was a kind, motherly woman. She could be sharp when she wanted to be, but she was nowhere near as prickly as Sister Holmes.

She was in Richard Webster's room as usual. Effie could see Adeline's smirking expression out of the corner of her eye as she explained her predicament to Mary Lund.

'I don't know why you're asking me, you can't very well wander around the ward like that, can you?' the staff nurse sighed. 'Go on, and be quick about it.'

As Staff Nurse Lund left the room, Adeline smiled. 'What a glamorous job you have!'

'Stop teasing Nurse O'Hara,' Richard said. 'I bet you couldn't do her job.'

'I really wouldn't want to!' Adeline shuddered. 'I can't

think of anything worse than spending every day up to my elbows in blood and bedpans.'

'You don't mind looking after me,' Richard pointed out.

'That's different,' Adeline replied, planting a kiss on his cheek. 'I love you.'

And I don't see you doing much looking after him either, Effie thought. Adeline's idea of nursing was sitting by the bed holding his hand and looking pretty. Effie could never imagine someone so exquisite administering an enema or mopping pus out of an infected wound.

'Anyway, you'd better run along and get changed,' Adeline dismissed her, nose wrinkling in disgust. 'I can smell you from—' She stopped speaking abruptly, her gaze fixed on the doorway beyond Effie's shoulder.

Effie turned around. There, just outside the door, leaning heavily on two sticks, was Adam Campbell.

He looked different, dressed in his everyday shirt and trousers. Older, more manly, and very good-looking.

'What are you doing here?' Effie asked.

'I came to say goodbye. I'm going home today.' But he wasn't looking at her as he said it. He was staring at Adeline. Effie was suddenly horribly aware of the comparison between them, her still in her stinking vomit-soaked apron.

There was a moment of tense silence. Then Richard said, 'Hello, who are you?'

'It's no one.' Adeline shot to her feet and hurried to the door, shutting it in Effie and Adam's faces. 'No one we know anyway,' they heard her say through the door.

'Are you sure? I thought I recognised him . . .' Richard's voice was uncertain.

Effie looked back at Adam. He was still staring at the door, a thunderstruck expression on his face. She felt a sudden pang of intense dislike for Adeline.

'So,' said Effie, desperately trying to bring Adam's attention back to her, 'you're going home?'

'Yes.' His reply was distant, his eyes still intent on the door. 'Richard really doesn't remember anything, does he?' he murmured.

'Not yet,' Effie said. 'But I'm sure he will, in time.'

'Poor devil.' Adam shook his head. Effie saw his troubled face and could tell at once the thoughts that were going through his head.

'You mustn't blame yourself,' she said. 'You didn't ask him to get in that car and drive into a wall, did you?'

'I suppose not,' Adam agreed heavily. 'But if only I hadn't told him about being in love with Adeline – it was so selfish of me.'

'Adeline was the selfish one,' Effie insisted firmly. 'You were just trying to put things right.'

He finally shifted his gaze to meet hers, his mouth twisting. 'Why do you always jump to my defence, even when I've been so awful to you?'

'You weren't that awful.' Effie looked down at herself ruefully. 'At least you didn't vomit over me, like some people.'

'True.' He cleared his throat. 'I wanted to see you before I left because I wanted to give you this.' He reached into his pocket and drew out a slim book, which he handed to her.

Effie looked down at the cover. '*Collected Love Poems*,' she said quietly.

'I got my father to bring it in for me. I know you said you didn't pay any attention to poetry at school. I just wanted you to find out what you were missing.'

'Thank you.' Effie did her best to sound cool, but she could feel her face heating up with pleasure.

They stood for a moment, neither of them speaking.

Then she said, 'Was there something else you wanted? Only there'll be murders if Staff Nurse Lund comes along and sees me talking to you.'

'Right. I'd better go, then.' He shifted his weight from one stick to the other, but stayed put in the corridor.

Then, just as Effie was beginning to despair, he suddenly said, 'Actually, there was something else. I wondered if you'd like to go out with me one night?'

Effie stared at him. 'Me? Go out with you?'

He frowned. 'You don't have to look so appalled. Just a simple yes or no would do.'

'No! I mean, no, I wasn't appalled. And yes, I'd love to go out with you.'

'Good.' He smiled. 'I'll arrange it then.'

He walked away slowly. Effie stared after him and was still hugging herself with joy outside Richard Webster's door when Staff Nurse Lund returned and caught her.

'Are you daydreaming, Nurse O'Hara?' she asked.

'No, Staff.' Effie pulled herself together quickly.

'Then why haven't you got changed yet? And why is this door closed?' she demanded, pushing open the door to Richard Webster's room. 'You know we always keep the doors to private rooms open.'

'Yes, Staff. Sorry, Staff.' Effie was so happy she would gladly have taken the blame for anything.

Adam Campbell had given her a book of love poetry, and he'd asked her out! Even she didn't have to sit and ponder what that meant.

She was halfway down the passageway to get changed when Adeline caught up with her.

'What did he want?' she demanded.

'Who?'

'Adam, of course.' Adeline's pretty face was tense with impatience. 'Why was he here? Was he looking for me?'

'As a matter of fact, he was looking for me,' Effie said. 'He wanted to ask me out. On a date.'

'A date? With you?' Adeline looked confused. 'But why?'

'I suppose he must like me,' Effie replied. The pleasure she felt on watching Adeline's face fall was second only to hearing Adam ask her out.

Chapter Thirty-Two

In his time as a medical officer in Casualty, David McKay had seen all manner of injuries. He had picked pieces of grit out of eyes, extracted beads from ears, and once retrieved a hat pin stuck in a woman's enormous buttocks.

But now he faced his toughest challenge – trying to dislodge a quantity of orange peel that was wedged up a small boy's nostrils.

'I don't understand,' he said, perplexed, as they waited for the anaesthetic to take effect. 'How did it all get up there?'

'Saturday morning pictures,' the boy's mother replied with the weary resignation of someone who'd lived through it all before. 'I should know not to give him an orange. He always sticks the peel up there.'

David glanced up and caught Helen's eye across the couch. Her face was poker straight as she aimed the lamp at the boy's nose. But he could see the telltale twinkle in her eyes.

'He's a little bugger for sticking things up his nose,' his mother went on. 'Last year he stuck one of his brother's lead soldiers up there, and we didn't even know until it turned septic.'

'Sounds nasty,' David said. He picked up the nasal speculum. 'Right, let's see what we can do . . .'

As he leaned forward, Helen moved too and he caught the light scent of her hair mingling with the fresh starchy smell of her uniform.

And that was when it all started to go wrong.

It should have been a fairly easy job, and yet somehow David contrived to make a huge mess of it. His hands were shaking so much he dropped the forceps twice. He could feel beads of sweat gathering on his brow as he struggled to extract the piece of orange peel. All the while, the child's poor mother watched him askance. She didn't question him, but her worried glance said it all. She probably though he had delirium tremens.

Finally, after several attempts, he pulled out the last piece of peel.

'There.' He held it up, triumphant.

'Thank the Lord,' the boy's mother breathed. David didn't know which of them was more relieved.

'Try sending him to the pictures with an apple next time,' he called after them, but the woman was already ushering her son out of the consulting room. Helen followed them, closing the door with a quick smile at David.

He sank down on the couch and buried his head in his hands.

'David McKay, you're such a fool,' he murmured. And he wasn't talking about his lack of finesse with a pair of forceps.

What was the matter with him? Jonathan Adler once said David made Helen nervous, but now he was the one who shook like a leaf in her presence.

And he knew why, of course.

He'd been horrified when Jonathan first suggested he might have feelings for her. But slowly he'd realised his friend's assessment was correct.

It wasn't what David wanted. He'd intended to live out his years in the doctors' house as a happy bachelor, enjoying the company of women but never getting close enough to fall for one.

But then Helen Dawson had come along and ruined everything. Right from that first day she'd got under his skin in a way no other woman ever had. Which was why he'd started looking for reasons to reject her.

When he meets the right woman, he'll do the chasing. That's what Esther had said. But the trouble was, when David McKay had met the right woman he'd promptly run a mile.

And by the time he'd given in and accepted that he had feelings for Helen, it was too late. She was engaged to someone else.

In a way it was a relief because it meant he wasn't tempted to make a fool of himself. But in another way it made being close to her quite unbearable.

At the age of thirty-five, David McKay had never lost his heart to someone before and he couldn't say he was enjoying the feeling.

But he was nothing if not practical, and had already worked out what the remedy should be. All he needed was his friend Jonathan Adler's help.

Jonathan was highly amused when David put his idea to him.

'You mean it? You want Esther to introduce you to one of her friends?' His dark eyes gleamed like glass buttons.

'Do you think she'd mind?'

'Mind? I'm sure she'd be delighted. She's been feeling a little under the weather lately, so I'm sure this will be just the pick-me-up she needs.'

'Oh?' David was immediately concerned. 'What's wrong with her?'

'Nothing serious, she's just been a bit tired and rundown. But as I said, finding a woman for you will do her the power of good. You know she's been desperate to get you married off for months.'

'I don't know about being married off!' David laughed. 'I just think it would be good for me to have some female company, that's all.'

'Quite right, too,' Jonathan agreed. 'But I wonder, do you really think it will work?'

'Work?' David frowned.

'I mean, will it be enough to help you get over Helen Dawson?'

David sighed. 'For the last time, I have no feelings for Helen Dawson!'

'Please yourself.' Jonathan sent him a shrewd look. 'But there's got to be some reason for this change of heart. And I'm guessing our esteemed sister has more to do with it than you want to admit!'

Chapter Thirty-Three

On a warm April evening Frannie caught the bus home from Liverpool Street after another disappointing Peace Society meeting. Every week, there seemed to be fewer and fewer people there. They'd made plans for another protest in Hyde Park, but it was as if no one had the heart for it any more.

On the way back to the sisters' home, she thought about calling in at the Porters' Lodge to see if there were any messages for her, then decided against it. After nearly a month, she'd given up expecting to hear from John Campbell. And she had more pride than to go looking for him. He'd made it very clear that anything they might have had between them was over.

Frannie would have liked to see him again, though, just to ask him why it had happened. His sudden rejection had been all the more hurtful and shocking because it was so unexpected. One minute they were growing close, and the next – he was gone. Over the weeks since, Frannie had searched her mind for the reason, but couldn't come up with anything that satisfied her.

At the sisters' home a few of the windows glowed with light, but most were in darkness. The more elderly ward sisters tended to retire to bed early while the younger ones were still out, either together or with their admirers.

Frannie was letting herself into her own little flat when she heard a door open at the other end of the corridor, followed by shuffling footsteps.

'Miss Wallace?' It was supposed to be a whisper, but Veronica Hanley couldn't manage anything quieter than a boom.

She loomed out of the darkness, her tall, square figure blocking out the light from the street lamp outside the window. She hadn't earned the nickname 'Manly Hanley' for nothing.

'Have you heard the news?' she asked.

Frannie paused, her key in the door. 'What news?'

'They're closing down the hospital.'

'April Fool's Day was three weeks ago, Miss Hanley!' Frannie laughed. Then she saw the Assistant Matron's earnest expression. 'Are you serious? Where did you hear that?'

'Miss Trott was telling us about it at supper. If war breaks out, we'll be closing our doors and sending everyone home.'

'Oh, well, that explains it. You know you can't believe anything Miriam Trott says. She's inclined to exaggerate.'

Frannie let herself into the flat and Miss Hanley followed her.

'But it isn't just Miss Trott. It's all round the hospital,' Veronica Hanley insisted. 'I'm surprised you haven't heard about it.'

Frannie looked up into Veronica Hanley's plain, square face, fringed with sensibly short grey hair. Miss Hanley didn't usually allow herself to get upset over nothing.

'There must be some mistake,' Frannie told her. 'Have you spoken to Matron about it?'

Miss Hanley looked uncomfortable. 'I tried to talk to her after supper, but she said I would have to wait until tomorrow morning. To be honest with you, Miss Wallace, I find it very hard to talk to her about anything these days. She's very – distracted.'

Frannie considered this. She hadn't seen much of Kathleen recently, apart from her morning ward rounds. They were supposed to be going to a choral concert together the previous week, but Kathleen had cancelled at the last moment, saying she was too busy.

'I wonder – do you think you could talk to her about this?' Miss Hanley pleaded. 'I know you're a particular friend of hers, so I thought she might discuss it more freely with you.'

'I'm not sure—'

'Please, Miss Wallace? I don't suppose the rumour is true, but it's causing a great deal of consternation among the staff. It would help put all our minds at rest if you could find out for sure.'

'Very well,' she sighed, putting on her coat again. 'I'll go and talk to her now. But you do realise she'll probably laugh at me for coming to her with such a ridiculous idea?'

Miss Hanley smiled nervously. 'I hope so, Miss Wallace,' she said.

But Kathleen Fox wasn't laughing when she opened the door to her flat a short time later. She was wrapped in her dressing gown, her chestnut hair loose around her tired face. She looked as if she'd just woken up.

'Frannie?' she frowned. 'What are you doing here?'

'I'm sorry, were you in bed?'

'No, but I was just about to have a bath. Come in.' Kathleen stood aside to let her into the narrow hallway.

'I'm sorry for disturbing you so late.'

'It's quite all right. What can I do for you?'

Standing there in front of her, Frannie suddenly felt very foolish. 'It's nothing, really. But I've been talking to Miss Hanley . . .'

Kathleen smiled wearily. 'That sounds ominous!'

'She's heard a silly rumour that the hospital might be closing down.' Frannie waited for Kathleen to laugh, but she just stared at her. 'Apparently Miriam Trott has it on good authority from someone, who heard it from someone else – you know how these things go. Anyway, I've been sent to talk to you about it. I know it sounds utterly ridiculous but—'

'It's true,' Kathleen said.

Frannie's mouth fell open. 'What?'

'Nothing's been decided yet, of course. But the Trustees have discussed certain – arrangements, in case of war,' Kathleen confirmed.

Frannie stared at her. This woman wasn't the Kathleen she knew and loved. There was no warmth in her voice at all. She sounded distant, strained.

'You mean it? They're going to shut this place down?'

'I told you, nothing has been decided yet. It may well be that it turns out to be a lot of fuss over nothing.'

But Frannie wasn't listening. 'I can't believe you'd ever agree to such an absurd notion,' she said.

'It's nothing to do with me. It's the Trustees' decision.'

'But you're on the Board of Trustees. You could say something, speak up for us—'

Kathleen's expression faltered for a moment. Then she said, 'I don't want to talk about this tonight. I'm too tired.'

She turned away and walked into the sitting room. Frannie followed her.

'Kath, what's happened to you? Why are you being like this? The most dreadful thing in the world is about to happen, and you don't seem to care at all. What's wrong?'

'Who says it's the most dreadful thing in the world?' Kathleen's voice rose. 'It's just a building, nothing more. Who really cares if it closes down, or if the Germans bomb it to the ground? Some of us have worse things to worry about—'

She stopped herself then, mouth closing like a trap. Frannie took a step closer to her.

'Kath?' she prompted gently. 'Kathleen, you're scaring me. Please tell me what's wrong. What are you so worried about?'

Her friend turned round to face her, and Frannie gasped at the bleak despair in her eyes.

'Oh, Fran, I think I'm dying,' she whispered.

Chapter Thirty-Four

Frannie's legs buckled beneath her and she sank down into the nearest armchair.

'But I don't understand . . . what . . .' Her mind groped for the right words, lost in a fog of panic.

'I've been ill for some time.' Kathleen sounded surprisingly calm. 'I'm in a great deal of pain.' She laid her hand on her abdomen. 'And over the past few months I've been bleeding . . . I tried to ignore it at first, but recently it's got worse. It's been going on for a few months now.'

'A few months?' Frannie stared at her friend, scrabbling around in her mind for an answer, some explanation that would make everything all right.

'It might not be as serious as you think,' she said bracingly. 'Could it be the change? You're about the right age for it, surely?'

Kathleen shook her head. 'I thought of that. But the pain is so bad now, I can scarcely think with it. And then there's this . . .'

She took Frannie's hand and pressed it against her abdomen. Under the folds of her dressing gown, her belly was solid and swollen. It was all Frannie could do not to snatch her hand away in shock.

But Kathleen must have noticed her reaction, because she gave a sad little smile and said, 'You see?'

Frannie withdrew her hand. 'All the same, there are

other explanations,' she insisted. 'You're a nurse yourself, Kath. You know as well as I do that it doesn't have to mean the worst—'

'Fran, I know. I've been through all this before. My mother died of carcinoma of the uterus when I was fifteen. I helped nurse her, so I saw what she went through. It's exactly what I'm going through now.' She wrapped her arms around herself in a gesture of self-protection. 'It happened to her mother, too. The family curse, she always called it. I suppose I've just been waiting for it to happen to me.'

'Then you must see a doctor,' Frannie said, immediately practical.

'No.'

'You don't have to go down to the Sick Bay with the other nurses. If you ring up Mr Cooper, I'm sure he'd—'

'I don't want to see a doctor, Fran.'

Frannie stared at her, bewildered. 'Why not? You can't go on suffering like this, Kathleen. You need to get it sorted out. I would have thought you'd know that, with your history.'

'That's just it. It's because of my history that I know it's already too late.' Her voice was flat.

'You don't know that,' Frannie insisted in her briskest voice, the one she used for chivvying depressed patients. 'Just because your mother couldn't be treated, that doesn't mean you can't be.'

'My mother was treated,' Kathleen said. 'I watched her for three years, undergoing all kinds of treatments, getting weaker and weaker, struggling and hanging on to life. She knew nothing could be done, and so did the doctors. But she did it for us, for my father and brothers and me, because she didn't want to leave us.' She swallowed hard, her throat moving convulsively. 'I know what she went through,' she whispered. 'I used to listen to her crying when she thought none of us could hear. All the treatment did was prolong her suffering. Why should I put myself through all that pain and humiliation?'

Because it would mean you still had a chance! Frannie cried out silently. If it were her, she was sure she would grab every chance she could, cling to every last shred of hope. And yet Kathleen seemed so resigned, as if she'd already surrendered to her fate.

'You won't know for sure until you see the doctor,' Frannie insisted stubbornly.

'Don't you think I've tried?' A spark flared in Kathleen's grey eyes. 'So many times I've picked up the telephone to the Sick Bay. I even tried to talk to Dr McKay once after a Trustees' meeting.'

'So why didn't you?'

'Because I'm scared!'

Frannie stared at her, unnerved. This wasn't the calm, wise Kathleen Fox she had always known. The energetic young Matron, always so full of practical good sense, had been replaced by a terrified middle-aged woman with a pale, drawn face and bitten-down nails.

'But you don't have to be,' Frannie soothed her. 'It might not be as bad as you think, Kath.' Her mind still clung to hope, even if Kathleen's didn't. 'I'll come with you, if you like?'

Kathleen shook her head. 'I can't do it. I'm sorry, Fran, I know you think I'm being silly, but I can't sit there and listen to him saying it.' Her mouth twisted. 'Ridiculous, isn't it? I must have delivered that news to patients' families a hundred times over the years. And yet I can't bear to hear it myself.'

'That's probably why,' Frannie said. Before she'd gone into orthopaedics, she'd worked on a medical ward. She could remember every single time she'd had to comfort a heartbroken husband or wife.

But even while she sympathised with Kathleen, she still couldn't understand why her friend wouldn't want to grab at any shred of hope that was offered to her.

'I can't understand why you'd rather not know,' she said.

'I realise it makes no sense to you, but it's the way I feel. If I'm right and there is – no hope,' Kathleen's voice faltered over the words, 'then I'd rather accept my fate than have to undergo treatment that won't achieve anything.'

'So you'd rather live with no hope at all?'

'If that's the way it is – yes.'

Frannie looked at her friend's calm, martyred face and anger flared inside her. It wasn't Frannie's way just to accept things, and she didn't think it was Kathleen's way either. Frannie had always thought her friend was a fighter, just like her. But now, faced with the biggest fight of her life, Kathleen had let her down.

'This isn't like you, Kath,' she said. 'The woman I know wouldn't be such a coward.'

'A coward? Is that what you think I am?' Kathleen turned on her angrily. 'Do you know what it takes for me to get up every morning and face the world? All I want to do is to run away and hide. But I don't. I put on that uniform and do my ward rounds. I settle the petty disputes between the sisters and reprimand the students for breaking thermometers, and I listen to everyone else telling me their problems when all the time I just want to scream inside . . .'

She put her hands over her face, as if to shut it all out. At once, Frannie's frustration disappeared and she rushed to comfort her. Kathleen was supposed to be her best friend. How could she not have noticed her suffering so much?

'Oh, Kath, I'm so sorry,' she said, gathering her into her arms and stroking her hair, calming her as if she were a child. 'But you're not alone any more. I'm here now. I'll help you.'

In the back of her mind, she still planned to tell the doctors. If Kathleen wouldn't fight this, then Frannie would fight it for her.

But as if Kathleen could read her thoughts, she pulled away and said, 'Promise me you won't tell anyone about this?'

'I—' Frannie tried to lie, but the words wouldn't come out. 'I can't watch you go through this and not do anything to help you,' she said. 'You're my friend, Kath. I – I don't know what I'd do without you.'

'If you're really my friend, then you'll do as I ask.' Kathleen faced her resolutely. Her grey eyes were shadowy hollows, rimmed with red. 'Promise me,' she insisted. 'Promise me you won't say a word to anyone about this?'

Frannie stared at her helplessly. It wasn't in her nature to sit back and do nothing. But it wasn't in her nature to betray a friend either.

'I promise,' she said.

Chapter Thirty-Five

'How do I look?'

Effie did a quick pirouette at the foot of her friend Jess Jago's bed, to show off her new dress.

Jess looked up from the book she was reading and surveyed her through narrowed eyes.

'Like a dog's dinner,' she said finally.

Effie pulled a face. 'I don't know why I asked you.'

'You look lovely,' Devora Kowalski said. She sat cross-legged on her bed, darning some black woollen stockings.

'Thank you.' Effie admired herself in the mirror again. 'I just hope he's worth it,' she murmured.

The dress had cost her a whole week's wages, but it was gorgeous. Daisy printed rayon in the same sky blue as her eyes, with a sweetheart neckline, tiny red buttons down the front and a shirred midriff to show off her waist. Adam had never seen her out of uniform before, and Effie wanted to make a good impression. She'd taken special trouble over her hair, too. It had been torture to tame her cloud of dark curls into soft waves.

'Where's he taking you?' Devora asked.

'I don't know yet. We're meeting outside Great Portland Street Tube station, so it must be something fancy.'

'He's probably taking you to the zoo,' Jess muttered, head still buried in her book.

Effie stared at her, appalled. 'He wouldn't!' She had

borrowed Katie's best calfskin sandals and didn't think her sister would be impressed if they came back covered in dirt and heaven knows what else.

'Of course he wouldn't,' Devora said, shooting a warning look at Jess. 'Maybe he's taking you out to dinner somewhere fancy? Or dancing at the Café de Paris?' she suggested.

Effie looked at her reflection in dismay as she added more lipstick. She loved dancing, but everyone said she had two left feet.

'I doubt if he'll be doing the foxtrot with a newly repaired femur,' Jess reminded them.

'That's true,' Devora said. 'It'll be dinner then. Or the theatre. Or cocktails in the American Bar at the Savoy!'

'How do you know so much about these places?' Effie asked her.

Devora sighed. 'I read the society pages. It's the closest I ever get to a night out.'

As student nurses, none of them had much of a social life. When they weren't working, they were either studying or sleeping. At least Jess had a boyfriend, Sam, who she sometimes went out with. The nearest Effie and Devora ever got to a date was when they went to the pictures with each other.

So far as Effie knew, Devora had never had a boyfriend. But that didn't stop her from being an expert on matters of the heart, thanks to devouring endless advice columns in her women's magazines. She had solemnly advised Effie that a lady should keep a man waiting if she wanted him to be more interested in her. But Effie was so worried Adam wouldn't be interested in her at all, she arrived at the Tube station early.

It was a relief when she saw him crossing the street towards her, leaning heavily on his stick.

He looked her up and down. 'You look very smart.'

'Do you like it?'

'It's very – nice.' He seemed more amused than impressed. 'A bit dressed up for where we're going, though. People don't usually make that much effort.'

'Where are we going exactly?' Effie asked.

'Oh, didn't I tell you? I thought I'd mentioned it. We're going to a poetry recital.'

Effie's heart sank to her calfskin sandals. 'No,' she said. 'You didn't mention it.'

'Yes, it's a very special event. A poet from Madrid has written an epic verse about his experiences in the Spanish Civil War. This is his debut performance.'

'How exciting,' Effie muttered through gritted teeth.

All the way there she thought Adam must be joking. At any moment she expected him to turn around and laugh and say he was taking her to the pictures instead. Or to the theatre, or even just for tea and a bun. Anything but this!

How Jess and Devora would laugh at her, she thought as she seethed with resentment at the back of a stuffy church hall. It was hot and crowded, and Effie could feel her hair wilting and her rayon dress sticking to her perspiring skin.

And all the while the speaker droned on. Effie pretended to study the programme in her lap as her eyelids drooped.

Finally, after what seemed like hours, it was over.

'What did you think?' Adam asked eagerly as they emerged into the fresh air.

'It was – different,' Effie said tactfully.

'It was, wasn't it? He's an inspiration, don't you think? Such power – and such courage.' Adam looked so enthusiastic, Effie wondered if she'd dozed off during the performance and missed something interesting. 'As soon as I found out he was coming to London, I knew I had to see him.' He smiled at her. 'You see? I told you you didn't know what you were missing.'

'I do now,' Effie muttered.

She shouldn't blame him, she told herself. He wanted to do something special for her. It wasn't his fault she couldn't appreciate it.

And Adeline would probably have loved it, she thought.

Adam must have noticed her expression, because his smile faded. 'You didn't really enjoy it, did you?' he said flatly.

He looked so crestfallen, Effie rushed to console him. 'It wasn't that bad. I'm just not used to poetry recitals and suchlike,' she said.

'Of course. I should have thought of that. If you're not used to hearing poetry then it's bound to take you a while to learn to appreciate it.' He smiled sadly. 'I'm sorry,' he said. 'This was supposed to be a nice evening, to thank you for looking after me.'

'We could still have a nice evening,' she said.

'How?' he looked gloomy.

Effie grinned. 'Do you know the American Bar at the Savoy?'

Effie felt very swish, sitting in the stylish bar among the cream of chic, wealthy London society, enjoying her first taste of a dry Martini. A curving, mirror-trimmed bar ran the length of the room, with glass shelves lined with more colourful bottles of spirits than she had ever seen in her life. Reflected in the mirrored walls, they seemed to go on and on for ever.

'This is more like it,' she beamed.

'Is it?' Adam looked around. He still seemed rather unsure of himself, she thought. 'I've never been here before, but I know Adeline and Richard used to come here often . . .'

'Do we have to talk about Adeline?' Effie interrupted him.

'I'm sorry.' He looked shamefaced. 'I am making a mess of this evening, aren't I?' he said ruefully. 'But it's difficult for me not to think about her. I still have feelings for her, you see. Even though it's obvious she felt nothing for me.'

'Perhaps she did . . . in her own way,' Effie said carefully.

His mouth twisted. 'You don't believe that,' he said. 'No, you were right when you said she used me. She never had any feelings for me. She was just bored, that's all.'

Effie twirled an olive around on the end of a cocktail stick. 'I'm sorry, I shouldn't have been so unkind.'

'No, I needed to hear it. I'm grateful to you for your honesty.' He lifted his gaze to meet hers. 'I just wish I hadn't made such a fool of myself, that's all. And more than anything, I wish I hadn't hurt my best friend.'

Effie hesitated, then said, 'What happened . . . on the night of the accident? You've never really told me.' She'd never liked to ask while Adam was in hospital. But now she felt they could speak more openly.

'I decided to tell Richard the truth. He was my best friend. He'd taken me under his wing when I first came to London. He was rich, well connected – he introduced me to lots of his friends. I felt I owed it to him to be honest.'

'About you and Adeline?'

He nodded. 'I fell in love with her from the first moment I met her. She was the most beautiful creature I'd ever seen. But, of course, I didn't do anything about it. As I said, Richard was my best friend. But then he had to go to Scotland for a couple of months on family business, and Adeline and I were left in London on our own, so—'

'So you seduced her?' Effie said. Even though she'd said she didn't want to talk about Adeline, this was more intriguing than one of the torrid stories in Devora's magazines.

Adam smiled. 'Is that what you think of me? A great seducer? I'm sorry to disappoint you, but I'm hardly Rudolph Valentino.' He shook his head. 'It was Adeline who seduced me. Not that I wasn't willing,' he added. 'As I said, I'd loved her from the first moment I saw her. I genuinely believed she'd fallen for me, and that our love was meant to be.'

Effie looked into his green eyes, so sincere and full of emotion. She could imagine how flattering it must have been for Adeline, having someone so devoted to her that he would betray his best friend.

'It was a very passionate affair,' Adam went on. 'I'd never felt like that about anyone in my life, I didn't even know it was possible to feel such an overpowering love for anyone. I knew it was wrong, but I couldn't help my feelings. I was mad with love for her. I knew we were meant to be together.'

Effie sipped her drink, wincing at the sharp taste. 'And so you decided to tell Richard?'

His gaze fell away. 'I had to. I couldn't go on lying to him, it wasn't right. And I thought Adeline wanted to be with me. That's what she told me, or I would never—' He broke off. 'I thought I was doing it for her,' he said. 'I wanted her to tell him, but she said she couldn't bring herself to. I thought if I did, it would save her all that heartache . . . But I suppose the real reason she didn't tell him was because she didn't want to.' Adam's expression was bitter.

He explained then how he'd decided to tell Richard one

night, when they were on their way home from a party. 'We were driving back to London, and we'd both been drinking, and – I don't know, it just seemed like the right time.' Adam shrugged. 'I don't know how I expected him to react, but he went berserk. He put his foot down, started acting like a madman. He kept screaming that if he couldn't have her then neither would I.' He screwed his eyes shut, reliving the moment. 'Poor Richard,' he whispered.

'Not just him,' Effie said. 'You could have been killed too, don't forget.'

'I would have deserved it,' said Adam in a low voice. 'Perhaps it would have been better for everyone if I had died that night.'

'You mustn't talk like that!' Impulsively Effie put out her hand to cover his. He stared down at it for a moment, but didn't take his hand away.

'Why not? I've made a mess of everything, haven't I? My friend nearly died, and the woman I love doesn't even care about me.'

The woman I love. In spite of it all, he still loved Adeline. Effie pulled her hand away. She didn't know why his admission should hurt so much, but it did.

As he took her home, Adam said ruefully, 'I'm sorry if you've had a wasted evening.'

'It wasn't completely wasted,' she assured him. 'I got the chance to show off my dress at the Savoy!'

'You looked very nice.' His eyes met hers for a moment, then he looked away. 'I've made a mess of this too, haven't I? What girl wants to sit listening to me bemoaning my lost love all night?'

'I didn't mind,' Effie said. 'Anyway, I'm prepared to give you another chance.'

His mouth curved. 'That's very generous of you.'

'Isn't it? Only this time I choose where we go.'

He eyed her warily. 'What have you got in mind?'

'Never you mind.' She tapped the side of her nose. 'But wherever it is, it'll be a lot more fun than a poetry recital!'

Chapter Thirty-Six

'You wanted to see me, Matron?'

Kathleen looked up at Gertrude Carrington, sister of Hyde, the Female Chronics ward, standing in the doorway of her office. She glanced at the clock on the wall. Half-past seven on the dot. Trust Sister Hyde to be punctual to the second.

'Yes. Please come in, Sister.'

Gertrude closed the door carefully behind her and crossed the room to stand in front of Kathleen's desk, hands folded in front of her. She was in her sixties, tall, gaunt-framed and utterly fearsome. Her grey hair was drawn back under her starched bonnet, the jaunty bow under her chin a stark contrast to her bony, unsmiling face.

Kathleen picked up her pen in an effort to prevent her hands from shaking. She wasn't looking forward to this. Sister Hyde was one of the old school. She had been at the Nightingale for as long as anyone could remember, and probably several decades before that.

She wasn't going to like what Kathleen had to say. But it had to be done.

She invited her to sit down but Gertrude Carrington dismissed her offer with a stiff, 'I'd rather stand, if you don't mind, Matron. It wouldn't be proper.'

Kathleen smiled. 'As you wish.' She paused for a moment, then said, 'As you have probably heard, the Trustees have put plans in place for the hospital in the event of war – which, unfortunately, seems ever more likely.'

Gertrude Carrington's nostrils flared, but she said nothing. She wasn't going to make this any easier, Kathleen realised.

'We have already made arrangements to transfer the medical school down to Kent, and over the coming months we will be reducing the number of hospital admissions, and closing down wards as and when it is possible to do so,' she went on. 'But as you can imagine, that isn't practical for the Chronic wards.'

Strictly speaking, the Chronic wards were for patients with long-term or terminal conditions. In reality, they were the elderly men and women who had nowhere else to go. Often they were alone in the world, or had been abandoned by their families. They were the forgotten, the confused, the infirm and the weak.

And Sister Hyde protected them with the ferocity of a lioness.

'So what will you do with them, Matron?' Gertrude Carrington's tone was polite, but with an undertone of steel.

'We have decided to disperse them to other hospitals.' Kathleen busied herself consulting her notes so she wouldn't have to meet the older woman's eye. 'So far, we have managed to arrange beds for them at St Agatha's in Sidcup, St Giles in Guildford and – the St Albans Public Assistance Institution.'

There was a lengthy pause. 'The workhouse.' Gertrude Carrington uttered the words through stiff lips. 'You're sending them to the workhouse.'

'Now, Sister Hyde, you know there's no such thing these days,' Kathleen told her briskly. 'These are all perfectly good hospitals, where our patients will be well looked after. And it will be a lot safer for them out of London, if war comes . . .'

She trailed off in the face of Gertrude Carrington's

basilisk stare. Sister Hyde had the power to make Kathleen feel like a foolish probationer again.

'I don't know if you are aware, Matron, but many of the elderly patients on my ward and on Male Chronics grew up in fear and terror of the workhouse. They have lived all their lives in the shadow of it. If you send them there, it could kill them.'

'Very well,' Kathleen said. 'I will find other hospitals.'

'Wherever you send them, the journey will probably kill them anyway,' Gertrude said. 'But then I suppose that would solve your difficulty,' she added in an undertone.

Kathleen put down her pen. 'Sister, please. I'm doing my best.'

'I beg your pardon, Matron, but you're not. If you were doing your best then you would have put an end to this nonsense straight away, instead of letting the Trustees get away with closing the hospital down when there is absolutely no need.'

Kathleen stared at the elderly nurse as she stood before her, ramrod straight in her immaculate grey uniform. 'How dare you take that tone with me!'

'I'm sorry, Matron, but it's about time someone told you the truth. I have spent my whole life caring for these people, and I'm not going to abandon them to an uncertain fate just because some self-important fool of a Trustee tells me I should. And I must say, I'm surprised you don't feel the same,' she added.

I do, Kathleen wanted to shout back. Any other time she might well have stood up to Constance Tremayne and the other Trustees. But not now.

Pain gnawed at her. The aspirin she had taken first thing had failed to dent the urgent stabbing in her belly. She could barely think of anything but the constant, grinding agony.

She held on to her temper. 'This wasn't an easy decision,' she said. 'But the Trustees have to consider the safety of the doctors and nurses who work here—'

'Then ask *them*!' Gertrude cut her off bluntly. 'Ask those doctors and nurses if they would rather be here, saving lives where they belong, or cowering in the countryside praying for it to all be over. Because I know which I'd choose!' She faced Kathleen, her blue-grey eyes full of fire. 'Did you know there has been a hospital on this site for five hundred years? Long before it was ever called the Nightingale, long before Florence Nightingale ever picked up a lamp. It's lived through wars, bombings, fires and God knows what else, and has stood firm through it all. Because we don't run away when things get difficult. We turn around and face them.'

Kathleen winced as pain lanced through her. She gripped the edge of her desk to stop herself from crying out.

'That will be all, Sister,' she said through clenched teeth. She could feel beads of sweat gathering on her upper lip.

But Sister Hyde didn't move. She stood there, towering over Kathleen, looking down at her with icy contempt.

'You know, when you were first appointed Matron everyone thought you were too young and inexperienced,' she said. 'But I saw something in you. I thought you would be good for this place. I thought you would bring fresh ideas, new blood, something to keep it alive for years to come. I never imagined you would be a coward.'

'That will be all!' Kathleen raised her voice above the pain that screamed through her body.

The door closed behind Gertrude Carrington, and Kathleen finally allowed herself to collapse forward, her head in her hands. Behind her, rain fell steadily out of leaden skies, pattering against the window like gravel thrown at the glass.

Sister Hyde was wrong, so wrong. Kathleen loved this hospital, had cherished it for five years. She had shaped it, cared for it, defended it. It was her whole life. How could anyone believe she would want it to disappear?

The pain subsided, washing away like waves receding from a shore, and Kathleen took a moment to catch her breath and reflect. It was the second time recently she'd been called a coward.

Was that really what she was? She'd thought she was being heroic, soldiering on, but now she realised she was running away from her problems.

Perhaps, as Sister Hyde had said, it was time to turn around and face them.

Chapter Thirty-Seven

James Cooper had just finished his rounds on the Gynae ward when Kathleen found him.

'Matron.' He looked up from scrubbing his hands in an enamel bowl, a smile crinkling the corners of his intense blue eyes. He was in his forties, tall, dark and handsome in his expensive pin-stripe suit, with just a touch of rakishness about him. His charm was all the more lethal because he seemed completely unaware of it. 'What a pleasant surprise. I didn't realise you were doing your round this afternoon.'

Kathleen glanced past him to where Sister Wren stood looking very peeved. The ward sister disliked sharing the chief consultant's attention with anyone else during his twice-weekly visits. She also disliked Matron turning up unannounced.

'I was looking for you, Mr Cooper.' Kathleen lowered her voice. 'I wondered if I might have a word with you in private?'

Now she was here, she was already beginning to regret her decision to speak to him. She crossed her fingers in the folds of her black dress, hoping he would say no, he was too busy. If he told her to come back another time she would have the chance to escape . . .

'Of course.' He shook the water from his fingers and reached for the towel a student nurse was holding out for him. 'Come along to my office.'

James Cooper's office was sleek and beautifully furnished, as befitted a consultant of his high standing.

The walls were lined with framed certificates attesting to his qualifications and achievements. Two very comfortable-looking leather armchairs flanked the fireplace. His desk was empty, save for a pristine blotter and a gilt-framed photograph of a beautiful, dark-haired woman. The window gave a fine view over leafy Victoria Park, bathed in brilliant early-summer sunshine.

On the other side of the office was a couch half hidden behind a green hospital screen. Kathleen shuddered, remembering why she was here.

James Cooper closed the door and invited her to take a seat in one of the armchairs, then sat down opposite her.

'What can I do for you, Matron?'

Kathleen clutched her shaking hands together and pressed them into her lap. She took a deep breath to steady herself.

Tell him, the voice inside her head urged. *Just say it and get it over with.*

He waited, his handsome face smiling and composed, blue eyes searching hers. Kathleen opened her mouth to speak, and—

'I wondered if you'd had any thoughts about the evacuation plan yet?' she said.

His face clouded over. 'The evacuation plan?'

'Yes. We – need to start drawing up a schedule of when we can start to send patients home.'

'I see.' His voice lost its warmth. 'I didn't realise it was a matter of such urgency? As far as I know, no one has declared war on anyone yet.'

'Yes, but it's as well to be prepared, don't you think?'

'If you say so. But you'll need to speak to Sister Wren about it, not me,' he dismissed impatiently.

'I will.' Kathleen stood up quickly, and only just stopped herself from yelping with pain.

'Is that all? Mr Cooper asked.

'Yes. Yes, it is.' She clenched her teeth and turned hurriedly for the door. 'Thank you for your time, Mr Cooper.'

Coward. The word echoed around her brain as she cleared the space between the armchair and the door.

'Miss Fox?'

She jumped at the sound of her name. Her hand was already on the door handle, ready to escape. 'Yes?'

'You could have spoken to me about the evacuation plan outside, you know.'

She heard him cross the room to stand behind her. She could smell his cologne, subtle and lemony, as he stood behind her shoulder, but she didn't dare turn round to look at him in case he saw the agony written all over her face. Instead she stared at the hand he'd placed on the door. His nails were well manicured, nothing like her own which were shamefully ragged and bitten-down.

'What do you really want?' he asked.

His voice was so deep and gentle, Kathleen felt herself melt. There was something about his calm presence that reassured her, that actually made her believe he could help.

Without meaning to, she suddenly found herself telling him about her pain.

'I'm sure it's nothing,' she said hastily. 'Just my age, that's all. You expect this kind of thing as you get older, don't you?'

She allowed herself to glance at him, expecting more reassurance. But his face gave nothing away.

'Let's have a look, shall we? If you could undress behind the screen and lie on the couch . . .'

'Oh, no!' Kathleen panicked. 'Surely there's no need for that now?' Her hand was already scrabbling for the doorknob again. 'I'm sure you must be very busy. I can easily come back later . . .'

'There's no time like the present, is there? Besides,' he added with a knowing smile, 'I suspect if I let you get away now, you'll find an excuse not to come back.'

Kathleen's shoulders slumped in defeat. 'You're right,' she said.

'Then let's get on with it, shall we?'

It should have been mortifying to find herself on Mr Cooper's couch, but Kathleen was in so much pain she was past caring. She lay there, biting her lip to stop herself from crying out, staring up at the elaborately corniced ceiling as he examined her. Only once did a whimper escape her as his warm hands pressed her swollen abdomen.

He looked up at her sharply. 'Does that hurt?'

'A little.'

'More than a little, judging by your face.'

Finally, he finished his examination. 'You may get dressed,' he said shortly.

Kathleen uncurled her fingers that had been gripping the edges of the couch and sat up, wincing with the effort. As she dressed, she could hear the splash of running water from the other side of the screens.

'As I said, I'm sure it's nothing serious,' she began, when she'd finished dressing. 'Just my imagination, I expect . . .'

She emerged from behind the screens and looked at James Cooper. She was waiting for him to say she was right, it was nothing to worry about. But his grave face told a different story.

'With your permission, Matron, I would like to operate straight away,' he said.

Chapter Thirty-Eight

Around teatime on 15 May, Dora Riley hobbled into Casualty in the throes of labour.

Nick was with her, carrying her bag in one hand, the other arm protectively around her shoulders.

'She was digging a hole in the backyard for a bloody Anderson shelter when her waters went,' he told Helen grimly. 'I told her not to do it, but would she listen?'

'We needed to get it put in,' Dora protested. 'I thought I might as well get on with it, since I had nothing better to – ooh!' She stopped in her tracks, doubling over.

'Dora?' The colour drained from Nick's face. 'Do something!' he pleaded with Helen.

'I'll fetch Dr McKay.' She turned away, but Dora put out a hand to stop her.

'I'm fine,' she insisted. 'It's just labour pains, that's all. I don't even know why he brought me in.' She shot a dark look at her husband. 'I told him I only need my mum and my nan to help me when the time comes . . .' She stopped talking again, drawing in a sharp breath between her teeth. 'Ooh, that was a bad one.' She tried to smile.

'So is our new maternity department not good enough for you, Nurse Doyle?' Dr McKay approached them, smiling.

'It's Mrs Riley to you, Doctor,' Dora told him primly. 'And I'm sure your maternity department is lovely,' she added. 'It's just I don't want all the bother. My mum had all her babies at home, and so did my nan. I don't see why I shouldn't do the same – ow! That bloody hurt!' she cursed under her breath.

Helen glanced at Nick's helpless expression. He looked as if he was suffering every contraction with his wife.

'Are the pains getting worse?' he asked worriedly.

'No, you fool. It's your hand gripping my arm that's hurting!' Dora tugged herself free. 'You're going to draw blood in a minute, if you're not careful.'

She looked at Helen and they both burst out laughing.

'Just get me home, for gawd's sake,' Dora said. 'I'm having this baby in my own home and my own bed, and that's – aah!' She stopped dead again.

'Those contractions seem to be coming thick and fast,' Dr McKay said. 'I think we'd better check how far along you are, just to be on the safe side.' He nodded to Helen. 'Take Nurse – I mean, Mrs Riley – up to the labour ward, will you? I'll telephone and let them know you're on your way.'

'I'll take her,' Nick offered immediately, but Dr McKay barred his way.

'You're an expectant father today, Mr Riley, not a porter,' he said. He turned to one of the student nurses. 'Nurse Forrest, could you arrange a cup of tea for this young man? And I don't think a spot of brandy would go amiss, either. The way he looks, we may end up admitting him too, in a minute!'

Up in the labour ward, Helen helped Dora undress and get comfortable in bed.

'I really don't want a fuss,' she kept saying. 'Look at me, putting you to all this trouble . . .'

'It's no trouble,' Helen assured her. 'It's what we're here for, remember?'

Dora smiled weakly. Her freckles stood out like dark pinpricks against the milky pallor of her skin.

'Are you nervous?' Helen asked.

'A bit,' Dora admitted. 'But I'm more worried than anything. This wasn't supposed to happen for another three weeks. It will be all right, won't it?' she asked anxiously. 'That the baby's come early, I mean?'

'Of course,' Helen said. 'You know these things never go exactly to time. It will come when it's ready.'

'It's my own stupid fault, digging that hole,' Dora muttered, gnawing at her thumbnail. 'Nick warned me not to do it, but I wouldn't listen. I had to be stubborn . . .'

'You, stubborn? Never!'

Dora looked at her ruefully. 'I'm not the only one. You were the one who walked out on me, remember – ow!' She groped blindly for Helen's hand as another labour pain swept over her.

Helen checked the watch on her bib. 'Dr McKay was right, they're definitely coming quicker now.' She glanced at the door. 'What's keeping my brother, I wonder? Perhaps I should go and check . . .'

'No!' Dora gripped her hand tighter. 'Stay with me – please? I feel better when you're with me.'

Helen gazed into her friend's muddy green eyes. Dora was a proud East End girl, and not the type to ask for help unless she badly needed it.

'Of course I'll stay,' promised Helen. Even if Dr McKay gave her a telling-off for it, she wouldn't abandon her friend.

'Thank you.' Dora smiled gratefully. 'And I'm sorry I stuck my oar in about you and Christopher,' she added in a rush. 'I meant what I said – I am happy for you.'

Helen smiled, the argument that had kept them apart already long forgotten. She was so relieved to have her old friend back. 'Thank you.'

Just at that moment, William swept in. 'What's going on here?' he said, picking up her notes. 'I hear you've been digging trenches?'

'It was an air-raid shelter,' Dora muttered.

'All the same, not a good idea in your condition.' He scanned her notes. 'Let's have a look at you, shall we?'

Still holding her friend's hand, Helen watched a shadow cross William's face as he examined Dora. Her heart sank.

Dora noticed, too. 'What is it?' she demanded. 'What's wrong?'

His brittle smile fooled neither of them. 'Nothing,' he said. 'Just a bit – unusual, that's all.'

Dora turned panicked eyes to Helen. Her fingers tightened, biting into Helen's flesh.

'For God's sake, Doctor, you're forgetting I was a nurse,' Dora said. 'I know when something's wrong, and when it ain't. Just tell me, please!'

William glanced from Dora to Helen and back again. 'Prepare yourself,' he said. 'I think it's twins.'

Five hours later, Winifred and Walter Riley came howling into the world, tiny and utterly perfect, both with intense blue eyes and dark curls like their father.

Helen presented them, washed and wrapped in their knitted shawls, to their proud but stunned parents.

'Blimey, I reckon we're going to have to knit some more matinee jackets!' Dora grinned up at Helen as she took her son in her arms. Her red curls clung damply to her freckled face. She looked tired but happy, and none the worse for her gruelling labour.

'And here's your daughter.' Helen placed little Winifred in Nick's arms.

He stared speechless down at the baby. He didn't have to say anything. His look of stunned pride and love said it all.

Dora caught Helen's eye. 'Reckon there's another girl in my husband's life now!'

'I'll leave you alone for a minute.' Helen hurried away before they could see the tears in her eyes. Not that they would have noticed. They were so wrapped up in themselves and their happiness, they wouldn't have noticed if she'd danced a jig in front of them.

And that was how it should be, thought Helen. They were a perfect family, the four of them together. Those babies would have everything they ever needed, growing up with parents who were so utterly devoted to each other.

That was what she wanted for herself, too. One day, she wanted to have a baby of her own, and to be able to share it with a husband who adored her as much as Nick did Dora.

William was washing his hands in the cleansing area.

'Mother and babies doing well?' he addressed Helen's reflection in the mirror.

'Very well, thank you.'

'How about the father? Has he calmed down? I had the awful feeling he was going to kick the door down and throttle me once Mrs Riley started screaming.'

'He's very happy.'

'Good,' William said. 'Because I for one would hate to see him when he isn't.' He groped for the towel. 'Speaking of happy couples, when are you going to tell Ma and Pa your little secret?' he asked.

Helen sighed. 'Not again, William!'

'Well, you're supposed to be engaged, aren't you? It seems rather rum that you haven't even told your own parents yet. Unless you're having second thoughts?'

'Certainly not,' Helen said, dumping the tray of instruments down and running the taps.

'So why the big secret? I hope you're not going to spring another surprise wedding on them like the last time, are you?'

Helen looked up at him sharply. 'That was hardly my fault, was it?' she snapped. 'Charlie was dying.'

William's smile disappeared. 'No, you're right. I'm sorry, that was uncalled for.'

'Yes, it was. Very.'

She turned her back on him and started washing the instruments. All the time she was aware of her brother watching her expectantly.

'All I'm saying is don't wait too long,' he said. 'You know Mother will take a while to get used to the idea.'

'I daresay she will.' Helen was dreading the idea of telling Constance. Her mother had made no secret of her disapproval when Helen had married Charlie, so heaven only knew what she would say when she found out her daughter was planning to marry his cousin. 'Look, I'll tell them when I'm ready,' she said shortly. 'I thought I might wait until Christopher comes home, then we can tell them together.'

'And when will that be?'

'In a couple of weeks, I think.'

'You think? You mean you aren't counting off the days in your diary?'

She turned to face him, her arms still immersed in hot water. 'What's that supposed to mean?'

'Nothing.' He shrugged. 'You just don't give the impression of a girl who's hopelessly in love, that's all.'

'Yes, well,' she said, turning back to the sink. 'Not everyone is as giddy and romantic as you are.'

William sighed. 'Oh, Helen,' he said. 'If you can't be giddy and romantic when you're in love, when can you be?'

Chapter Thirty-Nine

Frannie was pleased to see her friend looking so well again. The drawn, scared woman was gone, and the smiling, energetic Kathleen Fox was back. Her cheeks bloomed pink and healthy, and her grey eyes sparkled with their usual merriment as she lay against the pillows in her flower-filled room off the Gynae ward.

'It's like a florist's in here!' Frannie laughed, breathing in the heady scent.

'I know. Everyone's been so kind. Even Mrs Tremayne sent me flowers.' She nodded towards a mean little bunch of carnations on the window sill.

'Who are those from?' Frannie asked, admiring an extravagant bouquet of roses, jasmine and lily of the valley.

'Mr Cooper.' A blush rose in Kathleen's cheeks. 'Poor man, I don't know what he must have thought of me, sobbing all over him in his office.'

'I daresay you're not the first,' Frannie said.

'I know, but I'm Matron. I'm supposed to be above that sort of thing.'

'You're also human,' Frannie reminded her.

'All too human, I'm afraid.' Kathleen looked rueful. 'Oh, Fran, I feel so foolish,' she said. 'To think I made so much fuss, thinking I was going to die, when all the time it was only fibroids.'

'You weren't to know. Even Mr Cooper wasn't sure until he operated.'

'I suppose.' But Kathleen didn't look convinced as she

chewed her lip worriedly. 'I still wish I'd sought help sooner instead of getting myself in such a state about it.'

'I did try to tell you.'

'I know,' Kathleen sighed. 'But I wasn't thinking clearly. I'm sorry for losing my temper with you, Fran.'

'You have nothing to apologise for. I'd be just the same in your position. Besides, it's probably me who should be apologising,' she went on with a grin. 'As I recall, I didn't talk to you in quite the way a sister should address a matron!'

'No, but I needed to hear it. You gave me just the kick I needed.' Kathleen paused for a moment, then said, 'Thank you for keeping my secret, too. I know I put you in a difficult position, asking you not to tell anyone about my illness.'

'I'm not sure how long I could have kept my promise,' Frannie admitted. 'I'd already almost broken it by the time you went to see Mr Cooper!'

'I had a feeling you might.'

Kathleen went quiet for a moment, and Frannie saw the troubled look in her grey eyes. 'What is it, Kath?' she asked.

'Nothing. I'm just being silly. It's just – I wish he hadn't had to perform a hysterectomy, that's all.' She gave a sad little smile. 'I know it sounds daft, and there was never any question of my having children at my time of life, but still . . .'

'The chance was always there?' Frannie finished for her.

'I told you it was daft, didn't I?'

'There's nothing daft about it, Kath. I think it's something we all think about from time to time. The life we could have had, if only . . .' She'd certainly been thinking a lot about it herself lately.

As if she knew what Frannie was thinking, Kathleen said, 'You haven't heard from John, then?'

'No, and I don't expect I ever will. John gave me no illusions about that.' She shook her head sadly. 'I just have to accept that it's over and done with. If it ever started in the first place!' she added wryly. It had finished so suddenly, she had begun to wonder if it had all been in her imagination.

'I don't understand it,' Kathleen said. 'He was besotted by you, anyone could see that.'

'Obviously not.' Frannie shook herself. 'Anyway, it's you we're thinking about now,' she said briskly. 'I've brought you some presents . . .'

She unpacked the bag she'd brought for Kathleen, containing books and magazines and some sweets.

'Turkish Delight, your favourite,' she said. 'But don't tell Sister Wren, because they're her favourites, too!'

'You'd better hide them in that case!' Kathleen grinned conspiratorially. 'Or we could eat them now.'

'How are you getting on with Sister Wren?' Frannie asked, as they dived into the box. 'She's specialling you herself, isn't she?'

'Yes, she is. But between you and me, I don't think she enjoys it very much.' Kathleen brushed icing sugar from the front of her nightgown. 'She keeps asking me if I wouldn't be more comfortable in the Sick Bay.'

'I expect you make her nervous.'

'I think she's more cross because she can't hide in her sitting room and read her romance novels in peace! Poor Sister Wren,' sighed Kathleen. 'It must be every ward sister's worst nightmare, having Matron come to stay!'

Once Frannie had gone back to work, Kathleen was soon bored again. It might not have been so bad if she'd been put on the main ward, she thought. But Sister Wren had decided that only a private room was good enough.

Kathleen wasn't sure how she would cope for three weeks staring at the same four walls. It would drive her completely mad, she was sure of it.

Sister Wren was no help. She made sure she visited frequently but was always very brisk, as if determined to show what an efficient nurse she could be. Kathleen would have liked to chat while she succumbed to her not so gentle ministrations, but never had the chance.

Then, in the middle of the afternoon, just as Kathleen was flicking disconsolately through the magazine Frannie had brought her, salvation arrived in a faded pink satin dressing gown.

'All right, love?' A woman stood in the doorway, cigarette in hand. She was pretty but tired-looking, half an inch of dark roots showing through her platinum blonde curls. 'No fun for you, stuck in here on your own, I'll bet. I've just put the kettle on – fancy a cuppa?'

Kathleen stared at her. 'Um – yes. Thank you.'

'Won't be a tick.'

She disappeared. Kathleen was just wondering if she'd imagined it when the woman returned with a cup of tea.

'Here you are, ducks. I'll just put it down here then I'll pull that table up for you – no, don't you do it, love, you don't want to bust your stitches, do you?' She dragged the bed table into place and put the cup down.

Kathleen stared at it. 'You make your own tea?'

'Oh, yes. Us lot that can get up take it in turns. We like to help out where we can, see. And Sister doesn't bother with us, as long as we stay out of her way.' She settled herself down on the edge of Kathleen's bed and pulled her dressing gown tighter around her. 'Besides, it does us good to stretch our legs. Most of us ain't used to sitting on our arses being waited on all day.' She smiled at Kathleen. 'I'm Vera, by the way.'

'Kathleen.'

'Nice to meet you, Kathleen. Fancy a smoke?' She pulled a cigarette packet out of her dressing-gown pocket and offered it to her. Kathleen shook her head.

She watched, dazed, as Vera unhooked the notes from the end of her bed and consulted them. 'What you in here for, Kath? Ooh, fibroids, eh? My sister had them. Painful buggers, they are.' She replaced the notes. 'I might have to have all mine taken away, too,' she announced. 'I've got a weakened womb, so Mr Cooper reckons. Well, I'm not surprised after thirteen kids, are you? The doctor reckons another one could kill me. "Mrs Maloney," he said, "if you have one more child it will be the death of both of us." So I said to him, you'd best sew it all up while you're about it, because that's the only way I'm going to stop my old man having his conjugals!' She cackled with laughter. 'You married, ducks?' she asked , peering at Kathleen through the plume of smoke rising from her cigarette.

Before Kathleen could answer, Sister Wren appeared, looking flustered.

'Mrs Maloney, what are you doing in here?' she demanded in shocked tones.

'Keep your knickers on, Sister, I was just making Kathleen a cup of tea.'

Sister Wren shot Kathleen an anxious glance. 'Really, you know you're not allowed out of bed.'

'But—'

'I can't think what's got into you, I really can't. As if I would ever allow patients to wander the wards willy-nilly, helping themselves to refreshments!' Sister Wren muttered, hastily ushering her towards the door.

Vera turned back to Kathleen. 'I'll pop down again later, love, then we can have a proper chinwag,' she called over Sister Wren's shoulder.

'You'll do no such thing!' Sister Wren mumbled a quick, embarrassed apology to Kathleen before she disappeared.

Kathleen lay back against the pillows and listened to the ward sister and Vera arguing all the way back up the ward. She smiled to herself. Perhaps Wren ward wouldn't be such a dull place after all.

Frannie had just returned to the sisters' home that night after a busy shift when she was met in the doorway by an irate Miss Hanley.

'There you are, Miss Wallace. I'm very glad you're here at last. Someone has just telephoned for you.'

'For me?'

The Assistant Matron nodded. 'And very persistent he was, too. Called four times in the last hour. I told him you wouldn't return until after nine o'clock, but I'm sure he didn't believe me. I was sorely tempted not to answer after the third time.' She looked most put out.

'I'm sorry,' Frannie said absently, but her mind was already racing. 'Who was it?' she asked.

Miss Hanley handed her a piece of paper. 'I've written it all down here. He was most insistent that you should contact him as soon as possible.' She eyed the telephone balefully. 'I expect he'll ring up again in a minute.'

But Frannie wasn't listening. She was staring at John's name and telephone number, written out in Miss Hanley's careful copperplate script.

He answered on the first ring. 'Campbell.'

A thrill went through Frannie when she heard his familiar deep voice again. She took a steadying breath. 'John, it's Frannie.'

'Oh, thank God. I wasn't sure if you were avoiding me.'

I could say the same to you, she thought. 'I must say, I'm surprised to hear from you after all this time.'

She heard his heavy sigh. 'I know – I'm sorry. I tried to stay away, but then I realised I couldn't.'

'Why, John? Why would you want to stay away?' Even though she wanted to, Frannie couldn't keep the hurt out of her voice.

'It's difficult to explain.' There was a long pause, and she could sense him groping for the right words. 'There are things about me . . . things I couldn't tell you.'

Her blood ran cold. 'What sort of things?'

'It's easier if I see you. Then I can explain.' He paused. 'May I see you, Frannie?'

She wanted to say no. She wanted to tell him she'd wasted enough heartache on him. She felt as if she were on the edge of a precipice, about to dive in. She took a deep breath.

'When?'

He sighed with relief. 'Thank you.'

'I'm not making any promises,' she said. 'I just want to know the truth.'

There was a long silence. 'The truth,' he promised. 'All of it.'

Chapter Forty

Very few people ever dared to disagree with a hospital consultant. So when the neuro-spinal expert Mr Masters had decreed that Richard Webster would never get out of bed, would never be able to speak or use his hands again, it didn't occur to anyone to disagree with him.

But Richard Webster had done the unthinkable. He had defied doctor's orders and made an excellent recovery. His memory was still patchy and his speech a little slow, and he had allowed Mr Masters the slim satisfaction of being right about the need for a wheel-chair, but in most other respects he was back to normal. Now, on a warm day in late May, he was ready to go home.

Effie was pleased for him as she packed up the belongings from his locker. But she couldn't help feeling sorry for him, too. He was such a nice young man, and she knew the future wouldn't be easy for him.

Richard was still optimistic about it. 'At least I'm alive, which is more than anyone expected,' he grinned. 'And it's more than I deserve, too, after what I did. I still can't imagine what possessed me to take the car out on such a filthy night. And to be driving so fast, too – it doesn't make any sense to me.' He looked troubled.

'I wouldn't worry about it, darling.' Adeline, as usual, was quick to step in. 'It doesn't matter why it happened, does it? As long as you're getting better.'

'I suppose not. I just wish I could remember, that's all.'

Richard sighed. 'Oh, well, I daresay it will come back to me one day.'

Adeline caught Effie's eye and looked away guiltily. Effie wondered how long she could go on brushing the truth about the accident under the carpet. It seemed very cruel that she was keeping the truth from him just to save herself.

Effie had tried to talk to her about it, but Adeline wouldn't listen.

'You owe it to him to tell him what happened,' Effie had told her. 'If he remembered about the accident, then it might help him remember other things about his life, too.'

'You're wrong,' Adeline insisted. 'It would only upset Richard, and I don't want that. And don't you even think of telling him,' she added, pointing a warning finger at Effie.

'It's not my place to say anything.'

'No, you're right, it isn't. So mind your own business.'

But she'd still been very watchful of Effie, hardly daring to leave her fiancé's side in case the other girl said anything.

Now, as they prepared to leave, Effie could see the relief written all over Adeline's face. No doubt she thought she was safe at last.

Just as they were about to go, Richard turned to Effie and said, 'I've got something for you.'

'For me?'

'To thank you for everything you've done for me.' He handed her a small, velvet-covered box. 'Adeline chose it for me. I hope you like it.'

Inside the box was a necklace, a curious golden-brown striped stone on the end of a delicate chain.

'It's a Tiger's Eye,' Adeline said. 'It's supposed to have special powers, to help you overcome difficult obstacles in life.'

Richard watched Effie closely. 'You do like it, don't you?'

'It's lovely.'

It was beautiful, but there was something slightly repellent about it, too. The oddly shaped stone was too dramatic, not at all the kind of thing Effie would usually wear.

'You must put it on. Here, I'll help you.' Adeline went to fasten it around her neck but Effie took a step back.

'We're not allowed to wear jewellery on the ward,' she said. 'But I'll put it on later, when I go out,' she promised Richard.

At that moment Sister Holmes appeared with a porter to escort them down to the front doors. Effie slipped the necklace into her apron pocket.

As Sister Holmes followed the porter, Adeline paused and turned to Effie.

'I don't suppose we'll be meeting again,' she said coldly.

'I don't suppose we will,' Effie agreed.

'Are you still in touch with Adam?'

It was on the tip of Effie's tongue to tell her it was none of her business, but she couldn't resist boasting. 'As a matter of fact, we're going out this evening.'

'Oh, really? Anywhere nice?'

'We're going to the dog track, to watch the racing.'

Adeline's eyes lit up with amusement. 'The dog track? Gosh, how thrilling. Adam certainly knows how to treat a lady, doesn't he?' Then, before Effie could reply, she said, 'Be sure to give him my love, won't you?'

Effie watched her sauntering off down the passageway after Richard and Sister Holmes. At least this was the last time she would have to see Adeline's superior, smirking face.

And as for remembering her to Adam – well, Adeline had another think coming!

It was a warm early summer evening and Walthamstow Stadium was packed. Adam looked around him warily as they bought their entrance tickets and slipped through the turnstile.

'I'm not sure about this,' he said. 'It doesn't look like a suitable place for a lady.'

Effie gazed around her at the bobbing sea of flat caps. Most of the crowd were men, and some had turned to stare rudely at her.

But she wasn't that easily daunted. 'Don't be silly, we've paid for our tickets now. Let's go and put a bet on.'

It amused her to see how ill at ease Adam was in the jostling crowd. 'Bit different from your posh friends at the poetry reading, isn't it?' she mocked.

'I'm just worried about hurting my leg, that's all,' he told her loftily. 'I'm still not fully healed, you know. I have to be careful.'

'Go on with you. No one's asking you to run after the hare.' Dragging him behind her, she pushed her way to the front rail, overlooking the track. 'We should be able to get a good view from here.'

'How thrilling,' Adam said dryly. Effie glared at him. He sounded like the awful Adeline when he talked like that.

'You just wait,' she promised.

And she was right. As each race went by, Adam grew more and more interested. By the time the last race came round, he was hanging over the rail with her, cheering on the dogs as they streaked past.

'How do you keep winning?' he asked.

She tapped the side of her nose. 'I know a few things

about dogs,' she said. 'My uncle breeds champion grey-hounds back in Killarney.'

He sent her a look that was almost admiring. 'You never cease to surprise me, Effie O'Hara.'

Then came the eighth and final race.

'I like the look of Hard Luck,' Effie said, peering at her race card.

'Are you sure?' Adam said. 'Black Bombshell's the favourite.'

'I don't care, I want to put my money on Hard Luck.'

'Put a penny on each way. It'll be safer.'

She shook her head. 'I'm putting all of it on. To win.'

Adam shook his head. 'You're mad,' he said flatly.

They watched the last race in tense silence. Effie could feel Adam's disapproval coming off him in waves as they stood waiting for the dogs to be released. The electric hare started off, whizzing around the track, and then suddenly the traps opened and the dogs shot out, streaks of brown and black and grey under the stark lights.

Black Bombshell took the lead straight away, leaving the others panting in her wake. Last of all was Hard Luck, a wiry, silver hound with a long, clumsy stride.

'Looks like he's going to live up to his name!' Adam said.

By the time they'd got three-quarters of the way round the track, Black Bombshell was leading easily, and poor Hard Luck was still tripping over his feet.

'Well, that's that, then.' Adam sighed and started to tear up the betting slip. But Effie put out her hand to stop him.

'Wait,' she whispered, her eyes still fixed on the track.

'What's the point? You only have to look at him to see he's—' Adam stopped talking abruptly.

The men around Effie roared as, yards from the finishing line, Hard Luck suddenly found his stride and pushed forward up the field, streaking past the other dogs until he romped home ahead of Black Bombshell.

'What did I tell you?' Without thinking, Effie launched herself into Adam's arms. There was a moment of stunned awkwardness when they both froze, arms around each other, then pulled apart.

'Congratulations,' Adam mumbled, looking away.

Effie couldn't forget the look of panic in his eyes as she'd moved in to embrace him, but she was determined not to let it spoil her evening. She'd had a lovely time, she was two pounds richer thanks to her winnings, and she was so happy being with him.

'Well, did you enjoy it?' she asked as they made their way home on the bus.

'I suppose so,' he admitted grudgingly.

'It was more fun than a poetry recital anyway!'

He sent her a sidelong smile. 'You're a philistine.'

'Yes, but I'm a rich philistine,' she giggled.

'Next time we should choose something we both like,' he suggested.

Effie's eyebrows shot up. 'Next time?'

A blush rose from his shirt collar. 'We might as well, I suppose.' He shrugged. 'But it's not a date,' he told her quickly.

'What is it, then?'

'I don't know.' He looked embarrassed. 'Just friends?'

Effie turned her face towards the window so he wouldn't see her smile. She'd seen the look in his eyes when she'd hugged him.

She just had to be patient, she told herself. She would teach him to love again one day.

As they walked through the darkened streets to the hospital, she wondered whether to tell him about Richard going home. She was reluctant to bring up Adeline's name after they'd had such a lovely evening. But in the end she decided it would be unfair not to tell Adam. He was Richard's friend, after all.

'I'm glad,' was all he said, his voice distant.

'He gave me this – look.' She pulled the necklace from inside her blouse and held the stone up to show him. 'Between you and me, Staff Nurse Lund was livid because she only got a box of chocolates.' She stopped, seeing his grim expression. 'What's the matter?' she asked. 'Don't you like it? I wasn't sure about it at first, but now I think it's quite pretty . . .'

'I gave that to Adeline for her twenty-first birthday,' he said coldly.

'Oh.' Effie stared down at the Tiger's Eye stone. She suddenly wanted to wrench it from her neck and toss it as far as she could.

Adeline had done it deliberately to hurt Adam. Or to keep herself in his thoughts.

'I'll get rid of it,' said Effie, fumbling for the catch.

'No,' Adam said. 'Keep it. If she's given it away, it obviously doesn't mean anything to her.'

Effie glanced at his rigid profile. It might not have meant much to Adeline, but it obviously meant a great deal to him.

Chapter Forty-One

Frannie came out of the train station, stared around the flat Essex landscape shrouded in rain and wondered again what she was doing. She should never have agreed to come. She couldn't imagine why John had dragged her all the way out here.

She'd had a few days to consider her feelings since his unexpected telephone call, but still wasn't sure what to make of it all. She was deeply hurt by his unexpected rejection, but also intrigued enough to want to know what lay behind it.

Which was why, on her half day off, she had come all the way to this odd little village squatting in the middle of damp, unappealing marshland. Frannie had no idea why, but for some reason John seemed to believe that this place would make everything clear to her.

Doubts began to creep up on her again, and she was considering turning around and getting on the next train back to London when a car drew up and John stepped out.

The breath caught in Frannie's throat when she saw him striding towards her in uniform.

'Frannie.' He kept his distance but his green eyes were warm as they fixed on her. 'It's good to see you,' he said quietly.

'That wasn't the impression I got the last time we met,' she said. 'It seemed as if you couldn't wait to get away from me then.'

'I know. I'm sorry.' His gaze fell away from hers. 'You have to believe how hard it was for me to walk away from you like that.'

'So why did you do it?'

He didn't reply at first. Then he said, 'Can we go for a drive? I'd like to show you something.'

The village, such as it was, consisted of nothing more than a few streets straggling around the train station. John drove through it and out into the marshes beyond. Under the darkening, stormy skies the land was flat and uninspiring, miles of glistening purplish-brown stretching out to the horizon, dotted here and there with dismal little cottages.

'Where are we going?' Frannie asked.

'You'll see. It's not far.'

Finally he stopped the car on the edge of a murky-looking lake. Not far from them, further along the waterside, was a dilapidated-looking farmhouse, its whitewashed walls peeling. It was flanked by similarly neglected outbuildings, all built around a filthy yard. It looked as if it hadn't been lived in for years.

John got out of the car and came round to open the door for Frannie. She stepped out, her shoes sinking immediately into the spongy marsh ground. She pulled her hat down over her ears, shivering in the chilly wind that swirled across the flat land. It was as if the heat of the summer had never visited this grim part of the world.

'Where are we?' She tried to stay calm, but her heart was pattering against her ribs. 'It looks like the middle of nowhere.'

'It is, more or less.'

He looked down at her, eyes shaded under the peak of his cap. 'First of all, I wanted to apologise.' His voice was hoarse. 'I should never have walked away from you like that. I knew as soon as I did it that I'd made a mistake. I thought I could stay away from you. But then I realised you meant too much to me.'

'Why did you do it then?' Frannie fought to keep the hurt out of her voice.

He stared across the lake towards the house. 'I haven't been completely honest with you,' he said.

Fear crept up her spine. 'In what way?'

He turned to her. 'You have to understand, I didn't think I would ever see you again,' he said, his eyes pleading for understanding. 'And then when we met in the hospital – I just didn't know what to do. I knew I should tell you the truth, but at the same time I didn't want to lose you. And I knew if you ever found out—'

'John? John, what are you talking about? You're scaring me.'

A loud click behind her made her swing round. In the distance, she saw a man standing in the doorway to the house, a shotgun raised to his shoulder, pointed straight at them.

Frannie let out a cry of panic but John was perfectly calm as he turned slowly to face the gunman.

'For God's sake, put the gun down, you fool,' he called out wearily, his voice echoing across the marsh. 'I've brought someone to see you.'

'John? Is that you?' As the man slowly lowered the gun, Frannie saw his face for the first time. But even though it was clear to her, she still didn't believe it.

'Matthew?' she whispered.

Chapter Forty-Two

'Frannie?'

It was a vision, she thought, as she watched the figure striding out of the mist towards her, gun crooked over his arm. Birds wheeled overhead, their screams breaking the silence. She was imagining it, just as she'd imagined him in her dreams in the weeks and months after the telegram came.

But then he was there, standing in front of her, as real as he was when she'd kissed him goodbye at the railway station.

Matthew scowled at her, then at John. 'You promised,' he muttered. 'No one would ever know, you said.'

'Yes, I promised. And that promise has cost me dear over the years, believe me.' John's face was grim. 'But I'm not going to lie for you any more, Matthew. Frannie needs to know the truth.'

She was hardly listening. Her eyes were fixed on the man she'd loved and lost all those years ago. He was still handsome but had lost weight, his clothes hanging off his bony frame. His dark hair was too long, and his chin shadowed with stubble.

All kinds of emotions rushed through her – anger, hope, bewilderment, disbelief. She felt the ground sinking under her feet, and all at once John's strong hand was at her elbow, holding her up.

'I – I don't understand,' she stammered.

'He can explain everything.' She caught the hard look

John gave Matthew, and read the tension between them. Matthew's face was petulant, just as it always had been when he was forced into doing something he had no inclination for.

Finally, he seemed to relent. 'You'd better come in, then,' Matthew grunted. He turned and started towards the house. Frannie went to follow, but John stood still.

She glanced towards him. 'You're not coming?'

'This is between you two.' He glanced at the house. 'I'll be out here waiting if you need me.'

Frannie gave him one last look then walked slowly towards the house, moving on legs that seemed suddenly unable to support her. This was all so horribly unreal, as if she was floating through a dream. John seemed like the only solid, dependable thing around her, and she fought the desperate urge to cling to him.

Inside, the cottage smelled of damp and neglect. Barely any light permeated the grubby net curtains, filling the room with gloomy shadows. From what Frannie could make out there was one room downstairs, sparsely furnished with a single threadbare armchair beside the range, a kitchen table and two wooden chairs. Over in the corner stood a narrow dresser and an old stone sink.

A mangy-looking mongrel lay in front of the range. He lifted his head to look at Frannie and then let it droop, as if the effort were too much for him.

'Make yourself at home,' Matthew said. 'Sorry about the mess, I wasn't expecting visitors,' he added pointedly.

Frannie sat down at the table. In front of her lay a dirty plate with the congealed remains of a meal, and next to it an empty cigarette packet and an overflowing ashtray.

Matthew went to the range and picked up the kettle. 'Tea?' he offered, then smiled knowingly. 'Although I reckon we could both do with something stronger, don't you?'

He crossed to the dresser and took out a whisky bottle and two glasses. 'I suppose this has all been a bit of a shock?' he threw over his shoulder.

'Yes. Yes, it has.' Shock was putting it mildly. Frannie watched Matthew as he filled their glasses, terrified that if she took her eyes off him even for a moment he would vanish into thin air.

Her dazed mind still couldn't take in the idea that he was alive. For the past twenty years she'd thought about him often, wondering what he might have been like had he lived. But never, ever had she imagined anything like this.

'And I don't suppose John's told you anything?' She shook her head. 'He always was a man of few words, wasn't he? I don't know why he had to open his mouth now,' grumbled Matthew, putting a glass down in front of her. 'He swore to me he wouldn't tell anyone. This has put me in a very awkward position.'

He plonked himself down in the chair opposite hers, full of bad grace. Frannie watched him take a gulp of his drink.

'I thought you were dead,' she whispered through numb lips.

'That was the general idea.'

'But why? Why couldn't you let us know you were alive?'

'I couldn't very well be found after all this time, could I? People might have started asking some very awkward questions.'

'But I don't understand – why did you disappear? Were you injured?'

'Not exactly. Not in my body, anyway. But up here . . .'

303

He tapped his temple. 'Not that that meant anything to them,' he muttered bitterly. 'I was out of my mind with fear, but as long as I could point a rifle, that's all those bastards cared about.'

'So what happened?' Then, suddenly, it dawned on her. 'You ran away,' she said.

He glared at her over the rim of his glass. 'Do stop giving me that disapproving schoolteacher look, Frannie,' he snapped. 'I hated it when we were kids and I still hate it now. Let's just say I did what I had to do to survive.'

'You deserted,' she repeated faintly.

'So what if I did? You don't know what it was like out there. Living in filthy trenches, up to our knees in mud, running alive with fleas and rats. Not being able to sleep at night for fear and cold.' He drained his drink and poured himself another, his hand shaking. 'They all died, you know. Tom, Stephen, the Sowerby boys. One by one, they were all killed. I even saw it happen to little Frank Sowerby. He got caught up on barbed wire. The Germans shot him to pieces as he hung there.'

'Don't.' Frannie winced. She remembered Frank Sowerby sitting in the back pew of the church, shooting peas at the back of the curate's head.

'I know you don't want to hear it, but that's what it was like. I knew it was only going to be a matter of time before I ended up the same way, so I escaped. Who wouldn't, given the chance?' said Matthew defiantly.

Frannie thought of all the young men she'd nursed at the field hospital, men who hadn't run away. 'You would have been shot if you were caught.'

'Yes, but I wasn't, was I?' He smiled, looking pleased with himself. 'I got friendly with some sappers in our platoon, who told me there was a network of disused trenches and tunnels leading right back beyond our supply lines. They reckoned if someone knew the right route, they could get all the way to Calais without being spotted. Or at least, far enough that they could make a decent attempt at escape. I'm surprised no one else did it,' he shrugged.

Frannie picked up her whisky to take a sip, then examined the grimy glass and put it down again.

'And so you ran away,' she murmured. In a way, she couldn't blame him. As a dedicated pacifist, she didn't believe in sending innocent young men to fight. And Matthew painted such a bleak picture, she could imagine anyone being driven to desperation.

Anyone but Matthew. She tried to picture the supremely confident young man she'd known, the one who'd proudly boasted he was going to come home a hero, abandoning his friends and crawling on his belly through the mud to escape.

He must have read her thoughts. 'I don't really give a damn whether you approve or not,' he said, slamming down his glass. 'I'm telling you, I did what I had to do. I should never have been there in the first place. I realised that as soon as I got there. I was too bright for them, too clever,' he said, his dark eyes glittering with defiance. 'I wasn't cannon fodder like our friend John.' Frannie flinched at the cruelty in Matthew's tone, but he went on talking. 'John took to it like a duck to water. He was so dogged, so determined to do his bit. They made him a corporal straight away, did he tell you that? And didn't he feel proud, strutting around with those pips on his shoulder, lording it over the rest of us?' Matthew's mouth thinned in contempt. 'I suppose he was so used to buckling down and following orders in the orphanage, it was second nature to him to kowtow,' he sneered.

Frannie saw the jealousy in his face. She could only imagine what it must have been like for someone like

Matthew, always the leader, suddenly to find himself taking orders from a workhouse boy.

'But you were better than that?'

Matthew was so full of himself he didn't notice her sarcasm. 'Of course. Why should I take orders from someone who was barely fit to clean my boots in civilian life?' He lifted his stubbled chin. 'I should have been an officer,' he said, a whining note in his voice. 'Then perhaps I wouldn't have had to do what I did.'

'Did John know what you were planning?'

Matthew gave a snort of laughter. 'Of course he did. I offered him the chance to come with me. I thought we could escape together, but he was too busy playing the hero to do that.' Angry colour rose in his face. 'He didn't want me to go either. He even threatened to shoot me if I went. But I told him he might as well. I was going to be dead either way, so it didn't matter to me who fired the bullet. In the end he let me go.' His mouth curled, as if he despised John for it.

Frannie stared at him. 'You could have told us you were alive,' she said.

'How could I? I would have had to give myself up.'

'But your mother – it would have meant so much to her to know you were safe.' Poor Alice Sinclair had never recovered after that telegram. She had always been a strong woman, a capable farmer's wife. But after Matthew's loss she seemed simply to fade away. 'You know she died of a broken heart, don't you?'

Matthew looked away, and for the first time she saw a shadow of guilt cross his face. 'You can't blame me for that,' he muttered.

'And what about me? I waited for you.'

'I didn't ask you to. I thought you'd take the hint when I stopped writing to you.'

She stared at him, shocked. 'But we were engaged!'

'Oh, that. I gave you a cheap ring the day before I left for France. Lots of the lads were doing it. I thought it would be fun. To be honest, I thought you might give me something to remember you by in return. Show me what I'd be missing, and all that?' He sent her a meaningful look. 'But of course, being the disapproving schoolmaster's daughter you were, you wouldn't hear of it.'

Frannie cast her mind back to their last night together, when Matthew had given her the ring. She'd chosen to preserve it as a perfect, magical moment, and to push away the memory of the unseemly tussle that had followed, but now it all came back to her, the way he'd clawed at her blouse and tried to put his hand up her skirt. If he hadn't have been so rough and insistent she might have given in to him.

'We were young,' he said. 'I truly thought you'd forget about me and find someone else as soon as you found out I wasn't coming home.'

'I couldn't,' she said. 'I loved you.'

'You don't mean to tell me you've been pining for me all these years?' He sent her a look full of amazement and pity. 'Oh, Frannie! Oh dear, you poor girl.'

She hadn't meant to do it, but all the pent-up tension got the better of her. And when she saw the smirking expression on his face, before she knew what she was doing, she'd hurled the contents of her glass across the table and into his face.

'You're right, I was foolish to wait for you,' she hissed. 'But then, I wasn't waiting for *you*, was I? I was waiting for a hero, not a whining little coward who blames everyone else but himself for his misfortune.'

Matthew sat back, wiping himself dry. 'I think you'd better go, don't you?' he said coldly.

'Oh, believe me. I don't want to stay here a minute longer.' She got to her feet. 'You know, I used to dream about a moment like this,' she said. 'I used to think about what it would be like to find you again. But it was never like this.' She sent him a look of contempt. 'Now I wish you'd stayed a memory rather than find out what kind of a man you've become.'

As she left, he followed her to the door. 'You don't know what it was like for me,' he said. 'You have no idea what it's been like all these years, having to live like this. I should have inherited the farm after my father died, but I couldn't. Instead I've had to live here, in this ghastly little hovel, while my sister and her husband are living in my house and farming my land. I deserve better than this!' he cried, his voice carrying up into the vast, silent sky.

Frannie looked over her shoulder at him, standing in the doorway, self-pitying to the last.

'Don't we all?' she murmured.

John was waiting for her outside, leaning against the car, staring up at the clouds. He saw Frannie and sprang forward to meet her.

'How did it—' he started to say, but Frannie cut him off.

'I want to go home now, please,' she said.

'I'll drive you back to London.'

'No. I just want you to take me back to the station.'

'But we need to talk.'

'I don't want to. Not at the moment.'

They drove to the village without speaking. Frannie stared out of the window at the flat fields rumbling past, lost in her own thoughts. There was so much going on inside her head that she had no room for words.

She was aware of John beside her, but she simply didn't know what to say to him. He had colluded with Matthew all this time, caused so much unhappiness when he could have put an end to it so easily. How had he spent so much time with her and still kept such a secret?

As he pulled up outside the station, John said, 'Will I see you again?'

'I'm not sure.'

'I understand.' She expected him to argue, but he didn't. He sat staring at the steering wheel, looking utterly defeated. 'I'm sorry,' he said hoarsely.

Frannie gave him one last look as she got out of the car. 'So am I,' she sighed.

Chapter Forty-Three

Christopher was coming home from sea at last, and Penny Willard wouldn't stop talking about it.

'When does he arrive? I bet you're looking forward to seeing him again after all this time, aren't you? Imagine him being away for so long. I bet you can't wait.'

'No, I can't.'

Penny frowned at her. 'You don't sound too excited, I must say. I'd be over the moon if it was my Joe coming home.' She nudged Helen. 'I expect you've booked a nice little B and B, haven't you?'

'A B and—' Helen blushed, realising what Penny meant. 'None of your business,' she said shortly. 'Now, have you got that admission paperwork done for Mr Twigg yet? They'll be calling down from the ward in a minute, asking where it is.'

No sooner had she said it than the telephone rang. 'I expect that'll be them now,' Helen said as Penny picked up the receiver.

But it wasn't. Helen was conscious of Dr McKay at her side as Penny took down notes.

'Right . . . yes . . . six years old . . . and how bad are the burns?'

Helen had a sudden, horrible mental image of Christmas Eve. The charred, blackened wounds everywhere she looked, the little girl in the scorched pink party dress, gasping her last breath . . .

Panic washed through her, and suddenly her legs didn't

seem to want to hold her up any more. Helen gripped the edge of the desk.

'Did you say burns?' she whispered, when Penny had hung up the telephone.

Penny nodded. 'Little girl, six years old. Her nightdress caught light on the gas stove, apparently. Luckily they managed to get it off her, but she still has second-degree burns to at least half her body, and some lesser burns to her face.'

Dr McKay took charge. 'Right, get her straight through to the Accident Treatment Room as soon as she arrives. Doesn't sound as if the nightdress will need cutting off, but we'll need tannic compresses and – Sister? Sister, are you listening?'

Helen stared at him. 'I can't do it,' she whispered.

'Of course you can.'

'I – I can't.' She was already backing away. She was conscious of Penny gawping at her, but fear had taken a grip on all her senses and Helen no longer cared.

Outside the insistent clang of the ambulance bell grew louder. Helen glanced fearfully towards the doors.

'Sister, listen to me.' She tried to get away but Dr McKay caught her sleeve, pulling her to him. 'We won't lose this one. Trust me,' he said in a low voice.

Helen whipped round to look at him, dazed that he'd remembered. But she had no time to think about it as the doors crashed open and the ambulance men appeared, carrying a stretcher between them. They were followed by a hysterical young woman, not much older than Helen, a baby in her arms.

'I only turned my back for a second,' she was crying. 'Just for a second to see to the baby. And then when I turned round – you will save her, won't you? You will save her?'

Something about the urgency of the poor young mother's tone shocked Helen back to her senses.

'Nurse Willard, please look after this woman,' she ordered. 'Keep her calm, and give her hot, sweet tea. You might need some blankets, too. She's very pale,' she added in a low voice.

'Yes, Sister.'

Helen put her arm around the trembling woman and guided her into a chair. 'You sit there, love, and wait for me. I'll be out as soon as I can,' she promised.

As she hurried to the Accident Treatment Room, the young mother's imploring cries followed her. 'You will save her, won't you? Promise me you'll save her . . .'

In the Treatment Room, Dr McKay had already administered a shot of morphia and was scrubbing up while he waited for it to take effect. He shot a sideways look at Helen as she set about preparing the tannic-acid compresses. Her hands were shaking so much she could scarcely hold the brown glass bottle still enough to pour it.

'We will save her,' he said softly. 'The burns are extensive, but they're not too deep.'

'Neither were the other girl's.' The child on Christmas Eve had hardly been touched by the flames. And yet she'd still died.

Finally the anaesthetic took effect and Dr McKay set about removing the loose, blistered skin. All the while, Helen watched the child's face, the rise and fall of her chest, waiting . . .

'Her breathing is fine.' Dr McKay looked up briefly, reading Helen's thoughts. 'Clean this area with ether for me, and then start applying the compresses.'

Helen didn't move.

'Sister?'

She stared down at the little girl. 'She's cyanosed,' she whispered.

'Let me see.' He leaned over to look. 'Her colour is perfectly healthy,' he said.

'She's turning blue. Look, why can't you see it?'

'Helen, look at me.' She glanced up in shock at the sound of her Christian name. 'She is breathing normally and her colour is good,' said Dr McKay patiently. His brown eyes were warm over his surgical mask. 'Now, I need you to stay calm and help me. Can you do that?'

His voice was like balm, soothing her. Helen took a deep breath and nodded.

'I'm sorry,' she whispered.

Once she had applied the compresses and the little girl had been splinted to keep her body rigid, Helen set up a saline drip and tucked blankets and hot-water bottles around her to keep her warm.

She was sitting with her in the Recovery Room, trying to coax some sugar water past her lips, when Dr McKay came back in.

'You can't sit there all night, Sister,' he said.

'I know. I just want to wait with her until she's transferred up to the ward.'

'She'll be all right, you know.'

Helen looked at him. 'Will she, Doctor?' she asked. 'Will she do?'

He nodded. 'She will. Sister Parry will look after her.'

The silence lengthened between them. Helen knew she had to say something.

'Thank you,' she whispered.

'What for?'

'For making me do this.' She brushed a pale strand of hair off the little girl's face. 'I was so afraid . . . I didn't think I could . . .'

'It happened to me once,' he said. 'When I was a junior houseman, I lost a patient with a ruptured appendix. From then on, every time a patient presented with any kind of abdominal pain, I couldn't cope with it. I thought my medical career was over before it had begun, but the senior registrar made me deal with every abdominal case that came in from then on. At the time I thought he was the cruellest man in the world but it turned out it was the best thing he could have done for me.'

There was a soft knock on the door and the porter appeared.

'I've come to take the little girl up to Parry.'

A sudden thought struck Helen then, and she looked at her watch. 'Oh, my gosh! I completely forgot. My fiancé came home from sea today and I'm supposed to be at his party.' She jumped to her feet in a panic.

'Mustn't miss that, must you?' Dr McKay said. 'I'll walk out with you.'

It was past nine o'clock, and Penny Willard and the day staff had already gone. A solitary night nurse sat behind the booking-in desk, flicking through a textbook.

The doors opened and a dark-haired woman walked in.

'Can I help you?' Helen started to walk towards her, but Dr McKay stopped her.

'Actually, she's with me,' he said.

'Oh . . . Oh, I beg your pardon.'

Helen watched him going to greet the woman, leaning in to kiss her cheek. For some reason the sight shook her more than she wanted to admit.

Chapter Forty-Four

The party was already in full swing at the Dawsons' house when Helen arrived, late and breathless.

Through the sitting-room window she could see Christopher holding forth in the middle of the room, a glass of beer in his hand, surrounded by a circle of aunties and uncles. He must have been telling one of his stories, by the way they were all roaring with laughter.

Helen paused unseen for a moment to admire him. He looked so handsome, with his reddish fair hair and twinkling smile. It was hard to believe he was really hers.

'Here she is!' Christopher's voice rose above the general merriment as Helen came in. 'I was starting to think you'd stood me up!'

'Sorry I'm late – we had an emergency.' Helen nodded a shy greeting to the aunties and uncles, who all turned to look at her.

'Never mind, you're here now.' He put down his glass and held out his arms to her. 'Come and say hello properly to your old man, then.'

The next moment he'd gathered Helen into his arms and was kissing her long and hard, much to the delight of everyone around them, who whooped and cheered encouragement.

'Chris! Please! Not here.' She pulled away, embarrassed.

'Saving it for me in private, are you?' Christopher chuckled, loud enough for everyone to hear.

Two of the aunties grinned at her, and Helen felt the hot blush rise up her throat.

'How much have you had to drink?' she hissed.

'Listen to that! She's nagging me already and we ain't even wed yet!' Christopher announced to everyone. Helen did her best to smile along with the joke, but privately she was wondering why he had to keep showing off in front of his audience.

'So when is this wedding going to be, then?' Auntie Mabel shouted back. 'You need to give me plenty of notice so I can get me hair done.'

'Go on! What she means is she's got to get her old man's whistle out of the pop shop!' Auntie Midge laughed.

In the middle of the laughter, Christopher turned to Helen. 'I dunno, I'm going to have to ask my fiancée.' He pronounced the word slowly, letting it roll over his tongue. 'Come on, love, don't keep us in suspense. When's the big day?'

Helen felt everyone watching her expectantly. 'Um . . . I'm not sure yet,' she mumbled.

His smile faded to a frown. 'I thought you were going to book the church?'

'Give her a chance, Chris. I expect she's been busy, ain't you, love?' Nellie came to her rescue.

'Maybe she don't really want to marry you after all?' one of the uncles suggested.

Helen saw Christopher's merry expression cloud over, and stepped in quickly.

'Of course we'll be setting the date – as soon as Chris has asked my father's permission,' she said quickly.

'Quite right too.' Auntie Midge and Auntie Mabel nodded their approval. 'Told you she had lovely manners, didn't I?' Auntie Midge said. 'That's how a proper lady gets married – not like us, running off to the register office three months gone!'

The party was exhausting. Helen was already weary after her twelve-hour shift, and even though she did her best to smile and laugh with the others, inside she could only think of going back to the sisters' home and crawling into bed.

It was a stiflingly hot night, too, and she slipped outside into the backyard for some much-needed air. She was so weary she briefly considered leaving by the back gate and heading for the hospital, but she didn't want to disappoint Christopher.

What was the matter with her, she thought as she gazed up at the stars peppering the inky sky? She had just been reunited with the man she loved, the man she was going to marry, and all she could think about was going home.

But it wasn't the reunion she'd been hoping for all these weeks. She'd imagined them alone, walking hand in hand by the river, talking and getting to know each other again. But instead they'd both been tossed into the middle of this party. With so much drinking and singing and laughter and general mayhem going on around them, it wasn't surprising they'd hardly had a chance to say two words to each other.

Chris was different, too. Alone, he was the kind-hearted, charming young man she'd grown to love. But with a few drinks inside him and an audience to please, he turned into a brash, cocky stranger.

It was just the excitement, she told herself. He'd been away at sea for weeks, it was hardly surprising he wanted to kick up his heels and enjoy himself now he was surrounded by his loved ones again. It would all be better when everything had calmed down, and she could have him to herself again.

Raised voices coming from the kitchen made her look round.

'Look, no offence, son, but I'm just not sure about it,' she heard Uncle Harry saying.

'Why not? I'm a good worker, ain't I?' Her ears pricked at the sound of Christopher's voice.

'Oh, you work hard enough, I'll give you that. But it's that temper of yours. The other lads won't put up with it. And I don't want to be sorting out fights in my factory.'

'They put up with me before.'

'Only because you had your cousin to look out for you. Everyone kept away from you out of respect for Charlie. But now he's gone . . .'

'So you ain't going to give me a job, is that it?' Christopher's voice was thick and slurred.

'I can't, son. Why don't you stick to the merchant ships? You got a good thing going there.' Chris must have made some reply she couldn't hear, because Uncle Harry sighed and said, 'Suit yourself, mate. But don't say I didn't warn you.'

Helen stood in the darkness, hugging herself, not sure what to do. She didn't want to walk back into the kitchen because then they'd know she'd been eavesdropping. But she couldn't stand out in the yard all night either.

While she was still trying to make up her mind, the back door opened wider and Chris stumbled out. Helen watched him lighting up a cigarette. The flare of the match briefly illuminated his handsome features.

He looked up sharply as she stepped forward out of the shadows.

'Helen! Jesus, you gave me a fright!' He clutched his heart. 'What you doing out here?'

'Just getting some air.' She looked up at the sky. 'It's a

lovely night, isn't it? So warm. And did you ever see so many stars?'

'I ain't looking at the stars.' He put the cigarette down on an upturned bucket and came over to her. 'I'm glad I've got the chance to be alone with you at last. I've missed you, Helen.'

'I've missed you, too,' she said.

'Come here and show me how much.' He pulled her into his arms and kissed her. His mouth tasted of beer and cigarettes as he kissed her hungrily.

Helen pulled away, laughing nervously. 'Stop it! Someone might see.'

'I don't care.' His eyes glittered in the moonlight. 'I want you, Helen. I've thought about nothing else since I've been away.' He moved closer to her, his face brushing hers. 'I want us to find somewhere, just the two of us. So I can show you how much I love you.'

A nice little B and B. Penny Willard's knowing comment popped into her mind.

'I thought we were going to wait?' Helen said.

'I can't.' His voice was hoarse with longing. 'Jesus, Helen, I've been away at sea for weeks. You can't make me wait any more, it wouldn't be fair!'

As he moved in to kiss her again, there was nothing gentle or sensuous about it. It was as if he wanted to possess her, to prove she was his.

Helen put up her hands to ward him off, pushing against the solid wall of his chest. 'Stop it, Chris. I mean it,' she said.

'You can't keep me at arms' length for ever,' he whispered. 'Charlie might have had the patience of a saint but I'm just a man—'

The mention of Charlie's name was like a bucket of cold water over her, shocking her to her senses.

'Don't,' she snapped, pushing away his hand. Christopher lost his balance and staggered backwards, kicking over the upturned bucket.

'I was only joking!' he protested.

'I don't care. Don't ever talk about Charlie like that.'

'Oh, no, we can't have that, can we? Can't ever take the name of blessed Saint Charlie in vain.' Chris's face twisted, becoming ugly with malice.

'What's going on out here?' Nellie Dawson appeared in the doorway, peering out into the darkness.

'Nothing, Auntie,' Christopher called back, his eyes still fixed coldly on Helen. 'Nothing going on at all.'

The following morning Christopher turned up at the sisters' home, bearing a huge bunch of flowers and with a remorseful expression on his face.

'Helen, I'm sorry, I dunno what came over me, I really don't. It was the drink talking, that's all. You know I'd never force you to do anything you didn't want to do – I love you, you know that. You do understand that, don't you, Helen?' he pleaded. 'And as for all that stuff about Charlie – I'd never say a bad word against him, honest to God. I loved him like a brother, I did. And if I ever thought I'd done anything to hurt him or you—'

'I'm sorry, too,' Helen said. 'You're right, it's unfair of me to make you wait.'

'But I don't mind,' he assured her quickly. 'I'll wait for ever if it's what you want. I just want us to be happy, Helen,' he pleaded.

'So do I,' she said. And so she forgave him, because after a sleepless night facing the prospect of being lonely again, forgiving Chris seemed like the best thing to do. 'I just want to be happy, too,' she said.

'Come here and give us a cuddle, then.'

And so she let him take her in his arms, and they held on to each other fiercely. And Helen fought off the terrible feeling that she was clinging on not to the man she loved, but to a lifebelt in a sea of loneliness.

Chapter Forty-Five

'The coast is clear, Kath – fancy a cuppa?'

Kathleen looked up with a smile as Vera stuck her head round the door. She was joined by Cissy, who'd been admitted two weeks earlier after an ectopic pregnancy.

'Are you sure Sister isn't about?' asked Kathleen, throwing back the bedclothes.

'She's gone off to her sitting room to read her magazines. We won't see her for the rest of the afternoon with any luck!'

Kathleen slid her feet into her slippers, shrugged on her dressing gown and followed the two women to the main ward. After nearly three weeks, they still had no idea who she was, and Kathleen preferred to keep it that way. Once they knew she was Matron, they might treat her differently, and she didn't want that. She enjoyed being one of the girls too much.

As she made her way up the ward, Kathleen caught the eye of Jess Jago, one of the students. She gave her a conspiratorial smile and hurried off to the sluice. Even the young nurses seemed to have forgotten she was Matron. Without her black armour and starched headdress, she was just another woman.

She'd fallen into a comfortable routine with the other patients. Once Sister Wren had gone off to put her feet up, all the women who were well enough would gather together, either in Kathleen's room or around one of the other women's beds, to drink tea, smoke and gossip.

Sometimes they flicked through magazines, sometimes they sewed or knitted. They would comfort each other when they were feeling homesick or they'd had bad news, or give vent if Sister Wren had upset them. But most of the time they found something to laugh about.

Kathleen had learned far more about the women and their lives that she would ever have found out on one of her ward rounds. She discovered that Cissy was married to a coalman, had two young children and lived in Whitechapel. She found out that Vera had had her first baby at sixteen, and almost one a year since then. Ten of them had survived, three had been stillborn and one had died of diphtheria at five years old. She also found out that mousy Mrs Grange, who spent most of her day murmuring over her rosary beads, had been caught by her husband having relations with the milkman.

'You wouldn't credit it, would you?' Vera had whispered. 'It's always the quiet ones, ain't it?'

'Some people will do anything for an extra pint,' Cissy grumbled, then looked around at them blankly when they all cried with laughter.

As she got to know them better, Kathleen was constantly amazed by their resilience. Their lives seemed to be a constant struggle to overcome poverty and to keep their families safe and well. And yet they faced death, disease and everything else life threw at them with smiles on their faces.

But today, as they gathered around Elsie Watson's bed, the conversation turned to the war.

'My son's talking about joining up,' Elsie said mournfully. 'He reckons if he gets in now he'll be able to choose where he goes, instead of waiting to be told when he's called up.'

'My husband's the same,' Cissy sighed. 'He wants to

go in the Navy. Dunno why, he gets sick on the boating lake in Victoria Park! I don't want him to go. I dunno how I'll cope with two kiddies on my own.'

'I wish my old man had bloody well joined up years ago, then maybe I wouldn't have kept having kids!' Vera said.

'It's frightening, though, ain't it?' Elsie said, when they'd stopped laughing. 'Seeing 'em go off like that. Not knowing what'll happen to 'em, whether they'll come back safe.' Her voice was thick with emotion. 'No mother wants that for her son.'

'If this war is as bad as they reckon, there might not be anything to come back to,' another woman, Pauline Farrell, joined in, taking a drag on her cigarette.

'What about you, Kath?' Cissy turned to her. 'You got any loved ones signing up?'

Kathleen shook her head. 'My father and brother were both killed in the last lot.'

'Mine too,' Vera said. 'It's a bloody business, ain't it? Hardly seems fair. They all reckoned it was never going to happen again, and now look at us. At it again. Bloody men never learn.'

Cissy shuddered. 'It's all change, ain't it? I don't like change.'

'Who does?' Elsie said. 'It's horrible, not knowing where we'll be this time next year, or even if we'll be here at all.'

A glum silence fell around the bed. Kathleen considered her own future, too. After sleepwalking through the past few months worrying about her illness, she'd finally woken up to the upheaval going on around her.

Only that morning she'd had a frosty visit from Miss Hanley to tell her that one of the midwives in Maternity had given notice. When Kathleen had mentioned advertising for her replacement, Miss Hanley had said, 'Surely that won't be necessary, since Maternity will be one of the wards closing down?' There had been a reproachful look in her eye when she'd said it.

Now Kathleen looked around at the women on her ward and wondered where on earth they would have their babies in future.

'Still,' Vera said cheerfully, 'we know some things won't change.'

'Like your old man?' Cissy laughed.

'True,' Vera agreed ruefully. 'I expect I'll be in here this time next year, ready to drop another.'

'I thought you were going to have it all taken away?'

'You don't know my husband.' Vera blew a stream of smoke out of the corner of her mouth. 'He only has to look at me and I cop for a kid. I reckon I could get pregnant without anything there.'

'You're a bleeding medical miracle, Vee!' Cissy said.

They laughed. Only Kathleen was silent.

'You all right, Kath?' Vera asked.

'Yes, I'm fine. Just thinking, that's all.'

'You don't want to take any notice of this lot.' Vera grinned at her. 'They're all doom and gloom, but they don't mean it. Nothing's going to change around here. This time next year we'll all still be here, large as life and twice as ugly!'

Kathleen watched Vera as she took another deep drag of her cigarette. If only that were true, she thought.

Chapter Forty-Six

It was barely ten o'clock on a Sunday morning, but already another stiflingly hot day. The sun beat down from a brilliant, cloudless sky on the crowd gathered around Speakers' Corner in Hyde Park to listen to the leader of the Peace Society.

Frannie fanned herself with the pamphlets she was clutching, and longed for some cooling shade. She could feel the sun scorching her skin in spite of the straw hat she wore.

But it wasn't just the heat that was making her feel uncomfortable. The Sunday-morning occasion in Hyde Park was usually a good-natured affair, but today the crowd was growing restless. They were heckling more than usual, Frannie noticed, drowning out the speaker with their booing and catcalls.

'Nazi lover!'

'Get back to Berlin where you belong!'

'You lot are worse than Mosley's bunch!'

Frannie didn't blame them for being hostile. Although she was there to support them, even she didn't agree with the message of the Peace Society any more.

'All I'm saying is that if Hitler is allowed free rein there will be no need for war,' the man on the soapbox was saying, his voice almost drowned out by the jeering around him.

'Let him take over Europe and then he'll leave us alone, is that what you're saying?' someone shouted.

'If it's the choice between war and being left in peace—'

The crowd started jostling around Frannie, knocking her sideways. One man in the crowd shoved another, and the next minute a fight had broken out. As the fists flew, Frannie stepped in to try to sort it out.

'Stop it,' she begged. 'There's no need for this . . .' Then a flailing fist caught her in the side of the head and sent her spinning to the ground.

'Get out of the way! Let me through, damn you!' a loud voice, full of authority, shouted from the back of the crowd. As she lay sprawled on the grass, Frannie was suddenly aware of the crowd parting around her. A man in uniform appeared above her, blocking out the sun.

'Frannie? Are you all right?'

She squinted up at him. 'John?'

Strong hands grasped her, lifting her to her feet. 'For pity's sake, give her some air!' he barked at the crowd, who immediately backed away. John turned to her, his green eyes full of concern. 'Are you hurt?'

'Only my pride.' She brushed dust off her skirt and looked around her. 'And I've lost my hat.'

'Here.' He picked it up off the ground, dusted it down and gave it to her. 'Are you sure you're all right? You're very flushed.'

'It's just the heat.'

'Come on, let's get you out of here.' Taking her elbow, he steered Frannie through the crowd, which parted like the Red Sea before them.

'What are you doing here?' she asked, then couldn't resist adding ruefully, 'You surely haven't come to listen to the Peace Society?'

'Hardly.' He looked contemptuous. 'I came to find you. I went to the hospital but they said it was your day off. I had a feeling you'd be here.'

They had left the crowd far behind and were in a more peaceful part of the park, surrounded by fragrant rose bushes. Couples wandered by arm in arm, and in the distance Frannie could hear the clopping of horses' hooves.

'I've stayed away for as long as I could, but I needed to see you, to explain. Please, Frannie, may we talk?' he asked.

Frannie looked up into his imploring face. She wasn't surprised to see him. She'd been half expecting him since the day she'd left him at the railway station in Essex.

She nodded. 'I suppose so.' Much as she hated to admit it to herself, she had missed him. And now time had abated some of her anger, she was ready to listen to what he had to say.

He smiled with relief. 'Thank you. Shall we walk, or would you prefer to find somewhere to sit?'

They ended up in the café beside the lido. Frannie sipped her iced lemonade and watched the swimmers splashing about in the Serpentine. How she envied them. She could feel the perspiration trickling down inside her flowery summer dress.

'I wasn't sure you'd want to talk to me, or even see me again after what happened,' John began. He sat beside her, his gaze also fixed on the swimmers.

'I'm sorry I stormed off that day,' she said. 'I was rather shocked after everything that happened. I just needed time to think . . .'

'I understand.' He sent her a cautious sideways look. 'But I really wanted a chance to explain, to put my side of the story.'

'I'm listening,' she said.

He paused for a while, and she could see his mind working as he struggled to find the right words.

'I never meant to lie to you, you must understand that,'

he began. 'You're the last person in the world I'd ever want to hurt.' He stared down at his glass. 'When I made my promise to Matthew I never expected to see you again. And then when I did . . .' He paused again, then pressed on. 'It was so difficult for me, hearing you talk about Matthew and realising how much you'd suffered over the years, not knowing what had happened. You don't know how many times I wanted to tell you . . .'

'Why didn't you?'

'How could I? I knew you'd hate me if I told you the truth, and I couldn't bear that. But I also knew I couldn't go on living a lie. It would always be there between us. So I decided the best thing would be for me to leave.'

Out on the lake, two little boys were splashing each other, both shrieking with delight.

'I was so hurt when you did,' she said. 'I didn't know what I'd done wrong. I thought we were getting on so well.'

'We were,' John said earnestly. 'Too well, that was the point. I'd started to – have feelings for you,' he admitted slowly.

'I had feelings for you, too. That's why it hurt so much.'

'I know, and I'm sorry.' He looked wretched. 'But that's why I had to leave. The more I grew to know you, the more guilty I felt at keeping this secret from you. I thought if I walked away, I could put you and everything else behind me.' He smiled reluctantly. 'But as soon as I left I realised it was too late for that. My feelings for you were already too deep. I knew I had to come back and tell you everything. Even if it meant facing the consequences.'

He stared out over the lake. His profile looked as if it had been carved from stone.

'I'm sorry I took you to see him. It was the only way I

could think of to tell you. I wasn't sure you'd believe me otherwise.'

'I don't think I would have,' Frannie admitted.

'It must have been a terrible shock for you, seeing Matthew again after all those years?'

'Yes, it was. That was why I walked away. I needed time to think, to clear my head.' She glanced at him. 'I was angry with you, too, for lying to me.'

'And are you still angry?'

'No.' She didn't even have to think about it, she'd spent so much time reflecting on it already. 'I understand why you did it. You were trying to protect your friend.'

She understood that now, after keeping Kathleen's secret herself.

'I'm not sure Matthew deserved my protection, after what he did,' John said tersely. 'Sometimes I wish I'd just shot him on that battlefield.'

She looked up at him, shading her eyes with her hand. 'Why didn't you?'

He turned his head to face her. 'Because I made a promise to you,' he said. 'I told you I'd look after him.'

A lump rose in her throat, choking her. When she'd said those words to John, on that station platform nearly twenty-five years ago, she'd had no idea that they would change the course of their lives.

'I wasn't sure if I'd ever see Matthew again,' John went on. 'I honestly didn't know what had happened to him after that night. He went missing during an assault we were making on enemy lines. I didn't know if he'd done as he'd threatened and run away, or if he'd been cut down in battle. I thought perhaps he'd changed his mind and stood with the rest of us . . . But then, just after the war, I received a letter from him, asking for help. He'd made it back to England, but he had no money and nowhere to live. He couldn't go back to his family either. He'd lost everything.'

'He only had himself to blame for that,' Frannie said.

John smiled wearily. 'You mustn't judge him too harshly, Fran. That was typical Matthew, he never considered the consequences of his actions.'

He was right, Frannie thought. Even as a boy Matthew was impulsive, always coming up with good ideas, running headlong into things, then losing interest just as quickly. At the time she'd found it exciting. Now she knew better.

'So you decided to help him?'

John nodded. 'I'd bought a little cottage just after the war. At the time I couldn't imagine going back to the army. I thought I might give civilian life a go, maybe try farming my own land instead of working on someone else's.'

'But you gave it to Matthew instead?'

'His need was greater than mine.' John shrugged. 'Shortly after he contacted me, I decided to re-enlist. And Matthew needed somewhere to live, so . . .'

'So you gave up the future you'd planned, for your friend's sake?'

'The idea was that he would work the land for me, as a sort of tenant farmer. But he hadn't quite the enthusiasm for it I'd hoped,' said John dryly.

Frannie thought about Matthew, eaten up with self-pity in his tumbledown cottage, blaming everyone else for his misfortune. He probably hated being so beholden to John, a boy from the workhouse, for his existence.

'He's lucky he had you to protect him,' she said.

John smiled. 'I feel as if I've spent most of my life protecting him.'

That was true, Frannie acknowledged. It had been the same when they were children. Matthew would get into trouble, and John would always take the blame for it. Nothing was ever Matthew's fault.

'Anyway,' he went on, 'I didn't do it for him. I did it for you.' His eyes met hers. 'I kept my promise, Fran,' he said.

And look what it cost us, she thought. She wished she'd never asked John to look after Matthew. He hadn't deserved it.

John was still watching her, his eyes intent. 'Do you hate me?' he asked gruffly. 'Can you ever forgive me for what I did?'

'There's nothing to forgive,' she assured him warmly. 'How can I hate you for being loyal to a friend?'

He let out a sigh of relief. 'Thank you,' he said. 'I was so sure I'd lost you for ever, I hardly dared think I'd see you again. But do you – think there could be a chance for us?' he ventured cautiously.

It was the question Frannie had been dreading, because she didn't know the answer.

'I'm not sure,' she said.

He frowned. 'But you said you forgave me?'

'I do. But this isn't about Matthew. It's about how I feel.' She met his gaze steadily. 'I don't know if we can be together, John,' she told him honestly.

His face fell. 'You don't love me then?'

'Yes, I do.' She was only just beginning to realise how much. 'But that's what makes it so hard for me.'

'I don't understand.'

'It's not you, John. It's this.' Frannie looked at his uniform, her gaze fixed on the gilt buttons glinting in the sun. She'd had a great deal of time to think about what it meant to her. And seeing so many men in uniform on the streets of London had only confirmed her feelings. 'Twenty-five years ago I saw someone off from the station and he never came home. It broke my heart. I don't think I can go through that again,' she said sadly.

'You won't have to.'

'Won't I?' She looked up at him. 'We both know war is coming, and soon. It's everywhere we look now, isn't it? Are you telling me you won't be sent away to fight?'

'I'll resign my commission.'

'John—'

'I mean it, Frannie. I'll leave the army.'

'They wouldn't let you.'

'I only have another two years to go. Besides, I've done my bit for more than twenty years. They can do without me.'

'You can't,' she said wearily. 'You've told me before, the army is your life.'

'You're my life. You and Adam. The army nearly cost me my son, and it's only recently that I've started to get him back. I don't want the same thing to happen to us. And if that means giving it all up for you, then I will.'

Frannie stared at him. He meant it, she had no doubt. But she also knew it would kill him if he had to choose.

'I'm sorry,' she whispered.

His face clouded over. 'So you won't give me a chance?'

'I think it's best if we go our separate ways.'

'Very well, if that's your decision.' She wasn't sure what she'd expected him to do. But she should have known John wasn't the type to argue, or to make a fuss. He rose to his feet, suddenly rigid and formal and every inch an officer. 'I wish you well. I don't suppose our paths will cross again.'

'I don't suppose they will,' she agreed heavily.

'Goodbye, Frannie.' His face was expressionless, but he couldn't keep the hurt out of his eyes.

'Goodbye, John.'

As she watched him walk away from her, so stiff and tall, all her instincts cried out to her to go after him, to stop him walking out of her life for ever. But she forced herself to stay perfectly still.

If it hurt to see him go now, how much worse would it be if she had to see him off to war?

Chapter Forty-Seven

Two weeks into her stint on the Gynae ward, Effie was already beginning to hate it.

It wasn't the patients who got her down. The women on the ward were all lovely, full of fun and laughter and always very appreciative of every little service she did for them.

But Sister Wren was another matter. Nothing Effie did was right, not matter how hard she tried. And instead of taking her quietly to one side and warning her, Sister made a point of humiliating her in the middle of the ward and making her feel useless.

Effie's latest crime was to forget to put a cloth on Matron's supper tray. Miss Fox hadn't even noticed, but Sister Wren had, and she'd reduced Effie to tears in front of all the other patients because of it.

Afterwards, the women had gathered round to comfort her.

'Take no notice of her, ducks. It was only a tray cloth, for heaven's sake.'

'That sister's a bully. She'll get her comeuppance one day, you see if she doesn't.'

'Dry your eyes, love. Here, have a chocolate.'

Effie sniffed back her tears, straightened her shoulders and went back to work, but she kept her eyes fixed on the clock, longing for five o'clock when she went off duty. At least she had a trip to the pictures with Adam to look forward to. They were going to see *Wuthering Heights* at the Rialto for their third date, and Effie had high hopes that watching such torrid romance on the screen might finally make Adam realise he had feelings for her. Third time lucky, didn't they say? If not, at least she had Laurence Olivier as handsome Heathcliff to gaze at.

She arrived early at the cinema to queue for tickets, but as the clock ticked and the minutes passed, Adam didn't come. The doors opened and the queue began to shuffle forward. Effie looked up and down the street, but still there was no sign of him.

She left the queue and allowed everyone to file past her while she waited for Adam. Even when the 'House Full' sign went up and the doors closed, he still hadn't come.

'Been stood up, love?' The commissionaire in his smart gold-trimmed burgundy uniform smiled sympathetically at her.

'I don't understand it,' Effie said. 'He's usually on time.'

'I'd give him a piece of my mind, if I were you.'

Effie didn't want to give Adam a piece of her mind, but she was worried. It really wasn't like him to let her down. There had to be a good reason why he was late.

Once she started to think about it, her imagination conjured up all kinds of possibilities. What if he was trapped somewhere and couldn't get out? What if he'd had another accident? What if he was dead?

The thoughts circled around and around in her head until Effie knew she wouldn't rest until she found out for sure. Scrabbling around in the bottom of her purse, she found enough loose change for the bus fare to his lodgings in Pimlico.

By the time she'd knocked on the door of the tall, white-pillared house where Adam lived, Effie's thoughts were racing nineteen to the dozen. She didn't know whether to laugh or cry when he answered it.

'Effie!' He looked surprised to see her. 'What are you doing here?'

'We were supposed to be going to the pictures, remember?'

His hand flew to his mouth. 'Oh, God, I'm so sorry.'

'So you should be. I stood waiting for you for half an hour.' She planted her hands on her hips. 'Well? You'd better have a good excuse, Adam Campbell.'

She saw the uncomfortable expression flit across his face and instantly knew why he hadn't come. A prickle of unease inched its way up her spine.

'It's Adeline, isn't it?' she said flatly. 'She's here.'

He stared at her in astonishment. 'How did you know?'

'Never mind,' she dismissed the question. 'What's she doing here?'

'She turned up a couple of hours ago, in tears. Richard's memory came back this morning. He suddenly recalled everything – including what led up to the accident.'

'No!'

'He lost his temper with her, accused her of all sorts, practically threw her out on the street. So of course she came here. She was so upset, I couldn't very well send her away, could I?'

Couldn't you? Effie thought. 'I waited for you at the pictures,' she said in a small voice.

'I'm sorry. I completely lost track of time.'

I'm sure you did, Effie thought. She could imagine Adam being so entranced by Adeline's return that he'd forgotten everything else.

'Where is she now?'

'In my room.' He nodded to a door off the main hall. 'I've spent all afternoon comforting her. She's utterly distraught, poor girl.'

337

'I bet she is,' Effie said coldly.

He looked defensive. 'I've said I'm sorry for standing you up. But this was an emergency, you must see that?'

'You mean Adeline snaps her fingers and you come running like a lovesick puppy?'

His face clouded. 'It's not like that. She's a friend, naturally I wanted to help.'

'Yes, I bet you couldn't wait to be her knight in shining armour.' Effie couldn't keep the bitterness out of her voice.

'Well, if you're going to be like that—'

'Who is it, Adam?' Adeline's light voice, with its delicate hint of an accent, drifted down the hallway. Before he could make a move to stop her, Effie barged past and followed the sound.

In Adam's sitting room, the last apricot rays of evening sun flooded in through the tall windows, falling like a spotlight around Adeline Moreau.

She sat on the couch, a handkerchief pressed prettily to her eyes. When she saw Effie, her face fell. 'Oh. It's you.'

'We were supposed to meet,' Adam blurted out an explanation. 'I didn't turn up, and so Effie came to find me.'

'I see. I'm sorry,' Adeline said. But Effie was sure she caught a glint of satisfaction in those dark almond-shaped eyes. 'Oh, Adam, I know I'm being the most dreadful nuisance,' she sighed. 'But truly, this was the only place I could think of to come,' she whimpered, her lips trembling. 'I – I didn't know what else to do. I walked the streets for hours . . .'

She looked very well turned out for someone who had spent hours walking the streets, Effie thought. Her flowery dress was fresh and pretty, and her blonde hair artfully waved. Her make-up was suspiciously unsmudged, too.

'You did the right thing, coming here,' he said stoutly.

'Did I? Are you sure? I know I don't deserve your kindness, after what happened—'

'That doesn't matter.' Adam pushed past Effie and sat down beside Adeline. His arm went protectively around her shoulders. 'You know you can stay here for as long as you like.'

'Oh, well, that's very kind . . .'

'I'm sure Adeline wouldn't want to impose on you,' Effie said quickly, before the other woman had had time to finish her sentence. 'Surely you have family you'd rather stay with? Or a hotel?'

'Her family is in France, and she's not staying in a hotel. Not when she's in such a state,' Adam said firmly.

'No, Effie's right.' Adeline sniffed, dabbing invisible tears away from her eyes. 'I shouldn't be here. I'll go . . .'

'Don't be silly.'

She turned her limpid dark eyes towards him. 'Oh, Adam, you're so kind,' she sighed.

Effie watched them gazing adoringly into each other's eyes. 'I suppose I'd better be the one to go,' she mumbled, but neither of them seemed to notice.

She was halfway to the front door when Adam caught up with her. 'Where are you going?'

'Back to the hospital. Three's a crowd, don't they say? Besides, I expect you and your girlfriend have a lot of catching up to do.'

'Don't be like that.'

'How am I supposed to be? I—' Effie stopped herself in time. *I love you*, she had been going to say. But even she had more pride than that.

'What?'

'I just don't know how you could take her back, that's all. After everything she did to you. Or have you forgotten that?'

He glanced away. 'Of course not.'

'Can't you see why she's doing this, Adam? Richard doesn't want her any more, so she's trying to worm her way back in with you.'

'She wouldn't do that.'

'Of course she wouldn't. Because she's such a paragon of virtue, isn't she? Oh, wake up, Adam! You think you're so clever, but you have no idea when it comes to women. She used you before, and she's using you again. Anyone can see that.'

'It's not like that. Adeline isn't like that,' he insisted stoutly.

'Suit yourself. Just don't come crying to me when she lets you down again.'

As she turned to go, he said, 'You can't help who you fall in love with, Effie.'

No, she thought. No, you can't, can you?

She walked out of the door, proud of herself for not looking back.

'You're early.' Jess looked surprised when she came off duty just after nine o'clock and found Effie already in bed. 'I thought you'd be in the back row of the pictures with your boyfriend by now.'

After sobbing into her pillow for nearly an hour, Effie had washed her face and convinced herself that she could finally speak without crying. But as soon as she tried, the lump rose in her throat, choking her, and before she knew what was happening tears were spilling down her cheeks again.

Jess was at her side in a moment, sitting on the edge of her bed, arms round her.

'Oh, love, what is it? What's happened?'

'It – it's Adeline. She – she's come b-back.' Sobs

shuddered through Effie's body as she struggled to get her story out. Jess listened, her pretty face creased in sympathy.

'You mean to tell me he just stood you up without a by your leave – for that awful woman?' she said in disbelief.

'He didn't feel he had any choice,' Effie defended him, wiping her eyes on her sleeve. 'She just turned up on his doorstep, with nowhere else to go . . .'

'Of course he had a choice!' Jess snapped. 'He could have sent her packing. That's what he should have done.'

'He could never do that. He's too in love with her.' Effie had seen it, written all over Adam's besotted face when he looked at Adeline. He looked like a man who'd just woken up from a bad dream.

'Then he's a fool and you're better off without him,' Jess declared. She stood up and started unpinning her cap.

Effie watched her friend. She didn't feel better off. She'd only left Adam's lodgings two hours before, and already she was beginning to miss him dreadfully.

'I don't blame him,' she said mournfully. 'Adeline is so beautiful and sophisticated. Why would he ever want someone like me when he could have her?'

'You mustn't talk like that,' Jess said, through a mouthful of hairpins. 'You're a lovely girl and far too good for him.'

'No, I'm not good enough.' Effie picked up the poetry book, which had lain abandoned on her nightstand ever since Adam had given it to her. 'I'm not nearly clever or cultured enough for him.'

'Well, if he feels like that then he ain't worth bothering about,' Jess declared.

But Effie wasn't listening. She was already flicking through the book, her eyes searching the pages as if they somehow held the answer to all her problems.

Jess stopped in the middle of unfastening her collar studs. 'What are you doing?' she asked.

'Improving my mind,' Effie replied, not looking up. 'If being more like Adeline will make him fall in love with me, then that's what I'll do.'

She heard Jess sigh. 'O'Hara, you're not serious? Why on earth should you try to change yourself for someone who isn't even worth it?'

That's just it, Effie thought. He is worth it. And next time she met Adam Campbell, she would be ready for him.

Chapter Forty-Eight

Veronica Hanley had never had much sympathy for the 'new' Matron, as she still insisted on calling her after five years.

It wasn't that she disliked her personally, although in Veronica's opinion Kathleen Fox was too young, too inexperienced and far too frivolous to make a good Matron.

The main reason she didn't approve was because she didn't feel Kathleen Fox was right for the hospital. She had replaced the old Matron, a very worthy woman who had presided over the Nightingale since Queen Victoria's Diamond Jubilee. Veronica had served as her Assistant Matron for the last five years of her tenure, and she'd very much hoped that she might be given the chance to continue her good work after the old lady retired.

Except the Board of Trustees had decided in their infinite wisdom to appoint Kathleen Fox instead.

'A breath of fresh air,' they called her. A load of nonsense, in Veronica's opinion. Change for change's sake. What's more, Miss Fox wasn't even Nightingale-trained. How on earth could a woman who had received her training in the north of England ever hope to maintain the high standards of the hospital Veronica was so proud to call her own?

But much as she hated to admit it, some of the changes the new Matron had brought about were for the better. Veronica didn't approve of everything, of course. Miss Fox was far too soft, and she lacked the necessary gravitas of a good Matron. And the traditions of the Nightingale would never mean as much to her as they did to those who had been trained in its ways. But generally speaking Miss Fox hadn't been quite the unmitigated disaster Veronica had expected. Especially with her Assistant Matron by her side to guide and advise her.

Until now. She had never been more disappointed with Miss Fox than she was when she discovered the hospital was going to close – and that Matron had allowed it to happen.

Now, Veronica sat as Acting Matron in the Board of Trustees meeting, her heart in her stout black shoes, and listened to them making plans to dismantle the hospital – her hospital, the place that had been her home since she was a young student.

It was all she could do to stop herself shedding tears. But she knew her poor departed father, a colonel in the Indian Army, would never have forgiven her if she had allowed her stiff upper lip to tremble for a moment.

Instead, she concentrated all her emotions on disliking Constance Tremayne. She was the worst of them all. The other Trustees were well-meaning enough, but quite useless. It was Mrs Tremayne who wielded all the power.

And she had betrayed Veronica.

To think she had once admired Mrs Tremayne for her forthright manner and her determination to see things done properly. Constance had once been Veronica's biggest ally. She hadn't wanted Kathleen Fox appointed as Matron either, but for once she had been outvoted by her fellow Trustees. Both she and Veronica had been most disgruntled about it, and even though Veronica didn't like to admit it now, they had conspired to make life as difficult as possible for the new Matron. It filled Veronica Hanley with shame to remember how spiteful she'd been.

But now . . . Mrs Tremayne had bitterly disappointed

her. How could she do this? How could she sit there, so smug and self-satisfied, while everything they had worked for for years was taken apart around their ears?

The medical school was moving down to Kent. The wards were to be closed down, the poor Chronics were being scattered to the four winds, and everyone else had to fend for themselves. The nurses' Preliminary Training School was moving to Kent, too. But Veronica had just learned they would not be taking on any more probationers if and when the war started.

'No more probationers?' she'd said aloud, startling herself and the rest of the Trustees. 'But however will we manage?'

'We'll hardly need them, since there won't be a hospital for them to train in,' Constance Tremayne pointed out, slowly and carefully, as if she were addressing an idiot.

There won't be a hospital . . .

Veronica stared at Mrs Tremayne's thin lips moving. How could she say it so matter-of-factly?

Mrs Tremayne had turned back to the others and was speaking again.

'Excuse me, Mrs Tremayne?' Veronica raised her voice, interrupting her.

Mrs Tremayne turned to her with a strained smile. 'Yes, Miss Hanley?'

'What about the staff?' Veronica asked.

Mrs Tremayne looked at her blankly. 'What about them?'

'Surely they will have to go somewhere too?'

'I assume they will find positions elsewhere,' Mrs Tremayne dismissed the question briskly. 'Now, if we could move on to the next item . . .'

'And what about the ones who can't?'

Mrs Tremayne frowned, not trying to hide her irritation. 'I don't know what you mean,' she said.

345

'Several of the staff are past retirement age, or close to it.' She thought of her friend Agatha Sutton, the Home Sister, and Florence Parker, the Sister Tutor. How would they manage without any girls to look after?

'Then they will retire, I imagine,' Mrs Tremayne said, with a touch of impatience in her voice.

'But how? They don't have homes or families to look after them.'

'I don't know, do I? Really, Miss Hanley, this isn't our concern,' she dismissed.

'Isn't it? Well, it should be.'

Mrs Tremayne looked at her, startled. 'I beg your pardon?'

'These are proud, elderly women who have known nothing but nursing all their lives. They've sacrificed homes and families of their own so they could serve their hospital.'

Reginald Collins, another of the Trustees, cleared his throat. 'You never know, it might not come to that,' he said.

Veronica stared at him. Feeble little man, with his thinning hair and milky-white hands that had never done a proper day's work in their life.

'Of course it will come to that,' she retorted. 'There is going to be a war, you can be sure of it.'

'At least we agree on something,' Mrs Tremayne murmured under her breath.

'But you don't win a war by beating a retreat,' Veronica continued firmly. Her father the colonel would have scorned such tactics.

'Miss Hanley, may I remind you we're not fighting this war?' Mrs Tremayne snapped. 'This is a hospital, not an army barracks! The war has nothing to do with us.'

'That's where you're wrong,' she said. 'This war, if it

happens, will not just be fought by our soldiers at the front. It will be fought here, on our streets and in our homes. And every time we panic, or shut up shop, or close our doors, we are sending out a message, not just to the enemy, but to everyone around us, that there is something to fear.'

'Miss Hanley is quite right.'

Veronica looked up. Kathleen Fox stood in the doorway, proud and tall in her stark black uniform. Her face was almost as pale as the starched white linen headdress that framed it.

'Matron, what a surprise.' Constance Tremayne's voice was falsely bright. 'But surely you're supposed to be resting?'

'I had to come,' Miss Fox said. 'I need to address the Trustees on a matter of great importance.'

'Is it on the agenda?' Malcolm Eaton addressed the paper in front of him.

'It's about the hospital closure.'

Veronica heard Mrs Tremayne's stifled sigh. 'What about it?'

'It must not be allowed to happen.' Miss Fox's imperious gaze swept the table. Veronica was suddenly reminded of a statue of Boadicea she'd once seen. 'The Nightingale must not close.'

Veronica wondered if she'd heard correctly. And she wasn't the only one, judging by the stunned expressions all around her.

'But it's been decided,' Mrs Tremayne said through taut lips. 'You were all in favour, as I recall?'

'I'll admit I was,' Miss Fox conceded. 'But I was unwell at the time, and that clouded my judgement.'

'Nevertheless . . .'

'Nevertheless, I've had time to reflect on my decision

347

since then. And I've realised we are in danger of making a grave mistake.'

Her footsteps faltered slightly as she approached the table, and Malcolm Eaton gallantly offered her his chair. Mrs Tremayne didn't move, Veronica noticed. She sat rigid and upright, regarding Miss Fox through narrowed eyes.

'And may I ask what's brought you to this shattering conclusion?' she asked.

Kathleen Fox took a moment, gathering her thoughts. 'As you know, during my recent illness I've been spending time in a ward, and it's given me the chance to get to know many of the patients very well. I've come to realise how much this hospital means to them,' she said. Mrs Tremayne rolled her eyes but said nothing. 'This isn't just a building, it's a beacon to them. A place they've known all their lives, somewhere they trust.'

'Hear, hear,' Veronica mumbled gruffly.

'There are other hospitals,' Mrs Tremayne put in briskly.

'Not like this one,' Kathleen Fox said. 'Look at it from their point of view, Mrs Tremayne,' she appealed. 'These people are facing great changes in their lives. They're likely to be seeing their loved ones sent off to fight soon, and won't know if they'll ever return. One day the people we serve may even lose their homes, all their worldly possessions. They need something they can rely on. They need us,' she urged.

Veronica felt dampness on her cheeks, and was mortified to realise tears were sliding down her face.

Even Mrs Tremayne seemed slightly moved. She cleared her throat. 'That's all very well,' she said, pulling herself together, 'but we have to think of the staff. We can't very well make them stay, can we?'

'Have you asked them if they want to stay?' Kathleen asked her.

'Well, no, but obviously no one would want to put themselves in danger.' She abruptly stopped talking as Kathleen raised her hand.

'If you'll excuse me a moment?' she said. Her voice was quiet but they still watched her, transfixed, as she reached into her pocket and pulled out a thickly stuffed envelope.

'What's this?' Mrs Tremayne eyed it suspiciously.

'It's a letter, signed by the staff, urging you to reconsider this decision.' Miss Fox went to hand it to her but Mrs Tremayne drew back sharply, as if it were a dead rat. Instead Reginald Collins took the envelope and tore it open.

'There are a great deal of signatures on here,' he said, scanning the contents.

Miss Fox turned her calm grey eyes to Mrs Tremayne. 'Everyone has signed it,' she said. 'All the ward sisters, the consultants and the registrars, right down to the probationers and the junior housemen. All of them have put in writing their willingness to stay at the Nightingale, come what may.'

Veronica Hanley gave up trying to hide her tears, and sniffed loudly. 'With your permission, Matron, I should like to add my name to that list,' she said.

Kathleen smiled graciously at her. 'I should very much like that too, Miss Hanley,' she replied.

'Perhaps we could come to some kind of compromise?' Malcolm Eaton suggested.

'A compromise?' Mrs Tremayne fixed him with a withering stare.

Malcolm nodded, refusing to be daunted. 'Perhaps move the non-emergency staff and departments out of London, but keep the rest open?'

There was a lengthy silence. Constance Tremayne must

have known she was beaten, but she wasn't the type to go down without a fight. 'It's out of the question,' she said. 'I refuse to consider it.'

'Pardon me, Mrs Tremayne, but you're not the only one of the Trustees with a say,' Reginald Collins spoke up. 'In light of these developments, I think we should put it to a vote, don't you?'

Veronica beamed at him. How could she ever have thought him feeble? In her eyes he had suddenly become a dragon-vanquishing hero. But not as great a hero as Matron, who sat looking calmly about her, smiling at the mayhem she'd created.

As if she knew she was being watched, Miss Fox glanced up and caught Veronica's eye. To the Assistant Matron's astonishment, she winked.

And to her even greater astonishment, Veronica Hanley found herself winking back.

Chapter Forty-Nine

'Married?' Constance Tremayne said icily. 'You want to get married?'

Helen kept her eyes fixed on the Turkey rug at her feet. She didn't dare look at Christopher.

They were having tea with her parents at the Vicarage on a sunny Saturday afternoon, and it was every bit of excruciating as Helen had expected it to be.

Poor Christopher, she thought. He must be wondering what he'd got himself into. Her parents couldn't be more different from the kindly, boisterous Dawson family.

Her father was as welcoming as always, and did his best to make Chris feel at home. Her mother, by contrast, looked as if someone had shoved a particularly sour lemon in her mouth.

'Married,' repeated Constance Tremayne, shaking her head slowly. 'Well, this is the first I've heard of it.'

'That's why we're telling you now,' Chris replied cheerfully.

Helen sent him a shocked glance, which he ignored. Hadn't she warned him not to answer her mother back? Silence until Constance had finished expressing her opinions was always the best policy, in her experience.

But he didn't pay any attention to her warnings. He'd started off on the wrong foot when he breezed in, gripped her mother's hand in a manly handshake and said, 'Nice to meet you, Connie.' He'd then added to his sins by sitting down without waiting to be invited, drinking spilled tea out of the saucer and not using the jam spoon in the correct manner.

Helen turned imploringly to her father, who leaped into action.

'Well, that's marvellous news, isn't it? Absolutely first rate.' He stood up, slapped Christopher on the back and shook hands with him enthusiastically. 'We couldn't be happier, could we, my dear?'

All eyes turned to Constance. She inhaled a long breath, and Helen waited.

'Of course,' she said. 'We're very happy for you, Helen.'

Beside her Helen heard Chris's sigh of relief, but she could only stare at her mother. She felt odd, almost let down, though she wasn't sure why.

'You see?' he whispered to her. 'I told you she wouldn't be able to resist my charm!'

Helen smiled weakly back, but she could hardly take it in. Her mother must be sickening for something, it was the only explanation.

Helen got the chance to question her further when her father took Christopher out into the garden to show off his roses.

'Are you sure you're all right about Chris and me getting married, Mother?' Helen asked.

Constance smiled benignly. 'Of course, why shouldn't I be? He seems like a very pleasant young man,' she said. 'Very – what's the word? Confident.'

Full of himself, in other words, Helen thought. She was surprised her mother hadn't slapped him down.

'I hope you don't feel it's too sudden?' she tried again.

'Hardly sudden, dear. You've known each other several months. It's not as if you only met him a fortnight ago, is it?'

Helen stared at her in frustration. 'You do know he's Charlie's cousin?' she burst out.

Constance leaned over and laid a hand on her daughter's arm, silencing her. 'I know you're concerned about my feelings, dear, but don't be. I've learned my lesson,' she said. 'I took against Charlie when you first met him, and as you know I've always regretted not giving him more of a chance. I don't intend to make the same mistake again, I assure you. Besides,' she went on, 'you're a woman now. More than old enough to make up your own mind.'

Helen stared at her, stunned. She had just turned twenty-five years old, and in all her life she had never heard her mother say she was old enough to make up her own mind about anything.

So why had she chosen now, of all times, to decide that Helen could make her own decisions?

'Besides,' Constance said, 'I'm far too tired for another argument. I've already had one bruising encounter this week, and I simply can't face another.'

'A bruising encounter, Mother?' Helen said, amused.

'There's nothing funny about it!' Constance snapped. 'Thanks to Matron's overdramatic intervention, the Nightingale is now having to stay at least partially open, instead of closing entirely as I'd planned.'

Helen nodded. 'Yes, Dr McKay told us the good news.'

'Good news?' Constance's lip curled. 'It's hardly good news as far as I'm concerned, Helen. And don't mention that man's name to me either,' she added. 'I partly blame him for the situation we find ourselves in. If he hadn't got the Trustees talking about this in the first place—'

'Dr McKay is only doing his job, Mother. He happens to be very conscientious.'

'He's a troublemaker!' her mother said. 'He and Matron have set out to humiliate me.'

353

'Don't you think you're taking this too personally?' Helen reasoned. 'They only want what's best for the hospital.'

'And I don't?' Constance raised her eyebrows. 'Really, Helen, I'm very disappointed in you, taking sides with that man. I'm beginning to wonder if it was a mistake for you to move to Casualty in the first place.'

'I like it there.'

'All the same, perhaps it would be better for you to move back to Theatre.'

Before Helen had a chance to reply, the two men came in from the garden through the French windows, laughing together like old friends.

'Well, Helen, your young man can certainly tell a good story!' Timothy Tremayne chuckled. 'I wouldn't mind going to sea myself after listening to some of his tales!'

Helen looked at Chris, who winked back at her. He seemed so relaxed, as if he didn't have a care in the world. But she could tell he was trying hard to make a good impression, for her sake.

'We've been talking about the wedding,' her father went on.

Chris's grin widened. 'Your dad's offered to marry us in your church,' he said. 'I thought you'd like that?'

'What a lovely idea,' Helen said absently, her mind still on what her mother had said.

'It's just a matter of finding a date,' her father continued. 'Christopher says you want to marry as soon as possible?'

'Well—'

'We seem to have weddings every weekend at the moment. Lots of couples wanting to get married before the men are called up, I suppose,' Timothy sighed. 'But as luck would have it, a bride's mother rang me up this morning and said her daughter's decided on a register office wedding instead.'

'And we all know why that is, don't we?' Constance said with a knowing look.

'Quite, my dear.' Reverend Tremayne gave his wife a patient smile. 'Anyway, it means I have an afternoon free next month, if that's of any interest to you?'

'Perfect,' said Chris. 'Eh, Helen?'

But before she could reply, her mother chimed in with a very sharp, 'Out of the question. It will take much longer than that to plan even the simplest wedding. And besides,' she went on, 'if you marry with such indecent haste, everyone will think you're doing it for a reason.' Her gaze dropped meaningfully to Helen's narrow waist.

'Mother!' Helen blushed.

'I'm only telling you what everyone else will think.' Constance sniffed. 'But as I've told you, you're old enough to make your own decisions.'

Helen looked at Chris. 'What do you think?'

'It's up to you,' he replied with a shrug. 'You know I'd like to get wed as soon as possible, but it's your big day, and I don't want to spoil it for you.'

'That's settled then,' Constance interrupted them. 'You can get married later.'

Helen smiled at her mother. So much for being able to make her own decisions!

Chapter Fifty

'Call yourself a doctor? You didn't even know your own wife was expecting.'

David McKay laughed at his friend. After weeks of Jonathan Adler's saying his wife was under the weather and in need of a tonic, the true cause of Esther's mystery illness had finally revealed itself.

Jonathan had the grace to look abashed. 'How was I to know? After two years of marriage and no sign of pregnancy, it wasn't exactly expected,' he defended himself.

'Well, I couldn't be happier for both of you,' David said warmly. 'How is Esther?'

'Blooming, now she's over the sickness and lethargy.'

His wife might have recovered, but Jonathan didn't look as if he would ever get over the shock. His dark eyes had a dazed expression, and his face was pale in contrast to his black beard. He looked like a man in need of a stiff drink.

'We'll have to celebrate,' said David. 'But before you say anything, I'm not inviting myself to supper again,' he went on, as his friend opened his mouth to speak. 'I wouldn't expect Esther to slave over a hot stove in her condition.'

'You're surely not inviting us to that hovel of a doctors' house?' Jonathan laughed.

'No, I thought we could go out for dinner to the Café de Paris. My treat.'

'In that case, I'm sure my wife and I would be delighted

to accept your invitation.' Jonathan inclined his head graciously. 'Will the lovely Rebecca be there?'

'I daresay.' David caught his friend's searching look. 'So I'm sure Esther will be able to sit and scrutinise us at her leisure,' he said.

'We're just interested in how you're getting on, that's all. You've been seeing each other a few months now, haven't you? How is it going?'

'She's – delightful.'

Jonathan sent him a shrewd look. 'That doesn't sound too promising. She doesn't make your heart skip a beat, then?'

'No, and I'm rather relieved about that. I don't know why you should think cardiac arrhythmia is a good sign,' said David. 'Hearts skipping a beat are generally considered dangerous, medically speaking.'

Without thinking, his gaze strayed across the Casualty hall, to where Helen was checking a batch of newly sharpened hypodermic needles.

Jonathan sighed. 'In your case, my friend, I'd say most definitely,' he said.

Helen gazed down at the babies sleeping end to end in their cot. Two perfect little pink angels, each with a thatch of dark hair. 'They're so beautiful,' she sighed.

'They are when they're asleep,' Dora replied with a grim smile. 'But they're little perishers when they're awake and screaming in the middle of the night!'

Typical Dora, Helen thought, trying to hide her feelings. But her friend's freckled face glowed with motherly pride as she looked down at her sleeping babies.

Helen had never seen her look so radiant or so contented. 'Motherhood suits you,' she said.

'I dunno about that.' Dora gave an embarrassed shrug.

'I hardly have a minute to bless myself these days.' She ran her hand through her thick red curls. 'Lucky I've got Danny here to help me – eh, Dan?' She smiled at Nick's brother, who lingered shyly close by as usual. 'You should see the way he rocks them to sleep. I swear they drop off quicker for him than they ever do for me!'

Danny's pale face suffused with embarrassed colour, but he couldn't keep the pleased smile off his face.

'He loves those kids,' Dora said to Helen. 'Honestly, he watches over them like a proper little guard dog. Won't let a breath of wind blow on 'em. I dunno know what he'll do if we—'

'If what?' Helen asked.

Dora looked up, her muddy green eyes troubled. 'Nick wants me and the kids to go away to the country if the war starts,' she whispered. 'He reckons we'll be safer down there.'

'He's right, isn't he?'

'I suppose so,' Dora sighed. 'But I don't like the idea of going away. This is my home, with him and Danny. I don't like the thought of leaving them.'

'But you've got to think of the babies,' Helen reminded her.

'That's what Nick says.'

Helen reached down and stroked little Winifred's downy cheek. 'Where will you go?'

Walter let out a whimper and Dora bent to attend to him. 'Millie Benedict has written to invite us to stay with her,' she said quietly, gathering the baby into her arms.

'Really? Lucky you!' Millie Benedict, or Lady Sebastian Rushton, to give her her proper title these days, had been their room-mate while they were training. She was the daughter of an earl, and was now married to the youngest son of a duke. They lived on the family estate in Kent. 'Imagine living in a castle!' Helen said.

'That's just it – I can't imagine it,' Dora groaned. 'Can you picture me, sitting down to tea with her grandmother, the Dowager Countess? I wouldn't know what to say to her.' Her freckled face flushed at the thought.

'You'll be all right. You'll have Millie to look after you.' Helen smiled. 'It'll be fun. Just like the old days in PTS!'

'Only if you were there too.'

Helen caught her friend's look and knew what she was going to say. 'No,' she said, shaking her head.

'Why not? You said yourself a lot of the wards are moving down to Kent. I'm sure you could get a transfer if you wanted to. And it would be fun. Just like the old days. Go on, what's stopping you?'

'I can't,' Helen said.

'I'm sure there'll be bodies to patch up in the country same as here,' Dora said.

'Yes, but I'll be needed here badly once the war starts. Dr McKay thinks they're bound to extend the Casualty department. We'll have to take over space taken up by the Outpatients' clinics and train extra staff . . . What?' Helen stopped talking, aware that her friend was watching her with interest.

'Nothing.' Dora shrugged. 'I'm just surprised you're not keen to leave Casualty, that's all. I thought you and Dr McKay didn't get on?'

'He's not that bad, now I've got to know him better,' Helen said. 'And besides, this is nothing to do with him. It's about me doing my duty where I'm most needed.'

It was past ten o'clock when she made her way back to the hospital. It was a warm, starry night, and the full moon cast a silvery light. All around her the ward blocks were in darkness, curtains pulled shut, only the occasional green glow visible through a window.

It made Helen think of all the nights she had had to leave windows open for Millie and Dora to climb back in after lights out. The only time Helen herself had tried coming in without a late pass, she'd climbed through the wrong window and ended up trapped in the Home Sister's bathroom.

She smiled at the thought of Millie. Dora was right, it would be fun to see her again. But at the same time Helen didn't want to leave Casualty. As she'd explained to Dora, her place was there with . . .

Her place was there, helping to look after all the emergencies they were bound to get in once the war started, she amended the thought in her mind.

She had almost reached the doors to the sisters' home when she heard a voice behind her.

'Sister Dawson? Helen?'

The voice was so faint that at first Helen wondered if it was the breeze whispering through the plane trees. But the night air was sultry and still, and not a breeze stirred.

'Who is it?' She spoke softly, but her voice still sounded loud in the quiet of the evening.

'It's me.'

Helen swung round. 'Nurse Willard? What are you doing lurking here at this time of—' She stopped talking as Penny Willard stepped out of the shadows. 'Oh, Willard!' cried Helen. 'What have you done to yourself?'

Chapter Fifty-One

Helen hardly recognised her at first. Bruises bloomed purple, blue and black around the swollen, puffy mess that was Penny's left eye. Blood trickled like tears down her cheek.

'Thank God it's you,' she stammered. 'I've been waiting for you. I didn't know where else to go for help.'

'What happened?'

'I – I walked into a door.'

Walked into Joe Armstrong's fist, more like. Helen fought back the comment. 'I'll take you to Casualty,' she said. 'I know it's ambulance emergencies only, but I'm sure they mind—'

'No! I don't want to go there. The night nurses will be there, and they'll only talk.'

'But you need to get this treated.'

'I just need you to clean it up for me,' Penny said. 'I'd do it myself, but I don't want to go back to the nurses' home looking like this. Just a bit of gentian violet on it should do. Please?' she begged.

Helen sighed. 'Let's have a look at it.'

She pulled Penny into the lamplight and tilted back her head to examine her injured eye. Close to, it was even worse. The skin around it was shiny and taut over the grotesque swelling, splotched with vivid colour. Inside the narrow slit, the white of her eye swam bright scarlet with blood. As Helen gently touched her cheekbone, Penny hissed with pain and flinched away.

'It's badly cut,' Helen said. 'I think you might need sutures.'

'No!'

'Willard, please. Let me take you to Casualty. You need to get this examined properly.'

'I can't.' Penny jerked out of her grasp. 'I can't have them all gossiping about me, I can't face it.'

'Then let me take you to the Sick Bay,' Helen pleaded. 'Dr McKay can help you.'

'I don't want anyone else knowing,' Penny insisted. 'I came to you because I trusted you. If you won't help me, I'll sort it out for myself.'

She started to walk away. Helen watched her stumbling off into the night. 'Willard, wait,' she called out. Penny stopped, but didn't turn round. 'I'll help you,' Helen said. 'But we need to go to the Sick Bay.'

Penny shook her head. 'I told you, I don't want Dr McKay involved.'

'We won't tell him,' Helen said. 'I'll treat you there myself.'

The hospital's Sick Bay was at the top of the main building, away from the wards. Leading off a short corridor were four rooms, each made up with three hospital beds. At the far end was the consulting room, lined with rows of jars and bottles and furnished with a couch, screens and a desk. This was where the doctors and nurses reported to Dr McKay, the Medical Superintendent, when they were feeling ill. Not that many did, since all the nurses knew only a severed limb or a bad case of TB would ever count as a 'real' illness.

Luckily, none of the beds was occupied and the whole floor was in darkness. Helen could hear her heart thudding in her ears as she crept in, Penny following.

'We'll have to be careful,' she whispered. 'If Night Sister sees a light on up here she's bound to come and investigate. You pull the curtains, then I'll switch on the light.'

As Helen stumbled towards the desk in the darkness, Penny touched her arm.

'Thank you,' she whispered. 'I know you're taking a big risk to help me, and I do appreciate it.'

'I don't know if I will be able to help you yet,' Helen reminded her. 'I can clean you up, but if that injury is really bad you'll need a doctor to look at it.'

'I know.' But even though the darkness hid her expression, Helen knew Penny had no intention of seeing a doctor, no matter how bad her injury was.

'Close those curtains and let's see what we can do, shall we?'

Penny lay on the couch while Helen tended to her, gently swabbing the wound to cleanse it.

'How did this really happen?' he asked. 'Was it an argument?'

'I don't know what you mean. I told you, I walked into a door—'

'Willard, please. I'm not a fool.' Helen sighed. 'I'm taking a risk to help you, the least you can do is be honest with me.'

The fight seemed to go out of Penny.

'Joe didn't mean to do it,' she said. 'He just lost his temper, that's all.' She took a deep, ragged breath. 'It was a silly thing, some man started talking to me in the pub. I shouldn't have spoken back to him, I know Joe doesn't like me talking to other men. But I was only being polite, I couldn't very well ignore him—'

'You're allowed to talk to other people, you know,' Helen said. 'Joe doesn't own you.'

'He loves me,' Penny insisted stoutly. 'I've never had a man fight for me like that before. It shows he cares.'

'It's a strange way of showing it, to hit someone.'

'It was just this once.'

'Penny, I've seen the bruises on your arms,' Helen said wearily. 'I've seen the way you walk sometimes, as if your ribs are cracked. He's usually more careful than this, isn't he? He hits you where it won't show.'

Penny stared up at her, her face full of dismay. 'Do you – do you think anyone else knows?' she whispered anxiously. 'Oh, God, I'd be so ashamed if I thought people were talking about me.'

'I don't think anyone else has noticed.'

'Thank God.' Penny sighed with relief. 'I don't want anyone to think badly of him, you see. I mean, it's not Joe's fault. He just gets angry sometimes. But he does love me,' she said. 'He wouldn't bother with me otherwise, would he?'

She looked up, her battered face so full of hope it nearly broke Helen's heart. Without answering the question she finished cleansing the wound and bent to have a closer look.

'That cut isn't too deep, but it's bad enough,' she said. 'I think it's going to leave a nasty scar.'

'Let me see.' Penny struggled to sit upright and took the mirror Helen offered her. 'Oh, no! It looks awful. People are bound to notice, aren't they? What can I tell them?' She looked panic-stricken. 'I'll have to put off the wedding,' she said. 'I can't walk down the aisle with a big scar on my face, can I?'

Helen stared at her, appalled. 'You're surely not still going to marry him after this?'

A flush crept up Penny's neck. 'I told you, he's not always like this. Most of the time he's all right. I just have to be careful when he's in one of his moods, that's all.'

'So you're going to spend the rest of your life tiptoeing around, making sure you don't upset him?'

'You don't understand!' Penny thrust the mirror back into Helen's hands and started to get off the couch. 'Joe's the most loving person I've ever known. Most of the men I've gone out with have upped and left me, but not Joe. He really cares about me, wants to spend the rest of his life with me. That says something, doesn't it?'

'It says you're a fool if you marry him.'

Penny's face puckered with anger. 'I don't want to end up lonely and on my own,' she insisted. 'What will that say about me, if I end up a miserable old maid like Sister Wren or Miss Hanley?'

'It's better than being married to the wrong man.'

'Is it?'

Helen didn't have time to reply because at that moment the door behind her opened. There was a click and Helen flinched as the room was suddenly filled with blinding light.

Dr McKay stood in the doorway, his arms folded across his chest, his expression icy.

'Would someone mind telling me what the hell is going on?' he said.

Chapter Fifty-Two

There was a moment of horrified silence. Helen glanced at Penny. She was trembling.

'Well?' Dr McKay said. 'I'd like to know why I came back up here to fetch my bag, and I suddenly find two nurses in here without permission?'

Helen stepped forward. 'I'm sorry, Dr McKay,' she said, fighting to sound calm. 'It was my decision to come here and I take full responsibility for it. Nurse Willard was injured, and she needed urgent treatment.'

'I see.' Dr McKay's brown eyes turned to Penny's face for a moment. 'And it didn't occur to you to call me?'

'I—'

'It was my fault, Doctor,' Penny blurted out. 'I asked Sister Dawson to help me. She wanted to call you, but I wouldn't let her.'

I'm for it now, Helen thought, feeling his enquiring gaze on her.

'How bad is it?' he said.

She stared at him blankly. 'I'm sorry, sir?'

'The injury, Sister. How bad is it? You must have carried out some kind of assessment, surely.' There was an edge of impatience in his voice.

Helen pulled herself together quickly. 'The cut isn't very deep, but I'm not sure if it needs sutures, sir,' she replied.

'Let's have a look, shall we? If you don't mind, Nurse Willard?'

'N-no, Doctor.'

Helen caught Penny's quick, panicked glance as she settled back on the couch.

She watched Dr McKay as he bent over, examining the injury. Helen was still too terrified to allow herself to breathe. But at the same time she felt strangely relieved that he was here. His presence calmed her, made her believe he could make everything right.

He straightened up. 'Well, you're right, it is quite bad. But I think we can get away with a collodion dressing to hold it together. Fetch the bottle, will you, Sister?'

Still bewildered by this turn of events, Helen hurried off to find it. Behind her, she was aware of Dr McKay scrubbing his hands under the running tap.

'Shall I cleanse the wound a second time, Doctor?' she asked. 'It's starting to bleed again.'

'Yes, please, Sister. It will need to be quite dry to set the dressing.'

They worked closely together, he pinching the edges of the wound together while Helen dabbed away the blood. Then she carefully painted on the dressing.

'That's it. Now all we have to do is hold it together until it dries.' Dr McKay looked up suddenly, his face only inches from Helen's. His eyes were dark and fathomless and unexpectedly warm, and for a second their gazes held. Then, as if released from a magnet's pull, they jerked apart.

After Dr McKay had finished dressing the wound, he ordered Helen to make ready one of the Sick Bay beds.

'I'll give you something for the pain, and sign you off for a couple of days,' he told Penny. 'That should give enough time for the swelling to go down. Although you'll still have quite a shiner,' he warned.

'That's all right, I can hide it under make-up,' she said cheerfully. 'No one will ever know.' Helen and Dr McKay exchanged looks, but neither of them said anything.

'Isn't he wonderful?' Penny whispered to Helen who was putting her to bed later. 'I didn't think he'd be so sweet about it, did you?'

'No,' Helen murmured back. Although she had the feeling Dr McKay was still going to take her to task once it was all over.

Sure enough, he was waiting for her in the consulting room when she returned a few minutes later.

'You really should have called me, you know,' he said, a note of reproach in his voice. 'What if she'd cracked her eye socket?'

'I know – I'm sorry.' Now the panic was over, Helen realised how foolish she'd been. 'As I said, I take full responsibility for it.' She straightened her shoulders. 'I assume you'll be reporting me to Matron?' she said stiffly.

'Oh, for God's sake, Helen. Is that really what you think of me?' He gave an exasperated sigh. 'I meant I could have helped you, that's all. You can trust me, you know.'

They looked at each other across the room, and something seemed to shift in the air between them.

'I don't suppose you'd like a medicinal brandy?' he offered.

It was nearly midnight. The last place she should have been was drinking in the Sick Bay with a doctor. But it had been an evening of high emotion, and Helen was exhausted.

'Yes, please,' she said.

They sat in silence, Helen perched on the couch, Dr McKay behind the desk, sipping their brandy from china cups. But it wasn't a tense or awkward silence. It was companionable, almost comfortable, each of them lost in their own thoughts.

'I suppose it's too much to hope that this might finally

make her see the light where her boyfriend is concerned?' Dr McKay said at last.

So he knew what Joe Armstrong was like, too. Helen wasn't surprised Dr McKay had seen right through him. 'I'm afraid not,' she said. 'She was more worried about whether her face would be scarred for the wedding.'

'Good God.' David McKay shook his head. 'Silly girl. What does she see in him, I wonder?'

'I don't think it's him particularly. It could be anyone who shows her attention. She just doesn't want to be alone.'

'I can understand that,' he said.

Helen regarded him in surprise. 'I didn't realise you were in the same position,' she said.

'Oh, I'm not talking about myself,' he dismissed this. 'My father married again, shortly after my mother died, for the same reason. He was terrified at the prospect of being on his own, so he married the first woman who came along.'

'What happened?' Helen asked.

He sighed. 'Unfortunately, like Nurse Willard's fiancé, she turned out to be a thoroughly unpleasant piece of work. Led him a dog's life, and bullied my sister and me. My father spent the rest of his life trying to please her, until she finally sent him to an early grave. It taught me a lesson, I can tell you. As far as I'm concerned, it's far better to be lonely than with the wrong person.'

'Then you've obviously never been lonely.' Helen hadn't meant to say it out loud, didn't even realise she'd said the words until she looked up and caught Dr McKay watching her closely over the rim of his cup.

'Oh, I've been lonely,' he said softly. 'I hadn't realised just how lonely I was until someone special came into my life.'

Helen thought of the glamorous dark-haired woman

waiting for him in reception, and the way he'd greeted her, and felt a strange pang. 'I'm happy for you,' she said quietly.

'The wretched thing is, she's with someone else.'

Helen looked up sharply to find him staring straight back at her. She felt a jolt, a shock of recognition. She suddenly realised that this was inevitable, that everything she had known and experienced had led her to this moment.

The realisation that, without a single shadow of a doubt, she loved him.

And he loved her, too. She could see it in the kindling warmth of his brown eyes.

'Helen?' He murmured her name softly. Too softly. It sounded dangerously like a caress.

She put down her cup with a clatter and jumped up. 'I – I have to go.'

'Helen, wait—' But she was already gone, putting as much space as she could between herself and a situation which she knew would be her certain fate, and her undoing.

Chapter Fifty-Three

They lost another two patients on Female Chronics during the warm August night.

'That's five just in the week we've been here,' Effie said to Jess after they had finished performing last offices on poor Aggie Harman. It was always a sad job, and Sister Hyde insisted on its being done in absolute silence out of respect for the patient. 'It's almost as if they know something's happening, isn't it?'

'Don't be silly. They're just old, that's all,' Jess, ever practical, said as she loaded the washing things on to the trolley. 'Death is to be expected on a ward like this. Sister Hyde said so.'

'You're right, I suppose. Besides, most of them are too doolally to know what's going on.'

'Shhh!' Jess glanced around guiltily. 'Don't let Sister hear you say that. You know she's most particular about the way we treat the patients.'

'"Nurses, you must go about your duties diligently and remember to smile and remain cheerful at all times,"' Effie quoted back to her in Sister Hyde's gravelly, upper-crust tones. They heard the same thing every morning when the ward sister was handing out the work lists. 'She's continually telling us to smile, but I've never seen her do it. She always looks boot-faced to me.'

'I suppose it must be hard for her at the moment, knowing she's got to send all the patients away,' Jess said.

'Staff was saying she's nursed some of them for years. They must be like family to her.'

Some family, Effie thought. She couldn't see why Sister was so worried about a bunch of dribbling, rambling women who had to sleep in cots to stop them wandering off or falling out of bed. Most of them couldn't even ask for a bedpan, either. After a week of constantly stripping and remaking beds, scrubbing mackintoshes and soaking sheets, she'd had enough to last her a lifetime. She certainly didn't think she would ever become attached to these patients.

The poor women on Hyde might be unaware of their own bodily functions, but even they must have sensed the cloud of gloom that had descended over the hospital. The Trustees' plans had become more official since the government had issued an order that only acute patients should be admitted for medical care, and that they should be ready to send other patients home at a moment's notice should it become necessary.

But it wasn't just the patients who faced an uncertain future.

'I don't know how she expects us to stay cheerful when we don't even know what's going to happen to us,' Effie complained, as they headed for the sluice with the trolley.

'The latest I heard, they were evacuating us all to the country,' Jess said.

'How can they do that? Who's going to look after the patients?'

'I shouldn't think there'll be many patients left once they've finished sending everyone home. And if they do need extra help they'll just transfer all the staff nurses from the wards that have closed, I suppose. Those that haven't joined up,' she added.

'My mother is still on at me to go back to Ireland,' Effie

said. 'She's been reading in the papers about the prospect of thousands of people being bombed in London, and it's scared her stiff. As if she didn't have enough to worry about with our Bridget going off and joining the Red Cross. She's convinced her daughters are all going to be killed if she's not there to keep an eye on them.'

'Do you think you'll go?' Jess asked.

'I don't know,' Effie sighed. 'I don't want to. But if I don't, I'll probably just be sent off to some funny little corner of the country where I don't know anyone. If I can't stay in London I might as well be back in Killarney. At least I'll have my family around me. But I'd much rather stay in London, if I could. Just in case—'

Just in case Adam Campbell ever tries to find me again. She didn't want to say the words out loud, because she knew what Jess's reaction would be. Her friend had made it very clear that she thought Effie was foolish still to be pining for him. In her opinion, Adam Campbell didn't deserve such devotion.

But Effie longed to see him again. Ever since they had parted, she had thrown herself into self-improvement. Before she went to sleep every night, she made herself read and memorise one of the poems in her book. And whenever she had any time off, she took herself off to a museum or an art gallery. She had even foregone a night out dancing with the other girls so she could sit through another poetry reading in the hope that she might bump into Adam there.

She kept waiting to enjoy staring at paintings and old pots in glass cabinets, but so far it had all been deathly dull. But one day, she promised herself, one day she would be able to impress Adam, and her efforts would be worthwhile.

'I'm going to ask permission to stay on here,' she came

back to the present to hear Jess saying. 'It's my home, after all. I've got nowhere else to go.'

Effie eyed her friend sympathetically as she stood at the sink, washing the bowls. The Nightingale was Jess's only real home. She came from a rough part of the East End, a real den of thieves by all accounts. Her father was in prison and her stepmother had all but thrown Jess out on the streets. Becoming a nurse had changed her fortunes completely, so Effie could understand why she didn't want to give it up.

'Do you think they'll let you?' she asked.

'I don't know. But if they don't, I'll come back and volunteer as a VAD. They're bound to be able to make some use of me, with my training,' said Jess.

Effie gazed at her admiringly. As usual, Jess had it all worked out. She liked to think and plan, unlike Effie, who generally preferred to tackle life's problems as they were thrown at her.

But it was time for her to start making some plans now, she decided. 'I would like to stay and finish my training,' she said wistfully. 'Mammy says I can do it in Ireland, but it won't be the same.' For one thing, there would be no fun to be had with her mother watching her like a hawk.

Then another thought occurred to her. 'But what if there isn't a nurses' home here for us to live in?'

'I'm sure there'll be something, even if it's not what we're used to,' Jess said. 'Or if not, they might let us live out.'

'Live out?' A glimmer of hope began to flicker inside Effie. 'Oh, do you think so? Imagine if we could all get a flat together – you, me and Kowalski. Wouldn't that be grand?'

She was already making plans, wondering how she could somehow entice Adam to her sophisticated new abode, when Jess ruined it all by saying, 'But surely if your mother says you've got to go home, then you won't have any choice? Not until you're twenty-one.'

'That's true.' Effie sighed heavily, seeing her wonderful dream of independence slipping away from her. She felt sorry for Jess, with no family to rely on. But sometimes having a loving mammy and a bunch of interfering sisters did have its drawbacks.

Chapter Fifty-Four

On the morning of Friday 1 September Germany had invaded Poland, and everyone knew that war was inevitable.

But no one could have guessed it from the atmosphere in the Prospect of Whitby pub on Wapping Wall that night. There was a typical East End knees-up going on, and the Dawsons were in the thick of it as usual. One of the uncles thumped out a tune on the pub piano while another played the accordion. The beer flowed against a background of laughter, singing and dancing.

The merry sounds drifted out of the door towards Helen as she stood waiting for Chris.

The man she loved.

She said the words determinedly in her head, as if by repeating them often enough she could make herself believe them.

She did love Christopher, she was sure of that. But she also knew now that she wasn't in love with him.

She hadn't even realised there was a difference until that fateful night in the Sick Bay with Dr McKay. But that jolt of recognition when she'd looked at him, as if she had finally found the other half of herself, had made her all too painfully aware that there was.

It had also made her determined to stay away from him at all costs. Because the idea of being so consumed with love, of needing someone so badly, terrified Helen. She had been through that with Charlie, and losing him had nearly killed her. She couldn't risk her heart twice over.

And besides, she couldn't let Christopher down. He loved her and he wanted to marry her, and she had made a promise to him that she couldn't break. And she loved him, too, enough to know that they would make each other happy. Or as happy as she needed to be.

The night air was still and stiflingly warm. It was the hottest summer anyone had known, so the newspapers said. But there were no more stars to be seen, only endless grey barrage balloons floating silently in the sky above them. How quickly she'd got used to seeing them there! She hardly seemed to notice them these days.

'Waiting for me?'

Helen turned around and there was Chris, standing next to her. She was relieved to feel her heart lift at the sight of him. He was so good-looking, with his red-gold hair and laughing blue eyes.

It's better to be lonely than with the wrong person. She pushed Dr McKay's words from her mind.

'Where have you been? I was worried about you.'

'I had a few things to sort out.' Chris leaned down and kissed her. Not his usual devouring kiss, but the lightest peck on the lips.

'Shall we go in?' She started towards the pub but he stopped her.

'In a minute. Can we go for a walk first? There's something I need to talk to you about.'

He took her arm and they walked along by the river. The stench of the dockside factories hung on the still evening air.

Helen waited expectantly, but Chris's usual chattiness seemed to have deserted him.

'What do you make of this news about Poland?' she said, her voice falsely bright. 'I suppose it means war has to come now, hasn't it? I mean, surely we've got to do something . . . Did I tell you William is planning to join up? He wants to go into the RAF . . .' she gabbled on, anything to fill the uncomfortable silence that stretched between them.

Just as she was running out of things to say, Chris stopped walking and gazed out across the water.

'Beautiful, ain't it?' he said, nodding towards the silvery ribbon of the river snaking its way into the distance. 'Whenever I see it, I think of what it feels like to be on a boat, heading down there and out to sea. That's proper freedom. You don't know what's ahead of you.'

Helen looked at his profile, carved against the twilight, and suddenly she knew.

'You're leaving, aren't you?' she said.

He was silent again. Then he nodded. 'I've been offered a job sailing out to the West Indies.' He kept his eyes fixed ahead of him on the river.

'How long will you be gone?'

'A few months. Maybe longer, if it all works out.' He gave her a quick, sideways glance. 'But I have to leave tonight.'

It was only then that she saw the duffel bag at his feet. How could she not have noticed it before?

She turned her gaze back towards the tall cranes silhouetted against the night sky. 'What about the wedding?'

She already knew the answer, even before she heard his sigh of regret. 'I'm sorry,' he said.

'Sorry because we're putting off the wedding? Or because you don't want to marry me?'

He was silent for a long time. 'I tried, I really did,' he said finally. 'But I reckon we both know I'm not the marrying kind. I need my freedom too much, I just can't settle.'

She thought of him, moving restlessly from job to job, never staying in the same place for long. No wonder everyone thought he was trouble. On land, he was like a caged animal.

'I tried to make it work,' he went on. 'I wanted to do it, truly I did. I wanted what everyone else had, a wife and a home and a good job.'

'Is that why you wanted to marry me? To be like everyone else?'

'No!' He turned to her, his eyes serious. 'The minute I saw you, I wanted you,' he said. 'You were so beautiful, like an angel. And you intrigued me, too. You were so sad, I wanted to be the one to make you happy.'

'You did make me happy – you do,' she amended.

'Oh, Helen, don't make this harder for me than it already is,' he pleaded. 'We both know it's not going to work. I realised it that first night I came back. We see everything so differently . . . I could never be part of your world, and I don't think you'd enjoy being part of mine.'

A lump rose in her throat, choking her. 'But you still talked about getting married? We went to see my parents—'

'Like I said, I wanted to make it work. More than anything. I suppose that's why I wanted to be married quickly. Everyone always says I'm impulsive, and they're right.' He smiled ruefully. 'I wanted to marry you before I had a chance to think about it and change my mind. But now I have thought about it, I know I'm not being fair on you.' He gazed down at her. 'Believe me, love, if I was going to settle down with anyone, it would be with you. But it wouldn't work. I can't do it, even for you. I'm a wanderer,' he said. 'Sooner or later I'd let you down and hurt you, and you've already been hurt enough.'

Tears stung Helen's eyes, but deep down she knew he was right. She had been trying just as hard as he had to make things right between them. But if they'd stayed together, how long would it have been before one or the other of them became too exhausted to try any longer?

'Helen?' Chris put out his hand and cupped her cheek, turning her to face him. 'Don't be upset,' he said. 'You'll find someone to make you truly happy one day. Happier than I ever could.'

She saw a flicker of another emotion in his eyes then and it suddenly occurred to her that he knew. He understood the turmoil she'd been going through and had decided to make it easy for her. Either that or his pride had made him end it before she could.

But the next moment he was smiling again, and Helen told herself she had imagined it. How could he possibly guess her feelings, when she refused to admit them even to herself?

They walked back towards the pub together, holding hands one last time. When they reached the doors Chris turned to her and said, 'Well, this is where we came in. Bumping into each other in a doorway.' He hitched his duffel bag over his shoulder. 'Say goodbye to them for me, won't you?'

'Aren't you going in?' Helen asked.

He shook his head. 'They won't miss me,' he said, a trace of sadness in his voice.

He bent down and kissed her one last time, a kiss of such infinite gentleness Helen wanted it to go on for ever. But all too soon, he pulled away.

'Will I see you again?' she said, gulping back tears.

He smiled. 'I doubt it.' He winked at her. 'Be happy, Helen.'

And then he was gone. She watched him sauntering away from her, his duffel bag slung over his broad shoulder, as the sound of music and laughter drifted from the pub.

Chapter Fifty-Five

'Well, that's that then,' Mr Peckett said. 'Fancy declaring war on such a beautiful morning, too. They've got some ruddy nerve, ain't they?'

No one else spoke. They all continued to stare at the wireless, long after Mr Chamberlain had finished giving his speech.

They had been expecting it. But his sombre announcement that Britain was now at war with Germany had still come as a shock.

'God bless us all?' Mr Talbot muttered, from under his canopy of wires and pulleys and splints. 'God help us all, more like!'

'What happens now, I wonder?' Mr Peckett said.

'We carry on, of course,' Frannie replied with a touch of defiance.

But she could tell from the way they looked at her that they all knew this wasn't true. Nothing would be the same again. She already barely recognised the Nightingale Hospital, its walls banked high with sandbags and windows criss-crossed with sticky brown blast tape. In a few days the students would be evacuated. The patients would go home or, if they couldn't, would be moved to other hospitals far from the city. And she would find herself presiding over an empty ward.

But she wouldn't allow any of the worry she felt to show on her face as she turned to her nurses. They surrounded her, wide-eyed as scared rabbits.

'Look sharp, there are still things to be done,' she said. 'Matron will be doing her rounds soon, and then the porters will be on their way up with dinner. And after that we have to prepare for Visiting Hour . . .'

An unearthly droning suddenly filled the air, drowning out her voice and ruffling her composure. The nurses looked at each other in panic.

'Air-raid warning! Quick, what do we do?'

'Get the patients out!'

'I've forgotten my gas mask!'

'Nurses, please!' Frannie raised her voice to silence them. 'It'll be a false alarm, there's no need to panic.' She looked at them, all shamefaced before her. 'Goodness me, five minutes of war and you forget all your training. If you're like this now, I dread to think what you'll be like after five weeks – or five years!'

Katie O'Hara turned pale. 'We won't be at war that long, will we, Sister?' she said, her upper lip trembling.

'I certainly hope not.' Frannie tried to smile at her reassuringly. 'But we mustn't lose discipline just because of what has happened. We must always remember we are nurses at the Nightingale Hospital.'

'For now!' Frannie heard one of the students mutter, and turned on her furiously.

'You can go to Matron for your cheek!' she snapped. 'I will not have insolence or tolerate slapdash behaviour just because there is a war on, do you understand?'

'Yes, Sister,' they chorused half-heartedly.

'Good. Now get on with your work and I don't want to hear any more nonsense from any of you. And the next person to mention the war will also go straight to Matron!' she added.

She dismissed them and went to her office, Katie O'Hara following her.

'Excuse me, Sister, may I have a word?'

'Yes, O'Hara. What is it?'

'I wondered if I could have a half-day holiday on Friday?'

Frannie regarded Katie across the desk. She was shorter and plumper than her sisters, but with the same black curly hair and bright blue eyes. 'It's very short notice,' she said. 'I hope you have a good reason?'

'I'm getting married, Sister,' she said shyly.

Frannie looked at her sharply. 'Married?'

'Yes, Sister. My Tom has got his call-up papers, so we thought we'd get married before he goes away.'

A lump rose in Frannie's throat. She had a sudden vision of another girl waving a young man off at a railway station . . .

'Sister?' Katie O'Hara was watching her anxiously.

'Yes, yes, of course, O'Hara. I'll talk to Matron about it.' Frannie summoned a smile. 'And may I offer you my congratulations.'

Katie's smile dimpled her cheeks. 'Thank you, Sister.'

'But I suppose this means you'll be leaving us?'

'I suppose so, Sister. Although I'd like to stay on, or at least volunteer if I can? I mean, I'm happy to stay living in while my Tom's away.'

'We'll have to see,' Frannie said. 'I'll talk to Matron about it.'

'Thank you, Sister,' Katie said. Then she added brightly, 'You never know, we might soon have lots of married nurses!'

Who knows? Frannie thought wearily. Everything was so topsy-turvy now, anything was possible. They would have female doctors and male nurses next.

When Katie had gone, Frannie took off her bonnet and ran her hand through her hair, enjoying the coolness of the air against her scalp.

Outside in the courtyard ambulance bells were clanging. Frannie jumped up and pulled the shutters over the windows, muffling the sound.

'You can't ignore it, you know. It's everywhere.'

She swung round, shocked to see Matthew Sinclair standing in the doorway.

He'd smartened himself up a bit since the last time she'd seen him. He'd shaved, put on a clean shirt, and he didn't stink of whisky. But the sight of him still repulsed her.

'What are you doing here?' she asked.

'Well, since you took me by surprise, I thought I'd do the same to you.' He closed the door and plonked himself down in the chair opposite hers without being invited.

'Your manners haven't improved, I see,' she said.

'At least I'm not throwing whisky in your face.'

'You deserved it.' She stared at him. 'What do you want?'

'I thought you'd like to know John has been given his marching orders,' Matthew said. 'His regiment is travelling down to Southampton in three days' time, and then it'll be on to France, I imagine.' He laughed. 'You would have thought he'd have managed to swing himself a nice cosy desk job by now, wouldn't you? But not John. He always has to go and act the hero. I suppose he thinks the war can't start without him.'

Bitterness and jealousy were written all over his face.

'Why are you telling me this?' Frannie asked.

'Because I want you to understand what you're doing by pushing him away like this. I also want you to know that if you send him away without telling him how you feel, there might be no going back.'

Which is exactly why I can't tell him, Frannie wanted to shout. It was the dreadful feeling that she might lose him that had stopped her from following John that day in the park. And it had stopped her from picking up the telephone to him every day since.

But she didn't want to betray herself, least of all to Matthew. So she replied coolly, 'I really don't think that's any of your business.'

'That's where you're wrong,' he said. 'I know why you're pushing him away, Fran. It's because you're scared. You don't want to lose him like you lost me all those years ago.' He paused for a moment, then said, 'I did you a great wrong, and I want to make things right if I can.'

She sighed, 'If you're talking about the way you lied to everyone, I don't think—'

'No, I'm not talking about that,' he cut her off. 'If it hadn't been for me, you would never have been this afraid. Because then it might have been John you were saying goodbye to at that station twenty-five years ago. And he would have come home to you.'

Frannie stared at him, uncomprehending. 'What are you talking about?'

'You really don't know, do you?' Matthew looked at her in wonder. 'My God, for a clever girl you can be rather dim sometimes, Frannie.' He leaned forward and lowered his voice. 'John was in love with you, you idiot girl. He always had been, right from when we were all children. Surely you must have realised? It was obvious enough to the rest of us!'

'I don't know what you mean,' she murmured, bewildered.

'So you never noticed the way he looked at you, or the way he blushed whenever you looked at him? You never noticed what a tongue-tied fool he was whenever he tried to speak to you?'

'I just thought he was shy.'

'Shy? He was lovesick, dear girl. Honestly, it was

painfully funny to watch him sometimes. He would trip over himself not to go near you yet couldn't tear himself away from you at the same time.' Matthew shook his head pityingly. 'Not that he'd ever approach you,' he mocked. 'You were the schoolmaster's daughter, far too good for the likes of poor, humble John.'

She winced at his sarcasm. No one could ever accuse Matthew of being poor or humble, that was for sure.

'If I'm being honest, that was part of the attraction for me,' he went on casually. 'I quite enjoyed watching John squirm when I flirted with you.'

The truth dawned. 'Are you saying you were only interested in me to make him jealous?'

'Of course that wasn't the only reason,' Matthew said defensively. 'You were the prettiest girl in the village, and all the boys liked you. Even if you were a little bit bookish.'

Frannie was quiet for a moment, trying to take it in. She remembered how surprised and delighted she'd been when Matthew took a sudden and unexpected interest in her. Now she knew why.

'He was even worse when we went to France,' Matthew continued. 'As far as I was concerned it was a case of out of sight, out of mind. I was young, I thought I was going to die, so I reckoned I should have a bit of fun while I still could.' He grinned sheepishly. 'But John put a stop to all that. He stood over me, made me write to you. It was worse than being at school!'

'I treasured those letters,' Frannie murmured.

'I should think you did, the effort it took me to write them!' Matthew retorted. 'I told John he should start writing to you himself, and save me a job, but he always said you wouldn't want to hear from him. I suppose he was right, wasn't he?'

Frannie fought the urge to slap the arrogant smile off

Matthew's face. Even after all these years, he still reckoned himself superior.

But to her shame, she had to admit he was right. Like everyone else, she had been so dazzled by Matthew that she had never noticed John standing in his shadow.

But now she looked at her former fiancé she realised that behind the dazzling exterior there was nothing but emptiness. He was all front and show, the complete opposite of quiet, unassuming, heroic John.

'Anyway,' Matthew said. 'I came to tell you if it hadn't been for me, John would have come home to you. You could have got married, and—'

'Don't.' Frannie held up her hand, silencing him. 'I don't want to think about that now. It's too late.'

'But it isn't,' Matthew insisted. 'You could still be together if you go to him, tell him how you feel.'

'For how long?' Frannie said bitterly. 'You said yourself, he'll be sent to France soon. What if he doesn't come home this time?'

'You'll be heartbroken,' Matthew said simply. But then he added, 'But will you be any less heartbroken if you don't tell him?'

Frannie looked away, infuriated by his logic. 'Did John send you to talk to me?' she asked.

'Good God, no!' Matthew laughed harshly. 'He'd be mortified if he knew I were here. He's so proud and noble, he would never come and beg you for anything, no matter how much he might want to.'

The sneer in his voice made Frannie's hackles rise. 'Don't criticise him for being proud or noble,' she bit out. 'Just because you don't know what either of those words mean!'

To her surprise, Matthew slumped back in his seat, all the bravado gone out of him like air from a burst balloon. 'You're right,' he admitted heavily. 'I'm neither of those things. But I'm trying to do the right thing now. I've hurt the two people who loved me most, and I want to make it right, if I can.'

'And where did this sudden change of heart come from?' Frannie mocked.

Matthew lifted his gaze to meet hers. 'I'm dying,' he said.

His abrupt declaration took away all her anger. 'Oh.'

'It's all right, you don't have to try and look sorry for me. I don't need your pity, and I certainly don't deserve it. But I want to go to my grave knowing I did one good thing in my life.'

He stood up to go. Frannie looked at his yellowing skin and emaciated frame and wondered how she hadn't noticed before how ill he was.

'I won't take up any more of your time,' he said. 'And by the way, John doesn't know anything about my illness, so I'd rather you didn't tell him. I don't want him feeling sorry for me, too.' He smiled grimly. 'I really don't think I could stand any more of his charity.'

'How can I tell him, when I'm never going to see him?' Frannie said.

Matthew shook his head sorrowfully. 'You're as bad as John,' he sighed. 'Neither of you will ever admit how you feel.'

As he shuffled towards the door, Frannie said, 'Wait! Can I order you a taxi?'

He shook his head. 'No, but thank you. You're very kind.' He looked at her thoughtfully. 'Think about what I said, won't you? But don't leave it too late. Time's running out for all of us.'

Chapter Fifty-Six

'Well, we've been at war since yesterday, and so far no one's been blown up yet, thank God,' David said. 'The worst we've had so far is someone walking in front of a bicycle during the blackout. Long may it continue!'

He held up his wine glass in a toast. The others joined in, but he noticed Jonathan and Esther's smiles seemed more strained than Rebecca's.

He couldn't understand why. They had come for dinner at the Café de Paris, one of the few nightspots still open after everywhere else had closed their doors. They had enjoyed oysters and steak Diane, listened to some wonderful jazz music and were generally having a very pleasant evening, or so he'd thought.

'Come on, out with it. What's wrong?' he asked, putting down his glass.

Esther and Jonathan looked at each other. Esther gave her husband an encouraging nod.

'Go on,' she whispered.

Jonathan turned to his friend. 'The thing is, Esther and I have been talking and we've decided she'd be better off leaving London for a while. We don't want to take any risks in her condition.'

'Splendid idea,' David agreed. He smiled at Esther. 'Where are you thinking of going? Somewhere nice, I hope?'

'I have some family in Cambridge,' she replied quietly. 'My father is already there, and I promised I'd join him.'

'Well, that's a nice part of the world. And it's not too far from London, so you'll be able to keep an eye on her, Jonathan.'

As soon as he said the words and saw his friend's face darken, he guessed what was coming next.

'That's the thing, old man. I'm going with her.' Jonathan lifted his gaze to meet David's. 'I've been offered a job at a teaching hospital there.'

'I see.' David recovered himself quickly. 'Quite right, too,' he said. 'Couples should be together. What's the point in marriage otherwise?'

Esther smiled, but Jonathan's expression was still tense.

'Are you sure you're all right about it?' he asked. 'I hate leaving you in the lurch.'

He looked so anxious David couldn't help laughing. 'Good Lord, is that why you've ruined a perfectly good dinner?' he asked. 'What did you think I was going to do, Jonathan? Burst into tears? Obviously I'm utterly distraught. But we're friends, we're not joined at the hip. It's your wife you need to worry about, not me.' He winked at Esther.

She looked relieved. 'You see, I told you he'd understand.' She nudged her husband. 'David, you can't imagine the agonies he's been through, wondering how to break the news to you.'

Embarrassed colour rose in Jonathan's face. 'I was just worried, that's all. I didn't want you to think I was abandoning you. I know you'll need all the help you can get in the coming months. Especially as the hospital has been designated an official Casualty Clearing.'

'Oh, I'm sure we'll find someone to take your place,' David said airily. 'You're easily replaced.'

'But will they be able to tolerate your barbed sense of humour?'

'Probably not. But hopefully I won't have to tolerate their dreadful singing, either.'

The two men grinned at each other.

'You should go with him,' Rebecca joined in, looking from one to the other. 'I'm sure Jonathan could find a position for you, and then you wouldn't have to be parted.'

'Good idea,' Jonathan said. 'I'll tell them we come as a pair and can't possibly be broken up.'

'That's a very tempting idea, but I'm quite happy where I am, thank you.' David smiled and sipped his wine.

He'd thought Rebecca was joking, but she persisted, 'I really think this could be a good opportunity for you too. I'm sure a man of your talents could easily find a more prestigious position in Cambridge.'

David bristled. 'More prestigious than working in one of the best teaching hospitals in London?'

He looked at her. She was extraordinarily beautiful, with large coppery brown eyes and dark hair like satin. Just his type, in fact.

But there was something about her that rankled with him.

'Yes, but you could do better,' she insisted. 'I'm sure if you moved to another hospital you could find a consultant's post.'

'I don't want a consultant's post.' He wished she would shut up. He could sense the atmosphere changing. 'If I'd wanted to be a consultant, I would have done it years ago.'

'So you're happy to patch up black eyes and bruised knees for the rest of your days?'

Her scornful tone reminded him of his stepmother, constantly jabbing at his poor father, pushing him to do better, to achieve more, always to be something more than he wanted to be . . .

'Hardly,' he said tautly. 'As Jonathan said, we've been designated a major Casualty Clearing Station. Once the bombs start dropping I think we'll be praying for black eyes and bruised knees. Although I don't suppose being knee-deep in dismembered body parts is glamorous enough for you either?'

An angry flush spread up Rebecca's slender neck. Jonathan jumped in quickly to calm the situation.

'I'm sure David knows his own mind,' he said. 'Besides, if he went, there'd be no one left in Casualty.'

'Why, who else is deserting the sinking ship?' David asked casually.

There was a long pause. 'You mean you don't know?' his friend said.

David looked at him across the table and felt his blood run cold. 'Who?'

'Sister Dawson is going down to Kent. I'm sorry, I thought you knew . . .'

It was like a fist in the stomach, taking the wind out of him.

Rebecca laughed. 'David, you look as if you've seen a ghost! Who is Sister Dawson? Is she that dark-haired girl I've seen around? The tall one?' She looked from one to the other, an expression of bewildered amusement on her face. But David was hardly aware of her. All his attention was focused on Jonathan.

'Why?' he asked.

'Look, David—'

'Why?' he interrupted.

He could hear his heart thrumming in his ears. Suddenly all his attention was focused on one tiny pinprick of time and space.

Jonathan sighed. 'Her fiancé called off their engagement,' he admitted heavily. David sat forward. He could feel electricity surging through his body, making it hard for him to sit still.

'But why is she leaving?' he asked.

'I suppose she felt it would be easier.'

David caught the meaning behind his friend's look. She knew, he thought. He wasn't going mad. She had felt it too, that spark between them.

'It's probably for the best,' Jonathan said.

He was right, David thought. Helen would be safer in the country. But the thought of not seeing her again, of letting her go without telling her how he felt, was unbearable.

'What's going on?' Rebecca's voice had sharpened, her woman's intuition working overtime. 'David?'

He barely heard her. He was already on his feet. 'I have to see her,' he said.

'David, don't,' Jonathan warned. 'Leave the girl alone.'

'That's not what you said a few months ago.'

'I know, but she must have her reasons for leaving. Her mind's made up. It won't do you any good to go stirring things up now . . .'

But David was already on his feet. He took some notes out of his wallet and threw them down on the table. 'Here, this is on me. I have to go,' he said shortly.

'David? What are you doing?' Rebecca snapped.

He looked down at her. 'Something I should have done months ago,' he said.

Helen was in her room, packing. She and Dora were catching the train down to Kent first thing in the morning with the babies and Danny. Typically kind-hearted, Millie had immediately invited Nick's brother to stay at Billinghurst when she'd found out how worried Dora was about leaving him behind.

As she folded her clothes and laid them neatly in her suitcase, Helen kept telling herself this was just what she needed. She tried to be excited about staying in a castle and seeing her old friend again. But deep down she knew she was running away.

She had just finished emptying the last of her things from the wardrobe when the door flew open and David McKay stood there. He was wearing an evening suit, his shirt unbuttoned at the throat, a bow tie hanging loosely around his neck. His dark eyes were blazing.

She fought down the treacherous flare of excitement she felt. 'What are you doing here? How did you get in? You can't just walk in, I'll be trouble if anyone finds you . . .'

'What do you care? You're leaving anyway, aren't you?'

He walked into the room, slamming the door behind him. Helen took a step away from him, trying to keep as much distance between them as possible.

'Well?' he demanded. 'When were you going to tell me? Or were you just going to sneak off without saying goodbye?'

'I – I thought you knew,' she stammered.

'Do you think I'd let you go if I did?'

Her heart was crashing against her ribs. If he touched her, she would be lost.

'Why?' His voice lost its angry edge. 'Why are you going?'

Her mind grasped for the excuses she'd been preparing ever since she'd made her decision to go. 'I want to transfer back to Theatre . . . My friend is being evacuated and she wants me to go with her . . . I thought I might be safer in a hospital in the country . . .'

'Safer from what, exactly? From the bombs or from me?'

Helen clutched her hands together to stop them from shaking. 'I want you to leave,' she said.

'Not until you tell me the truth.'

She faced him across the room. His anger was all the more lethal for being so contained. He was still, but she could see the fire in his eyes.

'That night in the Sick Bay, the night Nurse Willard was attacked,' he said. 'There was something between us, wasn't there? You felt it too, I know you did.'

'I don't know what you're talking about,' Helen said flatly. But when she closed her eyes, she could still feel the electric thrill that had gone through her when they'd looked at each other.

'You did. I could see it in your eyes. Why won't you admit it?'

It was the hoarse pleading note in his voice that broke her, far more than his anger ever could.

'All right,' she admitted. 'I did – feel something. But nothing can ever come of it,' she added sharply.

'Why not?'

She couldn't tell him. She'd already exposed enough of herself to him. Any more and he would know all her secrets. And then she would be powerless against him.

'Please, go,' she begged.

'I can't,' he said simply. 'I can't walk away from you, Helen. You think I haven't tried? You think if I could just turn away and forget you, I wouldn't have done it a long time ago? I've watched you,' he said. 'I've been through agonies, seeing you with someone else. And now I've found you, you're pushing me away . . .'

'No!' She shook her head, as if she could shake the tormenting thoughts out of it. 'We can't be together. Don't you see, that's why I have to go.'

He crossed the room in a second, grabbing her wrists, holding her against him. 'Why? Why do you have to go?'

'Because I'm scared!'

She was scared now, his face only inches from hers, so close she could see the shadow of stubble on his jaw, see his pupils turning his eyes almost black. The truth was out, and it had left her shaking.

Slowly his face was transformed. Warmth kindled in his brown eyes. 'Why, Helen?' His voice was gentle, uncomprehending. 'What are you scared of?'

'This. Us. It's – it's too much.'

Once she'd said it, she realised why she had been so attracted to Chris. He was safe. She liked him, had even told herself she loved him. She wanted him physically. But he had never laid claim to her heart, and she'd known he never would.

But David McKay was different. 'You could hurt me,' she whispered to him.

His dark brows drew together. 'You know I'd never do that.'

'How can you be sure?' Tears clogged her voice. 'How can you make a promise like that? Charlie never meant to hurt me, but he still did. How do I know you won't do the same? I don't think I could live through that again . . .'

'So you think it's better to run and hide than to risk feeling anything?' His eyes searched her face. 'Don't you think I'm scared too? I've run away from love my whole life. I'm terrified of the idea of giving my heart to anyone, because I've seen what it's like when it gets trampled on. But I'm willing to take a risk with you, because I have no choice.' His voice was ragged with longing. 'I don't have any other choice because a life without you is no life at all.' His mouth curved into a small, sad smile. 'All I know is, I'd rather live a day of happiness with you than a lifetime without you.'

He took her hand and pressed it to his chest. She could feel the warmth of his body, the steady beat of his heart under the solid wall of muscle. 'I'm willing to risk it,' he said softly. 'Will you?'

For a moment she couldn't breathe. All her senses were screaming at her to say yes, to be with him, to answer the call of her heart.

'I can't,' she said, pulling her hand away and letting it drop to her side. 'I'm not ready . . .'

'And will you ever be ready?'

'I – I don't know,' she admitted sadly.

'Very well.' She heard him sigh but couldn't meet his eyes. She knew if she did she would be lost. 'Then I won't bother you again.'

He went to the door. 'Let me know when you are ready. If it's not too late by then,' he said shortly.

Helen stared at the door for a long time after he'd gone. The air still seemed to vibrate with the imprint of his presence.

It was already too late for her. That was the problem.

Chapter Fifty-Seven

Effie crammed the last of her belongings into her suitcase and slammed the lid shut.

'Well, this is it, girls.' She tried to smile bravely, but couldn't stop her lips from trembling.

Devora was crying too. Even Jess, who never cried, looked close to shedding a tear.

'I wish you didn't have to go,' Devora said.

'I don't want to,' Effie said. 'It's not fair you two are allowed to stay and I have to go back to Ireland.'

The day before, Matron had announced that any student above second year could stay on at the Nightingale if they wished, on the understanding that their studies would not continue until after the war was over. Or, if they preferred, they could transfer to another hospital outside London to finish their training in the normal way.

Most of the students had opted to stay except for Effie, who had already promised her mother she would go home in this eventuality.

'At least you'll qualify next year,' Jess reminded her. 'If this war carries on we might be thirty before we get our State Finals!'

'How do I have a hope of passing without you to help me study?' Effie replied.

Her sisters took her to the station to catch the train to Liverpool, much to Effie's chagrin.

'You don't have to take me all the way, you know. I'm not going to make a bolt for it!' she grumbled as they all got off the bus. The streets were full of men in uniform. Buses full of troops rumbled past, calling out to the girls. Effie smiled and waved back, until Bridget nudged her.

'Behave yourself,' she hissed. 'And you wonder why we have to put you on the train!'

Katie was very quiet, Effie noticed. She'd hardly said a word on the bus journey from Bethnal Green, which was unusual for her because usually she never shut up.

'You know, it's a shame I can't stay a couple more days, just to see you married,' Effie said to her.

'Not a chance!' Bridget broke in. 'I promised Mammy I'd see you on that train, and that's what I'm going to do. Now wait there while I go and buy your ticket.'

As she walked away, Effie turned back to Katie. 'Be sure to send me a photograph, won't you? And write and tell me all the details. I bet you'll make a beautiful bride,' she sighed.

Katie scowled at her. 'Oh, sod you, Euphemia O'Hara!' she snapped. 'Why did you have to pick now of all times to be so bloody nice?'

Effie stared at her, perplexed. 'What have I done now?'

Katie glanced past her to where Bridget was lining up at the ticket office, then fumbled in her pocket and drew out an envelope.

'I wasn't supposed to give you this,' she said, handing it over. 'It came for you last week. Mr Hopkins gave it to Bridget by mistake – God knows why, since no one in their right mind would ever send *her* a love letter!'

Effie stared down at the envelope. It was covered in hastily scrawled hearts and kisses.

'Anyway, I wanted to give it to you but Bridget said we couldn't because, knowing you, you'd get some romantic notion in your head and decide not to get on the train,' Katie continued. 'But since you've been so nice, I feel rotten about it . . .'

But Effie wasn't listening. She was too busy reading the letter. 'When did you say this arrived?' she asked.

'Last week sometime – Monday, I think. Look, Bridget's coming back. For God's sake, don't tell her I – Effie? Effie, where are you going?'

'I've got to meet someone,' she threw back over her shoulder, already hurrying away.

'Not again!'

Dora fumed as the train lurched to a halt for the fifth time. She stood up, jostled her way to the window and leaned out to have a look.

'Would you believe it, we've been pushed into another siding! It'll take a month of Sundays to get to Kent at this rate.'

It's all the trains carrying troops,' Helen said, fussing over baby Winifred in her arms. 'They have to keep shunting us to one side to let them through.'

'I know that,' Dora said, sitting down again. 'But if it takes much longer the babies are going to need feeding again. And how am I going to manage that on a crowded train, eh?'

The carriage was packed full of forlorn-looking children clutching cardboard suitcases, luggage tags dangling from their coats. The lucky ones huddled with their brothers and sisters while others sat alone, pale and frightened. The netting shelves above their heads sagged under the weight of baggage.

Helen handed the baby back to Dora and reached into her pocket for a bag of humbugs, which she offered round to the children nearest to her.

'Dora, I – I think Walter n-needs changing,' Danny said.

'Oh, that's all I need!' she said crossly. Helen stared across at her. She had never seen her friend in such a frazzled state.

Helen leaned across to her. 'Are you all right?'

'Of course I'm not all right!' Dora retorted, her green eyes flaring. 'Do I look all right? I've got two hungry babies, I've left my home, my family and my husband behind and don't know if I'm going to see any of them again. This war's only been going for three days and I'm already sick of it. And I'm bloody sick to the back teeth of being brave, too!'

Then, to Helen's utter astonishment, she burst into tears.

Helen took the baby from her arms and gave her to Danny, then squeezed into the seat next to her friend and cuddled her.

'I don't even know why I'm doing this,' Dora sobbed, her tears soaking through Helen's summer dress. 'I didn't want to go in the first place, but Nick insisted. I hate the country. It's too big and dark and it stinks of God knows what. I've been there hop picking and I didn't like it then and I ain't going to like it now.'

She stopped, exhausted by her rant, and caught Helen's eye for the first time. They stared at each other for a moment and then Dora started laughing. 'Oh, blimey, look at me!' she said, smiling bleary-eyed through her tears. 'What must I look like? In a train full of kids I'm the only one crying!'

'You're not the only one,' Helen said, wiping a tear from her eye.

Dora pulled out a handkerchief to mop her eyes. 'Are you having second thoughts too?' she asked.

Helen nodded. 'I really wish I weren't.'

'You never told me why you changed your mind and decided to come?'

'Because I'm a coward. Someone offered me everything I'd ever wanted and I was too scared to take it in case it was taken away from me again.'

'What you've never had you never miss,' Dora said.

'Except I do miss it,' Helen sighed. Just knowing what she and David could have shared if only she'd been brave was enough to make her hurt.

'It's a risk, you know,' Dora said, handing back the handkerchief. 'Every time you give your heart to someone, you take a chance that it's going to get broken. But if you don't, you never know what you could have had.'

David's words came back to her: *I'd rather live a day of happiness with you than a lifetime without you.*

The troop train rumbled past at last. Any moment now and they would be moving again, getting further and further from London with every passing moment.

'I can't do this,' said Helen suddenly. She shot to her feet and wrestled her bag from overhead, watched by a dozen pairs of wide, astonished eyes.

'What? Where are you going?'

'I've got to get off this train.'

'I'm coming with you.' Dora was on her feet too. 'Get the bags, Danny.' She scooped the babies out of his arms so he could grab their luggage.

'You don't have to come!'

'You're having a laugh, ain't you? If you think you're going back to London without me, you've got another think coming, mate! I want to get off this train just as much as you do!'

They climbed off, passing bags and babies between them until they were all safely on the ground. And not a moment too soon, as the train rumbled off.

They watched it disappearing down the track in a cloud of dirty grey steam.

'Ain't w-we going to the country no more, Dora?' Danny asked.

'Don't look like it, mate.' She shaded her eyes and squinted up and down the track. 'Where are we?' she asked.

'I don't know,' Helen admitted. Next to the railway line was a patchwork of grey rooftops, and beyond that in the distance the glistening ribbon of the Thames. 'Not too far from the city, though.'

'Thank the Lord for that slow train!' Dora grinned.

'H-how will we get home?' Danny asked.

Helen looked around her. 'I suppose if we went down that path there, we could find a bus to take us back to the city at least.'

She glanced at Dora. Now her initial bravado had worn off, Helen was beginning to wonder if this was such a good idea.

But she'd reckoned without her friend's optimism. 'That's good enough for me.' Dora smiled back at her and hoisted a baby higher on her hip. 'London here we come!' She grinned at Danny. 'Tell you what, though, Dan. I reckon we're going to have some explaining to do to your brother when we get home!'

Chapter Fifty-Eight

It took every last farthing of the savings Effie had stuffed in the top of her stocking to pay the taxi fare to Pimlico.

All the way she couldn't stop thinking about Adam's letter. He'd poured his heart out on the page, told her what a complete fool he was for letting her go, how much he loved her. He'd even quoted Robert Browning to try to explain the depth of his feelings for her. It was just the kind of wonderfully romantic letter Effie had always dreamed of receiving.

The taxi pulled into the leafy square fringed by tall houses with white porticos and Effie suddenly remembered the last time she'd come here, the day Adeline had arrived to take possession of Adam again. Effie's stomach churned with emotion, remembering how humiliated she'd felt as she stumbled down that flight of stone steps. All the time she'd hoped that Adam might follow her, tell her he'd been wrong ever to allow Adeline back into his life.

And now, finally, he had.

As she was paying the driver, the front door opened and he came out.

'Effie?' He looked stunned to see her. Effie was shocked to see him, too. She hardly recognised him in his khaki army uniform. For a moment they could only stare at each other, speechless.

'I didn't think you were coming,' he said finally. 'When you didn't reply to my letter, I thought you didn't want to see me any more.'

'My sister only just gave it to me,' Effie said, still transfixed by the sight of his uniform. 'You're really going then?'

'I don't have much choice. I registered as a conscientious objector, but the tribunal threw it out. Now I have to do six months' military training and I don't want to go.'

Effie stared at his sullen face and thought about all the porters and medical students at the hospital, going off with cheerful stoicism to do their duty.

'I don't suppose anyone wants to go,' she said.

'I daresay you're right.' Adam looked abashed. 'Thank you for coming to see me, anyway. It means such a lot to me.'

Effie glanced away so she didn't have to look into his green eyes. 'Adeline isn't here then?'

'I told you in my letter, didn't I? She's gone.'

'Did you really send her away?'

He nodded. 'I knew you were right, that Adeline was only using me, but I didn't want to admit it. My stupid pride, I suppose.' His mouth twisted. 'At any rate, as soon as you left I realised my mistake. I should never have let you walk out. Can you forgive me?'

'Yes, of course. That's why I'm here.'

'Really?' His face lit up. 'Oh, Effie, I can't tell you how happy I am to hear you say that—'

He took a step towards her, arms outstretched, but Effie sidestepped his embrace. 'I've been learning poetry,' she said.

'Oh, yes?' He frowned, half amused.

'I wanted to impress you, you see. I wanted you to think I was as cultured as you and Adeline.'

'You didn't have to do that.'

'I felt I did.' She paused. 'I learned a new poem last night, as a matter of fact. 'The Bargain', by Sir Philip Sidney.

405

Do you know it at all? *My true love hath my heart, and I have his . . .*' she quoted the first line.

He nodded. 'It's one of my favourites.'

'Mine too,' she agreed. 'You really feel the love in those lines, don't you? *He loves my heart, for once it was his own. I cherish his because in me it bides.*' She sighed at the sentiment.

'Yes, it's beautiful.'

'They love each other so deeply, it's as if they have each other's hearts beating in their chests. They feel each other's pain. Can you imagine loving someone like that?'

He paused a fraction too long. 'I do,' he answered. 'That's how I feel about you.'

He reached for her hands, but she pulled them away. 'No, you don't. You want to be in love with me, just like you wanted to be in love with Adeline. You're desperate to love someone. But you can't love me because you don't know me, not really.' She wrapped her arms around herself, suddenly cold in spite of the warmth of the day. 'I tried so hard to be the person I thought you wanted me to be,' she said. 'But then I realised, if I had to change that much you couldn't really love me.'

'I do love you, and you don't have to change,' Adam insisted. 'I love you just the way you are.'

'No, you don't.'

'Then *I'll* change. I'll try to be the kind of man you want me to be.'

She shook her head. 'Don't you see, Adam? Neither of us should have to change. We should love each other just the way we are.'

His broad shoulders slumped in defeat. 'What do you want me to do, then?'

'Find someone who makes you truly happy. Someone whose pain means more to you than your own.'

'That's what I want, more than anything. That's what I've always wanted.'

For the first time she allowed herself to meet his gaze. He looked so wretched, she thought with pity. Poor Adam, constantly searching for someone to love. She had thought she was the hopeless romantic, but now she could see she wasn't the only one.

But then his petulant side reasserted itself. 'I'm surprised you came at all, if this is all you have to say,' he grunted.

'I came because I wanted to say goodbye and to wish you well,' Effie said. 'As a friend.'

'A friend?' His mouth curled around the word.

She leaned forward and planted a light kiss on his cheek. For the first time he didn't flinch, but it was too little and far too late.

'Stay safe, Adam,' she said.

As she turned to walk away, he called after her, 'Wait! May I write to you?'

She shook her head. 'Better not,' she said.

She walked away, making sure not to look back until she reached the corner. When she did, he was still standing at the top of the stone steps, watching her, a forlorn figure in his khaki uniform.

For a moment, it was all she could do not to run back to him. But she knew it would be better for both of them if she kept walking.

My true love hath my heart, and I have his . . . The words echoed in her mind. It hurt her so much to say goodbye. But Jess was right, she thought. She and Adam both deserved better than that.

'You know, Mrs Durrant, I don't think I've ever met a child who uses fruit as imaginatively as your son,' David McKay said, wielding his forceps.

407

The woman looked offended. 'You were the one who told me to send him to Saturday morning pictures with an apple instead of an orange,' she accused.

'Yes, but I didn't expect him to stuff the core up his nose, did I?'

As he tried to extract the offending object, he was aware of Mrs Durrant's head casting a shadow over her son's face.

'What if some of the pips travel right up there, Doctor?' she asked anxiously. 'Will they grow in his brain, do you think?'

David paused for a moment, composing himself.

'I don't think they'd find very fertile ground, Mrs Durrant,' he said. 'Or indeed any—'

He froze, forceps poised, as the door opened and Helen Dawson stood there, a calm, beautiful vision in her stiff grey dress and goffered white bonnet.

At first he thought he was seeing things, and it was all he could do not to throw down his instruments and rush over to check if she was real.

But then she smiled and said, 'Sorry I'm late, Doctor. But I'm ready now.'

'I don't understand. Ready for . . .' He stopped speaking. The glowing warmth in her dark eyes told him everything he needed to know. She was ready to take a chance, to hand him her heart and trust that he would care for it as she would his.

He cleared his throat. 'Are you quite sure, Sister?' he asked.

'Very sure, sir.'

He smiled. 'We'd better get on with it then,' he said, picking up his forceps. 'We've got a lot of lost time to make up.'

The station platform in Colchester was crowded. Soldiers, their families, wives, sweethearts, all clamouring to say goodbye. No one wanted to be the first to tear themself away.

Frannie desperately searched the crowded platform but there was no sign of John. Why had she left it so late? She didn't even know for sure if he'd be here. For all she knew he might have already gone, could be on the shores of France by now . . .

She felt nausea rise in her throat and steadied herself. Don't give in, she told herself. Don't let the fear take a grip on you, not this time.

And then the crowd parted and she saw him. Standing apart from everyone else as usual, tall, handsome and strapping in his officer's uniform, surveying the scene with narrowed, watchful eyes.

His gaze skimmed over her, then snagged on her and pulled back until they were staring directly at each other. He stood for a moment, frozen. Only his lips moved, saying her name.

The next moment Frannie was running towards him. She didn't stop running until she was in his arms and kissing him fiercely.

The harsh blast of the whistle parted them. 'All aboard!' The train guard started down the platform, his flag poised.

John looked down at her. 'I don't know what to say,' he murmured.

'Me neither.' There was so much she wanted to say, so much she wanted him to know, it would take a lifetime to say it. And with any luck, a lifetime was what they would have.

'I brought this for you.' She reached into her pocket, pulled out her lucky pebble and pressed it into his hand. 'It brought you luck before, so I'm hoping it will bring you luck again.'

His fingers closed around it, holding it tight. 'I won't

need luck,' he said. 'Not if I know I've got you waiting for me.'

The train guard gave another harsh blast on his whistle. 'You'd better go.'

As he walked away from her, he turned and called back, 'I will come home – I promise.'

Frannie smiled. 'I don't want you to come home a hero,' she whispered. 'Just come home safe.'